BLACK ROSE

LARKIN'S BARKIN' BOOK 1

PETE ADAMS

Published 2021 by Gumshoe – A Next Chapter Imprint

Edited by Fading Street Services

Cover art by CoverMint

"The lunatic, the lover and the poet, are of imagination all compact"

— William Shakespeare - A Midsummer Night's Dream

BOOKS BY PETE ADAMS:

The Kind Hearts and Martinets Series: (Part one of the 14 book Hegemon Chronicles series)

Book 1Cause and Effect – *Vice plagues the City*

Book 2Irony in the Soul – *Nobody Listens like the Dying*

Book 3A Barrow Boy's Cadenza – *In Dead Flat Major*

Book 4Ghost and Ragman Roll – *Spectre or Spook*

Book 5Merde and Mandarins – *Divine Breath*

The DaDa Detective Agency - Sequel to Kind Hearts and Martinets: (Parallel series to form a part of the 14 book Hegemon Chronicles series):

Book 1Road Kill – *The Duchess of Frisian Tun*

Book 2Rite Judgement – *Heads roll, Corpses Dance*

The Larkin's Barkin' series – East End of London, gangster family, saga: (The first two novels form a back story to the 14 book Hegemon Chronicles series):

Book 1Black Rose – *A Midsummer Night's Chutzpah* – 1966

Book 2A Deadly Queen – 4 Wars

The Rhubarb Papers: A spin off Sequel to Kind Hearts and Martinets (The first two novels form a part of the 14 book Hegemon Chronicles series):

Book 1Dead No More – *Rhubarb in the Mammon*

Book 2A Misanthrope's Toll

PREFACE

A few years before I wrote the first draft of this book, summer 2015, I attended *Portsmouth Poise,* an Arts gathering organised by Ed Woodruffe, Trudy Barber and Elaine Hamilton. Each attendee was asked to select an item from various objects in a glazed cabinet and instantly compose a five-minute short story to be read later that evening. I chose a burned crumpet, a bite taken from it. It had the following note attached:

"*This homemade crumpet was one of a batch baked in the kitchen of the 'Cat and Fiddle' pub in Stepney, in London's East End, on June 8th 1924. Bessie O'Riordan, who ran the pub, made crumpets every year on her son Jack's birthday, because they were his favourite food. Unfortunately, Jack had been missing, believed killed in action since 1917, but she continued to make them every year in his memory.*

Regulars were given buttered crumpets to eat with their pints every June 8th, but in 1924, she burned the first batch. Bessie was about to throw them out when the owner's grandfather entered the pub and announced the birth of a son, Sam, to Bessie's surviving son. He asked her for one of the burnt crumpets to keep as a token to remember Jack, his grandson and commemorate the birth of Sam - the crumpet is now well beyond its sell by date and should not be digested."

I composed a short story and read it out; Chas Larkin was born. Returning home and, well into the night, I wrote the opening chapters of *Larkin's Barkin'*. I archived these chapters and my notes in order to complete the *Kind Hearts and Martinets* series. *Larkin's Barkin'* was intended to be a one-off crime thriller, but upon returning to the work in progress and, as the story developed and the characters grew strong in my mind, the seeds of a series was sown. Book two: *A Deadly Queen – 4 wars and Book 3 A Holy Death - Dead, Dying or Gorgeous,* will follow.

ACKNOWLEDGEMENT AND DEDICATION

The crumpet script was written by Colin Merrin, an East End lad himself and now, an exceptional artist painting in Portsmouth. Colin has told me since that the idea was inspired by an East End of London myth about a Stepney young man who did not return from WW1, and his mum, who ran a pub, made buns (not crumpets) on his birthday every year until she died. True or not, this myth was a great catalyst for this my ninth book, and I dedicate it to Colin Merrin.

The painting is of his Grandmother, Great Grandmother, and Uncle - the coincidence of East End matriarchs, with a boy between, was too much to ignore, even if the narrative bears no resemblance.

1916 by Colin Merrin

FOREWORD

In this story I introduce a concept of *The Black Rose* as a mythical Irish character. I ask forgiveness from the Irish people who I have taken to my heart after meeting my long-term partner, June Merrigan; Siiobhain ni Mhuireaghain, her Irish name. When we met, so many years ago, June had a jet black cat she called Rosie, named for the benefit of the English. The cat's Irish name was Roisin Dubh, *Black Rose.*

Wikipedia describes a *Black Rose:* "The symbolism in many works of fiction usually contrives feelings of mystery, danger, or some sort of darker emotion, like sorrow and obsessive love."

Crumpets - an Anglo-Saxon creation that originally were thought to be hard pancakes cooked on a griddle, rather than the spongy confection of today and very popular in Britain.

Chutzpah - Unusual and shocking behaviour, involving taking risks, but not feeling guilty; audacity, boldness...

It is not certain that everything is uncertain

— BLAISE PASCALL

PROLOGUE
THE CRUMPET

MISERY RIFE, FEAR ENDEMIC, BECAUSE OF A DODGY CRUMPET. Burned, one bite taken, preserved, and dating back to just after the First World War. The whiff of undertaker's formaldehyde would be sickening if ever you took it from the glass display case, sat on the back bar where it had pride of place. However, that crumpet stood as a marker of an uneasy peace in the East End of London. Lost and found, lost and found again, amongst the bodies of retribution and counter-attack, always recovered, signal in the strength of one family, the Saints.

The family factions, long established in the East End of London, were the Saints and the Larkins. The Saints, the larger, more established, villainous family, held in check, one could say, by the precocious, lunatic may be more appropriate, Larkin family, who knew no fear when all around knew they should. And so, the lines of friction between the two families became white hot and sparked whenever the crumpet went missing.

And the O'Neill's? Not much was known of this mysterious Irish immigrant family, said to hail from County Clare, West of Ireland and, seemingly uninterested in owning a pub and disinterested territorially. Yet nevertheless, they asserted an untouchable presence.

Regardless of the ephemeral O'Neill's, the familial territorial headquarters was always the pubs, Dad's and Arrie's, both colloquial names, long established in local culture and street mythology.

Dad's was located in Stepney, deep in the heart of the East End of London and, Arrie's, in what can only be described as an uncomfortable distance away, next door. The two mutually dependent, though independent, pubs, were competitors and, the proprietary families as adversaries, extraordinarily, had a shared support of each other. You could not raze one pub to the ground without the other suffering a similar fate. Or so it was thought.

It was from here in semi-detached disquietude that the Saints controlled the Docks, their ground, and the Larkins, the gambling houses, brothels, and most other satellite industries, servicing mainly the docks, the dockers and the sailors. So it was that the families needed each other in another twist of fate. Which was the most fertile business depended on your point of view. Either way, the businesses were *bombproof* in that the docks were untouchable and, you could maybe destroy one or two of the Larkin properties, but not all, and then you would have a war so brutal and what would be the point, after all, the Saints and Larkins were neighbours, literally.

The crumpet was the symbol of a capricious peace. Every now and then the confection disappearing and later returned, the Saints temporarily vulnerable.

To understand the ground, you need to comprehend the history of the two families, though it would be more appropriate to say that the *umbilical* reason for the current violent turbulence of street politics, would be just that, and, in that maelstrom of tinder dry factional streets, was *born* and *nurtured*, in a non-maternal sense, an unlikely nemesis. And so it was, from this most unusual and unexpected direction, the life-sustaining chord of palpitant peace, was cut. The bête noire scourge, emancipated. Although, as it transpired, the adversary was totally unaware he was even free or, was a preceptor of ruination, being insensitive to his latent genetic *chutzpah*. This was a man destined to be Public Enemy number one. To be pursued by the Metropolitan Police, Special Branch, MI5 and, closer to home, The Saints and, to a lesser extent, The Larkins. And in all of this, there was *The Black Rose*.

The Saints.

Bessie Saint had been the fierce landlady of the Dog and Duck Pub in Stepney, the East End of London. The locals, in the vernacular, called the pub a Rubbadub and, colloquially, Dad's, as in the initials of Dog *and Duck*, but mainly in memory of Dad, old Mickey Saint, Bessie's beloved and sadly departed husband. He was said to have copped it at Passchendaele in the Great War, November 1917. Dad Saint, Dad's owner, was dead. It was, however, business as usual, as in reality Bessie had run the pub and just about everything, as was the East End matriarchal way. Old Mickey thought he ran the family firm, but he didn't. The brains of the outfit was Bessie and she had taken on the role from Mickey's Mum and, before her, Nan Saint. Bessie was highly suited for the job and had been selected for Mickey. Extraordinarily, this *arranged* marriage produced a love match, at least this is what Bessie told everyone, and who would be brave enough to contradict her? Certainly not Mickey, who was not averse to a bit of kneecapping and murder, but only if Bessie said so.

When news reached Dad's of Mickey's demise, Bessie had been conspicuously devastated. Under her guidance, he had run a tight ship in the principal family businesses: control of the Docks; extortion; violence; robbery; with the occasional dispatching of the unwanted, those who had transgressed the unwritten law, Bessie's Law. And what was that law? Nobody knew, she was not one to write things down, administration not being her bent, though she was firmly on the opposite side of law and order in just about everything else. The Saints were gangsters and had a serious rep.

Since the demise of her husband, Bessie, overtly ran the Saints gang with an iron fist and, she ran a tight ship in Dad's. When her eldest son, Mickey junior, who would have been the natural de facto successor, was, towards the end of the Great Conflict, declared *missing in action*, a military euphemism for dead, Bessie was truly devastated. She didn't give a toss about her husband, but she missed her Mickey Junior sorely. She set a tradition to commemorate her beloved son Mickey's birthday, and, on the 8th June every year, she would bake his favourite crumpets. These would be shared in the pub where everybody would salute Mickey Saint, eat heartily of the tasteless and often burned, small and round, perforated, bread-like confection, either dripping with melted butter and a green parsley sauce liquor or topped with jellied eels. At regular intervals, as if eating the vile crumpets was not bad enough, you were expected to raise your pint glass in a toast and shout, "Mickey Saint - *the little devil*", because Mickey had been a dirty, rotten scoundrel. He had been evil through to his core and ever since he could toddle, Mickey Saint had scared the living daylights out of everybody he met. This was the Saints; a villainous family and they learned their trade early on in life.

And so it was, on the 8th June 1924, Bessie had burned a large batch of crumpets, as had become the tradition and the crowded pub was effused with the charcoal aroma of the nauseating *delice-confection*. The clientele, scared for their lives if they didn't attend this auspicious occasion on the East End of London calendar, were all in attendance, waiting to share in the ceremonial crumpets, when the door opened and in walked Mickey Junior, as large as life and twice as dangerous. Nobody knew where he'd been, what he had been doing since 1918, for it had been just a few weeks before the end of the war when he had gone missing. People later suggested stories, all in the realms of fantasy, but one thing was sure, Mickey, *the little devil*, was back, rolling in filthy lucre and ready to resume control of his *Manor*, as was his right, because Bessie deemed it so.

That auspicious evening, Bessie declared free drinks, and the party, which was to last well into a third day, got under way to the smell of more burning crumpets, singing, dancing, and the occasional bottle on someone's head (that unwritten law again). At one point, Bessie panicked and retrieved from the bin the blackened crumpet she had been eating when her son had miraculously appeared, she'd taken one bite out of it. This would be a keepsake, a charm and she set it on the back bar shelf, announcing, "This is one lucky fucking crumpet", and thus it was given its place in Dad's. And, over time, the revolting crumpet became imbued with powers beyond its indelicate taste as Bessie further announced, it was the *Saint Crumpet.* It was never to be touched by anyone other than a Saint, on pain of, well, loads of pain and, if you were lucky, death. Another *unwritten law* that everyone acknowledged need not be written down as they, in their turn, would pass *the knowledge* onto their children and their children's children, in the way of all good diabolical East End myths. But, on that day of great joy for Bessie, she doled out the Saint largesse in the name of charcoal crumpets as if they were a true East End delicacy, topped with jellied eels or the green parsley liquor, to cover up the black surface and, people ate them, mumming and aaahing in feigned delight, as if their lives depended upon it, which they did.

The party had been well into its second day when the door of the Public bar crashed open (can nobody open a door quietly?) and Ancient Mickey, the grandfather, entered and announced the birth of Sam, Bessie's first grandchild, whom Bessie immediately rechristened Mickey. This had truly been an auspicious time for the Saints and Bessie put this turn of great fortune down to the burned crumpet, not so much the jellied eels or the green sauce and, drawing everyone's attention to her, she pointed to *the* crumpet on the back bar shelf, the bite marks of Bessie's false teeth evident, and she announced to all that this crumpet would be the symbol of the future prosperity and immunity of the Saint family.

The customers in the crowded pub parodied great hurrahs whilst under their breath muttered in trembling fear, “Just what they needed, a bullet-proof Saint family dynasty”. Which is what they got. The success believed by everybody, but no more than the Saint ascendency, to be attributed to the burned crumpet.

And even to this day the preserved crumpet sat on the back bar of Dad's. It had pride of place in the Dog and Duck pub.

When I say, “until this day”, I should have said, up until this day. For this day, this ominous and dark clouded, foreboding day, someone had entered Dad’s in the dead of night and purloined the Saint family’s lucky charm and replaced it with a crumpet, similar in appearance, but one imbued with malevolent juju. You could say that on this portentous day, the Saints were doomed.

But what of the Larkins?

The Larkins.

As in the tradition of all westerns, or in this case EastEnderns, there was a rival to the established villainous family. That family, the Larkins, equally villainous some would argue and live to regret it, owned the Bottle and Glass pub, known to those who favoured a walk on the wild side, or even those who walked the tightrope between Dad's and the Bottle and Glass, called this pub, the thorn in the side of the Saints, Bum's; bottle and glass being cockney rhyming slang for arse and this over time, became Arrie's, as in Aristotle – bottle (and glass) – get it? Some would say you needed a language degree to live and, survive, in the East End of London, but truthfully you would be better off with an invisibility cloak, or just get the hell out, and some did.

Arrie's was a seedy pub, ironically, in the arse end of Stepney and, if you stood back and screwed up your eyes, the Victorian bottle green and brown glazed tiles, acid etched glass, gave the pub an air of *Hansel and Gretel* classic beauty. However, if you were of the mind to partake of a pint or two within Arries and wore a tin hat and pads, you might discover it was not just a pub with visual character, you would learn it was patronised by characters, all of whom would not pass stage one of any sainthood test, not being in the Saint clan for instance, test one, but would pass with flying colours any test you threw at them for knavery.

Nonetheless, and despite the rivalry, Arrie's stood next door to Dad's and both pubs had a different visual character, if not dissimilar characterful patrons, all villains, in one way or another.

Of course, villainy came in very different forms and, when you grew up in this area, you either set your mind to getting out as soon as possible or, if you chose to stay and get a sensible job, you mainly stayed indoors after dark. The alternative was you commenced your apprenticeship in various categories of turpitude, eventually specialising in some form or other. Violence was always popular, and could be combined with aggravated burglary, or intimidation and such like. Further up the hierarchy were people considered skilled, like safe crackers, sappers, known as Petermen, good at fusing and defusing bombs and, there were specialists in alarms, and so on. There were and always had been, informers, or grasses as they were known; grasshopper, copper shopper, to shop villains to the filth, police, or so the story goes and, these informants came in two categories of stool pigeon. Your ordinary weaselly double-crosser, making a living for what often turned out to be a short life, sourcing naughty information for often a pittance of cash, in exchange for feeding the police with underground intelligence. All grasses aspired to becoming a *Super Grass*. It was like a career ladder within the telling on people cognoscenti, but on the more perilously precarious edge. The earnings were greater, commensurate with the heightened danger, but at the end of a career as a super grass, if you survived to say, forty-five, you could be given a lot of money and witness protection. You could maybe be shacked up in a luxurious villa, in a part of the world with a sunny clime. Least, this was the aspiration, but only a few made it to those dizzy heights, though the police encouraged these vocational ambitions.

And the numbers were made up by the East End plebs. The sycophants, living the life they had been born to, hanging on, often for dear life, suckered into a spiral of associated crime or denial, both intellectually and if the police questioned you. Even if the consequent tentative alliance and radiant admiration with known criminals, of the various category, gave you a certain cachet, hangers-on rarely got beyond a nodding acquaintance with the upper echelons of evil-doers and, hardly ever with the big boys. The masses were there to make up numbers and to stand by and laugh at jokes when made by those who would sever a limb or two without blinking an eye, if you didn't convulse in excessive jollity at often very poor jokes. Why is it gangsters think themselves whimsically entertaining?

Such was life in the oft eulogised East End of London. Not fun. Not a big loving family, but a life on the edge, and tolerated only by developing a rare sense of humour, bordering on denial. Everyone liked a tin bath, (laugh).

And so, the myths were handed down in both the Saint and the Larkin family. Some did get out. Charlie Larkin's granddad had escaped, as he put it, having found himself a beautiful woman, Alice, who absolutely insisted she would not marry him or bring up a family if it meant continuing to live in the dog eat crumpet world of villainy. She was escaping also his family pub and reputation and, Charlie Larkin (the granddad) was her ticket out of the East End of London. A bonus for Alice was that he was a kind and generous man who loved the bones of his Alice.

Charlie's granddad had moved to Portsmouth, a sort of home from home for EastEnders, only with a bastardised country accent and they took over a pub and renamed it the *Bottle and Glass,* after the family hostelry back in London, not that it existed anymore. In the Blitz, the Luftwaffe had done the Saints a service by bombing Arrie's and leaving Dad's remarkably unscathed, even the crumpet, and that was also seen as auspicious.

The Larkins steadfastly resisted selling the freehold of the bomb site and, eventually rebuilt it in a style that overshadowed Dad's both physically, architecturally, and emotionally – it was a modern design with all mod cons, hot and cold running blood.

And that was where the good sense ended, for Alice's eldest son, Charlie, who on visits to the family in London, trained hard to be a scumbag. Eventually Charlie returned to his so-called roots after his mum and dad tragically died.

Charlie, blind to all good sense, not least going back to the villainous way of life, married Betsy, a brazen Dockland tart. They had six kids and lived in a *cosy* East End hovel. The youngest child was called Chas, a diminutive form of Charlie, and he was a runt of a boy. Chas would ask why they did not go to Portsmouth and live with that family? He was, of course, cuffed for his impudence, the seaside home for Chas a distant fantasy. He was destined to remain in the East End of London, a place he hated, for alas, he did not have the chutzpah to leave and, probably never would. He was just like his Dad, so it was said, a famed cream puff.

1

THE YEAR, 1966

The Street

'Allo Chas,' drawn out and minacious. Mickey Saint junior at fourteen was not of big build, but he was menacing. It was in his genetic code. Even at this young age those fearsome bullying genes were fully developed into a playground gangster: Mickey Saint junior's manor.

Chas Larkin was frozen to the spot. Even though it was a warm summer day and the sweat drained down his petrified spine, he was chilled to the marrow. In his daydreams he imagined himself in another part of the world. Somewhere safe at least. He didn't ask for much, just to be safe. It was how he survived. He regressed into his dreams of a safe haven and, when he couldn't do that, he did things he thought might be lucky, like avoiding the cracks in the pavement.

Whenever he managed to get in some words to his self-absorbed mum, asking could they move, maybe to the countryside, she laughed at him. "We're EastEnders", and, "this is where we live", she would say, waving her arms about her as if the still bombed out East End of London was a glorious place to be and Chas should be grateful. He wasn't. The place was the pits and he hated it. It scared him. "But I don't like it mum", a statement that would be met with further derisive laughter and his mum would flounce, telling her friends, in his presence, mimicking a whining childlike voice "But I don't like it mum", to the great amusement of her audience, and deep embarrassment of Chas. She would flick his ear, or clump his head and, if she was drunk as a skunk, she would give Chas a right-hander that could knock him from Sunday to Monday.

'Cat got yer tongue?' Mickey Saint assayed as he strutted around the paralysed Chas, grasping his school satchel tight to his chest. It didn't hold anything valuable, but he had learned it could shield a blow or two. Mickey's gang leaned back, casually, hands in the pockets of their short shorts and laughed to the sky as Mickey prodded and taunted the trembling scaredy-cat, Chas Larkin.

Chas had no answer. He'd quite like a cat, but truthfully would prefer a dog. A dog could protect him. "Some chance", his mum had said, she had enough on her plate with six kids, of which Chas was the youngest and the burdensome runt of the litter, least this is what everyone told him, so he supposed he was. Chas was not sure what runt meant, but knew it wasn't good, because he didn't know of anything good. Nothing was good in his life.

Mickey flicked Chas's nose with thumb and forefinger, looking to his gang to bathe in accustomed glory as Chas rocked backwards in fear, which move gave Mickey the distance to wind up a haymaker. Chas knew it was coming, it always did, he wished he could run, to seek temporary respite in one of his many hideouts he had acquired as a means of self-preservation, but that wasn't going to happen. You try running with eyes that looked in different directions, where do you go? And he wouldn't get far with a club foot. His left foot twisted, not seriously, but enough that the sole could not be placed fully flat on the ground. Eventually he had been given a big shoe that had the sole and heel shaped and raised up. Chas was not sure what was worse, the sight of the club boot that so clearly did not match the shoe on his other foot, or his inability to walk like other kids, although he practiced, every day, desperate for some semblance of normality, which to Chas was the ability to blend into a *safe* background. Of course, it was the boot that everyone spotted first, the rest just followed as a natural consequence. It was Chas's lot and, he had just to get on with it was the sage advice from a distracted and uncaring mother. No maternal safe haven there.

Mickey's blow landed square on the runt's jaw. Chas was laid flat and had just enough time to curl into the foetal position before Mickey and each of his sick sycophants, popped in a kick or two as they passed by on their way to school.

Chas was going the other way; he had a doctor's appointment. He often did. He was what his mum called, "a sickly wimp of a runt", going on to say, in an amusing manner, that "her Charlie should 'ave drowned him in the Thames at birth, it's what they would've done in the old days". Then she would tell all how she was a martyr to the kid, like she was the victim, it was she who had the task of raising a child so demanding, and she'd clip Chas around the ear again for being a burden to her. Her solution to everything, if she wasn't flat on her back pissed, or shagging her way around the East India docks. Regularly, she would drag him off to the doctor's surgery as though he were a trophy, enabling her to suck in sympathy and caring endearments like a sponge. For her, not him; nobody cared about him.

'Get up 'orf the fucking floor, them cloves were clean on a week ago. What will the doc fink?'

Chas raised his bruised, emaciated, and deformed, elongated frame, to face his mum. If his self-esteem would allow it, and were he to stand upright, Chas considered he would be tall, but his body, like his ego, was seriously dented and emotionally curved inward, as if to form a hunchback's defensive shell. He leaned into his mother as she tugged his ear and pulled him towards the doctor's surgery, his tiny pleas choked off in a cloud of cheap, brassy perfume and the acrid aroma of lacquer from her beehive hair. He knew better than to tell her he hurt, his mother didn't care, and he often wondered why she so regularly took him to the doctor.

His mum was a looker, he had to agree with that. She dressed stylishly and often he wondered how come she had money for such lovely clothes, yet his own un-glad rags came from the *Salvation Army*? Another question he would never ask, as he clumped along following his mum who had not released his ear, and he buried his tears, buried his pain, and stifled his anger. Chas Larkin knew no other way. He repressed his so called fourteen years, so that inside he was still a small and vulnerable boy. He had no idea how old he was, or even his birthday and, what would be the point.

The Doctor

'Allo Chas.'

Chas liked Thelma, the doctor's receptionist. She was a warm buxom lady with mountainous bosoms that Chas loved to sink into when he received her motherly embrace, before showing them into the consulting room. Always sending him off with a fond ruffle of his hair. It was the closest he got to any stirrings that might encourage the growth of his inhibited adolescence. Chas had regular check-ups at the Docs. His mother made an inordinate fuss about all of Chas's distorted limbs, organs, and bits and pieces. It seemed to him to be the only time she cared and, oh how she and the doc laughed at his stunted growth, his inability to make that step into manhood.

'Lazy eye.'

'Lazy eye?'

'Lazy eye.'

'Lazy...?'

'Lazy eye,' the doctor reaffirmed, a brief nod that permitted him a cursory squint up Betsy Larkin's skirt: stocking tops. There was nothing lazy about his eye.

'Lazy eye?' Chas mumbled, trying to offer some substance to his still high-pitched and squeaky voice. Betsy clipped her son's ear, the Doc seeming to approve the chastisement with a glancing blow himself whilst distracted by Betsy's physical charms. Chas said nothing, not even ouch. He was used to it, though his temper, which bubbled and grew within him, permitted a rebellious clump of his club foot onto the polished floorboards of the surgery. He felt a little better. He had always had a squint, so why now? Why had the doctor at last thought his eye needed attention?

'What shall we do?' Chas's mum asked insincerely. She

found the Doctor inordinately attractive and he had such a lovely touch.

Doctor Byrne sashayed to the front of his desk like a lounge lizard, perched on the corner, and leaned over, facilitating an improved inspection of the creamy white thighs of Mrs Larkin and, whilst remaining focused on the black nylon tops, he scrabbled around Chas's face to remove the National Health, circular, wire framed glasses, scratching Chas's nose in the process. A trickle of blood trailed, to be ignored. Chas said nothing, he was used to being clumped, scratched, and beaten up generally.

Betsy slapped her son again. It was her default action, although her response seemed to have a reasonable motive, at least in her mind and, taking the spectacles from the doctor, she admonished her son. 'Look at the state of these bins, yer filfy...' and she demonstrably lifted the hem of her flowery cotton dress and, leaning down, adjacent to the doctor's fly region, she exaggerated exhaling a throaty breath onto the lenses and, with excessive and suggestive vigour, she cleaned them. The doctor was thus afforded a clearer view of Madam Larkin's under garments, which was of course the intention and the resultant mounding in the doctor's trousers was noticeable. Not to Chas though, he was as blind as a bat without his glasses, compounded with a lazy eye he had just learned, but he knew what was happening. It had happened before and his disabilities he thought to himself, were more often than not used as an excuse for his *mother* to visit the doctor. Still, it got him off school for a short while. He hated school. It was torture, even though he was academically gifted. The teacher had said this, but his mother had not listened, after all, in the East End what use were sums and writing, and clearly Chas did not have the *where-wiv-all* to follow his brothers into the family business. He was viewed as a waste of space.

Doctor Byrne, hunched over, raised himself from his perch. Chas heard a ripping of sticky *Elastoplast* and, still distracted by the intimate lady view, now fully exposed, Doctor Byrne roughly taped up the lens that serviced Chas's good eye and thrust the glasses back to the intimidated boy, dismissively telling him to wait outside.

Betsy glanced at Chas and told him to fuck off to school.

Chas fumbled the floor to pick up his glasses that had received no purchase on his face as the distracted doctor had attempted to replace them. Having found them and put them on, he found that now everything was a blur. His one good eye, though often facing the wrong way, was blinded, to teach the other one a lesson. He stood and with outstretched hands, he fumbled his way to the door and into the waiting room. The door closed to a squeal of feminine exquisite pleasure, and then a thud.

Chas stood still for a moment getting his blurred bearings, fighting the desire to cry. He felt the warm embrace of the comfortably plump receptionist who tugged Chas into her ample bosoms. This was what Chas looked forward to on every visit to the Docs. It was his only comfort. Now he cried. He was for the moment, safe, and Thelma removed the plastered glasses and dabbed his eyes with a perfume drenched handkerchief, caressed his head and kissed his damp cheeks. 'Fucking the Doc, is she?' Chas nodded, squashing himself into her body and she hugged him tight as she walked him to the door. 'Lazy eye?' she asked, and Chas nodded again, knowing the embrace and the comfort would end as the indistinct image of the door neared. Just the last kiss to go and he will have to face school.

Thelma kissed Chas. He didn't know, but there was a strawberry pair of lips printed on his cheek. He wouldn't care anyway because he relished the warmth, the milk of maternal nurturing and Thelma's kindness. He'd been standing on one leg having learned this was lucky and, so he thanked the Gods as he cherished the last vestiges of the luck and, the receptionist's cuddle, the final wisps of her womanly scent. He loved it, but he had to get to school.

School

Although the streets were familiar, Chas's drastically reduced vision made his walk to school difficult, treacherous even. Busy roads had to be negotiated. Shouts and car horns filled his extrasensory ears, serving him well, but much occluded by the pulsing thump of his heart.

Eventually the familiar smell of dog shit and disinfectant told him he'd reached the school entrance, not the playground gates, they would be locked by now to keep the kids from escaping. It was a short flight of stone steps to the double doors of the imposing, if you could see, Victorian portico. He stepped inside, knowing what would be waiting for him.

'Larkin, you're late,' the stern voice of the school secretary echoed in the voluminous gothic vestibule. Chas needed a wee and was not sure he could hold on as the dragon neared. Sensing the fire of her breath, he was able to anticipate the swing of the slap, so it took some of the momentum and sting out.

'Me mum sent a note. I've been...'

Slap, he didn't sense that one. 'We got no note from that strumpet of a mother of yours.'

Chas waited, no slap, no more berating.

'Mrs Coggan, perhaps I can take Chas to his class?'

Oh, the wondrous breath of respite, the elation of escape. 'Miss, er, Doyle? Is that you, I cannot see very well, er.'

Slap.

'Mrs Coggan, enough of that now.'

Chas sensed the secretary withdraw from the vestibule arena of conflict, retreating into her lair, and he leaned into the gentle caress of Miss Doyle as she stroked his reddened cheek, a slight abrasion from her handkerchief as she erased the imprint of Thelma's voluptuous lips. 'Come along Chas, let me get you to your class.'

'Thank you, miss, but I need a wee.' Chas imagined the caring smile of Miss Doyle rather than witnessed it.

'Can you find your way to the loo? Lazy eye, is it?'

'Yes, miss, lazy eye,' and Miss Doyle spiralled away, just a gentle smoothing of Chas's cheek that he pressed into, to savour, until the dragon breathed fire through the glazed portal of her secretarial den, insisting he get a move on, and to ask his mum to contact the school. Well, he'd tell her, but fat chance she would comply.

Chas felt his way into the corridor and, assisted by the smell of poorly aimed urine and, inadequate disinfectant, he found the door, entered, and panicked. The distinctive aroma that was the Boy's toilet was compounded with the smell of cigarette smoke. This could only be Mickey Saint and his gang. Somehow teachers allowed him and his brethren to get away with murder, perhaps because they had murderous back-up outside the school. The teachers didn't care, just longing for the day when he and his entourage would graduate to the streets.

Mickey Junior whooped with glee when he saw Chas Larkin enter the lavatories. Chas considered legging it, but he couldn't see and his second beating up of the morning would probably be less debilitating than an accident running the corridor, maybe even a tumble down the stairs. So, he braced himself, but was unable to prevent whizzing in his pants, the resultant streaming down his legs unavoidable and visible. This act of incontinence was greeted by the Saints with convulsive derision and cavorting depraved merry japes, regaling Chas with names, all toilet humour based, the hoodlums not having an expansive knowledge of the English dictionary, and this served only to scare Chas more and to turn his bowels to water.

A soft Irish accent, a girlish lilt and, a gentle touch, ushered Chas back into the corridor. 'Roisin?' (*Pronounced Ro-sheen*) he enquired. Chas was the only person who called Roisin by her baptised Irish name, most called her Rosie, or Ginger Nut, and Chas's determination to name her correctly meant he was a firm favourite of this vivacious and headstrong girl from an Irish immigrant family. He respected this girl. She had withstood all the banter about her unruly mop of ginger curls, freckles, and her lanky ungainliness, generally with a swift right hander, followed up with a threat of a belt from her Dah, if any of the parents felt like taking issue with her, and the threat of the O'Neill family had sway.

The O'Neills, although new to England and this East End neighbourhood, were establishing a firm *don't touch* reputation, Dah O'Neil reportedly earning substantial money as a successful bare-knuckle fighter back in the Emerald Isle, and along with a host of equally capable and protective brothers, Roisin had confidence aplenty. Chas admired it, admired her. Not much else was known of the O'Neills and people presumed that eventually they would be *dealt with* by either the Saints or the Larkins.

In the meantime, their reputation preceded any O'Neill. 'Hey, Rosie, we were just 'aving a larf like,' Chas heard a cowering Mickey say, his disciple backup having faded into the toilet cubicles. Nobody messed with this red-headed lunatic who carried her fifteen years, maybe older, status to great effect.

'It's Roisin, Mickey, and I thought I told you to leave Chas Larkin alone, so?'

'It's okay, Roisin,' Chas mumbled, extending the end of her name out of respect, the dampness of his trousers and his wet legs causing him to feel a chill from the draughty corridor.

The Police

Miss Doyle, sensing she ought to check on the toilets, found Chas shivering and hunched in a crouch in the corridor. She embraced the wreck of a child and not letting go of her hug, she took him off to the gymnasium. After cleaning him, she gave him some lost property gym shorts, saying she would wash his school ones and dry them in time for when he went home. Chas was so grateful he cried more, welcomed the further tug into the waist of the teacher's skirts and lingered as she calmed and soothed him, but eventually, 'Okay, we've been some time. So, let's get you to your classroom.'

Chas murmured a reluctant yes, knowing full well that by the time he got to the classroom the Saint boys will have spread the word of his accident and he would have to bear this along with the additional ribald comments about his PE shorts. But the anticipated cacophony of cajoling lackey school children, all scared of the Saints and equally relieved Larkin took the brunt of the gang torment, did not happen. The classroom was silent. No Saint gang, just an attentive class facing the front, paying attention to the Headmistress while a police constable stood behind the formidable woman, springing backward and forward, heel to toe, hands clasped behind his back, occasionally dipping and bobbing up with bent knees, full of self-importance.

As Chas and Miss Doyle entered, the spell of torpid, benumbed attention, was broken as the kids swung their gaze, relieved, distraction had entered like the cavalry over the hill. Chas, intuitively knowing he had to seek shelter, dived under the skirts of Miss Doyle, to the immediate merriment of the children. The pressure valve was released, and the class engaged in a thunderous cachinnation of belly laughs that resisted even the stare of the teacher but was brought under immediate control when the headmistress clapped her hands.

'Larkin,' the Headmistress barked.

'Yes?' Larkin replied, his response muffled by Miss Doyle's skirted tepee.

'Come out now!'

Miss Doyle made to say something but was immediately hushed, and Chas felt he had no choice but to reveal himself and accept all that was obviously coming his way.

As Chas emerged, the teacher made a hand gesture to silence the children who were fit to burst again.

'Miss?'

'Larkin,' and the head looked to the constable, 'PC Arbuthnot...' she paused as the kids laughed at the name, then froze in response to the harridan's stare. Quiet achieved, she continued, 'PC. Arbuthnot has some questions for you.'

Chas's curiosity was piqued, but he knew enough to know that whatever the questions were, it would be a formality. The headmistress already swished the cane.

The constable opened up. 'Larkin, you took advantage of a distracted Mickey Saint and smashed him over his head with a lump of four by two in the toilets.' It wasn't a question, as Chas had already surmised, but he could not disguise his shocked face. It was a look that said, what on earth are you talking about and, *hope*, that the persecutor of his short life might be dead and on his way to a fiery hell. 'Saint is in hospital, in a coma, but he was sufficiently coherent as he was taken to the ambulance, to name you as his attacker, and this has been supported by his cohorts, all of whom you equally knocked about.' The Constable looked for a response, a denial, or a confession. Chas knew it made no odds either way, he was bang to rights regardless and was dreading what would happen now.

Chas's plaintive cry, "But Roisin," was met with confusion and was very soon dismissed. The Headmistress intervened as the class, Miss Doyle, and Chas were dumbstruck, not that Chas could see anything; all was a blur to him, his sight and his memory. Certainly, he had dreamed of the day he would be able to pound to death Mickey Saint and his gang and, in silent reflection, he thought a piece of four by two wood was a pretty good idea, but he couldn't remember doing it? Did he do it? And whilst he mused in his little dream world, he could not avoid a generating a nervous grin and, realising his error, straightened his lips in panic, but they mischievously curved upwards again, his previously crimped *innocent* countenance cast aside.

This was all the headmistress needed to affirm guilt and she beckoned the miscreant boy with a crooked finger that Chas could not see, but he did hear, 'Larkin, come here boy and bend over.'

He was drawn into the ingesting voice of the cane swishing crone, longing desperately for a saviour. There was the suggestion of a temporary reprieve as Miss Doyle made a plea for sanity to prevail but was immediately dismissed from the classroom. Chas felt doomed as his only ally departed, challenging the decision, but with no authority to countermand. It was the way of the world and nobody knew this better than Chas Larkin.

Chas felt the back of his collar being seized and, he was tugged so hard, momentarily, his one good foot left the ground. His club boot dragged noisily on the wooden floor of the dais as he was yanked to the teacher's desk, folded over and, to Chas's excruciating embarrassment, the headmistress tugged down his PE shorts expecting to bare Chas's underpants, but he had none. He hoped this would stop the Headmistress in her tracks, but it didn't. She gained additional strength from the shocked communal sucking in of breath from the class of children, who up until now had hardly dared breathe. She held Chas's head down and began swishing, barking in time admonishing comments as she stroked painfully hard. Chas cried out to stop, but this seemed only to enthuse the demented woman who made the strokes land harder. So, he stopped and bottled up all his cries and feelings and dreamed he had the four by two and could strike back. It was how he weathered and suffered the searing pain, which made it difficult to focus even on a safe haven as the Head explained, stroke by stroke, that after this beating he will be taken to the police station and charged with attempted murder.

All Chas could think was this would be a relief. Could a police cell be a safe haven? Eventually, the swishing stopped, and, beyond his internalised sobs, he now thought, what would his mum say? And then, what was the silence? He heard Roisin's voice. That distinct lilt was increasing in vehemence as it got nearer and louder. It was a sound he had never heard before; she was raging.

He dared to look behind him and, across his striped lambent bottom, he saw in a blur, a red-headed Valkyrie land a powerful swinging punch to the chin of the headmistress who went careering across the classroom stage. The copper went to grab the girl, but she stopped him with a fearsome stare and, through gritted teeth said, 'Don't you lay a feckin' finger on me bluebottle, or you will answer to me Dah and his O'Neill brothers.'

The copper stepped back and began to weigh up the multiple threats that faced him. The O'Neills were still an unknown quantity, but the Saints were brute force incarnate, what you call in the law enforcement field, a rock and a hard place.

In the meantime, Roisin had lifted Chas's shorts, threatened the class blue bloody murder in the form of the wrath of the O'Neills if they grassed, 'And that goes for you, woodentop,' she added to the floundering copper. He nodded his understanding and passed an advisory glance to the headmistress who looked back at the unfolding events from the floor, not realising more was to come for her as Roisin grabbed the woman's hair and towed her, feet scrabbling to catch up with this slip of a teenage gangly girl, who seemed to have such amazing strength. Roisin forced the woman to the desk, where she was folded over, and prone, the headmistress felt a cold draught as her skirt was lifted and Roisin tugged down her old girl's bloomers and set about caning the viperous woman, calling out with each stroke what would happen to her should she consider becoming a "duck's arse" and grass on her.

Considering Roisin had only been in London a short while, her assimilation of the cockney slang was quite remarkable and that was all Chas could think as he relished the humiliation of the headmistress. Although he did consider with stark realisation that his trip to Kilburn, the Irish sector of London, in a futile attempt at running away, had borne remarkable fruit. Pleased now he had walked all of that way not treading on one cracked paving flag.

2

CHAS WALKED HOW YOU WOULD IMAGINE, BLIND AS A BAT, slewing his club foot, and favouring a smarting bottom. Roisin guided him to the school entrance hall, told the secretary in no uncertain terms, to sign them out as sick, watched it done, threatened the bully guardian of the official school portal that O'Neill hell would visit her if she rumbled any of this, after which she steered Chas down the concrete steps to the street. He was free. He was safe. And Chas felt a rare exuberance, for the time being anyway, for he knew there would be consequences, there always were.

He looked to Roisin, her face a blur but he knew what she looked like, he even dreamed of her. Although only a year or so older, she was so much taller than his crippled body. He always wished he could iron it straight, but this would expose him even more. Roisin had the rangy, lanky frame of a lass nudging her mature years, a radiant womanhood already evident. A passionate looking freckled face that flared to reinforce the shock of unruly red hair and, the thing Chas most loved, her emerald eyes. They were so soft and loving when directed at him. He could not understand why this girl had become his protector. He was too scared to ask lest it be unlucky, and she disappeared. She told him the faeries had sent her and, it was all Chas needed to complete a daydream and send him off on another one, one that embraced his growing love of the Irish.

Roisin stood looking up and down the road, as if considering which way to go, or maybe looking to see if the police were tailing them. Chas wanted to put distance between him and the school. All he could picture in his mind's eye was the Headmistress and School secretary charging down the steps to pull him back and beat him again, the police swooping to feel his collar, a charge of attempted murder. After a brief time that seemed like forever to Chas, Roisin made up her mind and, with Chas's hand in tow, she lugged him along the pavement. Although his ambulation was awkward, he felt wondrously safe; nobody laughed at him. Nobody dared.

Roisin noticed Chas's difficultly in walking, stopped and looked at him as though absorbing all of his hurt, a beautiful caring face. He couldn't see it clearly, but knew it to be narrow with high, defined cheekbones tipped with freckles, not soft, but warm. 'What's up Chas, is yer arse sore, so?'

Oh, what a lovely accent she had. 'Yes,' Chas replied.

'So, you're struggling to walk?' He felt her eyes bore to the core of his soul. 'There's a chemist down the road, we'll call in there,' and she started off again, tugging Chas who walked in an almost indecent manner, legs spasmodically stretching out, then brought into tiny steps, returning to an extended gait. Roisin's heart went out to this poor emaciated and crippled boy. She would protect him forever. She'd had an older brother who had been similarly malformed, and the family talked of how he had been tormented mercilessly by children, and even adults, until he could take no more. It was spoken of only in hushed tones in her family, suicide being a mortal sin in the Catholic Church. Her brother had been refused a Christian burial, and she still did not know where he had been interred. The family kept it a secret. She hated the Catholic Church for this and hated with a vehemence all priests. She knew what they were doing, and one had tried it on with her, just the once. She told the priest what she thought about that, just before she kneed him in his child molesting bollocks and smashed his head against the altar.

They reached the pharmacy, and without hesitation Roisin tugged Chas through the door. This girl knew what she was doing, and he followed, breaking his hand contact for a brief moment to turn around once as he entered. He needed to maintain this lucky streak. She looked back at him in a confused manner, took his hand again and traversed the aisles, stopped, looked, selected something, moved on, picked up something else. Chas followed her to the counter, he heard the till chime the sale and, thinking he would head to the daylight and return to the street, he was surprised to be drawn to the back of the shop. He was convinced he had trodden on some cracks in the plastic tiles, and this worried him, but trusted in his spin at the door to carry the good luck on. It did, Roisin knew what she was doing and in her he trusted.

They reached a back aisle that was darkened. She had removed the bulb from the low ceiling light and, taking a stool to one side, she pulled Chas to her, cuddled him and, gently turning him around, she lowered his shorts and then with tender hand strokes she rubbed a soothing balm into his red raw arse cheeks. He smelled lavender. It reminded him of his Nan's house, the floor polish she used. Nan, on his mother's side, had always been kind to Chas, and when she died a couple of years back, Chas lost his only familial ally. Oddly, Chas was not embarrassed, and he could not explain this. He liked the sensation of having his bum rubbed and it appeared to him this was going on longer than was absolutely necessary, not that he was complaining. He felt an unfamiliar tingling response.

'That should do the trick Chas. Are you enjoying this, so?'

In a croaking voice, Chas managed to say he loved the intimate feeling and was annoyed when the Chemist told them to bugger off. She pulled up Chas's PE shorts as he stood, and then, right in the face of the shopkeeper, she said something unintelligible to Chas and clearly to the shopkeeper as well. He thought it was the Irish. Regardless, it had the desired effect as the Chemist retreated, likely to the toilet to rub his own bum.

Roisin said she would take him home, but Chas stood his ground. She looked back and ruffling his hair she reassured him all will be okay. He wished he could believe her. However, he went along and as he hit the pavement and fresh air, he began his spasmodic and clumsy gait.

'What is it, Chas?'

Chas looked like she might be beautiful but dim-witted. 'If you tread on the cracks you will have bad luck.' It seemed obvious to him.

'Did you tread on any cracks this morning on your way into school?'

Chas thought, 'Only the one when I was beaten up by Mickey Saint the first time.'

'So, avoiding the cracks up until you met that feckin' arse Saint didn't help you much?'

Chas thought on, did cracks go over to the following day as he had trod on a crack as his mum had dragged him from the off-licence, home.

'Chas, superstition is not worth the stress, and I should know being Irish, but what the hell,' and she took Chas's hand and skipped the paving flags avoiding the cracks with Chas, laughing and joking, tumbling occasionally and gathering a great deal of future misfortune as she scooped him up and lifted him over a crack, treading on it herself, for his defence she said. They reached his house just as a shifty looking man trotted down the steps, sporting a satisfied grin that disappeared as Roisin tripped him. He went flying across the cracked pavement. Every flag was broken and Roisin, after telling the dirty old punter to feck off, looked at the pavement, seeking an explanation from Chas.

'Mickey Saint. He heard of my superstition and broke the entire pavement to make it difficult for me to get in or out of my house,' Chas answered, speaking from the largely intact cobbles of the road. Chas gestured his sightless head to a plank that lay against the kerb. Roisin lifted the plank and laid it down so Chas could step over the crazy paving onto the stone steps.

'You dozy bastard.' It was Chas's mum, in a tawdry nightie that might be alluring to a sex-starved blind man, but to Roisin, it was simply seedy. 'Wot you doin' 'ome so soon?'

'I, er, er...' Chas teetered, trembling on the narrow plank.

Roisin stepped in for him and walking across the cracked pavement with not a care in the world, she went up to Chas's mum, 'Mrs Larkin, I'm Roisin O'Neill.'

Chas's mum took in this knowledge as if it mattered not a jot, although the myth that was the O'Neill clan was growing in mysterious strength. She ignored the warning bell and Betsy laughed.

'Chas has had a little trouble at school...'

Roisin was interrupted as Chas's mum back handed her

son across the cheek. 'What've I told yer about being good?' He fell from the plank.

'Stop it, and if you know what's good for you, you'll not hit Chas again. Am I making myself clear?' Chas, as he stepped back on his plank, sensed his mum momentarily feel the power of the O'Neills and wisely become scared, but soon regained some of her Larkin composure, telling Roisin to "fuck off".

Roisin turned back, stomped the steps, and got right into the older woman's face, 'Say that again,' the threat and menace patent.

Mrs Larkin told Chas to get indoors, and he went, but before he disappeared to the scullery, to his place, he thought he heard his mum apologise to Roisin. It felt good and then he heard Rosin instruct that if the police come calling to interview Chas about the attempted murder of Mickey Saint Junior, she was to get a message to her, and at that, Roisin turned on her heel, skipped the steps and, treading on every crack, zigzagged away.

3

FROM HIS CROUCHED POSITION BESIDE THE COAL SCUTTLE, NEAR the pantry door, he heard his mum stomping the hallway and, in a blur, she swirled into the kitchen, whereupon, losing no momentum, she marched to Chas and with all of her might, belted him. It affected his hearing, but he thought she said, "Now, if you tell that bog dwelling Irish strumpet I've hit yer, I'll do for yer, and chuck yer in the Thames, got it?" Chas nodded yes and she hit him again, 'And don't you forget it. Now, what's this about the filf coming round, and what the fuck have you done for Christ's sake?' Chas started to say he wasn't sure, but it seemed like he was being accused of hitting Mickey Saint with a lump of four by two... he stopped as his mum intervened. 'You 'it him with a Jew?'

'Nah, mum, a lump of four by two wood.'

'Shit a fucking brick,' and Chas's mum looked at her son

differently, a crumb of respect? Then reality dawned. Not the police calling, that was normal, but if the Saints came knocking on her door that would be it for them. They would need to get outta Dodge, and that would not happen. How could that happen? They were trapped. Maybe she should call on her family, but they would be reluctant to start a war.

'It'll be alright mum, the O'Neills...'

'Fuck the O'Neills,' she screamed, looking like for the first time in her life she was truly scared. 'You fucking idiot,' and she swung at Chas so hard his glasses smashed, and as his head hit the wall, he was completely blinded.

'Mum, I can't see.'

'Shut up you poxy bastard. Can't see? Of course you can see.'

'Mum, I can't,' and Chas cowered lest he be hit again. He heard his Mum pace away and the bottle of gin chink against a glass, then crash down as she began drinking.

Chas knew that to stay around and explain himself would be not only futile, but could become even more dangerous, for as the gin was imbibed and absorbed by his mum's crazed brain cells, she would take out all of her anger and frustration on him. So, dragging the burdensome weight of his foot behind him, he felt his way to the hall and the street door, out onto the top step. He turned and pulled the door, not to shut it, as this would make a noise, and using the railings as his guide, he tentatively made his way down the steps and began the blind journey to the doctor's surgery.

Ordinarily a five-minute walk, it would take longer, and he hoped and prayed his memory would serve him as he gave up on the cracks in the pavement. Needs must.

As luck would have it, despite the crazy broken biscuit paving, a kindly neighbour saw him, and taking Chas's arm she steered him to the surgery, guided him into the reception and into Thelma's safe clutches. 'She's done for him this time. The fucking mare,' Mrs Bates said to the receptionist. 'Reckon he'll need the hospital, poor mite,' and the neighbour stroked Chas's hair and, quite shocking Chas, she kissed his bruised cheek.

Thelma telephoned for an ambulance and then the police. Ironic really, as the custody of Chas's mum might save her from any Saint Reprisals and, more scarily, Chas imagined, Roisin's retribution. Not that the police custody would last long as it was considered normal to batter your kids, but a few formalities would be required before Chas's mum would be released, likely with a caution, having screwed half the coppers in the custody suite.

Chas knew the score and accepted it as his lot in life.

The Palestinian, Naadhira, was a flourishing, highly educated woman, and after qualifying as a doctor and anglicising her name to Nadia, she responded to a sense of duty, and a desire to pay back the country that had taken her in and educated her. She took a post in the deprived East End of London, at the Royal London Hospital, Whitechapel Road, but also, as good fortune prevailed, despite Chas's inadvertent treading on the unrepaired pavement, she also specialised at Moorfields, the London Eye Hospital. Nadia received Chas into casualty and after she had treated his immediate injuries, she intended transferring him to Moorfields. Nadia diagnosed a detached retina. She was confident this could be repaired, along with the lazy eye, all pretty much ground-breaking surgery, especially in this deprived area, but Nadia was very capable, as was the consultant she worked under. Thelma, standing in as parental loci, encouraged the bold step. What did Chas have to lose?

In the meantime, and in the same hospital, the Saints had a pow-wow. Mickey junior was still out for the count. A coma the doctor said and advised the family to keep talking to him. They didn't talk to him, they never did, but in the Saint family tradition, the matriarchs talked over and across the prone boy's bed and, if he was able to comprehend, he would likely approve of the war drums as his mum and grandmother preached retribution, regularly tapping the glass dome that resided on the bed. It was the crumpet dome, brought along for luck.

Beside the bed, the doctor had his own fearful problems.

He had to tell the Saints that all evidence was pointing to little Mickey Saint not coming out of the coma and, if he did, he would more than likely be a cabbage.

'What?'

'A cabbage, Mrs Saint,' the Doctor replied.

'Fuck me sideways,' and she looked at her son, 'he can't stand cabbage.'

The doctor chuckled, and all things considered, this was a mistake, which he realised just before the chair fell upon his head with considerable force, he was lifted semi-conscious by his white coat lapels, raised up and slammed to the wall, whereupon he considered he had better become a grass and tell on Chas Larkin. It was his only hope. 'Chas Larkin is in casualty at the moment. His mum did for 'im,' and in his panic, the Doctor, who was actually a refined middle-class man, spoke in the local dialect. Still pinned against the wall by one of the Saint lads, he watched as the womenfolk considered their options. The men awaited instructions, bristling, wanting to dispatch the doctor from the room, preferably on a trolley and then down the stairs. They could be so creative could the Saint men. 'He's to be taken to Moorfields, but if you're quick, you might get there before he leaves?'

Madge Saint, Mickey's wizened and diminutive Nan, and de facto head of the family, weighed up the best response, gave Bessie, the younger, a knowing nod, and to her grand-sons she instructed, 'Get down there now, and I don't want to see yer unless it's to tell me the fucking runt's brown bread. Dead as a door nail, preferably having suffered before fucking 'and.'

The order was given, and a very relieved doctor slid down the wall and, through swirling stars, watched the Saint crew of thugs leave the room. He felt sick. Concussion or guilt, he wasn't sure, but decided to have a little lie down as Nan Saint booted him in the head with her cherry red *Doc Martens*. It was a measure of the intellect of the Saint clan that none considered, in kicking the doctor senseless, they were depriving the young Saint of his medical care. Doctors to them grew on trees and, if they upset the Saints, they could be *hung* on that tree from whence they came and, of course, went, celestially speaking.

He was a drip, he knew, and if he didn't, he only had to look in the mirror at his goofy teeth, crooked nose, and different eyebrows; one a slug and the other a hedgehog. Why he chose to live in the East End of London he questioned often, but of course it was oft told to him, by the cognoscenti of the NHS, that he was not the sharpest scalpel in the medical drawer, and so, as nobody else wanted to do casualty in this roughneck, redneck, neck of the woods, he had to take what was offered him. He was told about the extraordinary and famed wit of the EastEnders, but as far as he had learned, that came because you laughed at the shit jokes or you never breathed a chuckle again. He had a small flat in the hospital and, as he was always on call, he rarely, if ever, stepped out of the relatively safe confines of the hospital. However, Doctor Wentworth had things to learn, like, you are never safe in this part of London, especially if you had a Saint and a Larkin residing in the same hospital, one having done for the other, albeit it was the children of the rival neighbour clans.

Chas felt safe, Roisin was watching over him and currently she had positioned herself beside the double doors that accessed casualty as sentry. Thus, the tinderbox *Okay* casualty *Corral*, soon to be host of a fearsome Saint and Larkin scene of retribution, was compounded by the presence of an O'Neill. Roisin was far from seraphic, although Chas thought she had the face of an angel, she was a youngster of that legendary County Clare, street-fighting, family. All was set for a playground fight, likely to the death and all of this the goofy doctor was unaware. That is until the double doors banged open at the far end of casualty revealing the Saint boys, framed in the portal, snarling, tooled up with pistols and one sawn-off shotgun, threatening apocalyptic repercussions for the slight done to their family and as an afterthought, the bashing in of the head of Mickey. And then the double doors, on powerful self-closing floor-springs, additionally impelled by Roisin, sprung shut and hit the gangsters full in the face, causing them to discharge their weapons. Unfortunately for them, though fortunate for everyone else, the slamming doors caused the shotgun to blow off the foot of Jimmy Saint, causing Jimmy to shoot his brother, Stevo, in the chest, who in turn shot his other brother, Percy, in the family jewels.

'Call the police,' Dr Wentworth shouted from behind a nurse.

'Don't be daft, so,' Chas heard Roisin reply, 'they'll all be on the take and scared shitless, that's the Saints so it is, yer feckin' goofy twat.'

The doc responded, 'Call an ambulance.' He knew how daft this was as he said it and looked to Nadia, 'Sorry,' and followed the Palestinian surgeon to the pile of bodies at the door, one already set to push up the daisies, the other two brothers writhing and crying atop of him.

'Stop moaning and let me have a look,' Nadia ordered the Saint boys. She bent down, calling Wentworth to her side. 'Check him, looks dead.' Wentworth checked and confirmed the diagnosis then stepped over the body of Stevo who had taken the shot directly to his heart and had commenced his journey to hell. 'Tourniquet on his leg, now,' and Wentworth responding to Nadia's order, applied a makeshift tourniquet to Jimmy's thigh so it would halt the pumping blood from the mess that had been his foot. Nurses rushed with dressings and morphine, while Nadia did what she could for Percy, who screamed in an unusually high-pitched timbre. She thought they could save him and had a fleeting amusing muse that his injury would save most of the women in the area as well. She grinned, which did little to comfort the writhing, peckerless, Percy Saint.

In the meantime, Madge Saint had heard the muffled sound of gunfire and relaxed back into the armchair brought to her by the battered and bruised doctor. She had good and reliable grandsons. She tapped the crumpet, thought for a brief moment about little Mickey, and as she caressed the glass dome, so Mickey's eyes flickered, and he mumbled something incoherent. It was a nervous reaction in the coma, not that the Saint ladies realised this, and the doctor was not about to inform them. As far as Bessie and Madge were concerned, Mickey was coming back to normal. They were not too worried about brain activity as they needed a thug in Mickey. There never was any chance of him becoming the highbrow intellectual in the family, and the bang on the head may even have helped, and this was the extent of the medical wisdom handed down in the Saint dynasty. But this serenity was soon to be jagged as Bernie appeared, poking his head around the door in his trademark dozy manner. Bernie was the slow one of the Saint boys, Bessie had six of them, Bernie, just turning twenty, spoke in a deep and laboured manner and was nicknamed after *Bernard Bresslaw,* a comedian who play acted as thick as two short four by twos, his catchphrase being, "I only asked...".

'What is it, Bernie, *I only asked*?'

'Mum, call me by my name, Johnny, please.'

'Fuck off, Bernie, *I only asked*, and I wish yer old man had worn a johnny, so I didn't get lumbered wiv you, you fucking thicko. So, what is it?' Bernie looked scared, not unusual Bessie thought, but became aware that her son had wet himself. 'Bernie, what's 'appened? Is that bleedin' Larkin dead?'

'Mum.'

Madge stood, strode to her dipstick grandson, and cuffed him. 'You've pissed yerself you bleedin' pansy, now, what d'yer want to tell me?' And she smoothed his fluffy cheek and soothed the blossoming red hand mark.

'Nan, mum,' his large head flicked between the two matriarchs, 'Stevo's dead, not Chas Larkin.' He waited nervously for a reaction, stepped out of haymaker range, and after a while, continued despatching his bad news. 'Percy's been shot in the orchestra stalls and Jimmy's had one of his plates of meat blown off.'

Bessie took a moment to take this in. She looked to see if her thicko son was having a laugh, but he looked deadly serious. 'Say that again.'

Bernie went to repeat the bad tidings, but was knocked sideways by his mum's notorious right hander, 'Mum?'

'What the fuck 'appened?'

'The doors mum, the fucking doors.'

'What?'

Bernie rapidly considered what he should say. 'Someone must have slammed the doors on Jimmy, Stevo, and Percy, causing them to shoot each other...'

'Who?'

Bernie again tried to think what he should tell his mum. 'Well, there was a darkie doctor and another goofy one, but I heard Chas call out for that Roisin girl to "let 'em 'ave it", so my guess would be the Irish kid, Rosie, she goes to Mickey's school,' he thought, 'I think... so they say.'

'I know, I know, I've 'eard about 'er, the Larkin sprogg said it was 'er what did for Mickey and not him... can't see it meself, a girl?' Bessie responded, now pacing the room, her mind already moving on from the plight of her sons. She could always have more, even if she was knocking on a bit, for her it was like shelling peas and, she had grandkids from her girls, growing up, but for now, her mind turned to retribution and a need to find out more about these O'Neills. They were rapidly becoming an enigmatic local legend.

Her eyes turned to the crumpet as little Mickey Saint mumbled something incoherent but sounded like the crumpet had been nicked and replaced with another, an unlucky one. Bessie lifted the glass dome and sure enough, following close inspection, the bite mark was different. You had to know, and Bessie did. This was different and she said, 'Someone's 'arf inched the lucky crumpet and replaced it with a replica...' she paused to think on '... and this one's got bad juju.'

The police did attend the casualty scene, they could hardly not, secretly praising the Lord there was one less Saint, another who would likely be singing soprano in the choir and, as a consequence not likely to be a distraction for them, with another hopping his way around the East End, making him easy to catch.

They took evidence from their main witness, Johnny Saint, aka, Bernie, *I only asked*, and he was convinced the carnage was a result of a drip of a doctor, an Arab surgeon, and one of the O'Neill clan, the waif Rosie, or whatever her name was? It was a dilemma for the police, what to actually brush under the carpet, and, in the end, good sense prevailed, and they called it a tragic accident. After having examined the door springs and observing they were wound really tight, they concluded this caused the doors to close and the Saint boys to misfire their guns and, having declared the incident so, they retired to Arbour Square police station to keep a low profile. Things would be hotting up between the Saints and the Larkins and they needed counsel from on high. This was way beyond their pay grade.

As Chas Larkin was being readied to be despatched to Moorfields, Roisin reassured him not to worry about her, the O'Neills would protect their *Roisin Dubh*. Roisin told Chas this was her nickname in the Irish. Translated it read, *Black Rose*. Chas loved it, loved being watched over by the Black Rose. Safe at last.

4

'Inspector, I need to get this boy to Moorfields. He has a detached retina that needs urgent attention.'

The uniforms that remained in the hospital were now attended by a Detective Inspector Casey. The boy looked a state and Casey stood aside as the porters lifted Chas into a wheelchair and began rolling him to a waiting ambulance, Nadia and Thelma following.

Casey called out, 'Shouldn't his mother be with him?'

Nadia looked back at the kindly detective, obviously new she thought, at least to these parts. 'It was his mother who did this damage. Well, her and a thousand other people in the neighbourhood, namely the Saints. Isn't it about time the police did something?'

Casey walked to Nadia and whispered, 'I will, I will,' he was Irish. Chas heard the exchange and all of a sudden felt comforted by the accent. 'First thing will be to go and see his mother and read her the Riot Act.'

'Yeah, you do that, why don't you, and after she has shagged her way around your police station, she will be back out and nailing this poor boy, again and again, until he dies.' Nadia felt bad following this rare loss of her temper, she thought DI Casey looked like he actually did care. 'Sorry.'

'No, yer okay, so,' and Casey rubbed his face, pulled at an eyebrow while he pondered, not realising he was being closely observed.

'When did you last sleep, Inspector?' Nadia continued, looking deep into the bloodshot eyes of the policeman. 'And this bruising around your eyes...' she stroked his forehead and felt around his eye sockets '... what happened?'

Casey was wary as he returned the stare into the deep brown eyes of this perceptive doctor. 'Lack of sleep, I suppose?'

Chas sat in his wheelchair, head tilted toward the conversation taking place above him, sensing, rather than observing, the exchanges, aware there was kindness from the doctor and softness in the policeman. Kindly attitudes from people with authority? All new to Chas.

Nadia hemmed. She was not so easily fooled. There was something else in the detective who looked down to Chas and then to Dr Wentworth, distracted. 'We need to take him now, Inspector,' and turning to her colleague, 'Wentworth, you run casualty for the time being?' Wentworth nodded.

'Good, and you...' she turned to Casey and prodded his chest '... I want to see you again.' And they left, Wentworth struggling to hold open the heavy double doors that had tough floor springs, while the wheelchair had to manoeuvre around the dead body. Looking back to Casey, Nadia casually remarked along with a head gesture to the dead gangster, 'Do something about this please.'

Casey had been recruited to the Metropolitan Police because of his knowledge of the growing perceived threat from the IRA. The detective inspector was from the West of Ireland and supported Irish nationalism, but not the brutal tactics of the IRA. His family had espoused this view on many occasions and had paid the price. His father shot, and a niece, his sister's girl, killed in a car bomb. This made Casey sensitive to the cause but motivated to stop those who felt violence was the way to achieve what they wanted. It wasn't. Casey could see this, and now it looked like an offensive was to commence in England. Once again, he could understand why, but could not abide the killing of innocents, as would almost certainly be the case if they started a bombing campaign in London. This was a realistic threat and, although not much was known by Scotland Yard, DI Casey had been dispatched to the East End. It was well known that this underprivileged area of London harboured many malcontents within its dark and shady streets, slums, and bombed out dwellings, still not restored or rebuilt following indiscriminate attention by the Luftwaffe. Combine this with the immediate proximity to the City of London, the finance markets, shipping companies, and Establishment Corporate Company Headquarters, then the situation could be volatile. The authorities were wary, even if active campaigns had not yet begun, they were expected.

(The first attack by the IRA in London was in July 1970, but concern that the 'Troubles' in Northern Ireland would eventually reach England was feared long before that first bombing).

It was thought that the strengthening of the local police was to challenge the gangs, notably the Saints, and to a lesser extent the Larkins, but this was merely a convenient front. So, no eyebrows were raised as the Force grew in anticipation of a war between the two families.

There was nothing more DI Casey could do at the hospital, so he decided to interview the mother of Chas Larkin and, calling at the house, he could not resist walking along a plank that seemed to span the pavement where every flag was cracked. It momentarily amused him, before he was alerted. The door to the Larkin house was suspiciously ajar.

With the toe of his shoe, he pushed the door fully open whilst shielding himself beside the portal flank wall. The

Larkins were known gangsters. He had been informed Chas's immediate family were mainly petty criminals, more support players if anything, but he was naturally cautious. Betsy Larkin was a known tart, operating in and around the docks, an area controlled by the Saints. The Larkins, he knew, were more into the gambling houses and brothels. What made Casey particularly curious was the Larkin boy had mentioned a *guardian angel*, a girl called Roisin O'Neill. Was the *Black Rose* here already?

There was no response from his calling out. He drew his handgun. He was a rare copper, but because of his involvement in seeking out terrorist plots, he was permitted to carry a weapon, which was most unusual in the London police. The uniformed officer behind him expressed shock at the production of a gun and wondered what he had wandered into.

'Jesus!' he exclaimed.

Casey nodded for him to take up his vacated place aside the door as he stepped across the threshold and into the house. The house was a bodge repaired, bomb damaged house. One of those deemed structurally okay but barely habitable, and this suited the racketeer landlords. Another of the Larkin businesses, not that this stretched to fixing up a property, even for one their own. Casey permitted himself a wry smile, jerry rig repairs for a Jerry bombed house.

He poked his head into the disgusting parlour then moved onto the middle room, the main living area, even more disgusting, and choking on the putrid stench, he leaned cautiously into the scullery, nervously smiling, it looked like a bomb had hit it. But his good humour faded when he took in the image of a mangled and bloody body that he presumed to be Betsy Larkin. A lead pipe lay beside the body. There was no hint of disguising or removing what appeared at first sight to be the murder weapon.

He called the constable and instructed him to run to the nearest call box and report a murder, to get a team out to secure the house, the doctor, and a meat wagon. The young Bobby disappeared, pleased to be away from a scene that sickened him.

Casey stepped cautiously over the debris to the body, wary that in an IRA murder they would sometimes leave a booby trap device and, this had all the hallmarks of an IRA murder. One of the first things he will ask the doctor. The dead woman appeared to have had her kneecaps broken and her shin bones went in unnatural directions. The face had been beaten to a pulp, making recognition almost impossible. This was a message, and he was pretty sure the message would be conveyed by the troops after they returned to the police station, and he was sure he would have to interview Chas Larkin, sooner rather than later. It looked like he may have been right in the middle of the attack and may be able to give them a steer on who was responsible. If nothing else, it explained his injuries.

At Moorfields, Chas was admitted, Nadia signing him in, mentioning that his mother would be along after the police had interviewed her and, presumably, she had shagged her way round the police officers, not realising Betsy was no longer alive. Not that this would deter the most determined of coppers, but, as it turned out, she was no longer a looker.

Nadia went into the examination room with the consultant. She had called him at home and asked if he would attend, she being of the opinion that if they didn't operate straight away, Chas Larkin could lose his sight. The consultant confirmed her diagnosis. They could deal with the lazy eye at the same time as the detached retina and, asked for Chas to be prepared for immediate surgery. Nadia and the consultant left to ready themselves.

She was surprised to see DI Casey waiting outside in the corridor. 'What are you doing here?' she asked, probably more abruptly than she intended.

'Chas's mum has been murdered, the house turned over, and I think this could be where Chas got his injuries.' He held back as he looked upon Nadia's shocked face. Then dropped his bombshell, 'Can I speak to him, please. Just briefly in case he can tell us anything?'

'He is very poorly. Likely suffering from delayed shock and if he isn't, he will be.'

DI Casey gripped the edge of his eyebrow between finger

and thumb and pulled the skin. Nadia saw this as a nervous reaction, which explained his black eyes. 'Just for a moment, please. You can be with me.'

Nadia felt this man would be sensitive. He was not like the coppers she knew in this area, and she agreed. 'I will be there and if I think he is getting distressed, I will insist you stop.' Casey nodded agreement, but Nadia wasn't finished. 'If his mother is dead, who will sign the consent forms for his operation? His surgery is urgent.'

'I called the Welfare Office of the council and they are sending someone, so he will get his treatment.'

Nadia was impressed at the breadth of this copper's thinking and consideration. 'Thank you, very thoughtful,' and she touched his hand. He flinched, like he had been burned, and likely he had. 'Okay, let's do this, he's due his pre-med,' and she steered the detective into the room where Chas was propped up on a pillow on a trolley, unaware of what was happening, other than he had lost his glasses, it being the first thing his mum had smashed, and he was convinced he was blind, though his feelings of dread eased as he was comforted by the voice of Nadia.

'Chas, we can fix your eye, you have a detached retina, probably from a blow you suffered on your head and, while we are at it, we can correct the lazy eye. We are going to operate in a minute, so please, do not worry. I will look after you.' She touched his hand and began to talk more intimately, 'I have Detective Inspector Casey here. He wants to talk to you about the attack on you and your mother.'

'How is she?'

Nadia knew this question would come and she did not know how she would answer, but Casey did. 'I'm sorry, your mother died.'

Nadia tightened her grip on Chas's hand and whispered, 'I am so sorry Chas, but you will get all of the help you need. Where is your father?'

She was interrupted by a violent reaction from her patient. 'Not my fucking mum. Roisin, how is she? And my dad? Who the fuck knows where he is? He wouldn't give a toss anyway.'

'Roisin?' Casey asked in a calm, modulated voice, a lyrical softness of the west of Ireland.

Chas clammed up. He'd said too much, aware of tears running down his cheek.

Nadia called an end to the interview and shooed Casey out of the room and once in the corridor, the door closed, she said to Casey, 'You need to look into the history of this boy. I suspect he has been serially abused, bullied, and you can start at the school because it looks like in the last day or so, he has been caned most brutally. A fourteen-year-old boy. And if you don't do something, then I will.'

Casey took Nadia's hands and held them to his chest. 'Rest assured, I will look into all of this. This is more complex than just an issue of child abuse... as serious as that is,' and dropping her hands, Casey pinched the skin surrounding his eye.

Nadia took his hand away from his eye and pulled his arms to his side. Satisfied she had him pinned down, she commenced smoothing the bruised skin. 'You must stop this. I can see you worry and giving yourself pain helps you focus, but there are other ways without resorting to self-harm.'

Casey looked deep into Nadia's eyes, took the doctor's hands again, brought them up to his mouth and kissed them. This shocked Nadia, not because she was offended, but because she liked it.

'I can help you,' she whispered.

Casey snorted and Nadia tried not to be offended. 'You can help?'

'Yes.'

'How?'

'I can teach you other ways of dealing with the circumstances of your job and your life and, when you are ready, I will.' Then she surprised herself when she leaned in and gave the man, taller than her by at least a foot, a hug, but recoiled when she felt the hardness of his shoulder holster. 'Who are you?' she asked, stepping away, shocked.

'I'm not sure myself,' he replied in a sombre voice. 'Will you help me...' and he opened his jacket to reveal the holstered weapon, '... my job is harder than you could imagine.'

Nadia returned to the original embrace and tipping on

her toes, she kissed him. A light kiss, but she lingered, and it said all that she wanted. She liked this man. 'Yes, I can, and I will, help you.'

'Excuse me, I'm from Child Welfare. You need me to sign some consent forms?'

A short and stout woman in tweeds and brogue shoes, stood, legs akimbo, body language saying she took no nonsense and certainly did not approve of canoodling in hospital corridors.

'I had better be off,' Casey said, staring down the Welfare woman who looked like she had just stepped out of the Kennel Club and, to wind the woman up a bit, he leaned in and kissed Nadia goodbye. She blushed her farewells and he was gone, into God knows what danger, and already she had started to fear for him.

For Casey, he was buoyed. Was it because he was tingling at the kiss with such a beautiful woman, or was it because he felt he had a strong lead, and not for the murder of Betsy Larkin, oh no, this had bigger implications? If he was not mistaken, his intelligence out of Cork had been correct. They were looking for *The Black Rose*, and all roads lead, albeit circuitously, to the Saints, via the lad, Chas Larkin.

5

CASEY HEADED TO ARBOUR SQUARE POLICE STATION. HE thought he had better show his face, especially as he had only been stationed here a couple of days, discovered a murder, and called out local resources. If he was a good guesser, he would also surmise he was not liked and would never be popular. For one he was Irish, called a *bog dweller* on his first day, and then *Bones*. A derivation of *Casey Jones*, a TV series about a train driver and whenever he walked in, he had to endure very poor renditions of the terrible, though catchy, theme tune.

'Bones, Commander wants to see yer. So, I'd get the Cannonball Express up the stairs if I were you.' Casey thanked Old George, the Desk Sergeant, as politely as he could muster, but there was more as he watched the sergeant tap his chest. 'He's not a lover of guns. So, I'd be on yer metal, mate.'

Casey stopped in his tracks, returned to the counter, and faced up the Sergeant. 'That would be Detective Inspector to you, or Sir, and don't you forget it, or you'll be number one on my list.' He drew open his jacket and tapped the holstered gun, whilst staring down the copper who was out of the Ark and clearly had a problem with high-ranking officers being parachuted into his nick, cutting up a storm on his Manor. And then he was Irish.

Casey waited and eventually heard the anticipated response, 'Sorry, Sir.'

'It's okay, Sergeant. I understand, a Mick, bog dweller, dumped into your nick, and with a mysterious rep, eh? Maybe a pint after work, we can sort things out between us, fancy that?'

'Yes, thank you, sir.'

'Suppose I'd better see why the commander has a wasp up his arse,' and Casey spun on his heel and bog trotted to the stairs, pleased to hear the sergeant chuckling behind him. Wherever he went in England he had to earn his stripes, and in some places, it took longer than others. Arbour Square might take some time? It seemed a prejudiced nick to him, the Irish and Black immigrants, but he would win. He always did. He thought about Nadia and his tummy did a flip. What was that all about? He resisted pinching his eyebrow as he replayed her words in his head, loving the sound of her refined English voice with the hint of an exotic accent.

Although the procedure was relatively new, it was not difficult, and Chas was soon back in a single room off a side ward. A copper had been posted outside the door, Nadia grateful, she had worried about that. Casey seemed a thoughtful man and she wondered if she would see him again. She liked him and, it was clear he liked her, but any relationship between a white man and a coloured girl would be frowned upon, before getting to the religious differences, although she and her family had an open mind on these matters; they needed to have, in order to live here.

She saw Chas settled, his eyes bandaged, which she told him would only be for a day, maybe two and, she was confident he would see better than ever before. Chas was cheered by that thought, more so as he expected a visit from Roisin.

Casey knocked and entered but was informed by the commander he has to wait for the "Come". Casey stepped back out, much to the chagrin of the senior police officer, knocked and waited, knocked again, and heard "Fucking

Come" and Casey went in and took a seat in front of the substantial desk.

The commander was about to speak when there was another knock on the door and the PA entered with a tray of tea and chocolate biscuits.

'I did not say *come* Phyllis.'

'Oh, fuck off, you soppy sod.'

'I did not order tea, either.'

Phyllis gave him the look that said *fuck off you soppy sod*, and she went up and playfully slapped the bloated cheeks of the commander. 'Brendan wanted tea.' She turned to face Casey, 'Got you some lovely chocolate biscuits an all, an all.' Phyllis trying her luck at the blarney.

'Fanks sweet'art,' Casey's attempt at cockney, 'yer gorgeous, so yer are,' there was only so much mimicry he could manage.

The commander sighed as Phyllis wobbled her beautifully round arse, contained in a tight skirt, at the commander and disappeared.

'Lovely arse that girl.'

'Commander?'

'Sorry, did I say that out loud? Pour us a cuppa will yer, sunshine.'

'Jeyziz, feckin' 'ell, a cockney commander,' Casey thought, but spoke.

'I beg your pardon, Casey?' the commander responded,

and the ice was broken. It didn't usually take long for the Irish charm to work its magic on any hierarchy.

'Okay, okay, I want yer to know I don't take kindly to *Mavericks* on my patch, but you've come with a recommendation that even I would not question. But to give yer an 'eds up, I will be watching you,' and he used two fingers at his eyes, reversed them and pointed them at Casey. Message conveyed. 'Now, how the fuck did you manage to get chocolate biscuits outta Phyllis? I only get given the bastard plain ones.'

Casey smiled. 'Yer feckin' eejit, she fancies yer. Give her a bit of the glad eye and you'll likely get more than a chocolate, Oliver,' and Casey winked, and stood. 'Now if you don't mind, I need to get downstairs, sort out a space, and get working.'

'Don't go waving your pistol around either.'

Casey turned at the door, 'I don't think it's my pistol Phyllis is interested in,' and he knocked on the door and called back "come", 'get my drift *sunshine,'* and he was off, to get *Operation Black Rose* underway. Maybe he would call in to see how Chas Larkin was doing, but really, he had gotten all he would likely get out of the poor lad. However, Nadia was a completely different matter. His tummy flipped again.

Chas fingered his bandaged eyes. 'Leave that alone now, so.'

'Roisin, you came.'

'D'yer tink I would leave yers all to yerself now?' She stroked Chas's hand.

All in all, Chas thought, this had to have been the best day of his life. He'd had a visit from Thelma and Mrs Bates, *why, oh, why could not one of those women have been my mum*? And now, here was Roisin. He was as comforted by her Irish lilt as he was by her physical presence, and he thanked the Lord for the day this girl appeared in his life. Thelma and Mrs Bates gave him warmth and comfort, but Roisin gave him hope. Hope his life might change. She was a pathway out of his misery, and, hallelujah, his mum was dead. A brilliant day, all things considered.

6

CASEY SKIPPED DOWN THE STAIRS TO THE FIRST FLOOR THAT held the CID office. He had a lightness in his heart. Standing outside the double doors to the hall like room, and gazing through the porthole window, he smoothed his forehead. He resisted the urge to twist the skin of his eye socket. Instead, he screwed up his resolve. He was about to step into the Lion's Den where immigrants were only tolerated by the locals and *Blacks* and *Micks* were bottom of the list for acceptance. He never could get his head around this blatant prejudice. Arm out straight, he pushed a leaf of the door and stepped in, faux bravado disguising his jangling nerves. He had a job to do. He would not let his family down and, he could not do this on his own. He needed these people on his side.

He was greeted with *diddly-diddly* singing and broken

arm dancing, totally unauthentic. Not the point. He stood, legs akimbo and allowed them their juvenile fun. His lack of rising to the bait clearly disappointed and the merry japes faded when he was confronted by a woman, tall, likely mid- to late-thirties, attractive in a robust way.

'Yes?'

'DS Wade.' The dark-haired, no-nonsense woman stuck out her hand and they exchanged a firm handshake.

'Can you show me where my desk is please?' Casey resisted asking her for a cup of tea, knowing many men thought this was all women in the force were good for. He didn't. He'd worked with some very good women back in the old country. Looking around him, he noticed he was no longer the total centre of attention. Wade didn't move. 'Is there anything else?'

'Yes sir. I'm to be your *bagman*.'

There were ripples of stifled laughter around the room as Casey looked his allocated assistant up and down. So, this was the reason for the silent mirthful observation. She seemed unperturbed by his reticence, or the laughter. Wade stood straight-backed and legs firmly planted. It was rare to have a woman detective, and to rise to Sergeant meant this lady would have had to beat down great resistance and misogynistic banter, some of it not so light-hearted. So, he was addressing a strong personality. Casey guessed she had been promoted to Detective Sergeant in order to take this position with him, a Detective Inspector foisted upon a well-established team. 'And you've made a recent surprise rise from Detective Constable to Detective Sergeant?' Wade nodded, a little confused. 'You volunteered for this?'

Enthusiastically, Wade responded, 'Yes sir.'

'Nobody else wanted the job then?'

'Er, no sir.'

'Thought as much. What do you know about what we are tasked to do?' It was clear from the blank expression Wade had volunteered for the promotion and had not a clue what the job involved. 'Are you firearms trained?'

'Yes sir...' her energy waned. 'A little time ago.'

'Familiar with the territory?'

'Born and bred.' Wade stood to attention, pride for her East End heritage.

'So, you know the Saints?'

Circumspect, 'Of course. You here for them?'

It was Casey's turn to be coy. 'They, and the Larkins, have fingers in most things. So, I imagine the family heads will rise to the surface sometime. This could be dangerous.'

Wade seemed unperturbed. 'Yes, sir.'

'Look, Wade, no offence, but you need a few more years before you tackle something like this,' and Casey started to walk on, thinking he would find his desk on his own, aware also he was once again the focus of attention.

Wade stepped to one side to block Casey's progress. 'Sir, the commander said I was to be your bagman.'

Dodging to the left, Casey said, as he passed Wade, 'Don't want one. Don't need one.'

Wade allowed her new DI to wander around looking for a vacant desk. There were none. She stepped over to a corner office that looked like a room used to deposit anything that needed to be out of sight and out of mind, opened the door, and beckoned. 'Your office, sir.'

Casey swerved to meet Wade at the door, looked into the crammed box room, and returned his gaze to face up the laughter that silenced immediately. He may be a bog dweller, but he was a senior officer. He stepped inside the room, sidled around to a vacant space and summoned Wade to join him. She did.

'Close the door.'

She snapped it shut, sidled to a small gap in the floor that preserved her personal space and shrugged her shoulders at the sound of raucous laughter from the main room. Casey made his mind up, he liked her. Maybe she would have what it takes.

'Tomorrow morning, early, before anyone else gets in, we will meet here and throw all of this stuff into *their* room. We will set up my desk and another that will be for you. You will work in here with me.' Wade looked startled. So, Casey explained, 'First off, I don't know who I can trust out there and, if we are going to do this, we need to bond. You need to hear all that is happening. I can trust you?'

She nodded, 'Of course.'

He decided to see if he could trust her. 'You're a lesbian?'

'Sir!'

'Whatever you say will stay here with me. We need to trust each other. So?'

'Yes.'

'Just so you know, I'm perfectly okay with that. Not all bog dwellers are Neanderthals.'

Wade smiled, it looked like a load had been taken off her shoulders and, she was beginning to think this might work out well for her and, in an office, away from a room full of pre-historic men, who certainly didn't understand a person's sexuality

'What's your name?'

'Flora, sir.'

'Well, Flora, stop calling me sir unless we are with the brass. My name is Padraig.'

She stopped him, 'I thought it was, Brendan?'

He smiled and she thought he had a lovely warmth to his face, but it was a face that likely concealed a thousand secrets. 'I let people think that. Brendan is my middle name, but I was christened Padraig, which would give everyone over here, carte-blanche to call me Paddy. Do you see?' She nodded. 'I want you to call me Paddy.' Now this did surprise her. 'Would you like to know why I agree to this?' She nodded again, desperately trying not to gawp. 'Because I want you to get some credibility with those feckin' eejits outside.' He waved in the direction of the Hall of the cave dwellers, all to a man, looking back at them through the half-glazed screen, 'They will be amazed, but all my friends call me Paddy anyway.'

'Thank you, sir... er, Paddy.'

He smiled, that lovely smile again. 'Okay, are you up-to-date with the boy Larkin and the murder of his mother?'

'I am.'

'Good, brief me as we drive to Moorfields Hospital. He's out from his op and I think a brief chat is needed, don't you?'

She nodded again, thinking she had become a nodding donkey in the past five minutes, but was excited, feeling a bubble of great energy in her stomach. They both shuffled around the congested room to get to the door, which Casey held open for Wade, she passed through, and said, so it could be heard across the room, 'Thanks, Paddy, I'll just get my jacket.'

You could have heard a dinosaur drop.

7

As they drove, Casey probed more about Wade and her life, appreciating it must have been tough in the police. He was not even sure her path would have been eased by the fact she was attractive. She had dusky skin, her mum had been Maltese and yes, she was fed up with the *Malteeser* jokes. However, her dad had been a true cockney, a tall man and she had inherited his height, strength and, Casey was beginning to think, the East End famed wit. This woman would likely make a good *bagman.*

As they approached the children's ward, Casey was alerted by the lack of activity. He grabbed Wade's upper arm, 'Hang on, this is not right,' and he took his gun from his shoulder holster and handed it to Wade. 'Can you handle this?'

'Yes.' and she discharged the hilt magazine, checked it, slammed it home, flicked the safety off.

'Good. I'm going in and shortly after, I want you to carefully see what is happening. I left a guard on Larkin's room earlier,' and Casey walked casually to the ward doors.

'Paddy,' he looked back, 'careful yerself,' and he rolled a salute as he bashed through the double doors, noticing as he passed through, the uniformed copper on the floor being treated by Nadia. The policeman was lying in a pool of his own blood.

'Whoa, what's this?'

Nadia looked up, 'They're in...' she couldn't finish her sentence because a goon was shouting at her to shut up, waving a gun around like a kid with a sparkler. Gesturing with the gun, he indicated for Casey to get to the wall, which Casey did, joining two crying nurses, and a tea lady, sans trolley, which stood in the middle of the short ward. She was an elderly woman looking like she could take on the whole world with her teapot if she had half a chance. He could hear shouting from Chas Larkin's room.

Wade peeked through the porthole of the ward doors and weighed up what was happening, decided to bide her time. That time came quicker than she imagined. A man fell from a side room clutching his head. The gunman was momentarily distracted, and she took her chance, kicked the door open, crouched, aimed, and fired. The gunman dropped like a stone. Casey ran from the wall and kicked the gun away, spun, kicked the other thug in the balls and whilst he writhed in agony, he took the cuffs thrown by Wade and secured him. In the hectic moments he had heard an order from Chas Larkin, "Roisin, run ". He looked, but too late.

'Flora, chase after whoever was in Larkin's room,' and he pointed to the other end of the ward, another set of double doors that lead to a fire escape stair.

Dashing to the door, she looked through the porthole, could see nothing, opened the door and, gingerly, with the gun held out in front of her, she stepped out onto the metal fire escape. Whoever it had been had made a clean getaway. She returned to the ward, now under control, slipped the safety on the gun, and returned it to Casey. He had his arm around Nadia. The copper and the gunman were dead. The second assailant was shouting, demanding medical care, calling Wade a murdering bitch. Nadia parted from Casey and walked to the man on the ward floor and swung a pearler into his gonads, it didn't silence him, but it did give him something to think about, whilst he sung hallelujah in a high-pitched treble.

Wade dialled 999 from the nurse desk. Nadia was back in Casey's embrace again, crying.

'Support's on its way,' Wade said.

'Nice shot, Wade. I was going to suggest a refresher course. Don't think that'll be necessary.'

The nurses shuffled the children out of the ward, not one crying, all in a state of great excitement. They had enjoyed the played-out scene of goodies and baddies, full of the desire to spread the word of what they had witnessed, none realising the danger they had been in. Uniformed police began to arrive, and Wade set about instructing them what to do. They seemed reluctant to take orders from her, so Paddy opened his jacket to expose the shoulder holster, they got the message.

'Thanks, Paddy, but I could have handled those fucking turnips.'

'I know, Flora, I was just saying if you wanted to shoot one of them in the foot or the balls, I would lend you my gun,' and he looked to the dead gunman. The police officers got about their business more diligently.

'I think a brief word with Chas?'

'No, Brendan, or is it Paddy?'

'Padraig, Nadia. I would prefer it if you called me that, it is my name.'

'Well, Padraig, Chas will likely be even more traumatised. So, if you are going to talk, I want a child psychiatrist with him.'

'Wendy's a trick cyclist and she often treats children.'

'Who?'

'Wendy is my, er, girlfriend, Paddy,' and she looked at Nadia for a reaction.

'Wendy Richards?' Nadia asked, unmoved by the declared relationship.

'Yes, do you know her?'

'Know of her,' and Nadia looked at Casey, 'she would be good for Chas Larkin.'

In the meantime, a pair of detectives had arrived, idling by, waiting for instructions from Casey, the senior officer.

'You two, take witness statements, do not go near the patient Chas Larkin, and I want a doubled-up, armed guard on his room. This has Saints reprisal all over it, but you do nothing else until I say so, okay?' They nodded acceptance of their orders. 'I want to see your report first thing in the morning.' They nodded again to the disappearing back of the new DI bog dweller who seemed rather distracted, steering the beautiful, coloured doctor out of the ward. They resented being told what to do by an interloper, knowing they had to obey.

'Come on, you lot, and take that geezer to our nick,' Wade pointed at the thug on the floor still grasping his naughty bits, 'and bang him up. Paddy and I will be interviewing him in the morning, got that?' DS Wade ordered.

The Detective Constables looked at each other, riled at being told what to do, now by a girl, who up until today, had been good only for menial tasks, but according to what they had learned so far, *this girl* had shot and killed a Saint hired hand. They were impressed and at the same time, delighted. The Saints would not take kindly to that.

Outside the ward, Wade walked to Casey who was having a tete-a-tete with Nadia. Casey turned to Wade as she approached, 'Flora, what's a safe pub for coppers around here?'

'The Green Man's a filth pub, usually given a wide berth. The last thing the Saints or Larkins need is a war with the old Bill.'

'Nadia, I want to ask you out on a date, but in this instance can we start with a drink this evening? When do you get off?' Nadia looked taken aback, but Casey was continuing, addressing DS Wade. 'Can Wendy and you join us at the Green Man, Flora?'

'Wendy? Why?'

'I want to talk about what we are involved in. Wendy has a right to know, I take it you live together?'

Wade was further impressed by this man's perceptiveness, not that she was a lesbian, for she had never truly disguised the fact, but not cool to broadcast it. No, she was impressed he had instinctively detected she was in a permanent relationship, albeit necessarily discreet. 'Yes, we do, and a drink at the Green Man would be okay, I'm sure.'

'Detective, what on earth is going on here?' Nadia showed her resilience, having been close to dissolving into tears and, now this man was asking her out on date and, in a police pub?

'Wade, make sure those woodentops are doing what you asked them to do, then go home. I will see you at the Green

Man, say, seven thirty, eight... before the Arbour Square shift change.'

'Right you are, Paddy,' and DS Wade had to work hard to contain her excitement at all that had happened to her that day, topped off, she had killed a man. She couldn't wait to tell Wendy, although she may have to curb her patent glee, maybe not mention killing someone?

Nadia and Casey watched Wade disappear into the children's ward. 'Now, Padraig, what is going on? And I haven't said yes to a date yet.'

Casey put his arm across the doctor's shoulders. She wondered if she should shrug it off, but didn't, it felt nice, and she needed a hug. 'Nadia, I want to take you out. I'd like to get to know you, but as you have seen today,' and he fluttered his hand, 'my job can be a bit dodgy.'

'A bit!'

He smiled. 'Where do you live?' She told him, 'I will pick you up at seven-ish. Come with me to the pub, I want to talk to you and Flora, and if this Wendy...'

'Wendy Richards.'

'Thank you. Well, if she is there, then I can do the proverbial with one stone.'

'Two birds?'

'Well, technically, there will be three birds.'

'Paddy, I am not a bird, I am a woman.'

'Okay, two birds and a woman. I'll pick you up at your place, okay?' and he left Nadia pondering if she had in fact agreed and, whether she should call him Paddy if he annoyed her.

'Piece of work ain't he?' Wade observed.

Nadia looked deep into the eyes of this detective sergeant who struck her as a very capable woman, not a bird. 'Yes. Is that good or bad?'

'I'm going with good, and by the way, I'm okay being a bird. Come along tonight you can meet my bird,' and chuckling, Wade left the confounded doctor, sensing trepidation mixed with stirrings of excitement.

8

Back at *Dad's*, the Dog and Duck pub, the Saints matriarchy licked their wounds, while the men drowned their sorrows waiting to be told what to do. What preoccupied Nan, Mum, and a gaggle of aunts, daughters, and nieces was not that they had lost one of *their own*, or even that one of the lads was also not likely to make it, or at the very least would have a high-pitched voice, another a limp, and Mickey Junior was in a coma. What obsessed them was the crumpet had been taken and replaced with a replica. A good one they acknowledged, but this facsimile had seriously bad juju, as had been evidenced these past few days.

'What have we heard from our man arrested at the hospital?' Grandma Saint asked, speaking from her rightful place at the head of the table.

'Not been easy, they've got him banged up with guards

not on our payroll,' Ma Saint replied. 'We did hear from a nurse on the ward that Chas Larkin was saying it was some girl called Ro, sheen, O'Neill. Seems she has a liking for the Larkin runt and has set herself up as his protector. Didn't someone say this Rosie tart had been involved in the toilets with Mickey? Sorted out the headmistress at the school as well?'

'Sumfing like that.'

'We'd better track this girl down. She's causing us a lot of unnecessary,' and Ma Saint called out to one of the brothers in the public bar. 'Maybe she took the crumpet?'

'Mum?'

'Bri, find out all you can about this Ro Sheen O'Neill?'

'Ro Sheen?'

'Ro Sheen, yes, you gone bleedin' deaf?'

'Nah, nah mum, just little Mickey was mentioning someone called Rosie O'Neill at his school, but she was just a fucking kid. Older than Mickey, but just a kid and, a bleedin' girl,' and Bri allowed himself a sly grin.

Bessie Saint beckoned her second eldest down to her and Bri lowered his head. His Mum belted him one, 'You fuckin' tosspot. Never underestimate a woman, whatever 'er bleedin' age. Got that, have we not taught you nuffink?'

'Sorry, mum.'

'I should fink so. Now, go, and do what I told yer.'

'Mum?'

'Yes?'

'What was it again?' Bri wasn't the brightest of the dipstick Saint brethren, all of whom were challenged intellectually, a state exacerbated by never listening at school.

'Find out about the O'Neill family, especially this Ro Sheen. They're new to our manor so someone should be noticing them. What do they do? Where do they live, and what would they do to us if we sort out this fucking girl of theirs?' Bri turned to leave, still none the wiser, they had looked for the O'Neills only last week to no avail. The new family had a growing reputation, but people had no knowledge of them. If that was the case, even after a few broken fingers, then the O'Neills would be a force to be reckoned with, eventually, but Bri's main concern was how to tell his Mum and Nan.

'I don't drink, I'll have an orange juice.'

'Don't drink?'

'I'm a fucking Muslim, yer bleedin' eejit, Paddy,' and Nadia looked at Casey, both perplexed those words came out.

'And Muslims don't drink?'

'No, Padraig, we don't,' she sighed.

'Fair enough, orange juice it is,' and Casey went to the bar whistling as though he had not a care in the world.

When he returned with her orange juice and his pint, she

questioned him. 'It doesn't bother you I'm a Muslim? What are you, Catholic?'

Casey was about to sip from his pint and seemed surprised at the question. He put his glass down on a beer mat and answered, 'Why should it bother me? And, yes, I'm a Catholic, though seriously lapsed. I have little time for the Catholic Church, even more so with the feckin' priests, and I could not give a toss about your religion. Frankly, I care not for any religion. They're all trouble.'

Nadia chuckled into her orange juice, 'I agree. Religion is the cause of much strife around the world and, I have...' she wobbled her head, '... fairly broadminded parents, but even they might be a bit taken aback if I brought home a man who was a Catholic, lapsed or no. The significant fact being you were not a Muslim, you swear like a fucking trooper, and...' she looked stunned, '... I seem to have caught that from you.' They both snickered as if it was wrong they should be laughing at such a momentous thing as swearing, but their animated jerking bodies drew the attention of the few patrons in the pub, all coppers, or ex-coppers.

Casey hoped it would get rowdy when the shift knocked off around eight, the background noise would mask what he needed to say in confidence, contrarily though, he also needed an audience. He had to lean across to Nadia as she was whispering, 'What?'

'I said, how did you know Wade was a lesbian?'

'She told me.'

'What, she just upped and told you did she?' Nadia thought Casey looked like he had been caught in the headlights, only just realising he was talking to a bright woman and not a *bloke* on a bar stool.

'Well, no, I guessed, and she confirmed.'

'And?'

'And what?'

Bloody men she thought, you have to drag everything out of them. 'And she told you she was living with another woman?'

'No, I guessed that as well.'

'Allah be praised for Christ's sake,' aghast at her mix up, 'at last you tell me,' and just then Wade and her girlfriend, Wendy Richards, walked into the pub, spotted them immediately and walked to the table.

Wendy was a stunningly attractive cherubic lass of mid- to late-thirties but looking a lot younger. She took a seat at the table and waited to be asked what she wanted to drink.

'Drink, sir?' Casey gave Wade an admonishing look, 'Sorry, Paddy, drink, and I am guessing you would like a soft drink, Nadia?' She introduced Wendy to Nadia and Paddy as she left for the bar, having insisted Paddy sit back down and shut up. Casey liked his working partner a little more.

After they had settled at the table and exchanged a few frivolities, Casey set out why he had asked them to meet. 'I wanted you here, Wendy, because it seems Flora is hell bent on working with me and you need to know what she might get involved in. Already today she has been in a shoot-out and killed someone.' Casey looked at Wendy as she looked in horror at Wade. 'Okay, she didn't tell you. Well, that ends now,' and he looked to Wade. 'Flora, you will need support from Wendy as and when and Wendy needs to know if and when she needs to worry. These things are important, so you can focus without worrying about what she might think.'

'Why am I here?' Nadia asked, just as a rowdy shift from Arbour Square nick poured into the pub for a few jars before wending their way home, more than likely a few sheets to the wind. When the throng saw Casey and Wade, they formed a huddled hush.

Casey expected this, excused himself and walked to the now crowded bar, everyone jostling for the barman's attention, but Casey won out. He had a booming voice, but it was the accent that attracted the man behind the counter. 'Barman, I want to buy each and every one of these officers a pint.' The hush remained, the perplexed looks on all the faces, amusing if you had the time to observe, or the inclination to amuse yourself. Casey didn't, he addressed the placid coppers, 'I am buying you this drink because DS Wade and I will no doubt need your help in the coming weeks, months, or years and I want you to remember...' He looked back and flicked his head for Wade to join him and she did, '... I expect you to remember this peace offering and be grateful for it. I know some of you are in the pay of the Saints or the Larkins, maybe both, but know this, if Wade or I call for assistance and do not get it...' and he opened his jacket to reveal the gun, '... I will find you and kill you, without a second thought. Know this and understand it. Now, enjoy your beer and leave Flora and me alone, okay?'

A resounding "yes, sir", and the gaggle returned to gabbling, while Casey and Wade returned to their table.

It was Nadia who spoke first, 'And you want me to go out on a date with you? You need your brains testing, and Wendy here can do it for you, because you are an A-one, first class, nut job and I want nothing to do with you. I will find my own way home thank you,' and she left, the coppers at the bar having heard every word.

'Well, Paddy, I'd say you blew that,' and Wendy chuckled, put her hand on Wade's hand and took it off immediately,' she did not want to be indiscreet.

Casey lowered his head to the table to offer a confidential note, not for the gathered coppers, 'It was important to me the local filth knew Nadia had blown me out. She does not have the nous to stay safe and now she cannot be seen as any future bargaining chip. I did not want her worrying about me, nor me worrying about her.'

'Okay for me to be worrying then?' Wendy interjected.

'Wendy, most of those thickos will not realise you are important to Flora, and if they do, they will likely leave you alone. With Nadia, she would give it all away, and I cannot guarantee protecting her, and if I can eventually persuade her to come out with me, it will be out of the area, quiet, and discreet. Well, you know about that don't you?'

The Saints men had been sent away, each tasked with sourcing more intelligence on the O'Neills. Nan still commanded the table and spoke to the granddaughter, 'Young Bessie, make some enquiries of the Brigades. What do they know? Have they heard of these London O'Neills and do they have some dope on this Ro Sheen girl? And someone get my fucking crumpet back.'

9

Scotch 'Arry was in amongst it, couldn't avoid it. It was his worst nightmare. He had Billy Big-Head shadowing him, which was most unsettling, it meant the Saints were onto him and, to compound Scotch 'Arry's misery, Billy wore his fish jumper. Billy wore this jumper when he was on a Saint mission, usually to *manalise* someone.

Scotch 'Arry was a mystery, widely thought, up until recently, to be a waste of space, not that he took up much space, even at the bar. He was tall and drainpipe thin, drank like a drain as well. It was his penchant for the ale with whisky chasers that meant he needed to be able to feed that habit with money and, cash was hard to come by if you're in the pub most of the time. So, he embarked on a career path, *telling on people*, a calling at which he was singularly unsuccessful, even though he frequented so many pubs in the East

End that he could pick up untold amounts of information useful to either the Saints or Larkins, and the better prospects for a more sustainable career, ratting to the police. *Untold* though was the one tiny flaw in Scotch 'Arry's chosen vocation, that in his relatively sober moments he envisaged himself rising to the dizzy heights of a super-grass, a new identity and accommodated in a villa in Spain. And that flaw was, nobody, in London at least, could understand a word he said.

Scotch 'Arry had an abstruse Glasgow accent, which probably would be okay if he didn't exacerbate his unintelligible speech with a distinct slur after imbibing and, since he quaffed lots and regularly, this was a serious flaw. Scotch 'Arry was a local joke, never taken seriously.

That is up until the last week or so.

Jock MacDonald was an undercover cop brought down from Glasgow to the Met by none other than DI Casey. They had met on a case in Belfast a few years back, got on, and kept in touch. Before coming to take up his post at Arbour Square, Casey had called in the local knowledge, and there, sticking out like a sore sewer, was Scotch 'Arry. An incomprehensible informant. Jock met Scotch 'Arry and they got on like a house on fire that could only be extinguished by pouring copious amounts of beer on the flames. Not many people could understand Jock either, but he had one advantage over Scotch 'Arry, he could write legibly, pissed or sober. Scotch 'Arry's writing was so cacographic he could have been a doctor, but under the tutelage of Jock, he was improving. Even had his own pencil.

An immediate friendship was struck between the sloshed undercover cop and inebriated snitch and, since nobody could understand either of them, the information flowed readily. Scotch 'Arry's wealth of intelligence cascaded like the proverbial gushing Font, fuelled by a generous bar tab, funded by the Met, until the drainpipe collapsed, and the Glaswegian kissing-cousin would lug his new mate back to his lodgings, before returning to his own garret to write up his reports.

It was this collaboration that sourced the knowledge of Roisin O'Neill and the infiltration of the O'Neill family into the tinderbox East End of London and, that evening, whilst Scotch 'Arry remained vertical, Jock was able to leave 'Arry for a short while to feedback to Casey. Scotch 'Arry was reporting that there was to be a campaign by the Saints, principally against the Larkins since the Saints were convinced the Larkins harboured Roisin O'Neill.

Casey received Jock's note in his room at the Section House, a building adjacent to the police station that had rooms for single police officers. It was sort of a seedy hotel, though it was more akin to a boarding house ruled over by a desk sergeant who enforced the rule, no men on the women's floor and anything happening, he needed to be told. Sergeant Drake was, ironically, a *duck's arse*, a grass who told on the police, in return for copious quantities of cash from either the Saints or the Larkins. He wasn't fussed who paid, and pretty soon he reckoned he would have enough money to retire to the sunnier climes himself.

Sergeant Drake read the note from Jock before passing it onto DI Casey and that accounted for the presence of Billy Big Head standing with Scotch 'Arry at the bar when Jock returned. The jungle drums had worked and the Saints' most efficient weapon, an intellectually challenged battering ram with a big fish jumper, had been despatched.

DI Casey roused himself, read the note, dressed, and headed for the police station next door, via the telephone box on the corner of the Square. He put a call through to Scotland Yard, roused a trusted support team and they would meet at Arbour Square before hitting the streets.

Into the station, a cursory and cautious word to the desk sergeant, up the stairs and into the empty CID room and across to his office. It was still stuffed to the gunnels with all kinds of detritus, some of which he hurled out, in order to get to a phone. No sign of a chair so he perched on the corner of the desk, got through to the Comms room, and requested they call in DS Wade and, while he waited for his new bagman and reliant support from the Yard, he began emptying his office and setting up the two desks, back-to-back, so Wade and he could face each other. A radical arrangement he thought necessary as the Nick leaked like a colander. He wheeled in two of the best chairs from the CID room for Wade and himself.

Wade arrived, having been shaken from her bed with little time for any accoutrements, though a brush through her bushy black hair might have been good, Casey thought, but her mood was elevated by Paddy's housework. He had loaded every CID room desk with the evacuated rubbish, and she couldn't wait to see the faces of the CID men when they arrived in the morning. 'Well, Paddy, nice job.'

Casey nodded a curt acknowledgement and got straight down to business. 'Sit, I was going to brief you in the morning, but I'll run through it now. You'll see why, but first you should know we are a part of a new anti-terrorist Met Team.' Casey pinched his eyebrow while he observed how Wade would react, but he already had a shrewd idea.

Wade looked nonplussed, but equally excited, 'Okay...' and demonstrating her comprehensive knowledge of the Met, and especially Scotland Yard. 'What are we called?'

Casey smoothed his eye socket. 'You know the Yard well. Though we have no formal name, we will have loose links to Special Branch, who in turn are not so loosely connected to MI5, with a bit of muscle from the Sweeney.'

Now this did take the wind out of her sails, but demonstrating further her incisive thinking, 'Loosely Paddy? The Flying Squad? You do know the Sweeney Todd are loose cannons, don't you?'

Casey nodded, 'Well done, right question,' and he pushed to get to know his new assistant's intellectual prowess further. 'What do you understand by the term, "loosely"?'

Wade paused in thought, leaned forward in her lovely new chair that swivelled, elbows on the desk, and cupped her chin in her hands. She had resented the call this evening as she had been in the process of reconciliation sex following an enormous row with Wendy after they had returned from the pub. Wendy had expressed her anger at finding out that her partner had volunteered for a dangerous post without consulting her. For Wade this had mixed messages, the most important being that Wendy truly loved her and worried for her safety, setting their relationship onto a new footing. Though she had hated the row, she had been mightily impressed with the fury Wendy could muster. Wade preferred to muddle on and let things come out in the wash, whereas Wendy had made it very clear this would not be acceptable to her. The problem Wade tussled with now was how much she should tell Wendy as it would appear she was in deeper than she could ever have imagined with Wendy as well as some new police attachment that had the word *terrorist* in it.

Casey watched Wade process her thoughts, allowing her time to reach her conclusions. He knew she would be working out how much she could let Wendy know and half suspected they had rowed that evening. 'You have to be circumspect on how much you tell Wendy,' he said, interrupting the hiatus and observing the shocked response on Wade's face, and knew he had hit the mark. 'So, "*loosely*" what do you think?'

Fascinated with Paddy's ability to interpret her thoughts and the sensitivity of the man, she wondered if this was a quality a police officer needed in order to be good at such a specialist job? The one she was about to embark upon.

'If you're worried whether you have the ability to do this job, let me put your mind at rest. You are just starting out, and I am impressed so far. The rest you learn as you go along, but, and I say this with all seriousness, develop a second sight, a gut feeling because danger will come at you from all sides, the local gangs, terrorist groups, and, as I have seen this evening, from amongst our own in the police. So, "*loosely*"?'

'Our own, this evening?'

'Feckin' 'ell Wade, answer the bloody question!'

Wade jumped at his outburst and noticed he immediately grabbed for his eyebrows and screwed the skin mercilessly. 'You have to learn to stop doing that.'

'What?'

'Your fucking eyebrows, you prairie 'at!' He looked shocked, 'Sorry, sir.'

'Prairie hat?'

'Twat, sir.'

'Sir?'

'You guvnor, are a Radio Rental, Prairie 'at, and just so you know, it means you are a mental twat.'

Casey laughed, '"*Loosely*"?'

Wade sighed, this was worse than arguing with Wendy and she felt like giving her new Guvnor a right hander. 'Loosely, I imagine, means the powers that be are keeping a discreet distance in case it blows up,' and she thought about the terrorist threat, '... literally, in their boatraces.'

'Boatraces?'

'Oh, for Gawd's sake, you'd better get yer learning 'ed on for the slang, or you will not understand a fucking fing, *boatrace*, face... okay?' Casey grinned. He definitely liked his new bagman. 'And, I imagine, we need the intelligence of MI5, the resources of Special Branch, and, the Flying Squad would always cover our backs and, while we are at it...' she was calming and reciprocating Casey's beautiful blarney smile, '... don't call me a *bagman.* I'm a woman with balls enough to take on most of the girls' blouses in this nick, so, I think we have marked each other's cards enough tonight. Why don't you tell me why you called me in?'

10

SCOTCH 'ARRY WORRIED FOR HIS LIFE. THE FISH JUMPER WAS filling his vision. He slugged back his pint and chased it immediately with a whisky, and it scorched his vocal cords, not that anyone could tell. It was as if he had a natural unintelligible, rasping, soul singer's voice. Where was Jock, a drink addled thought, feeling more than a little exposed with the immediate proximity of Billy Big Head. He could not take his eye off the vertical whale of a fish knitted on the thug's baggy Aran jumper, perplexed as to why it was not horizontal and swimming along cable knit waves and, every time he tried to make for the door, so the fish would block his way.

Billy was a brainless thug, what might be called in sensitive teacher conversation as special needs and, he compensated for his lack of education and grey matter with a diametrically opposite forceful nature. Not quite like Lennie in the novel *Of Mice and Men,* for it could be argued Lennie had a soft nature, and if Billy had a sensitive side, people were yet to see it. If Billy said, "I only want to stroke your hair" it most certainly would not be a shampoo-like caress. It would end up with him caressing your brains like a meat mincer, not that he knew what brains were, except they made a mess on the pavement and the police seemed inordinately interested in them until they had been paid off, and the road sweeper given a substantial bung.

The patrons of the pub currently hosting Scotch 'Arry and Billy Big Head, and Jock whenever he returned, were rightfully nervous also. If Billy came into your pub it was not likely he was there for convivial conversation between friends, a sharing of banter on the merits of West Ham or Millwall football clubs, and so, the other customers kept a wary eye on Billy and the nearest exit.

It was a peculiar sight, the narrow limbed, elongated Scotch 'Arry, next to the humungous frame of Billy, who ironically, had a tiny head, certainly not in proportion to the thug's sizeable body. The best way to describe Billy, and many have cited this similarity but out of earshot of the Saints enforcer, was he was like a rotund, fully inflated balloon, where his head was the tiny knot that tied the neck and, amazingly, Billy had unfortunately been blessed with ridiculous hair that so resembled the lips of the balloon beyond the knot in the neck. This observation being an example of the EastEnders wit and sense of irony and, if you didn't get it, or more importantly, laugh, the irony would extend to an iron bar across your own balloon lips. However, although you would be well advised not to mention any of these patent visible characteristics in front of Billy, you could be permitted a tiny titter at the resemblance of Scotch 'Arry to one of those skinny balloons clowns have, just before they turn it into an animal that defies description. And, if any of the pub customers were good guessers, and I would guess they all were, Billy was fixing to twist and turn Scotch 'Arry into some funny-shaped animal any minute.

Casey and Wade continued their conversation until the phone rang and startled them back to reality.

'Casey, who's calling the *Golden Shot?*' Wade derred, it was a new game show on TV, contestants telling a crossbowman to move up, down, and sideways and then to fire at a target; it was a huge hit. Wade watched as Casey listened in, made a couple of scribbled notes, and said, 'Is he downstairs?' He nodded to himself and hung up.

He stood to get his raincoat, it had been fine drizzle when he'd walked from the Section House to the nick, and he noticed Wade had come in with a wet umbrella. It was the sort of weather in a British summer that could confound those who did not know it; an apparently benign drizzle can soak you to the skin. 'Time to meet another member of the team,' Casey said to a rising Wade. 'How's yer Glaswegian?' He set off for the door.

It was coming up to eleven, pub kicking out time, unless they had a lock-in at the Gallows. Either way, it spelled danger for Scotch 'Arry, Casey thought, as he descended the stairs to the entrance vestibule of the nick to meet Jock. Wade, playing catch up, was surprised at the speedy leap into action of her Guvnor.

Leaning against a wall in the vestibule, Wade noticed a pair of bored, stranger, plain clothes coppers. They were looking on fascinated, as a soggy and animated Jock paced up and down, regaling a confused Desk Sergeant with his Glaswegian diatribe, which swung and focused on Casey as he arrived. Casey began to get his notebook and pencil out so Jock could transcribe what he was saying, but it seemed Wade's talents extended beyond telling her Guvnor to do one in an equally befuddling cockney rhyming slang.

'He said, Scotch 'Arry is at the Gallows pub,' and she further explained it was a villains' watering hole, 'and he's got Billy Big Head as a shadow and, it's likely to go down anytime soon with it not looking like sunshine and fucking roses for Scotch 'Arry.'

'Aye that's it, hen,' a rare moment of clarity before Jock slipped back into the incomprehensible, except to Wade, who then translated.

'He says the Saints are out in force, turning over the Larkin knocking shops and gambling dens, looking for the

O'Neills. All hell is breaking loose,' she stopped because Jock looked like he had more, but he was interrupted by Casey.

'Outside, now,' and Casey looked up at the desk sergeant, then across to Jock and Wade, and all of them understood. Old George, the desk sergeant's face either showing offence at not being trusted, or it could have been anger at the loss of potential intelligence, which would have earned him a few pounds from the Saints.

When they got outside, they huddled, the blue lamp casting an eerie sheen across the wet pavement, as they agreed a plan of action.

'Should we not have supporting troops, Paddy?' Wade asked, looking at the two wet rag officers and a Scottish inebriate, none of whom reassured her one bit.

Casey sloped his head at Wade, 'You know who you can trust do yer? The Sweeney shouldn't be too far behind,' and he indicated to one of the dozy twins to call the Yard and direct the flying squad to the Gallows pub. Wade set off to follow Jock and Paddy as they headed for the villainous pub, a few blocks away, Wade sensibly asking what the plan of action would be and receiving no answer from the puffed-out members of this so called elite anti-terrorist unit.

The Gallows was still open, though the landlord could be heard calling time, telling his patrons to "Fuck off home to their beds". Casey and Jock were making horrendous horsey snorting noises as they sucked in the rain-saturated air. 'Oh, fuck it,' Wade said to her crippled colleagues, straight armed the pub door and there was immediate recognition of a copper, albeit she was plain clothes.

The landlord ceased his expletive ridden cry and called out to his boozy patrons, asking if they could pretty please pop back to their hovels and he will be their best friend and went directly to the copper. 'I'm getting them out now, no need for any fuss.'

She silenced the landlord with a fierce stare. 'I'm not here for licensing hours...' and she stopped and turned as Casey walked in wearing a black balaclava that covered the whole of his face save for two eyeholes and an opening for his mouth. He strutted directly to the bar where Billy Big Head had Scotch 'Arry around the throat, relishing slowly throttling the unintelligible grass.

The pub hushed so all heard, which was Casey's intention, and facing up Billy, Casey opened up in his full Irish brogue, 'You Billy Big Head?'

Billy thought for minute, then replied, 'Yeah, wot of it, Irish?'

'And you're a Saints man?'

Billy dropped Scotch 'Arry who made a scuttling, indiscreet exit, trailing a diarrhoea drenched perfume in the smoke and ale sodden bar atmosphere.

Billy answered he was a Saints man and then with a rasping sound, like the air squeezing out of the Billy balloon. Casey had the thug's neck, and he tightened the grip as he levelled his gun at Billy Big Head's little head and shouted so that everyone could hear, 'The O'Neills say hi,' then he blew Billy's little head off his big shoulders.

Wade screamed, Jock put his arm across her shoulders and hustled her from the pub and down to the street corner where they stopped and watched the clambering exodus from the Gallows pub. Patrons scattered to all points of the compass, notably one or two headed for the semi-detached Saints and Larkin pubs, Dad's and Arries. There was no sign of Scotch 'Arry, he was scotch mist, just Paddy now sauntering away from a scene of chaos, not a care in the world, slowly removing his balaclava once he was a distance from the Gallows. He slouched, leaning on a corner of brickwork waiting for Wade and Jock to reach him, both clearly in shock. Jock not so much; he'd worked with Casey in Northern Ireland.

'Fucking Ada, Paddy, when I said you were radio rental, I fink that was a fucking understatement. You're a full blown, loony.'

Casey rounded on Wade, 'Was Billy feckin' Big Head about to do for Scotch 'Arry?'

'Well, I suppose we will never know for sure, now will we?' She took a deep breath, tried to calm her inner self. 'But it certainly looked like it. Jeez Paddy, there will be a war now.'

'Yes, there will, but the Saints, who will likely team up with the Larkins, will be fighting the O'Neills, who sweet-'art...' he slipped temporarily into the local parlance, '... do not exist,' and back in his Irish accent, 'we made 'em up, so.'

He thought for a bit, 'Except maybe, Roisin Dubh. She is haunting this place somewhere and, our best chance of finding *The Black Rose,* is Chas Larkin.'

It was probably the adrenaline beginning to subside, but Wade could not stop herself convulsing into laughter, especially when Casey followed up by suggesting she not mention this to Wendy and asking if anyone fancied fish and chips. He assured her nobody in the pub would squeal on him, not that he could be recognised, for fear of retribution from the O'Neills; swift and deadly. She saw the sense, relaxed, and wondered about this *Black Rose* for the briefest of moments before her thoughts turned to going home to fuck the brains out of Wendy. So, she skipped the fish supper and left to do just that.

Jock and the two back-ups disappeared out west, home to Scotland Yard, appropriately, not that anyone could understand him there either, which also suited everyone, especially Jock.

Casey went back to the station, stayed for enough time to satisfy himself that the shooting was being attributed to the O'Neills, then retired with a bottle of Jameson's to the Section House that was emptying as the troops had been mustered to deal with a gangland killing, and the anticipated fallout. Casey fell into bed and drank from the bottle; he was knackered.

Maggie Saint, a young cousin and one of the barmaids at Dad's, went to respond to the bashing at the locked door of Dad's, but not before she had summoned help from some tooled-up Saint ladies. All the Saint men were out on Larkin bashing missions and scouring the area for the O'Neills, who would likely be hightailing it back to Ireland if they had any sense. She opened the door to an out of breath man she recognised but could not recall his name, which mattered not as the man wasn't staying. He was there only to impart bad tidings and, since messengers of doom-laden news had a habit of being blamed for any unacceptable content and, being done in for it, he intended to scarper. The man shouted his news, 'Billy Big Ed's just had his little head blown off by one of the O'Neills,' and the messenger turned and fled, leaving a shocked young lady to report back to the Saint matriarchy.

11

Roisin sat with Chas Larkin well into the wee hours. She held his hand and talked of the beauty of Ireland. She called it the Emerald Isle, because, she said, "It rained all the feckin' time". It got a chuckle out of Chas who struggled to sleep. The bandages were coming off in the morning and despite reassurances from Nadia, his lovely doctor, he worried he would be blind. Nadia also said she was going to recommend a surgeon to look at his club foot. She thought it might not be as bad as at first thought and she did wonder if he exaggerated dragging the foot, emotionally, rather than as any overpowering physical need. Still, the minor distortion, she had said, can be straightened, with some simple cuts and setting in plaster in stages, to eventually straighten the foot. He had a mixture of hope and trepidation. Roisin, however, saw it all as encouraging and when she left, just before the detective arrived, she had instilled in him a breath of hope that he cherished.

'Have I missed Roisin?' Casey asked.

Chas felt safe with this policeman, he didn't seem to be in the pay of the Saints or his own family and, had saved his bacon yesterday. 'Yes, she's been here a lot of the night. We talked of Ireland. It sounded lovely, and if I get my sight I would love to visit, maybe even live there. What time is it?' Chas was thinking of his bandages being removed.

'Six thirty, and you would love Ireland. The people would embrace you, Chas. The Irish are a loving people, have massive hearts.'

Chas was silent and Casey wondered why. He had the lad talking and didn't want him to stop, 'What is it?'

Chas summoned up the courage to ask a probing question that seriously impressed Casey, 'If they have such big hearts, why are they killing innocent people with bombs and shootings?'

Jeez, Casey thought, easy ones first eh. 'Chas, that is a long and very difficult question to answer and it stretches back into the distant past where the Irish, my grandfather being one of them, had to fight for Independence from Britain. The British ruled our country with a fist of iron and left it divided, North and South.' Casey realised he might be conveying his own innate anger to the child, so sought to lessen any anxiety. 'It was all a long time ago, but for some, feelings run deep for the historic hurt, especially for the divided Ireland. But not all Irish people believe in the way of the gun and the bomb. Essentially the Irish are a peaceful nation, you have to believe that. Do you Chas?'

Chas thought for a moment, thought of Roisin, of her wonderful loving heart, counterpoised with her sudden flaring to violence to protect him. Yes, he could see what this policeman was saying. 'Yes,' Chas said, 'I just wish we could all live in peace.'

Casey felt his heartstrings being tugged. This young boy who had endured so much in his short life, could empathise with a people who had suffered and most importantly, he shared with the boy a desire for peace achieved by negotiation, not violence, and that was often so difficult to understand. Even he struggled and sometimes felt the need to resort to violence, reassured himself always it was for the greater good, like yesterday evening in the Gallows Pub.

He sensed he was getting through to Chas Larkin and so pushed a little further, giving of himself, in order to receive. 'I am against those who would terrorise and kill innocent people, Chas. Would you like to know why?' Chas murmured he would, and Casey pulled his chair closer to the bed in order to confide painful information. 'You've heard of the IRA?' Chas said he had. 'The IRA have a belief to unite our country, it was divided by the British back in the mists of time and this is resented by many people who live in Southern Ireland, my home. Some of the folk in Northern

Ireland, however, feel just as vehemently to be a part of the United Kingdom, Britain. Do you understand?'

Chas said he did, 'And that is why they fight?'

'Why some fight. Whereas others, the vast majority, try to resolve things peacefully.'

'Are the IRA coming to England?'

A perceptive question from this astute boy and it warranted an honest answer, 'It is possible the IRA will bring their fight to England. They see the British government as integral in the resistance to the reintegration of the North and South. It is more complex than that, and if you look deeply, there are feuds, Catholic against the Protestant religion, the larger and stronger protestant population in the North, seen as marginalising and bullying the smaller catholic community. Do you understand what I mean?'

'Yes, a bit like the Saints and my family, the Larkins.'

'Very much like that and, because the enmity has existed for so long, like the Saints and Larkins, it is sometimes difficult to take a step back. To allow peaceful good sense to prevail.' Casey remained quiet for a while, listened to the boy's laboured breath. Convinced Chas was made of stern stuff, he continued, 'If it is any consolation, I believe good sense will prevail. There are very brave people talking on both sides, under the radar, working for a settlement. How soon that will happen heaven only knows, though I believe it will come. In the meantime, I, and many other people like me, Irish and British, work hard, behind the scenes, to stop the hurt.' Casey's breath caught, and Chas noticed.

'What is it, what else is it, sir?'

Clever or intuitive, Casey was not sure, but Chas Larkin impressed him. And so it was, with a lump in his throat, Casey answered honestly. This boy deserved that, especially as he could very soon be the centre of a maelstrom, not of his making, but innocently caught up. 'I lost a niece, killed by a bomb, and my father was shot by a Northern Irish group. We call them terrorists, whatever side of the border or religion they stand for. So, you see, it has hit me personally and, at first, I reacted violently, to my shame, but after a while I resigned to fight for peace and reconciliation. I still wonder sometimes if I have made the right choice.'

'What's your name?'

Casey was choking, he had not revealed so much to anyone before. He felt he could talk to this child, something about the boy that he could not put his finger on, but he deserved a truthful answer. Casey screwed up his eyebrows, so the pinched skin really hurt, 'People here know me as Brendan Casey, and if I trust you with this confidence, are you able to keep this secret my lad?' Casey winked and wondered why as the boy could not see. Chas confirmed he could and would, he had kept secrets all of his life. 'My name is Padraig, people I like, and I especially like you, I let them call me Paddy, and so you can call me Paddy, and son...' he paused, took a laboured breath, '... I promise I will look out for you. You are special indeed,' and Paddy sobbed, lying his head on the boy's bed and, after a short while, he felt the comfort of hands soothing his shoulders and, surprisingly, a kiss on his neck. He looked up into the deep brown, soulful pools of Nadia's eyes and she cried with him; her people suffered too, and she empathised with this tormented man and his heart wrenching story she had overheard. She tuned into another tortured soul.

DS Wade got to Arbour Square just after eight on a brightening morning, thankful the persistent fine rain had dried up. It could drench not only your clothes but your spirit. The police station was abuzz, the jollity of the piss-taking yesterday in the CID room belayed by a night dealing with attack and retribution, Saints -v- Larkins, and where the fuck were these O'Neills? Wade could not resist a chuckle as she made her way to what she imagined was the Anti-terrorist office or was it a tiny cubicle in the corner of this vast room, full to brimming with fulminating detectives watching her casually stroll through piles of furniture, boxes, and one old bike, that Casey had distributed the previous night.

She said nothing, stepped into the anti-terrorist broom cupboard, closed the door, leaned back against it, sighed, metaphorically wiped her brow, and consigned to oblivion the dire atmosphere she had left behind. She returned with full strength the glowering, before closing the blinds to the partition window; she was cocooned in Paddy's and her realm and walked across to the modest window that looked out onto Arbour Square Gardens. If you could shut your eyes, ears, and mind to the dystopian lawlessness all around and the frequent smogs that still prevailed despite the Clean Air Act, this part of London, her home, had a beauty.

She sat at her desk and recalled the chaos of last night and the wonderful sex of her homecoming. She said nothing of events in the Gallows pub to Wendy, felt bad about it, but what could she have said, by the way, that Irish fella you liked so much, just walked up to a fat thug and blew his head off? No, that would likely have put a dampener on things, and she chuckled to herself when the door opened, and the commander stepped in.

She stood, 'As you were, Wade,' the commander said, closing the door. 'Well, quite a night last night and you and Casey missed it,' he looked deep into Wade's eyes.

Wade marshalled her thoughts, it helped to pass the time while the commander considered what to say next. Did the commander know something? Did he know Paddy fucking Casey actually caused the Saint and Larkin ruckus to ramp up to boiling point? And then she questioned herself. She had not really given all the implications much thought, what did that mean? She knew Billy Big Head was a nasty piece of work and it was only a matter of time before someone did him in, but a copper assassin? And she chuckled to herself picturing the scene as Paddy had casually legged it, away from a fat bloated body with no head, and all she could visualise was the stupid fish on Billy's Aran jumper.

'Something funny, Wade?'

Oh God, she had to get herself together. 'No, sorry sir, just a passing thought.'

The commander was not interested. 'Casey not appeared yet?'

Wade was wondering herself but thought she had better cover for him. 'I think he was calling into the hospital to make sure the boy, Chas Larkin, had a good night, was safe and if he could get any further information out of him.' She could not disguise a grin.

'Spill the beans sergeant, what amuses you?'

'There is also an attractive doctor treating Larkin, and I think he may have his eye on her, if you pardon the Moorfields pun,' and the commander and Wade shared the amusing thought just as Casey walked in, closing the door on complaints, and jeering from the CID officers, not able to appreciate a joke turned back on themselves.

'Something funny?'

'Oh, shut up, Paddy, where've yer been?'

'Wade, please, you're talking to a senior officer.' The commander answered.

Wade shot up out of her chair and stood to attention. 'Yes sir, I'm terribly sorry, sir.'

The commander shared a naughty boy glance with the blarney officer, Paddy's good humour being attributed to his retribution on the CID office, which was not actually the case. The source being of Palestinian origin and called Nadia, 'You're alright, Wade. So, Paddy is it?' the commander finished off.

'If I like you, you can call me that,' Casey replied, 'and you might just pass muster, Commander. So, don't let me down, or I will take that privilege away.'

Wade watched on as the commander laughed some more; someone had definitely left a feather up his backside this morning she thought, and that feather may be called Phyllis.

'Okay, sorry. Casey, Wade, fill me in on what is happening at your end when you can. I'm afraid I may have to leave you to your own devices for a few days, did you hear about the murder at the Gallows last night?'

'I did hear something,' Casey replied, looking at the shocked visage on his detective sergeant. 'Not much doing at the moment, ducks in a row, lie of the land, so, if you get my drift?'

'I do...anyway, let me know if you need me for anything.' He looked quizzical, 'Wade, working in with you, Paddy? A bit unusual?'

'Works for us, keeps the feckin' eejits away,' and he looked in the direction of the CID room.

The commander nodded, turned to leave, opened the

door, and stopped, 'Right you are then, Paddy, carry on,' nodded to Wade and said, 'Wade...' and he left.

The squad of tired and dishevelled detectives watched on, still mesmerized as to what had happened, last night, the rubbish strewn back into their office, Wade and Casey working in the same office, and the commander departing with a huge grin across his face and calling Casey, Paddy. Their world had been turned upside down in little more than forty-eight hours, and Casey took a little amusement in the fact that it was about to get a whole lot more *interesting*.

The phone rang.

12

THE CALM FOLLOWING THE STORM. A TIME TO TAKE STOCK, weigh up the damage and to plan retribution. A meeting of the clans, taking place next door to each other. The Saints in their pub, Dad's, and the Larkins, Arries. Nobody thought to walk next door with a flag of truce, to parley a ceasefire or even a peace settlement, but one thing they agreed upon, not that they openly shared this agreement, was they each sought the O'Neills. The Saints for the dealing out of pain and retribution, and the Larkins, well, they thought they should be first to make an alliance with this powerful family. For the time being anyway.

A nervous Nadia called on Chas Larkin. She had come to like the lad who'd had such a diabolical upbringing, and she really wanted this operation to have worked: the detached retina, and the lazy eye. She had the consultant with her who was confident all would be okay, and so it proved. The staff nurse unwound the bandages and, after a brief moment of flickering eyelids, the broad grin on Chas's face was all the reward Nadia needed. The consultant looked closely, flicking a pencil beam of light here and there, asking Chas to follow his wandering finger, after which he declared the boy's eyes cured. He ruffled the Larkin mop of black hair and left, the nurse following.

Nadia watched the door close, subconsciously holding Chas's hand, the boy gripping firmly like he didn't want her to leave. Nadia found it unnerving having an armed police constable stationed in the ward, guarding Chas Larkin's room. Here was an innocent caught up in so much, and she wondered just how his brain coped, and then, was he coping? She looked at Chas, smiled, received back a beatific grin and her heart skipped a beat. Nadia shared some comforting words of encouragement to Chas, assuring him this was a permanent repair, and then touched on the sensitive subject of his mother's funeral, and where he would live after he was discharged from the hospital.

His face turned to thunder. 'I don't want to go to the funeral,' Chas answered, his reply not seeming at all unreasonable to him, his emotions churning.

'I know your mum gave you a difficult time, Chas, but you should go. It will enable you to say goodbye and close a difficult chapter in your life.' Chas appeared to understand, and not for the first time Nadia was impressed with his maturity. She did wonder if Chas was older than he was said to be and made a mental note to chase up his birth certificate. This would not be the first time she had come across a child in this area, stunted in growth and, held back from school for some time in order to help the family in whatever business it would need a small boy for. She had also witnessed stunted puberty and hoped his new circumstances would help Chas along there as well. Chas had not been incorporated into the villainy side of the Larkins, because of his deformity, she presumed, and previously he would have no use even as a lookout, so it was likely he had been used as a domestic skivvy. She would find this out as well and made a mental note to have some say in where the boy went to live. It could make or break Chas Larkin.

While his doctor drifted, thinking her own thoughts, Chas weighed up his options. Whether to go to the funeral and what would happen there, or not attend and incur the likely violent wrath of his brothers and uncles. The violence would be more psychological if he attended and he could deal with that, had been dealing with that all of his crumby life.

'Would you like me to go with you, Chas?'

Chas nodded yes, a wan smile breaking onto a serious face. 'Could be a bit iffy, miss.'

'I'll be fine Chas. So, you up for this?'

'Yes,' he replied, knowing this was the lesser of all evils and, he liked being with Nadia and, once again the fleeting smile dissolved.

'And?'

'I've heard all that has been going on. The policemen, when they changed shifts were talking in whispers, but I could hear. A funeral like this might attract attention. Not just from the police, but from the Saints, and I wouldn't want you to be caught in the middle of that.'

'I'm sure the police will be there to make sure it is safe. I will let Paddy know I am going with you and he will,' and she broke into a little Irish, 'to be sure.'

'Make doubly sure, miss.' Her turn to smile, it was infectious. 'You like him, don't you?'

'I confess I do, Chas,' she replied, a warm sensation tingling through her.

Wade answered the phone, 'Yes he's here,' and she handed the phone to Casey, mouthing it was his squeeze. Casey took the phone, and hand over the mouthpiece, mimed back "Squeeze"? Wade giggled, he had a lot to learn, 'Yer bird, yer twist and twirl, girl, girlfriend, dipstick,' amused at his bemused response.

'Nadia, what are you laughing at?' He listened and responded, 'Are you my mother of pearl?' and he looked at Wade, who followed her half of the conversation, excessively diverted at the embarrassment of her guvnor.

'She's obviously picked up on the local lingo, Paddy,' she remarked, to take the look of wonderment off his face and he was clearly enjoying the relaxed merriment from Nadia. 'How's Chas?' Casey asked, and repeated to Wade that Nadia had confirmed what she had reassured Paddy of the evening before, the operation had been a success, and then his face changed to fulminating concern. 'Nadia, you can't do that...' he listened, '... yes, we will have a strong presence.' He whispered to Wade, enquiring about a police presence at the Larkin funeral and getting a nod, and whispered back, she imagined so, shrugging her shoulders. Casey went back to the squabbling Nadia, irritated he had left her hanging on. 'I'm sure both the Larkins and Saints will respect family funerals, but we do not know how they will react in the light of last night's events.' Anger flushed through his face as it slowly dawned on him that if Nadia was going to be his *squeeze*, she was going to be no dewy-eyed pushover. He hung up after agreeing to a whole raft of things which entertained Wade more than it did Casey.

'What has she asked you to do?'

'What hasn't she asked?'

'And you agreed to all.' Wade flicked her lush eyebrows, a feature much loved by Wendy, as she emphasised the look to indicate that her guvnor was done up like a kipper, and seemingly not minding in the least. 'So, what's up?'

'She...' and he lingered, obviously picturing the stunning lady doctor in his mind, '... she, is going with Chas to his Mum's funeral tomorrow afternoon...' and he ran out of words, but Wade hadn't.

'Jesus.'

'Precisely, and don't forget Mary and feckin' Joseph.' Casey picked up the phone, bashed the rest several times, deriving satisfaction out of the clatter, and eventually spoke to the desk sergeant. 'It's Casey, you will have a presence at the Larkin funeral?' He nodded and seemed satisfied with the response, looked to Wade. 'They will have a big presence.'

'Will we be there?'

He shrugged his shoulders. 'There may be a few punters from the Gallows attending and we wouldn't want to rattle any cages in that department just in case the balaclava didn't do the trick.'

'No, fair point.'

'Maybe I can tuck myself away in the van?'

'We gonna hit the Larkin funeral, Nan?'

Madge, Grand-matriarch Saint, despaired sometimes about the blokes in her family, 'No.'

'Why?'

'Because.'

'Because what?'

'Because I fucking say so, that's because why.'

'Oh.'

'That's it, is it? Not curious as to why we will not hit the Larkins?'

All of a sudden Bernie, *I only asked*, wondered why he had no brains, not realising that he likely did, but after a lifetime of being told he was as thick as two short planks, he believed what he was told, which is what the Saint womenfolk intended.

'Why, Nan?'

'Jeez, give me fucking strength,' and she clipped the errant thicko grandson around the head. 'Because me lad we have a funeral tomorrow at the same cemetery. Unless you've forgotten, one of yer bruvvers copped it a few days ago and because we don't do that sort of thing, do we?'

'No, Nan.'

'And what else?'

Now this did throw Bernie, then he remembered the magic word, 'Please?'

She clumped him again. He was always being clumped. All the boys were clumped, and many folk were of the opinion this could account for them all being brain dead. 'Because we are looking for the fucking O'Neills, aren't we?'

'We are?' and he ducked, not so stupid then, but Madge got him as he came up. 'Can't we do both at the same time?' he responded, rubbing his elephant ears. Madge thought about that whilst Bernie prattled on, and then he said something that did get her attention, '... And then we can get that Chas Larkin, he knows one of the O'Neills, everyone says. This Rosie girl, remember?'

'Bernie, come here, that is not a bad point,' and Bernie went in for an anticipated grand maternal embrace but was clumped again.

'Ouch, Nan, what was that for?'

'Because.'

'Because why?'

'Because I fucking said so...'

'Is the bleedin' runt coming, Nan?'

'D'know.'

'Where's his dad?'

'D'know.'

''Ave they caught who did it?'

'D'know, no, I fink.'

'Chas apparently says it was some Irish kid, Rosie sumfink?'

'Who told yer that?'

'D'know.'

'Well fink.' Jack thought. 'Well?'

He shook his head, 'No, d'know.'

'The filf 'aven't got a bleedin' clue, surprised they ever catch anyone.'

'It's gotta be these O'Neills, everyone's talking about them, but nobody knows where they are. How could they hide so well?'

'D'know,' Nan Larkin was preoccupied. 'These O'Neills seem to be on the side of our family, saved Chas, and blew the head off that bastard Billy Big 'Ed,' she was thinking on and expressing those thoughts openly for any response.

'Will the Saints target Betsy's funeral, Nan?'

'D'know. No, likely not, as one of their boys is being buried tomorrow. So, it's quid pro quo.'

'A quid? For what?' Jack was thinking there was money to be made.

'What you on about, earning a Sov?'

Jack interrupted, 'You said quid pro sumfink.' It was a sad fact that the Larkin boys were as thick as the Saint boys. A balance in a way.

'Come 'ere,' Jack did and his Nan dobbed him on the nose. 'You bleedin' thicko. Now, you were always close to Chas weren't yer?'

'D'know, was I?'

'Yeah, Betsy always left him wiv yer when she was out shagging, didn't she?'

'Did she?'

'Oh, for crying out loud... anyway, if he's at the funeral, chum up to him and find out about this Rosie and her family. Tell him, to tell them, we should meet up, friendly like.'

'Not sure I'll be able to remember all that Nan.'

Nan flicked Jack's nose, 'Just tell 'im we want to meet the O'Neills, okay? Can you remember that?'

'D'know.'

That evening, Roisin visited Chas. It had not been difficult to dodge the copper on his door. Chas was so impressed with his Irish saviour, she always knew what to do and, unlike anyone else, she knew exactly how he felt about his mum and, together they hatched a plan. Chas was so impressed with the resourceful devilment of Rosin Dubh.

13

NADIA BOUGHT CHAS NEW CLOTHES. HE'D NEVER HAD NEW before, always *Salvation Army* stuff, or hand me downs, many generations old, and by the time Chas got them they were nothing more than rags. This was something special. Long trousers, grey, formal. He felt so grown up. White shirt, black tie, black shoes, one with a shaped insert for his club foot, and they matched. He had never felt his foot so comfortable before. He did think that if ever he had money, he would get proper shoes made for him, at least until he could have the operation Nadia had mentioned.

The hospital barber had been in and given him a trim, and the nurses, seeing that he looked the business, stood back, and admired the young lad and said so, raising Chas's esteem. Chas was an attractive young *man*, Nadia thought, and given half a chance and a fair wind, shuck his dysfunctional family and get his head sorted with Wendy Richards, he could make something of himself.

Nadia shushed the nurses away, stood back, and admired him. 'You look gorgeous Chas Larkin,' a smile grew, '... quite the young man.' There were signs of facial hair that the barber had shaved and hair elsewhere and this reinforced her theory. Chas had been deliberately held back and was a lot older than they had been told. She had asked Paddy to find out and he had found it impossible to argue with her. He'd been tongue-tied, like kippers, when they've been done up, apparently, just before being smoked. Chas, however, was done up to the nines and certainly cut a fine figure of blossoming adolescence, the man beginning to emerge at last, only fading bruises to mar the image.

Paddy had insisted Wade collect Nadia and Chas from the hospital and drive them the short distance to the cemetery and, on this auspicious and solemn occasion, the sun shone to reflect Chas's upbeat mood. He was burying his mother. The woman who had been his blight, and he looked forward to seeing her coffin disappear. His mum, gone forever.

Wade dropped them at the cemetery gates, parked the car, and, checking her weapon was accessible in her handbag, she stepped a speedy gait to join Chas and Nadia as the family lined up behind the hearse. Chas had been consigned to the back of the line of mourners, his rank in the family and in life, marked for all to see. More humiliation. Wade had a three sixty look around: a strong uniformed police presence, a black Maria police van parked about a hundred yards away, inside she knew Paddy was watching out for them, and armed officers a short distance away.

Before the cortege got moving, a couple of tarts teetered up to Chas, elbowing the copper out of the way, which is what Wade would have expected. She had filth written all over her, whereas, she thought, Paddy had another aura about him that she hadn't worked out, yet. In the meantime, she listened in to the conversation between the dockyard floozies and Chas and relaxed as it looked like these painted ladies, mutton dressed up as lamb, older than the image they wanted to convey, seemed fond of Chas and hugged him, and the whiff of cheap perfume cloyed. Chas seemed inured.

'Where, where is it?' one of the tarts asked, and Chas tapped the inner breast pocket of his jacket. 'You jeffing mad?'

Chas muttered under his breath, scuffed his shaped right shoe in a clockwise direction and then anticlockwise, his main line of defence against the dark arts for today, Nadia not able to dissuade Chas of the futility of superstition.

Ritzy sighed, 'What you gonna do?' Ritzy was a mate of Chas's mum, worked the docks, her name was Sarah, but people called her Ritzy because she was a cracker. Well, she used to be, but being a prostitute can take its toll, out, semi-clad, in all weathers with her back to the wall, physically and financially.

Chas murmured more inanities. He rarely spoke anything clearly and Nadia noticed that although these were tarts with heart, Chas had regressed within himself. It was his natural form of defence she imagined and resolved to discuss this with Wendy this evening. For Chas, he knew if he didn't perform these little rituals, he would likely be pounced upon by anyone around, beaten up, or the very least be jeered at. At least if people jeered at his murmurings, it didn't seem so bad. So, Chas stood on one leg. He knew this was lucky.

Chas looked a lost soul, which he was and had always been ever since his Mum had cut the appearance of apron strings and eventually sent him to school. School was a convenience for a lot of the tarts as most worked at night and, if they weren't shagging for money, they were thieving and, during the day they slept, waking to spend their ill-gotten gains in the pub. No need to look out for the kids, they were at school and the teachers can look out for them. Chas's mum, known in the docks as Sweetie, earned her living on her back, day, night, anytime she could get it. She always needed money. Sweetie generally drank away her earnings, slipping Chas a bob or two when he called at Arrie's for some cash to get something to eat. Of course, he was ribbed something rotten whenever he came calling for his mum, not just because he was overly tall for his age. Even hunched, he was a gangly, semi-blind deformed oik, had a squint and a club foot, and as a consequence, being bullied was his accepted lot in life.

'You're barkin' mad, Chas,' Ritzy remarked.

Chas recalled his childhood in that fleeting moment, like he was drowning and as he surfaced, Nadia saw a smile that was more a salacious grin. He wasn't mad, he'd had a tormented life and since he had met Roisin, he knew he would grow. She had said, in the local parlance and with a wonderful Irish intonation, "Chas darlin' you're not mum and dad, you're as sane as anyone living in this God forsaken hole." Chas believed in Roisin, and as this thought energised his body, so he stood erect, confident in the support of *The Black Rose*.

Nadia observed the change and marvelled some more at the boy becoming a man. However, Chas shrank into his hunch as the cortege moved off at a snail's pace, life, or was it death, moving again, his only comfort, Nadia, his doctor, and Roisin. She would be watching out for him and the red-headed firecracker was. Chas couldn't see her, but she was there. Their plans unfolding except someone had clearly started. Blowing the head off Billy Big Head. Chas giggled as he pictured this, and the people surrounding him in the cortege frowned. This was not appropriate, but it did affirm the belief that Chas Larkin was barkin'.

It was a long slow schlep to the Larkin family burial plot. The Larkins had a large section for themselves, ironically, adjacent to the Saint plot and, as the hearse, the following mourners, and hangers on approached, so they could see the freshly dug grave for the recently deceased Saint boy. Paddy watched on from the distant police van, looking through a smoked glass window with binoculars. He saw it all unfold.

As the hearse approached the burial ground there was a deafening high-pitched screech and the hearse came to a stuttering halt. Reacting to the Valkyrie-like howl, the already nervous hearse driver and attendee, dived from the car and rolled away just as the coffin in the back exploded. It was not a massive explosion, just enough to blow the coffin and Betsy's remains into smithereens, splattering the hearse interior and windows with infinitesimal parts of the Larkin tart. Her last movement.

The entourage dived to the ground and rolled away, taking cover behind nearby gravestones lest this attack be followed up with gunfire. Paddy saw the hearse motionless, smoke belching from the open front doors and, standing stock still, the only person not to dive for cover, respecting the obliterated corpse, was Chas Larkin. He stood, Paddy noticed, erect, no curvature in his back, unwavering, unmoved emotionally, until he began to convulse in manic laughter. Paddy leapt from the van to run to the scene and saw Nadia stand to comfort Chas.

There was nobody else around, they had either scarpered

or were hiding. It was a desolate scene. Paddy had his arm around Nadia and her arm was around Chas, hysterical, with what seemed to be his first ever thoroughly enjoyable event in his dogged life. Wade steered them to the police van, and into the back, to be whisked away, Nadia suggesting they should go to see Wendy at her hospital office. "Chas will need counselling" she'd argued.

Chas looked at Wade, Paddy, and then Nadia. 'What a fucking tin barf that was,' and maybe it was the tension of the moment, or the leaching of adrenalin, but it did seem as though it was funny.

The merriment was equally enjoined by the Saint lads as they quaffed ale and toasted what they thought had been a right royal result and, they'd had to do nothing.

Madge looked on from her table in the snug bar, a small room between the public and saloon bar, intended originally as a demure space for demure ladies. What a laugh that was too, but the Saint womenfolk always gathered here for their family pow-wows, and one was needed now as they would almost certainly get the blame and that could mean they would be facing a war. It was well known that explosives and arms were a Saint family trade, set up by the great granddad Mickey Saint, he of the crumpet fame. He had returned from Ireland into the family bosom and the family business in the docks, bankrolled to acquire and export, ordnance, something he had proved particularly adept at and even impressed the late departed, much missed and famed, Bessie Saint, the older.

News of this morbid event was all over the evening papers, and the BBC Home Service repeated bulletins on the wireless, and then, the joyous news the police were looking no further than a family, new to the East End, called the O'Neills, and sought any information that would assist them in the enquiries

---

This broadcast also surprised the team in the CID room and caused the commander to leap from his chair, feel for his heart, apologise to the kneeling Phyllis as he did up the button flies of his uniform trousers and, with a flush interpreted as anger, he barged through the CID room to the Anti-terrorist broom cupboard. A brief chuckle as he saw the newly appended, handwritten sign that read, Aunty Terrorist Unit, and he was still chuckling as he barged in, to interrupt Wade and Casey, beside the window, heads locked in a conspiratorial huddle.

Casey reacted to the flustered commander and told him to take a seat. In the confined space, the three of them shuffled past each other so the senior officer could sit in the vacant Wade chair, no longer a swivelling cushioned affair on wheels, but a wooden one with four uneven legs, another amusing intervention from CID. She would swap that back when they were distracted.

The commander, now sitting, diminutive compared to the standing Casey and Wade, felt immediately psychologically diminished, which was Casey's intention, as both terrorist officers began pacing, dodging each other as they passed. He made a faltering start, trying to assert his rank and authority, but was interrupted by Casey, 'Been listening to the wireless?

The commander blustered a reply, affirming that he not only had heard it, but wanted to know who told the BBC, and he tailed off as dawn broke. 'It was you...'

Paddy convulsed directly at the bloated and florid cheeks of the commander, Wade more circumspect, thinking he was laughing like Chas and, not for the first time, thought Paddy had a death wish. Not only from the street, blowing the head off Billy Big Head, but also his complete lack of regard for police hierarchy. But she need not have worried as far as the police were concerned, although she did have her concerns that Paddy may have been recognised at the cemetery when he ran, not to her and Chas Larkin, but more than likely to save Nadia, as the commander sighed and accepted his lot, and this lot, the Aunty Terrorist Unit.

Still, he felt he needed to have his say, 'When you talked me into this, it was because you told me that under our own noses the Saints were importing and exporting guns and explosives. That the Saints had been funded by the IRA for some fifty years. You thought this would be exploited by the IRA in a campaign here in London and, we have had the odd safe or two blown, but blowing up a fucking funeral? You think it was these O'Neills?'

'Calm down dear...' the commander fulminated at the put you down expression, but ironically, decided to keep his powder dry, '...we have it all under control.'

'You do?' and the commander looked at Wade who shrugged, which did not instil confidence in the senior officer, and to Paddy, who waved crossed fingers in the air. 'Oh, fuck me gently,' he said, and decided to return to his office and his PA, a notable hush in the CID office as he opened and closed the door to Aunty's room.

'So, it was you who briefed the BBC news.'

'A "reliable source" I think they said.'

'Source my fucking arse. What do you hope to achieve?'

'I hope, my dear Wade, to avoid a war between the Saints and Larkins and have them, in tandem, focused on the O'Neills...'

'Who don't fucking exist?' Wade thought for a bit, 'Except maybe for this Roisin girl?'

'Exactly, Wade.'

Wade looked at her guvnor like he had a screw loose. 'You're jeffing mental,' and she drilled a hole in the side of her head with her index finger to reinforce her view that she was working with a mentally deranged tosspot and here she was, accepting her lot and not overly displeased.

'Well, I'm off home. Wendy said she dropped Nadia and Chas back at the hospital. I imagine the boy needs a bit more rest and recuperation and, hopefully, Wendy will have got him to stop laughing at the thought of his mum splattered all over the inside of the hearse.' She sighed as she waved to Casey, 'Tatty bye, Paddy.' And in a swirl, she swanned through the CID room, down the stairs, through the vestibule, and out into the street to be met by a throng of newspaper reporters, who shouted a barrage of questions at her, all of which she diplomatically dealt with without any loss of momentum. 'Fuck off the lot of yer,' and she was gone.

Casey watched all of this from the modest window in their office. He grinned, well pleased with his bagman, or was Wade a bagbird? Now that did make him laugh, as he sat down to think through the next steps of his strategy, but was distracted by thoughts of the Nadia kind, so he packed up and went to see his *squeeze*, passing through CID who were now taking surveillance of the Saint funeral the next day more seriously.

14

'HE SAID ROISIN HAD BEEN TO SEE HIM, BUT I DIDN'T NOTICE her. The copper on the door suggested it must have been when he went for a wee. That's a bit dodgy isn't it, and should you not have two officers, Paddy? In case, you know?'

Casey was intrigued. He was aware Roisin was a slippery young woman, but this was close to *now you see her, now you don't*, but he also knew the copper on the door was not the sharpest knife in the drawer and probably had more than an eye on the nurses, indeed he had caught the fellow himself and given him a rollicking. Having said more or less this to Nadia, he also imparted that he thought Chas was no longer at risk. 'The Saints are preoccupied with their funeral, high noon tomorrow and trying find the O'Neills.'

Nadia was not reassured.

The Saints were the go-to people if you needed a gun or a

little bit of gelly, to blow a safe or some stubborn doors, but nobody, up until very recently, had taken advantage. The Saints were letting it be known that some of their guns and explosives had gone missing and the culprit had a window of opportunity to return the stuff. Whoever it was had transgressed the unwritten law, and this is what pre-occupied Casey.

'Paddy...' He had drifted in thought. Nadia removed Casey's hand from his eyebrow, and with gentle fingers she smoothed the skin to the bruised area. 'You have to learn not to do this when you are stressed. I have spoken to Wendy and she will give you some strategies, and I will give you another, if you keep on doing it, I will not walk out with you.'

'What?'

'You heard.'

'You will walk out with me?'

'Yes, but not if you continually have two black eyes. I'll give you two weeks to get used to breaking the habit, okay,' and she tipped onto her toes and kissed him, full on the lips. His breath was taken away. 'Now, I said we would call around to see Wendy and Flora. I trust you are okay with that?' He nodded. He had lost all power of speech following that kiss. 'Good, I think it is important we get some insight into what is happening with Chas Larkin, he is displaying some strange characteristics, and Wendy is uncertain as to what the causes are.'

'He is... she is?' Casey could not see what was strange

about the lad's behaviour. ‘If I'd had a mum like Betsy Larkin, I would roll in the aisles if she'd been blown up in her coffin.’

'Paddy!' He derred. 'Come here,' and she steered him into a quiet corner of the hospital corridor, whereupon she showed him what he might expect if he could stop bruising his eyebrows.

There was a loud rap on the acid-etched, glazed, double doors to Dad's. The Saints pub had been closed as a mark of respect for the loss of a son, grandson, and major thug. They expected trouble as the Larkins, next door, would be holding a wake in memory of Betsy, and they could not be sure what reaction there would be to her coffin exploding, but at the moment all was quiet, the doors of Arries, like Dad's, remained firmly shut.

Madge signalled for Bernie to open the door, counselling to be careful, but nobody expected to see Nan Larkin.

'Can I come in?'

Bernie looked back to Madge, his own Nan, who snapped her mouth shut, and going immediately onto her guard, beckoned Nan. Nan Larkin stepped around the tall, for two short planks, Bernie, who stood mesmerized, and she made her way to Madge's table in the snug bar. Bernie was stunned, never before had a Larkin stepped foot in *Dad's*, though someone had stolen the crumpet, and that may have been a Larkin.

Nan sat opposite Madge who waved everyone away. 'I never expected to see, you.'

'No, I imagine not, Madge, but here I am, and if you're worried, we're sure you were not responsible for the bomb in Betsy's coffin.' She shrugged her shoulders, 'To be honest, nobody liked her, and we intend to have a few drinks next door to celebrate her final resting places...' she chuckled, '... still, she went out with a bang.'

Madge appreciated the humour, defusing what could be a tense and dangerous situation. She looked up from her familiar spot in the Snug, where she could see in the Public bar her family gathering, all tooled up. She called out, 'You'll not be needed, and put the bloody guns away,' and returned to Nan, who reassured her this was a flag of truce meeting. 'So, what is it we need to talk about?'

'Madge, we've held an unsteady peace, yes? You and me, the two families, sticking to our territories, you the docks, and we all know about your arms dealing, and my family the gambling and whorehouses.' Madge nodded, it was tense, but peace had held. 'I also know you are missing your crumpet.'

Now this did surprise Madge. 'How'd you know that?'

'Because I had a little whisper with Ritzy and she said Chas, the fucking numpty, has it, and had it with him at the funeral today.'

'Stone the fucking crows... the little tow-rag.'

'Yes, and I agree with you.'

'You do? What do you propose?'

There was quiet for what seemed like ages before Nan Larkin answered. 'Betsy was not liked and, whereas Charlie, my lad what married the fucking slapper, is a bit of a numpty, his boys are okay and work well in the firm. The runt, however, is a waste of space, causing more trouble than we all need at the moment. So, if he were to end up in the Thames, face down, no Larkin would bemoan his loss, if you get my drift?'

Madge nodded. 'I do Nan. Why he wasn't chucked in when he was born, I don't know.'

'Me too darlin', I told my Charlie, but apparently Betsy insisted on keeping the little fucker, probably to milk all the sympathy she could, which she did, ad infinitum, forever and ever amen and never let the little sod grow up,' she shrugged her shoulders and made a sourpuss face, 'well, you know.'

'Too right, drove most of us up the bleedin' wall wiv 'er moanin' and jeffing on.'

'So, I'm here to tell you we will not disrupt the funeral of your grandson tomorrow, and you have our condolences.'

'Thank you.' Madge was touched.

'We can go our separate ways as and when, but for now we need to pool our resources to find these O'Neills or they will take over from both our families. I can see it: divide and rule, and all that. There are drugs coming onto our Manor and we think this has to be the O'Neills... and...' here Nan smiled, '... I will get your crumpet back.'

'I'd appreciate that, but what will you do with Chas? Not in the Thames?' Madge was not averse to a bit of killing but thought it would be hard for any grandmother to order the killing of her grandson. When he was born, chucking any deformed infant into the Thames was accepted, but now the lad was well into his teenage years, older as both Madge and Nan knew, well, that was a different matter, and the police would need a lot of paying off for that. It had been a joke how Betsy had held the boy back, stunted and runted, they used to say.

'No, I've arranged for him to be taken in by the Christian Brothers.'

Madge could not prevent an audible intake of breath, 'Jesus, Nan. The Christian Brothers? That home has one hell of a rep, and a boy like him, not bad looking in a deformed way, well, he will end up being used and abused. You know that?' and Madge smiled, appreciating a well-drawn up plan to deal with the bastard, for whom she had the tiniest of respect, for he had purloined their crumpet, but needs must.

Nan grinned menacingly, thinking of the torturous times the boy had in front of him, well and truly locked up, the key thrown away. He'd been a thorn in the Larkin side for too long and, the risk he had taken in pinching the Saint crumpet, well, that was a step too far and could have brought the whole house of cards down, which is why Nan was in the

Saint pub, confessing all. 'We will get the crumpet for you before he goes. Wanda and Ritzy are going to see him early tomorrow and, the Brothers and Welfare will collect him from the hospital tomorrow shortly afterwards, before that nosey A-rab doctor can interfere.'

Madge scraped her chair back as she stood, the grandmother and matriarch of this notorious family had a notoriously huge bum, a noted feature of many of the Saint women. The men loved a big backside on their women, so it is said, or maybe, so they are told more likely. 'It's a deal, Nan,' and the two matriarchs shook hands. 'Get the crumpet and we sit down and talk about the O'Neills. We've sent enquiries to Cork, should hear back anytime.'

Madge walked Nan to the pub door and to the surprise of all who watched on from behind the bar counter, the two women hugged. They knew each other from school and, unbeknown to most, maintained a distant but close friendship. It was the only reason there had never been an all-out war before, the families were close in an adversarial way.

Nan returned to Arries where Ritzy and Wanda were guzzling as much free gin as they could suck up, the booze calming the nerves of the two tarts, an agitated Ritzy wondering what on earth possessed her to tell Nan that Chas had the crumpet. The answer was simple, she was scared, as well as needing a bit of cash. She liked Chas, but the guilt would pass, helped on its way with a drop of mother's ruin. Wanda? Well, she couldn't give a toss about anything.

Nan interrupted their nerve- and gin-laced reverie. Standing beside their table, the petite Larkin dowager asserted her power, leaned in, topped up their glasses, and held onto the bottle. 'The last for tonight. I've something I want you to do tomorrow morning, real early like, and I need you to have a clear 'ead. Got it?' Both ladies said yes, believing they could stay relatively sober this once, the offer of cash helping, but not so much as the menace of Nan Larkin; you do not cross Nan.

'Can we take the long way around, walk along the river a bit?'

'I was planning on taking a taxi. It's a fair trot,' Casey was actually worrying they would be seen together. He didn't want her being used as emotional blackmail.

'Down by the Tower, along a bit, and then get a taxi that would be good, and safe? I know what you are doing, and I understand, but I want to walk with you,' she smiled, and stopped him grabbing for his eyebrows.

Casey conceded. It was a lovely summer evening, the setting sun on their backs and, arm in arm, they wended their way along the Thames north bank, a brown turgid river, its menace below the surface, above, evident bomb damage from the war slowly being replaced with new buildings.

Nadia enjoyed being with Paddy, even if he did appear on edge. When they reached Wapping High Street, they hailed a taxi to take them into Stepney, near the Mile end Road and The Royal London Hospital, pulling up at a terrace of well-proportioned houses with the odd two or three missing. Like a once set of glorious teeth having experienced the Luftwaffe flying dental team. London still suffered a living accommodation shortage and many of those surviving houses were often divided into flats. Flora and Wendy had a first floor flat in a modest three storey house of Georgian proportions.

Wendy popped down to usher Paddy and Nadia up the stairs and into the front living room where Wade was on the telephone. It was not commonplace for people to have a phone, but Wendy was often on call and Wade needed to be able to be contacted in case of a police matter, which was what was happening now as she crooked her finger to Casey. She asked the caller to hold, and put her hand over the mouthpiece, 'It's Lenny Johnson, detective constable from our nick, they want to interview Chas Larkin about the murder of his mum. They're informing us as a matter of courtesy. They intend to call into the hospital tomorrow morning.'

Casey was about to respond, but Wendy interrupted them. 'He's not ready to be grilled by a set of apes...' she paused, realised that Wade and Casey were a part of this team of police primates, and so modified her response, holding out mea culpa hands, '... sorry, I mean some are a tad Neanderthal, and, well, Chas is in a difficult... er, a dark place.'

Casey told Wade to say they would call back and fix up a time in the morning, and either she or he would be present, but this did not find favour with Wendy, or Nadia. 'You can't do that. I will not allow it,' Wendy asserted, supported by Nadia.

'Just tell them Wade...' and he took the cold stare from Wendy and the daggers from Nadia in good part, whilst Wade placated the young Detective Constable and replaced the phone.

'You cannot ride roughshod...'

Paddy halted reaction from Nadia, loving the animation in her face, 'Nadia *A mhuirnín,* darling. I have no intention of allowing their size twelve clodhoppers anywhere near Chas, and I am surprised it has taken them this long to ask for an interview.'

'Did you just call me darling?'

'I did, I did.'

Nadia seemed to reflect on this progression in their relationship. 'Well, I'm not your bloody darling, not yet my *Panda Boatrace feckin' eejit,'* Casey and Wade were both amused at the cockney, cod Irish, accent from a Palestinian woman. Nadia had picked up a lot from him in their short acquaintance, and Paddy loved that she challenged him, much as any

Irish woman would, love in the eyes beneath a short-fused rebuke. 'And take the stupid grin off your face. I'm not happy you're playing games with a child and, manipulating Wendy and me for your intrigue, whatever that might be, but I am damn sure it will be dangerous.'

Casey struggled, massaging his errant grin into a more acceptable countenance, let his hand drop as it started to move to his eyebrows, and looked to Nadia. She seemed satisfied with his facial remodelling, and smiled, seeming also to tolerate his reciprocal look of delight, which Nadia graciously permitted.

Wade stepped up to the plate, 'So what are we going to do?'

Casey felt cornered as the three women turned to him, seeking a plan that he hadn't worked out yet. He played for time, 'The murder team will be bemused that they have not had a clear perpetrator in the frame for the murder of Betsy Larkin. It would be natural to find a host of clues in what was most definitely a crime of intense passion, hatred even. If it didn't sound so ludicrous, and if Chas Larkin were not so badly injured, and blind, it would seem logical to look at him as the culprit.' There was an intake of breath, not so much from Wade, she had already thought this. 'But the feckin' eejits have not made that step yet, although it is only a matter of time. We need to get Chas Larkin to a refuge somewhere and question him ourselves, in a more benign, safe place.'

'He talks all the time about a lass called Roisin O'Neil,' Nadia said. Casey hemmed. 'Well?'

'Wade, phone back and tell them we will meet them at ten thirty tomorrow at the hospital, then let's sit down,' and his focus was on Wendy.

ROISIN DUBH

THE BLACK ROSE

15

THE NEXT MORNING WADE AND CASEY WERE IN EARLY, THEY had ducks to get in a row. Around eight the CID room began to fill, and Lenny Johnson popped his spotty head around the door to confirm the arrangements to interview Chas Larkin. He started to make some gentle enquiries for background and was told to fuck off by Wade. He fucked off. No match for this strong woman.

As the door to the tiny office closed, Wade answered the phone and handed it to Casey, 'It's Nadia, and she's in a two and eight.'

'Two and eight?'

'State.'

Casey reached for the phone and immediately began to proffer calming platitudes that were obviously, to Wade, not working, and she allowed her eyes to roll at her boss's ineptitude in speaking to women. 'Okay, okay, Nadia. I'll come over.' Nope, that wasn't right either. 'Alright, what should I do?' he asked.

Wade thought, at last, and looked at Casey beseechingly as he hung up the red-hot phone and rubbed his ear, 'Trouble?' Casey's lips straightened while he considered how to relay the information that he was only just taking in. 'Come on, Paddy, cough.'

'That was Nadia.'

'No bleedin' kiddin'.'

'Yeah, okay,' Casey pinched the skin around his eye socket and Wade shouted at him to stop. 'Sorry.'

'Don't be sorry, just think of another way to focus other than giving yerself two black eyes. Now, what's happened?' Casey dropped his hands from his eyes, and she thought he was about to demonstrate some Irish dancing, which would be more amusing than self-harming in front of her. 'Well?' Wade demonstrating some of her famed frustration that Casey was beginning to learn about.

'Nadia examined Chas this morning and he is making really good progress; his eyes are responding well.'

'Well, that's good isn't it?'

'Yes.'

'So, what's the problem?'

'I'm getting to it for feck's sake.'

'Well get a shufty on will yer sunshine.'

'I will if you'd just shut-up and let me get a feckin'

word in.'

'Sorry.'

Casey calmed, reflected on what he had been told and how to convey this to Wade. 'The Welfare lady turned up, with a priest, seems the Larkins are Catholics.'

Wade couldn't see what the difficulty was, not realising Casey needed time to get his words out, 'So, the kid's a roman candle, what's the big deal?'

'Give us a chance, will yer.'

'Sorry,' Wade blushed, but could not conceal her frustration.

'No problem really, except I can't stand the Catholic Church, but the priest was there representing the Christian Brothers and they're taking Chas Larkin into...'

He had no chance to finish. Wade shot out of her seat, 'Fuck,' she exclaimed. The chair teetered and she stuck out a hand to steady it before it fell.

'That's what Nadia said. She thought taking Chas Larkin would be a bad idea.'

'To bleedin' right it's a bad idea, that 'ome has a diabolical reputation for abuse. We've been trying to get it shut down for ages, but wheels within wheels,' and she flapped her hands in despair. 'I'm convinced some of the top, top brass, are involved somewhere along the line. Not to mention local so-called *personalities* taking too close a personal interest in the kids.' Casey looked shocked. 'You might well look taken aback. We had better do something.'

'That's what Nadia said, but what? What can we do?'

'What was Nadia doing at the time?'

'What?'

'You heard, where was Nadia? Could she not have stopped them?'

Casey fumed, considering his next moves as well as being angry at the implied criticism of Nadia. 'She was wrestling with two dockyard tarts, the ones who came up to Chas at the funeral, who were trying to take something from Chas. I think she said it was a crumpet?'

'Shit on it, Chas has the Saint's crumpet? Well, that accounts for a lot.'

'It does? A feckin' crumpet?' The phone rang. 'I bet that's Nadia again, wanting to know what I'm doing,' Casey said as he answered the phone, listened, then exclaimed, 'What? Where? What?' He hung up, Wade looked for an explanation, but Casey was again lost for words and mumbled incoherently.

'What?' Wade interjected, hoping to knock him back into the land of the living before she knocked his block off, their working relationship moving onto another level.

Casey shook his head in disbelief, 'It seems...' and he shook his head again, and almost chuckled, frustratingly, '... not actually clear, but that was the duty sergeant, he has had a report that a car has crashed on Commercial Road. It was a car carrying a priest, a welfare officer and, a young lad who, he was informed, was Chas Larkin. The kid is supposed to have grabbed the steering wheel and forced the car off the road into a lamppost and then leapt out, calling "Roisin", and then fecked off.'

It was Wade's turn to be stunned. She phewed and demonstrably wiped her brow, before saying, 'Chas would know about the Christian Brothers. Everybody does which makes it even more confounding why nothing is done about it.'

Wade and Casey looked at each other, Casey responded, almost under his breath, 'Jeyziz Mary and feckin' Joseph.' Then he leapt up and energetically headed for the door, 'We'd better get down there. I don't like the idea of Larkin and The Black Rose on the streets.'

The Saints were gathering in Dad's, a few drinks before the funeral cortège left for the cemetery. The glass domed display case lay on the bar awaiting the return of the crumpet. Ritzy and Wanda were late, 'They should've got the crumpet and been back 'ere by now,' a sober Madge said, whilst all around imbibed.

This did not bode well.

Ritzy entered on her own, Wanda having legged it, and

she walked stutteringly to Madge's table. 'Well?' Madge asked.

'The bloody A-rab doctor stopped us, and wiv a couple of porters, she frew us out. We waited a bit, finking we might 'ave anuvver go when all of a sudden Chas Larkin was dragged out by a bleedin' priest and some dozy posh cow who said she was Welfare.'

'Where'd they take him?' Madge knew the answer. Ritzy shrugged, took a step back, but too late, Madge leapt to her feet, slapped the dockland doxy hard across her face, and the prostitute went flying across the bar where she lay, more than two sheets to the wind with all of that wind knocked from her sails. Madge decided they had enough contacts in the Christian Brothers Home in order to get the crumpet returned and, to ensure Chas Larkin suffered before he was done in, resolving his deformed body should be chucked into the Thames, a fitting, if belated end.

The ice cream van lay unattended, exactly where they expected it to be. The local kids used to fantasise about breaking into the yard and helping themselves to an ice cream, except no ice cream was ever left overnight. Several had tried, got caught and sent to Borstal without even a yummy lick. Chas and Roisin had no interest in illicit ice cream; they wanted the van. Roisin could drive although you wouldn't know it, as she slewed all over the road, hit a few parked cars and, scared the bejeezus out of anyone thinking of crossing the road and even a few pedestrians as the van occasionally mounted the pavement, but slowly, they made their way.

Roisin dropped him off at the broken-down old house. 'It's too dangerous,' she said, 'and if we have to leg it, well...' and she looked at Chas's club foot, '... you wouldn't get far before they nabbed yer.'

Chas argued his foot was not so bad, but reluctantly agreed and allowed Roisin her head, to carry out their wonderfully diabolical plan.

'Have you any idea where they could have gone?' Casey was on the scene of the dramatic escape, while behind him and the traffic officers was a car hugging a bent over lamppost, steam hissing from a burst radiator. The two uniformed coppers had arrived, parked their patrol car, and, more interested in guiding traffic past the crash site, they had no clue where the miscreant had gone, neither had the Welfare Officer or the priest, both of whom nursed their bumped heads. 'Christ on a bike, you guys are feckin' useless.' He looked to Wade, ignoring the offended posture of the priest, 'You?'

Wade shrugged; it was an impossible question. 'The thing is, Chas Larkin was always being beaten up and must be expert in finding places to hideaway, but one thing is for certain, he would have a bloody big interest in the Saints' funeral.' She left that hanging in the air for a while, '… And, if what you say is right about this *Black Rose,* she would have an interest in disrupting both the Saints and the Larkins, but why?'

It was Casey's turn to shrug, though Wade thought he had a shrewd idea, so she threw in a few of her own thoughts, to see if she hit a score. 'You think this is IRA linked?' She waited, no response. 'The O'Neills taking over...' paused, '... you said they didn't exist, so that's not it. So, what is it, revenge?' And she noticed his eyes light up. Bingo she thought. 'So, revenge it is and, maybe to take over the arms business?' Casey looked at Wade and clapped his hands silently, applauding her reasoning, maybe, but her conclusion, was that right? 'I think we should head over to East London Cemetery,' Wade suggested. 'Take a gander at the Saint funeral, yeah?' Casey nodded, and they left the two plod coppers protesting, as Casey commandeered their patrol car and headed to the Saint funeral.

16

THE PRE-WAKE AGITATION WAS SHAKEN OFF IN THE CARS FROM Dad's to the cemetery, the service in the chapel and, by the time the mourners reached the graveside, the mood was respectfully sombre and funereal. The women especially, shedding floods of tears for the boy thug they were burying. This mood of solemnity though was disturbed by the incongruously joyous rendering of *Greensleeves*, the mechanical tune ceaselessly repeated and broadcast over a tinny Tannoy system.

The mourners looked around for the source of this cacophonic grating tune, annoyed that someone could be so disrespectful, but the source of the agitation was not seen until it was too late. An ice cream van came into sight, careering at speed, down the central avenue, weaving around, occasionally veering off the path, taking out the odd memorial stone, the crashing and crunching adding to the raucous intrusion into the mournful silence. The path of this bizarre, incongruous, sight was followed by all the mourners as they remained gathered around the graveside, the coffin already lowered to its final resting place. The mystical look on the faces of the grieving Saints remained glued on the pale blue and cream ice cream van that seemed to be taking a shortcut through the cemetery. As the van neared, Madge, under her breath, expressed dire retribution when they found out who was responsible. However, instead of passing by as anticipated, at the last minute and just some fifty feet from the graveside, the van changed course dramatically, stunning those gathered around the grave as it drove directly into the mourners. Madge and a few other of the upper echelon matriarchs, central in this event and taking up prime graveside positions, were cast into the grave as the van slewed, taking more people with it before toppling, to teeter on the edge of this final *gelato* resting place.

The music continued to grate, only partially drowned by screams, people hurt, mourners angry, some others rushing to help. The driver's door opened to the additional sound of rasping metal from the buckled side and, people watched on, stunned, as a gangly red-headed girl leapt from the lurching ice cream van, shouting and screaming, a definite Irish accent, as she stepped over and on writhing people, to make an escape out of the cemetery onto Grange Road, and away, out of sight, long before the police presence could galvanise itself.

The Saints, and their entourage of mourners, momentarily fell into silence, just the deep baritone slur of *Greensleeves,* droning, like it was running out of battery, the creak of the dangling van forming a mausoleum-like lid and, the spookily eerie moans and groans from the depths of the grave, like the dead arising. This shocked inaction was broken as police officers swooped to aid the matriarchs out of the grave, having to thread the persons through the tiny gap left by the ice cream van floor pan. It was a miracle it had not fallen in completely and, they began dealing with the walking and the non-walking wounded. The prevailing sentiment was one of righteous anger.

The report of the incident was received by Casey and Wade over the crackly patrol car radio. Wade switched on the bell and they increased their speed for the last half mile or so to the cemetery. Swinging into the short drive, they could see the funeral party ahead of them, the gathering of confused mourners, like a murmuration of black starlings, swooping this way and that, around, what looked like, an ice cream van? And what was that awful din, *Greensleeves?*

Stepping from the patrol car, the visual scene was given voice, a crescendo of sound, screams and cries, threats and cursing, and a gathering of uniformed police trying to offer help before the ambulances began arriving to take the injured.

'Jeyziz,' Casey remarked, as he leaned back against the patrol car. He went to talk to Wade, but she was not there, she was in amongst the melee, helping people, trying to find out what had happened, the crazy story emerging, telling of the ice cream van, still playing Greensleeves, driving into the funeral obsequies.

As the ambulance people took over, Wade returned to Casey. 'This is going to blow, let's get out of here. They're saying a red-headed girl was responsible and ran off...' and she pointed to a side gate, '... we may be able to catch her up?'

Casey lethargically lifted himself from his seat on the car bonnet, wandered around to the driver's door as Wade jumped into the passenger seat, eager to get going. She gave Casey an old-fashioned look as he got himself comfortable. Why was he so bleedin' slow, she thought? Eventually he fired the engine, and they took off, steadily. 'Jesus Paddy, step on it for Christ's sake.' He returned her stare and then stabbed the accelerator, swerving left outside the cemetery, their bell ringing a pulse of alarm for anyone to clear them a path.

'Is this Roisin d'you think?'

Casey looked at Wade for the briefest of moments, he slowed, looking everywhere for sight of the fleeing attacker. ‘Has to be. I never expected this.'

'What shall we do, stop and have a picnic, maybe go back and have a ninety-niner from the ice cream van?' Wade was bit fed up with her Guvnor. 'Get out and let me drive you bleedin' pansy.'

Casey eased the patrol car to a halt, leaned over, switched the bell off, and adopted his *Rodin the Thinker* pose, his spare fingers drumming the steering wheel. The pursuit of *The Black Rose* abandoned it would seem.

'Nice 'ere isn't it, we should come more often, only next time bring a flask of tea?'

Casey looked at Wade, was she miffed? 'Are you miffed?' he asked sardonically.

Wade piled on the sarcasm, something she was quite good at, Wendy often said. 'No, not at all. I didn't fancy chasing public enemy number fucking one anyway, much rather sit and chew the fat with you. So, what do we do now, Sherlock?'

'We...' he turned to the steaming Wade, '...*we*? the first thing *we* do is make an announcement, which would probably be best leaked via some police officers in the pay of the Saints and the Larkins and, may I suggest that dodgy desk sergeant, Old George, to say we suspect the O'Neills. Add that we believe there is some sort of attack going on. Suggest also it may be territorial and then *we* get our arses over to Scotland Yard for a meet with the big wigs. This is happening quicker than I imagined.'

17

After calling back at the police station for the briefest of moments, and a casual dropping of informative remarks to Old George, Wade and Casey left for the day, intending to meet up at Wade's flat for dinner. Wade, Wendy, Casey and Nadia, a social evening what could go wrong? If Casey had any reservations, Wade dispelled them by mentioning that Wendy had insisted, and this was a plan agreed by Nadia. Smoked kipper anyone?

Roisin made it back to the bombed-out house Chas regularly used whenever he needed to go on the missing list. It was also convenient, being just across the street from the wall of the East India Dock and, coincidentally, or not, this was ideal for Roisin. Chas knew his way around the docks well.

Roisin returned with bread, ham, tomatoes, *Tizer* to drink and, for afters, a delectable *Lyons* individual fruit pie. Chas smacked his lips as he savoured the prospect of the food, he was used to only getting beans on toast at home, so this was a rare treat, coupled with the fact he was starving. As they picnicked, so they shared the humour of the Saint and Larkin funerals, and the past two days, seeing off the school, kids and teachers, especially young Mickey Saint, and the fear of the devil put up everyone so they would not spill the baked beans on them. Life was getting good for Chas and, a bonus, his mum was finally out of his hair. Chas Larkin's revenge was going well, and there was much more to come.

It was such a wonderful feeling of satisfaction.

Chas even loved the down and out hovel he was sheltering in. Leaning back against a timber panel to what was left of a first-floor staircase balustrade, he stared above him, a void that rose to nowhere, only a hole in the roof. He liked to look at the sky, the clouds as they drifted by and, talking to those clouds, he thanked Roisin for her help. However, she had some requests of her own and Chas was not only well suited to assist, but he was also eager and willing to oblige. The fact it was Chas's local knowledge and latent anger that was being harnessed by the rangy Irish girl, did occur to Chas. He even discussed it with Roisin. However, Chas felt that at last, he was a part of something. This was a cause he could support and, if it helped him avenge all the injustices done him, then all the better. He had a mission and, he shared it with the girl he loved and her paramilitary backers it would seem.

The Saints gathered back at Dad's, but this was not the wake it was meant to be. For a start Madge, who had been the first to fall into the grave and onto her grandson's coffin, had been hurt both physically and psychologically, taken away by ambulance, screaming and shouting in pain and anger until the sedative took hold. Those matriarchs now out of the grave and taken home by the undertaker's cars, were able to settle for a meeting in the Snug bar. The leaked message from the police was number one topic of conversation. The O'Neills were responsible for both sacrilegious attacks on the Larkin and Saint Funeral services, and it was agreed, the Irish family had to be dealt with and, maybe, just maybe, it could be a joint effort. The Saints and the Larkins teamed up, a joint goal.

Young Bessie, the youngest of the powerful women, just twenty-three and named after the late Dowager Saint, she of the crumpet fame and destined for the seat of power at some time, suggested it should be a serious consideration 'After all,' she said, 'the families rub along territorially, don't they?'

There was a nod of assent, and *young* Bessie, recognised for her mild manner and superior intelligence, was in the commanding seat. She had a subtle presence and held herself aloof as she stood and demonstrated her right to rule; a smart brain backed up with an underlying menace, albeit well disguised. She also had a long *friendship* with Maude Larkin. They had been at school together and, Bessie felt they had a bond and this bond had been encouraged by Madge, Maude saying to Bessie that her Nan supported them in this closeness also, so long as it was discreet.

Young Bessie instructed one of her ladies in waiting to call next door to Arrie's to invite Nan and Maude Larkin and their close confidantes, for a parley midday the next day. Mourning should be put aside; this was urgent. Her final command was viperous, a rare display of her innate family venom, 'And bring me Scotch 'Arry.'

Wade opened the door, admitted Casey and Nadia, steering them to the stairs, up and into the first floor flat to be greeted by Wendy and a mouth-watering aroma of home cooking.

Casey looked at Wade and raised an eyebrow, the bruising fading. 'Don't look at me Paddy, Wendy's the cook,' and Wade put an arm across Wendy's shoulder, pulled her in for a kiss that was gratefully received. Paddy blushed, and Wade, enjoying his embarrassment, asked what they wanted to drink. Casey handed over a bottle of wine and a bottle of Cream Soda; Nadia liked Cream Soda.

'Sit yourself down,' Wendy gestured, taking over. This was her domain, and Wade, Nadia and Casey sat while Wendy busied herself with the first course. Something new and exotic, prawn cocktail, and Wade poured *Blue Nun* wine for three. Nadia sipped her soft drink.

The meal passed with polite chit-chat. Wendy, on the rise in her career, meeting Wade, love at first site though cautiously approached, and then Nadia, her parents escaping Palestine, or more exactly their forced expulsion from lands seized by Israel. The struggle to settle in England, her elevation academically and the struggle to become a recognised doctor, not so much because of her colour, mainly her gender. Things were getting better, but very slowly, she said. Wendy could attest to also having struggled to get her position at the hospital, and the two professional women cemented a bond that had been growing.

They looked to Casey, his turn, but there was a reluctance. He seemed in a dream. Nadia nudged him, no effect, 'Padraig, come on...' nothing came except tears. Nadia picked up his hand and kissed it, a glance to Wendy, a surreptitious agreement to talk another time. Wendy had her eye on Casey, he had a lot to tell, to get off his chest, before he could move on. Nadia had asked her psychiatrist friend to sort that, she was wary of a man who carried so much emotional baggage, having had baggage of her own that she had had to jettison.

Wendy stood, 'Okay everyone, I've made a curry.' There were little murmurs of pleasure from Nadia and Wade. It was difficult to tell with Casey, but it looked like the prawn cocktail had already been a step into the culinary unknown for him, and now, curry? But he smiled for good form, and Nadia leaned over and pecked a kiss on his cheek. She whispered in his ear and told him he would like it. It was not so much reassurance as an instruction. A strong woman, Nadia.

Casey survived the curry and even said he enjoyed it after his sixth glass of water, and overly expressed intakes of whistling breath, weaving his tongue in and out, and around, all of which did nothing to cool his mouth, but it did amuse everyone else. 'I'm not accustomed to exotic food,' he said, increasing the mirth around the table.

'Better get used to it,' Nadia responded, 'if I am going to cook for you some time.' For Casey, his burning mouth was forgotten as he smiled, leaned over, and kissed her. 'Get off, not yet,' but Nadia took the sting out of her admonition with a glorious simper for her handsome, in a dangerous way, *bog dweller*.

Wade cleared the table. She returned from the kitchen, and announced to Wendy, 'I'll wash up before we go to bed.'

'You better had,' Wendy replied, looking like she meant it, but she had fish to fry and Casey appeared to be on the end of her rod and line as she leaned into the table and asked a pertinent question. 'Do you know where Chas Larkin is?' He was hooked, and she began to reel him in.

Wade sat back in her chair and warmed the interrogative frying pan, intrigued as to how her guvnor would answer the questions Wendy had drifted past her earlier on. She also needed answers about Chas Larkin, and even more about Casey. Who was he? His accent seemed too real. Why had he appeared in her police station? And why now? There was something not kosher, and Wade could not put her finger on it.

Casey looked stunned, thinking this was going to be a social evening. Leaning toward Nadia, for support, he got none, just an expression that suggested he should answer. Casey made a move to his eyebrows. Nadia grabbed his hands and steered them to rest on the table, her hands on top to assure everyone they stayed put. 'Yes, I think so.'

'You do?' Wade reacted, on the attack, and Wendy applied a similar holding back of her lover's hands, and thus both coppers were nailed to the table and forced to reveal everything to the medical profession. 'I'm okay, Wendy, thank you,' but Wendy was taking no chances.

'Paddy, tell all, please,' Wendy asked.

'I've had Scotch 'Arry look for him, and he has tracked him to a bombed-out house beside the East India Docks.'

There was silence around the table. Nadia released Casey's hands and he leaned back in his chair considering the interrogation over, but it wasn't. Wade tugged her hands from Wendy's grasp, looking upon her Rottweiler psychiatrist partner, about to launch herself onto her unsuspecting guvnor. She knew this look from Wendy, her questioning may be expressed in a soft and gentle manner, but there were barbs being swallowed; Wendy was an expert angler.

Nadia, in charge of the landing net, softened Casey in anticipation. 'Padraig, I will want to see Chas. I need to make sure he is doing okay. I imagine it would be too dangerous to readmit him to hospital, but please, let me go and check him out and, I want Wendy to talk to him.'

'Okay.' He looked to Wendy, 'You want to talk to him?'

Nadia sat back and allowed a less emotionally charged Wendy to takeover. 'You fucking idiot,' maybe not so calm, 'that lad has so many issues to deal with...'

Wade grabbed Wendy's hand, 'Steady love.'

Wendy turned on Wade. 'Don't you fucking love me, you filf, you've not a bleedin' clue what's going on with that boy.' She pulled her hand from Wade, she had counting to do, but not before Casey stuck in his twopenn'orth.

'Steady, protection of Chas has to be our priority. I also need to question him. I reckon he knows more than anyone thinks.'

'You think, do you, brains?' Wendy struck back, her head sloping deceptively benignly, and Casey felt pinned to the back of his seat preparing to reap a whirlwind. 'Of course he knows more, likely everything, but consider this, even allowing for the fact that he has been used and abused all of his sorry life, a physical and emotional cripple, and all of the piss taking that came with that, and knowing that the Saints and likely his own family are after him, as well as the Welfare and the bleedin' Christian Brothers,' and she said that like she was spitting feathers, '... why do you think this lass, Roisin, has hooked up with him, eh?' She paused, watched, and waited. 'Answer me that,' and she waited for the reply whilst observing Wade, there was a look in her eyes that she could not fathom, but soon found out.

Wade leaned over to whisper into Wendy's ear. 'Jesus sweet'art babes, you're bloody marvellous. I'm gonna fuck yer brains out tonight.'

Wendy looked rather pleased about that, kissed Wade, and whispered that she could do the washing up in the morning and returned to Casey. 'Well?'

Nadia stepped in, intensity in her deep brown eyes, penetrating Casey's armour, 'Well?'

It looked like Casey was casually considering his response and shocked everyone as he violently stood, the chair toppling over behind him as his fist banged down on the table. The coffee cups rattled and spilled their contents into the saucers, his face was contorted in anger. He said nothing, just stared and seethed.

'Padraig, stop it now!' Nadia's rebuke seemed to penetrate Casey's steely facade, releasing him from his torment and dilemma. He wanted to smash the place up and run away, after all, this was his normal response, but he was so captivated by Nadia he did not know what to do. His plan, when he came to the East End, *do what was needed and disappear*, required serious rethinking. This was the essence of his flare up, a sense he was wearing concrete boots; he'd fallen in love.

Nadia leaned over and collected the chair, righted it and, standing, she eased a rigid Casey back down and from behind, putting her arm around his neck, her face cheek to cheek, she spoke softly. 'Now, my darling, tell us all. We are your friends... we love you, and will keep you safe,' and she wobbled her head slightly, 'well, safe from your feelings that is. Wendy has serious concerns, and if you give her a chance, it might help you understand what is happening, here in the East End, with Chas, and...' she leaned around to look directly into his mad staring eyes that she noticed were beginning to brim, '... even yourself. So, please, my lovely man, tell us all that you know, and then let Wendy tell you what she thinks... okay?'

Casey eased himself out of his rigid posture, and told them, completely unaware of the shocked looks on the faces around the table. Not so much Wade, who sometimes thought, being a copper was a burden. She always wanted to know more and, with her sceptic's head on, she felt the baring of her Guvnor's soul was more like a prepared speech. When he had finished, pale and spent, Wendy offered her view on matters. Casey and Wade were intrigued, it made sense, even if everything appeared scripted.

Casey and Nadia left shortly afterwards and not a moment too soon as Wade dragged Wendy into the bedroom, her muffled pleas about the washing up fading as Wade laid bare the woman she loved.

18

THIS WAS WADE'S FIRST VISIT TO THE HALLOWED HALLS OF Scotland Yard and entering via the tradesmen's entrance took the shine off and she let Casey know this. At the very least they could have entered via the Public entrance, on the side street off Whitehall that gave the Metropolitan Police headquarters its name. Still in a frump, Casey steered Wade down into the basement, passing various plant and maintenance rooms, eventually halting at a door announcing itself as the *Caretakers' Rest Room.*

Casey looked at Wade, a serious frown, and in an admonishing tone, like he was talking to an over indulged child, he spoke as he exhaled a long held in breath, 'Look, listen and learn.' He breathed in, job done, calmed himself, and tapped on the door three times, paused, and then, a rapid knock, twice. There was a response from inside, "Who is it?" 'It's me you fucking tow rags.' Casey turned to Wade. 'The password... now wait'.

She waited, then heard, "Gercha Cowson". 'The password response?' she asked, her bad mood history and in danger of hysterics at the *Famous Five,* idiocy.

'Yes,' Casey answered, his focus on the door as the latch rattled and after several attempts and a considerable amount of cursing, the door opened.

'You should get maintenance onto that,' Casey suggested to a stout gent, not too far off retirement age or death, Wade thought, as she took in the look of a stout man totally gone to seed, dressed in a khaki overall coat. The image presented like a ghostly caretaker emerging from a horror film, a thick fog engulfing him.

Wade struggled to breathe as she made to enter the room, following Casey who had disappeared into the fug of cigarette smoke that congested her nostrils as it made a bid for escape to fresher air via the door and into the corridor. She choked back her disgust as she stepped back from the effluvium, very much like a London *pea souper*. 'Paddy, what the fuck?'

Pushing the stout caretaker to one side, Casey delved deeper into the fog, clearly knowing the territory, or maybe not so clearly as she heard a bump and then his curse. This was followed up with the scrape of poorly maintained sash windows being opened, and immediately the smoke began to clear, probably to settle on the River Thames, whilst affording her a first view of the room and the people in it. Her eye at first on the ceiling, she was reminded of London's major railway confluence of Clapham Junction, so many nicotine-stained pipes, ducts, bundles of cables, that the ceiling itself could not be seen. The walls, also with a film of noxious brown residue, looked as though they had once been cream, topped with a pale green base, institutional colours so familiar to her from school and her first police station. She had often wondered if the government had a load of this paint left over after the war and was steadily using it up, but it was more likely some dodgy civil servant had done a deal with a paint manufacturer.

Wade shook herself out of her suffocating trance, the smoke having cleared tolerably well, but not the repugnant odour and, once she had stopped coughing, an eerie silence and an apparition affronted her fully assaulted senses. She was the centre of attention of four men, cloaked in similar khaki coverall coats, all shapes and sizes, from a cancerous skinny man and at the other end of the scale, a florid faced, bloated man, looking like a cod that had sat at the back of the trawler, undiscovered for a year. And this motley crew sat around a filthy table that had several ashtrays full and brimming over onto a sticky back plastic table cover, like the moon surface with fag burn craters. The table was cluttered with old plates that had not been washed up since before the dinosaurs had finished their fish fingers in tomato ketchup and a pack of stained playing cards scattered. The semblance, a down and out, speakeasy, poker den.

'Paddy, gonna introduce us?' the portly doorman asked, a coy smiling, nicotine-stained grin behind a hand of fanned out tacky playing cards that Wade found incongruously endearing. He had a face a bit like her lovely granddad, who had sported fat wobbly cheeks and a grey haired, brown stained, moustache, just like this man.

'To be sure I will now.' Paddy answered, a stronger Irish accent than she had heard before, which made Wade think more on Paddy and his origins, as aged cod man floundered to Wade. Piles she thought, or maybe grounded fish always walk like that? The old cod put a comradely arm across her shoulders, which she shucked off, accompanying this with a look that said, do that again and I'll tear yer fucking scales off, comrade, and the old fish stepped aside, his fins raised in mock defence. Paddy, a broad and lovable, cheeky grin, pointed to the guardian of the room. 'Alf, this is Wade, Flora Wade, Detective Sergeant. You can trust her and only her, well her and me,' he thought, grinned, '... yeah, and me.'

Alf, dismissing Casey's humorous aside, shuffled to Wade and greeted her with an outstretched hand of Bowyers sausages. Wade took the hand and shook, surprised that it was neither clammy nor limp, but firm and friendly, and while he had the grip, he tugged her into the room and with a practiced swing of his leg that reminded her of *Charlie Chaplin*, kicked the door shut behind her. Wade allowed herself to be steered deep inside, aware the soles of her shoes made an incongruous sucking noise as she tramped the sticky lino floor. The room now felt like an old pub that had not been cleaned after several boozy nights, reeking of the scent of stale beer and fag ash. Once again, she was revolted and could feel her stomach contents bubbling into her throat. She swallowed to stave off her nausea. The remaining card players stood and, one by one, greeted her with a handshake, friendly grins of dodgy teeth, and she immediately forgot all the names; did she actually hear? It was like she had walked into a dream world, not a nightmare, but a scene that held all of her pet domestic hates. Wade was fastidious to the point of obsession, it was the only thing she and Wendy argued about and, she had left for work that morning leaving the washing up. What was happening to her she thought?

It seemed that everyone in the room waited patiently while Wade shuffled and ordered her thoughts, looking down to her feet doing jigs in sticky shoes. She looked up, recognised the stares for what they were, concern that she might be sick, alert to getting out of the way. Wade screwed up her resolve and waved a reassuring hand, 'Right, I'm okay.' The caretakers and Casey visibly relaxed, and out of the corner of her eye she saw a weaselly man reorder the cards on the table while nobody looked. She smiled her recognition of the cheating manoeuvre so expertly achieved.

'Right then, let's get to it,' Casey said as he stepped to a chest of drawers behind a random array of buckets, mops, and brooms. Alf joined him and together they effortlessly moved the tallboy furniture to reveal a hatchway that Casey pushed. It swung open on well-oiled hinges, the only thing in the room of maintenance people that appeared well maintained. Interesting? A passing thought for Wade, as she watched Casey duck down, pass through and disappear, and like a butler, Alf waved a flowery hand to suggest Wade follow. She did, also wondering if Alf would be able to get his bulk through, and if he did follow, he would get a good look at her bum.

'Oh, fuck it,' she exclaimed, ducked, and slid through with ease, and shared a titter with Casey as Alf, with much puffing and panting, squeezed his way in.

Once inside, Alf closed the hatch, and she heard the furniture being replaced by the card players; how will we get out? Casey answered Wade's querying look. 'There's another exit if we need it, but the chest of drawers is on castors, so it moves easily from our side if needed. We lift it because we do not want to wear a mark on the floor, a dead giveaway if anyone came into the room, which they wouldn't, because it is so disgusting.'

'Deliberately so?' Wade responded, cottoning onto the subterfuge.

Casey sloped a grin to confirm she had the right of it and waited patiently to let her have a look around the room that was more of an antechamber, devoid of any furniture or personality. 'We go through here,' and Casey lead the way via another room, and in a distant wall, another door made not for Snow White but for her seven dwarves and feeling like Dopey, she followed Casey into a vaulted tunnel that had likely been here before the Scotland Yard building had been constructed. It had a mediaeval feel, as did the cobwebs. Wade followed with a sense of claustrophobia in the confined space, but it was better than the caretakers' rest room at least. Anything was better than that filthy den, and she smiled at a diabolical deceiving stratagem. Nobody in their right mind would enter there if they could possibly avoid it.

'Come on,' Casey called back, knocking Wade out of her stunned inertia. With her head crooked, she proceeded along the low headroom tunnel, no more than five feet to the high point of the vaulted brickwork, and imagined, rather than saw, a scattering of spiders and Black Death rats. It sloped down and then evened out. 'We're just passing under the Thames,' Casey commented nonchalantly, not realising this exacerbated the sense of trepidation Wade already felt but she was a trooper and pushed on, trying to put off all thoughts of drowning should the roof cave in.

Eventually they rose and reached the end, greeted by a small, profiled door made of aged wood that had never seen a lick of paint. Casey tapped, the same code as before, the response similar. "Who is it?" 'It's me you fucking tow rags,' Casey responded. Wade heard "Gercha Cowson" from beyond, and the door opened into a small hall, with another open door, in the near distance. It was an entrance into a cavernous room, wide and long, and clean, thank the Lord, she thought, as she stepped into the brilliantly lit space to look upon serried ranks of typists, clerks, and officious looking civil servants. The men were togged in the obligatory pin stripe trousers, black waistcoat, and she presumed a black blazer stored somewhere. The women, starched, prim and proper and, walking like they had a big stick up their arse and that passing thought made Wade chuckle. What on earth was going on here? She had entered another world, which made her think again, just who is Casey? The room had glazed pavement roof lights in the ceiling, obscure glass brick setts that offered at least a semblance of attachment to the outside world. This reassured Wade just a little, as she scanned the room looking for escape points if she needed them, not that she felt threatened. If anything, the room had a benign Britishness to it that should have felt comforting, but it did not comfort her.

'Paddy,' a man exuding a tall and strong physical presence, dressed like he'd just walked out of Carnaby Street and decided the purple haze, flowery shirts with flyway collars, and orange, suede, drainpipe trousers, not only were a good match, but suited him. Wade would have to put him right on that, a passing thought of calling the fashion police, but said nothing as she followed Paddy and this man with the extraordinary, bandito, droopy moustache that made him look like Bill or Ben the flowerpot men, on a vintage Mexican wanted poster. Alf waved his farewell, saying he would get back to his work. "The toilets at the Yard would not clean themselves", he added. Wade thinking, they probably would have to.

19

Around mid-morning, Nadia received a message at the hospital as to Chas's whereabouts, reportedly delivered by an Irish girl with a mass of red curls, who, it seems, informed an intimidated porter that he would incur the wrath of the O'Neills if he split on her. Nadia was relieved as Scotch 'Arry had lost Chas, following the kerfuffle of the Saints and Larkins rousting everyone in the East End the previous night. 'Arry had been taken and interrogated, kept for about fifteen minutes, suspended upside down in an old cellar, before being released as nobody understood a word he said. He was actually confessing all. He had a low threshold for pain and just about anything else. Upon release, he was followed, which Scotch 'Arry expected, and lead his tailing company away from where he knew the Chas Larkin accommodation was likely located, to a distant terrace of bombed out houses and there he dodged in and lost them. By the time he got to the hospital, all he could do was follow Nadia as she paced in the direction of the docks, her raincoat billowing, making her an easy mark to follow. He made a mental note to tell Casey. She could also have followed a more circuitous route that might have been a little less obvious should a Saint or Larkin wish to tail her, but Scotch 'Arry was satisfied she had no furtive followers and watched her safely into the desolate shell of a house that had become Chas's home of late.

Nadia examined Chas's eyes while the lad tucked into the bacon sandwiches she had brought him, occasionally sipping the sweetened tea she poured from a flask. His face was still marked from the battering, though a lot of the swelling had subsided, just a fading florid yellowy purple tinge. His eyes, he told her, "Better than ever". She wanted him back in hospital, but knew that would not be a realistic proposition, also realising he was as safe here as anywhere, even if the place was filthy and unsanitary. Chas told her that the dodgy side of his family owned, or more than likely stole, a lot of the bombed-out houses, the owners having disappeared along with any paperwork, either killed in the blitz, or more than likely by the Larkins, who now owned a considerable portfolio of property in the East End. With the minimum amount of work done to make them habitable, the Larkin family rented out these shells of houses to people who had no choice other than to be grateful. The one Chas was in, he told her, was scheduled for demolition. It would be part of a new estate, sometime soon, but not yet, so it remained vacant, too far gone for even the Larkin landlord.

Nadia pulled aside a rag cloth curtain to a hole she presumed at one time had been a decent second storey window, the remnants of a Georgian sash frame, broken like a disjointed familiar skeleton, the glass body long gone, where sash chords dangled like stubborn entrails. Across the street she could see the dockyard wall, a secure perimeter interspersed with integrated warehouses. She had a full view of the Thames' wharves and marshalling aprons, a pleasurable distraction to gaze across the industrious tableau that were the East India Docks. Nadia was not, however, aware this house faced onto one significant warehouse, one which was owned by the Saints. Why would she know, and why would she know that it was no coincidence Chas had chosen this hideaway, especially because of its proximity to this warehouse and, that it was at the express request of Roisin. A request he had been only too willing to follow.

Roisin knew exactly what she was doing. Chas loved her, in a spiritual sense, dreamed of her continually, longed for her visits and would comply with her every whim, safe in the auspices of the Black Rose, forever grateful that on one of his many attempts at running away, he had reached only as far as Kilburn. It was here in west London he had encountered and been cared for by an Irish family, the O'Rierdons, who had taken him into their loving bosom and, after a few days of familial respite, was returned to Stepney. His mum, his family, such that it was, he had no friends, all unaware he had been on the missing list.

Like most of the property around, the Saint warehouse was bomb damaged, the docks being an obvious target and only now were these warehouses being repaired or rebuilt. However, this warehouse remained as it had been on Armistice Day and if you walked past you would not give it a second glance. It had little obvious security, other than it appeared redundant, not worth a second glance, but if you did express curiosity, the principal guarantee of immunity was that it was owned by the Saints, as expressed by a sign painted on the brickwork. You had to be mad to mess with the Saints.

Chas often wondered if he was mad, after all he had pinched the Saint crumpet at Roisin's suggestion. A clever idea in that he had replaced it mischievously with a replica, but that game was up, and to get into 'Arries pub now would be considerably more difficult. Roisin had reassured him he was fighting for a cause and, together they would take that battle to the East End Establishment, to secure their trading routes and, after that, into the City of London, the commercial lungs of the Capital City and the country. So, regardless of risk, he would break in again, one more time.

It had become almost legend, certainly passed down from father to son, that the Saints had Irish connections, all the way back to the mysterious return from the dead of Mickey Saint, *the little devil,* all those years ago. What he had been doing in Ireland after the Great War was not general knowledge, although many guessed. Mickey was a natural for the uprising, and he returned in order to feed arms and munitions to the IRA, in return for which he was handsomely rewarded. It was presumed, but not known, that this arrangement continued and those in the security services who knew this for sure, had either been disposed of, or bought off, to be later removed permanently. They took no chances did the Saints and, neither did the IRA for that matter.

Chas had, as a matter of necessity, learned all of the secretive ways around the part of the East End where he lived. He knew every nook and cranny, every hiding place, and how to discreetly access those concealments. And, where better to hide from your principal tormentors, the Saints, than in their own rarely visited warehouse property. He had of course realised early on that the O'Rierdons were only interested in his knowledge and that he could access the Saints depository of arms and ordnance. He had, however, discovered from this Irish family, that the Saints were double dealing with the Republican's money, supplying weaponry to both sides and that betrayal was frowned upon. Similarly, the main funder of the Irish resistance was a City funding institution, who, it turned out, was also funding both sides. So, it was important that other lines of supply be sorted, before ending the Saint relationship, also permanently. How Chas knew of this treachery was not because he had been told by the O'Rierdons, they had just confirmed his knowledge. It was because the loose-lipped Mickey Saint junior had said it one day whilst kicking the shite out of him, saying he would use his Irish connections to blow him and his family to kingdom come. It was, however, a surprise to find that the Saints had been double crossing their paymaster and that they were on the *rubbing out* list of the IRA, a circumstance he took immense pleasure in, and even more so, as he was to play a part in that exercise of elimination.

Chas had a clear vision of his mission and following a hobble into Kilburn, the Irish part of London, he was able to establish his *intelligence* credentials, at the same time securing his future. He visited regularly and, it was as he left the O'Rierdons house one winter's evening, a bitter cold night, his walk home secure in the pea soup smog that so frequently shrouded the city, he was tapped on his shoulder. He had jumped with fear, thinking he had been followed by one of his many tormentors, but it could not have been further from that reality. Stood before him was a young lass, long and lean, a glorious beaming smile, and this young woman was pleased to see him. She spoke in the strongest of Irish accents, and Chas Larkin was initiated into the world of *The Black Rose.* It was all he had ever wanted in life. A protector, someone who cared, someone to guide him. The thought he might be being used did occur to him, of course it did. Chas, although crippled emotionally and physically and hunched within himself, was not stupid, though he was treated as such, as were many enfeebled children, but he did not care, he now knew what he wanted to do with his wretched life, and it amounted, singularly, to revenge. He burned with a passion for retribution, it sustained him in his troubled moments, it drove him on, and that is what the O'Rierdons, and now Roisin, had seen and used and, Chas could not care less.

Scotch 'Arry had seen the blinding light following his Billy Big Head narrow escape. A near miss courtesy of the thug's assassination by a man in a black balaclava, a man he presumed to be Casey, and this followed by the upside down talking to by the Saints. The thing was, Scotch 'Arry, by this fluke of fate, and ironically, was now a firm and active ally of the law. Well, Casey anyway, and he was the law, wasn't he? Scotch 'Arry had no other affiliation. He was no longer a casual informant. He was employed, and his principal Casey mission at the moment was tailing Nadia, not Chas Larkin, and he provided his paymaster incoherent intelligence, whom in return rewarded the drainpipe Scotsman with enough money to survive. Scotch 'Arry had the common sense to steer well clear of the Saints and the Larkins, no more hanging around in the pubs for him and so it was he began his long haul into sobriety, and full employment. It was the first regular job he'd ever had following demob from the Scots Guards.

Hiding himself behind a convenient lamppost, marginally fatter, and a lot brighter than himself, he watched as Nadia left the broken-down house in the gloom of early evening. A fine rain fell as he began to tail her, but out of the corner of his eye he saw Chas Larkin walking deliberately, only the hint of a limp, across the narrow road to the Saint's warehouse. He maintained his pace, following the doctor though his curiosity was piqued, knowing this would also apply to Casey who may even spring for some additional cash for information such as this.

Wade followed Casey, who followed the flower power man up several flights of concrete steps of a fire escape, to the second floor, into and along a central corridor of half glazed, boxy offices, each with suited and booted persons beavering away with God knows what? Tick-tock, tick tock, clock watchers all. The three were met at the end of that corridor by a tall, slim woman, in a figure-hugging pencil skirt and shapely blouse accentuating her conical bosoms. She had her hair scurfed back into a tight, civil service, austere bun, and had no nonsense, black, horn-rimmed glasses that had just the hint of a curly tip at the ends, sat upon a firecracker face. Looking closely, and not shy of being observed, Wade was riveted by the woman's nylons, a straight line up the calves, disappearing into the realms of heaven. She was gorgeous. Casey noticed and smiled.

'Shut it,' Wade said, and Casey's grin widened.

'The major is expecting you,' the secretary said, business-like, prim and proper, just a thawing smile and sideways glance to Paddy. Wade noticed, oh well, he was attractive if that was your bent. Or not, she supposed.

They were shown into a spacious corner office, the view out of a large window across the Thames to the Houses of Parliament was stunning, distracting Wade for a moment, she therefore missed the proffered hand from a stiff military man, and he was embarrassed but did not waver in his imitation of a rigid stick. Wade returned her gaze to the man who had to be the major, a medium height, ramrod, beanpole, with a dirty bit moustache on a skeletal face, with sunken eyes that looked like he had just been released from a Japanese prisoner of war camp. The only concession to a relaxation of the austerity of post war Britain, a wavy quiff, the black hair held in place with glistening *Brylcreem* that plastered the remaining short back and sides to his pointy head.

'Ahemm...' the military man cleared his throat, still embarrassed. 'Floraaaah Wadeaaah I presume?' he managed to say in a protracted military baritone.

Wade, shaken from her reverie, returned the fixed stare into pinball eyes, a face with cheeks colouring and shaved within an inch of their life, the pencil thin moustache steady as a rock, looking as if it had been drawn onto the stiff upper lip using a ruler. 'Yes', Wade replied as she took the proffered hand. It was a good handshake, not excessively strong, likely respecting her femininity? So, she returned a hard squeeze to show him who was boss. He squeaked and Wade thought maybe he had been *Household Cavalry*, or *Washing Up Dragoons*, and giggled. This was all too weird. She glanced to Paddy, his face still plastered with his cheeky *Danny Boy* grin, which she supposed, worked on some people, but she was becoming inured.

Flower power man, after introducing the major, emphasising he was known only as "The major", suggested they should sit around the long rectangular, highly polished, conference table. The major took his seat at the head, whereupon Wade swung her hips to knock Casey off course so she could take the other end and they exchanged a touché smile. Paddy was enjoying working with Flora.

Chas settled himself into the burrow he had been using for years, in amongst boxes of Sten guns, ammunition, explosives, and other ordnance he knew not the identity of. But Roisin did, and over time she had instructed him in their use, most important of which was how to make a simple bomb. It summed up the life of Chas Larkin, that in this lair of deadly firepower, he felt safe. He now also carried a handgun, don't ask what name it was, these things did not enthuse Chas so much as it did Roisin, but she showed him how to handle it, the case of bullets slotting into the handle grip. "Flick the safety, point, and fire". Her instructions and the only thing he had not done was shoot the weapon. I mean, where could he do that? He just imagined it would be okay and interestingly, he was excessively comforted by the extraordinary weight of the pistol within the shoulder harness strapped to his skeletal body and concealed on his person.

Chas played with the handgun, pretend shooting the Saints and more than a few of his own family. Beside him was the small attaché case his Mum used to take with her when she went off for a weekend of shagging, drop dead gorgeous she thought she was, well she was now. Dropped dead and splattered far, wide, and not so handsome. Chas was pleased about that, and now her case was going to be drop dead, inside a bomb, and this afternoon he intended to make his first retaliatory strike. Roisin said to do it in the name of the O'Neills, and he would. He knew the form and would follow it to the letter, and he committed the telephone code to memory, and the message; *"The O'Neills say hi."*

The telephone on the conference table rang, the major yanked and barked a "Yes", not pleased at being interrupted, and patently enjoying the sound of his own voice as he briefed Casey and Wade. Wade struggled to stay awake. The major had a monotone, monotonous voice that droned, militarily repeating things as if he had idiots in front of him. He hemmed into the phone, nodded to himself then questioned the caller, 'German you say, or maybe Liverpudlian? What do you mean you cannot understand a word?' He listened some more, looked to Casey, and gestured with the handset, 'For you,' he said with an exasperated sigh.

Casey took the phone, 'Put him on,' and he waited, then listened. 'Slow down, okay 'Arry,' a casual aside to Wade that it was Scotch 'Arry, and she derred, that bit was obvious as she could hear the high-pitched unintelligible accent screeching across the room. 'Can you get back and watch the warehouse please. Nadia's safe at work?' He nodded to himself. 'I will let you know when Wendy Richards is going to meet Chas, and I will want you to watch over her too.' Obviously satisfied with the response, Casey handed the phone back to the major, who listened only to the dialling tone. He rattled the receiver for some reason, hung up and looked to Casey for an explanation, as did Wade, what was this about, "Watching over Wendy?"

'My man,' was all Casey offered.

The major accepted that sometimes he had to be patient to learn all that he felt he should know, and this was something he did not like, the feeling he was not actually in charge. But it was the way of things in this murky MI5 world. He was only an administrator after all, and frankly, that suited him, but it didn't suit Wade.

'Well?'

'Well what?' Casey replied.

'What is 'appening, oh mighty dipstick?' Wade waded in and went in for the killer blow, 'You fucking tosspot.'

The major looked stunned at the insubordination, 'Wade, that is a superior officer you are talking to.'

Wade leaned back in her seat, raised her eyebrows, and sloping her head, gave the major an enquiring look that he could not define, but he didn't need to as Wade followed it up with an in-depth explanation. 'In your fucking dreams, soldier boy,' and she turned to Casey who was grinning *affectionately*.

She was about to give him both barrels when he disarmed her, 'I'll tell you later.'

Wade could see this would have to do, and flower power man interrupted to defuse the tension. 'Paddy, what do you see happening now?'

'Don't know, wait and see?'

Wade sighed, and considered a response, but the telephone rang again. The major picked up, and with a pencil he scribbled a note onto a pad, hung up, and slid the note to Casey. Wade twisting her head to read the tiny, anally controlled writing on the note as it passed along the table, it said, *The O'Neills say hi.* 'The code?' the major asked.

Casey picked up the note, showed Wade. 'Yes,' he said. 'If this code is given, it means it is a serious attack by the IRA, and you will have whatever time they give to react. Wade looked for an explanation. 'The IRA are only looking to damage the infrastructure, not kill innocents...' and he shrugged his shoulders, '... they hope, but you know...?'

20

NADIA VISITED WENDY IN HER OFFICE AT THE HOSPITAL AND talked about her impressions following her visit with Chas Larkin. 'He looks remarkably well, considering, ignoring the bruises that are steadily healing. His eyesight is good, I would like to get him in and work on his foot, but that may have to wait, and when he does undergo the series of operations, he will need some support around him, but who?' She shrugged her shoulders, 'Don't know. At the moment he seems only to have this rather illusive girl, Roisin, for the odd bit of company.'

Nadia reflected and Wendy pressed, 'And?

'He showed me out of his hovel, and...'

'Yes?'

'He walked better, as if some newfound confidence helped him overcome his disability.' She pondered more while there was a stultified silence. 'I wish I'd had the surgeon look at his foot while we had him in hospital. I am no expert, and to be honest I never looked that hard, but it might not be as bad as I had first thought.'

'His previous hobbling walk may have more to do with his state of mind, his wretched life exacerbating what may be a minor disability?' Wendy suggested, and shrugged her own shoulders to say she wouldn't know until she had more time with the boy. Wendy chewed the end of a pencil as she considered her further response. Nadia leaned across the desk, took the pencil away and told her it was a disgusting habit, and she should stop it. Wendy chuckled, 'Flora says that,' and she smiled, thinking of the woman she loved and how she seemed hell bent on, "knocking her into shape" as she would say. Well, she would maybe stop chewing her pencils and nails, but Wendy was more subtly manipulating Flora into the woman she wanted, and Wade seemed not to have a clue, which suited Wendy.

'Well?'

Wendy pondered further while Nadia displayed her impatience and when she thought she had tantalised the attractive surgeon long enough, she gave her professional opinion. 'The kid's a fucking fruit cake.'

'Wendy!' Nadia was shocked.

'You understand we tend not to use that language anymore in my profession,' and Wendy disguised her amusement, but Nadia could not. Trying to be serious in front of

Wendy was a challenge, and she realised this psychiatrist was one very accomplished woman and not just in her profession.

'So, a loony?' Nadia responded, joining in.

'We also tend to refrain from calling them loonies or indeed mental hospitals loony-bins but, to answer your question, Chas Larkin could do with a therapeutic spell in a *Loony-bin*, preferably in the peaceful countryside, away from the toxic atmosphere of the East End of London and all if its malevolent connotations. Especially his pernicious family and, the bullying Saints, all contributing factors that are bad for Chas and, if I had him there, I could really work on the boy. I could get him sorted, but...' she paused and leaned back, picked up another pencil and shaped to chew so Nadia had to lean across the desk and stay in that position for a little while as she admonished her. She loved looking down the front of her blouse, a little titillation did no harm did it, she thought, and maybe she might not tell Flora of this, '... it would take a long time.'

Nadia, after a while, realised what was happening and sat back down, unable to disguise her blushes. She sensed a mild titillation, but nothing like the powerful sensation she felt when she noticed Paddy, unsubtly, looking down her blouse, or eyeing her backside as she walked, which she exaggerated for his benefit, especially as he thought he was being surreptitious. The bozo. 'Did you enjoy the view?' she asked Wendy.

Now Wendy reddened and decided to slip back into professional mode. 'The point I make, Nadia, is that I cannot pinpoint any exact diagnosis. Not until I have had some extensive time with Chas Larkin. He will obviously have been severely damaged by his upbringing. You already realise he is a lot older than generally surmised and, this stunted physical growth will be also as a result of his repressed emotional and psychological development.'

Wendy gathered her thoughts some more and Nadia allowed her this time. So far, she had said nothing that she had not already surmised herself. Nadia's patience expired, 'So?'

'Are you looking for me to predict how Chas will behave?'

'No, although when I talk to Paddy, I am sure he will ask that question...' she paused, looked up from her contemplative lap, '... so, Flora has asked this already?'

Wendy nodded, whilst steepleing her fingers and sucking both index fingers as concocted surrogate pencils. 'Chas is a ticking bomb,' and she thought on.

'And...?' Nadia asked, patience wearing thin. Wendy leaned forward on the desk and allowed Nadia a look down her own blouse, in case she was interested, one good turn and all that. 'And I'm not interested in your tits.'

Wendy wobbled her head, indicating this was Nadia's loss and of no consequence to her. 'I have said all of this to Flora, and...'

Nadia interrupted, 'You can't understand why Paddy and

Flora have not taken Chas Larkin into protective custody?' Wendy nodded again, no flirtation, a serious look of concern. 'Oh, for fuck's sake. You think Paddy and Flora are hanging the boy out to dry for their own use?'

Wendy remained leaning and sighed as she flopped back into her seat. 'Well, I think Paddy is, and Flora is going along with it. I think she is trying to understand just what she has gotten herself into.' Nadia could see Wendy was now troubled and left her time to say what it was she needed to say. 'I know my Flora and, she is excited by all this action and embroilment in whatever and may subconsciously turn a blind eye to some stuff? God knows. I already suspect something serious has happened, it troubles her, and she has decided to not only ignore it, but more importantly, not tell me.'

'And what do you think about Paddy?' Nadia enquired.

'Well, you like him. He is good looking, if you like that sort of thing, and I can see you do.'

'Oh, shut up, Wendy, you know what I am asking, and my intuition tells me he is dangerous.'

'But you are enjoying that danger are you not?' Nadia sighed. 'Got you done up like a kipper, as my equally dangerous Flora would say, eh?'

Nadia sighed an even longer exhalation of breath, refilled her lungs with a large and noisy drawing in of air through clenched teeth, expelled equally lustily as she said, 'Yes.'

The major thought for a moment, and then into the phone he summoned his secretary to bring in a subordinate whom he briefed with the code word, that a call when identified was to be treated as an emergency. He emphasised that a special number was to be established, to further authenticate the call as one to take seriously, before the code was used and the message issued. The subordinate left to carry out his orders.

'I presume you can get all of that information to the relevant people?' the major asked of Paddy, already knowing the answer, and knowing this was why Casey was here. He hated mavericks but recognised that in this shady and perilous spook world, such people were needed. He knew also Casey had appeared on his doorstep with this reputation and he was beginning to suspect Wade was similarly wired and in no time at all would be recruited into MI5.

'Yes,' Casey responded, 'you were the last link in the chain, and...' he paused and thought a bit more, '... I have already sorted this for you. I think a campaign is planned and it will start straightaway. I already have a telephone link installed into Arbour Square.'

At the same time Wendy and Nadia were shocking each other into reality, and Casey, to a lesser extent Wade, were explaining the reality of this new world to the major, the Saints and Larkins had their command meeting. The Larkins, respectful of the proposed working relationship, accepted the venue in Dad's. The panel of very strong women, some in the brains department, others, bruiser types. They were there to make up the brawn should one or two of the men folk need batting around the head with a metaphoric rolling pin. After only a brief sharing of views and intelligence, the ladies had to conclude they were no further forward than before the *seek, find, and fucking manalise the O'Neills* mission was instigated.

Bernie, *I only asked*, shuffled to stand in front of the women. A brave move, acknowledged by Madge Saint, now returned from hospital, and Nan Larkin. 'What?' Madge asked of her halfwit grandson, who stood easily six foot-six, and if he had not been so brow beaten all his life, could pass as a handsome young man.

Bernie tried to get them to say his correct name but was beginning to forget what it was himself, Johnny? A consequence of being bounced around the head every time he complained, as well as being a sandwich short of a picnic, which had that sandwich been replaced, he would realise he would be known as Bernie, *I only asked*, forever, and should just accept it. However, Bernie was not even aware he had a picnic and so he decided to venture his opinion to the female Star Chamber. He hesitated nervously.

'Come on, dipstick, spit it out. What pearl of wisdom has your one brain cell come up wiv? Madge pushed her grandson, continuing the emotional and psychological repression.

'I only fort...'

He pondered a bit too long and was shocked by the raucous laughter around the table, enjoined a moment or two later by the bouncer women, naturally slower of thought, but not of physical action, and all enjoying the notion that Bernie had thought of something. In amongst this great jollity, Madge asked her grandson to continue and impart his brain wave for all to hear. 'Come on Sherlock, what is it we've missed?' Bernie stamped a humungous petulant foot and turned to leave. 'Oi, bozo, back here now,' and Madge signalled for one of the bouncers to return the gentle giant to the death panel.

Bernie was patently nervous and wondered why he had not kept this thought to himself which, if he was honest, and he could not be, as homosexuality was frowned upon, even though it was tacitly accepted in his family, it was his boyfriend Eric who had suggested it last night, when he told Bernie to come home to bed as the O'Neills probably didn't exist.

'Told you your boy was a bit light on his feet, Bessie,' Nan Larkin said. Meaning he was not just chicken, but clearly a homosexual, in the parlance, a poofter, and she repeated the assertion that sounded more like an accusation. And that was when the brawl started. Saints and Larkin fighting women, glasses, ashtrays, and furniture went flying across the room as Bernie backed himself to the wall; contrary to received wisdom, he was no fool. He found some inner strength. 'Stop it now,' he shouted, stamped his foot again and waved his arms petulantly, and repeated, 'stop it you fucking idiots!' He had a deep resonating and booming voice.

Well, that did it and Bernie, convinced they would all attack him, made to run, but was surprised the womenfolk did stop, took stock, and looked at Bernie in a different light. Heads sloped in an understanding way. Blimey here we go Bernie thought and headed them off at the pass, 'Nan Larkin is right mum. I'm Stoke-on-Trent, bent, ginger beer, a poofter, homosexual, and you had better get used to it,' and turning on his heel, he looked back, wondering why it was so quiet. He gazed upon a shocked audience, which was no longer angry.

Madge and Older Bessie approached Bernie and he cringed, expecting a belting, and was taken aback when they hugged him, his mum saying, 'We know yer light on yer feet son, but we're pleased you have acknowledged to us all, and you can tell that woolly woofter, Limp Eric, he can come out of hiding as well. We will welcome him into the family.

Bernie was stunned, 'You knew?'

Bessie clipped her son around his dopy head. 'Of course I knew, I'm yer bleedin' muvver, for fuck sake,' and she kissed him on the cheek. Something she hadn't done since he could not remember when? He had a passing thought, had she ever kissed him? 'Now, come and sit with us women and tell us what you've been thinking, what we suspect is Limp Eric's idea, is it?' And Bernie nodded, sullen, confused. What had just happened? 'Okay, come, sit and spit it out,' and she steered Bernie for his first ever sit down with the matriarchal Star Chamber of these two powerful families.

A chair was righted for Bernie. He sat and waited while the remaining furniture was restored and a semblance of order achieved, broken glass shuffled to the sides with the booted feet of the bouncers, and when he sensed he had all of their attention, he said it. 'I, well, Eric, and I agree with him. We think the O'Neills don't exist.'

Well, that did it, and the whole assembly of women burst into more raucous laughter, matrons folded in two, in stitches, which lasted for near on five minutes, before Madge spoke to the huge lad. 'Fuck off, Bernie, you dozy bum bandit,' and she carried on laughing, stood, and walked to her grandson. 'Go home to Eric, boy, and remember, we love you even if you are a bleedin' Perry Como,' and she ruffled his hair, planted a grand maternal kiss, and sent the huge man on his way with just a chuckle or two, interspersed with comments to the room, "The O'Neills don't exist" and this was received with more energetic mirth as Bernie slunk away. He was feeling extraordinarily light on his feet, he couldn't wait to get back and tell Eric they could come out into the open.

Bernie made it as far as the bar as the matronly committee of local death and destruction broke up and joined the party in the lounge bar. Not all the Larkins returning to their own pub next door but enjoying some free drinks at the cost of their old adversary, a novel sense of camaraderie. Bernie was forced to have some celebratory drinks with the Larkins who stayed, his surviving brothers, cousins, friends, and hangers on, the news now being broadcast far and wide, confirming everything they already knew, even about the secret squirrel boyfriend.

Heartily reassured, eventually Bernie sneaked out and legged it for home, a spring in his step as he bashed though the front door of their terraced house, ran the stairs two at a time and into the bedroom to see Eric sprawled across the eiderdown, his brains splattered on the far wall with a scrawled note in Eric's blood and grey matter, *The O'Neills say hi.*

21

WADE AND CASEY HEADED BACK TO ARBOUR SQUARE. WADE was frustrated she could get no substantial and convincing answers to her legion of questions and, her persistence, distinctly irritated Casey, which provided her with some compensating satisfaction. However, she felt inexplicably excited? She would need to cool this before she went home this evening.

'Shit's hit the fan,' Old George said, as they passed through the police station vestibule, 'tread lightly in the CID room.'

Casey ignored the comments until he heard Wade questioning further the man whom he considered particularly untrustworthy. He always sensed he was being pumped for information that would be passed onto the best paymaster.

'How so, Sarge?' Wade asked, nonchalantly leaning on the counter.

Casey stopped on the bottom step and turned to listen in. Wade, he was learning, had a nose for these things.

'The boyfriend of Bernie, *I only asked* Saint,' and the Desk Sergeant winked knowingly, 'if you get my drift? You know, Limp Eric?' Wade nodded, knew exactly what he was talking about, and exactly what the old reactionary fart meant. 'Well, he's been found with his brains blown out in the house they shared.'

Casey wandered back, he was getting to know the personnel of both the Saint and Larkin family, and he recognised the nickname of one of the Saint boys. He now listened into the stultified exchange, the desk sergeant not expecting to be interrogated. He just wanted to wind Wade and the bog dweller up for amusement, seek any scraps of information that might fall his way, but now found himself being put on the spot.

Before Wade could press more, Casey stepped in. 'Bernie, homosexual?'

Wade offered Casey a frigid stare, to put him back in his box. 'Yes,' she said, 'common knowledge. I'll talk about it later,' and she took immense pleasure in the frustrated look on his face as he was left to wait for the substance of Wade's information. Serve the bugger right, she thought, malevolently. She returned to her casual interrogation. 'So, Sarge, what's the prevailing opinion, gang stuff? The Saints or

Larkins not keen on closet fairies?' And she said that with menace, knowing everyone in the station knew she batted off the other foot, as they would irritatingly say, too embarrassed to use the word *lesbian*.

'Probably? Though we also thought they knew and accepted Bernie, ' the sarge responded. 'Oh, and the commander wanted to see you both as soon as you appeared, so I would get up there if I were you, there's a sound of buzzing from his arse.'

Wade and Casey, intent on the commander's top floor office, headed up the stairs, just a mischievous peek into the CID room, scurrying busy bee detectives, but Casey's eye was drawn to a young detective, pinning crime scene photos on the wall. A picture attracted his attention. He summoned Wade to follow as he bashed through the swing doors and strutted determinedly across the floor to stand in front of the pictorial display, edging the young detective to one side. Wade caught him up, and they shared a look at the crime scene photograph with a dawning acknowledgement.

'Oi, fuck off you two,' words from an irritated and territorial detective sergeant. Wade obviously knew the man and his accustomed demeanour, confirming this with a knowing wink, and with a not so discreet hand gesture, which suggested they leave, go see the commander, and she strutted for the door. Sensing Casey was not following, she turned back to see him looking at the picture in more detail. 'Paddy,' she called out, 'the commander?'

Casey waved her concern away. He focused his attention on the young detective and stepping in front of "detective sergeant feckin' eejit" as he called the irritated man, who made to resist before Wade responded, to stop him. 'Seen anything *sir*?' emphasising the sir, and the furious Detective Sergeant stepped away, recognising when he was outranked and outmanoeuvred. Wade walked back to join Casey. 'Oh, I see.' She saw the scrawled note on the wall in the photograph, *The O'Neills say hi.* 'Can you get another copy of that photo for yourself please, Tony, we'll be taking this one,' and she snatched the photo off the pin board, looked to Casey, 'Commander?' And they disappeared, leaving a seething CID room behind them.

Chas Larkin lurked in a shady vantage point, a corner niche of the dockyard wall, where he could see the tarts lined up. There was a Polish boat docked and they anticipated good trade. Selecting his target, and emphasising his limp, as Roisin had suggested, Chas hobbled to Ritzy who was shocked to see him,

'Fucking 'ell, Chas, you're barkin' mad?' Chas smiled, and Ritzy was thrown off kilter. She had never seen this lad smile before and, it was not nice. Chas's lips curled in a contemptuous manner. She was unnerved. It was demonic and immediately she felt a shiver run down her spine. 'What?' Chas continued his manic grin. 'What d'you want Chas, you know everyone's looking for you, and in that I include your own family.' Chas still said nothing, just moved to pull aside an old raggedy jacket that hung off him like a horse collar, to reveal to the prostitute a shoulder holster and gun. Ritzy drew in a deep breath, 'Jesus Chas, you're right off your rocker.' She thought for a bit. 'Bloody Nora, wasn't you what done for Limp Eric was it?'

Chas slowly shook his head and in a low grumbling tone, no longer his high-pitched whine. 'That was the O'Neills.'

'Well then, you 'ad better keep out of the way of the Saints, cause they're gunning for anyone associated with the fucking O'Neills...' she paused as Chas lifted something from the inside pocket of his jacket, and this brought even more shock and awe to the tart with a heart. 'Shit a brick Chas, the Saint crumpet?' Chas nodded, and handed the crumpet to Ritzy who immediately dropped it on the floor as if it were red hot. In a way, it was calescent property indeed, even if it had been burned forty odd years ago. It radiated a symbolic *heat*.

Chas looked down at the incendiary crumpet. Nodded for Ritzy to pick it up, which she did, looking all around to ensure she was not seen, which was silly because she had a crowd of floozies surrounding her. All enjoying the tableau, and every one of whom were relieved they were not participants in the crumpet scene being played out before their eyes.

'I want you to take the crumpet back to the Saints, now. They're all gathered with some of my family, at Dad's. When you go in, I want you to make a big fuss, shout out you have the crumpet, draw everyone's attention, got it?' Ritzy agreed, and Chas went to his trouser pocket and pulled out a pound note and waved it in front of Ritzy. Nearly a week's takings on her back or against the dockyard wall, and the seriously impressed prozzies ooohed and aaahed in stunned amazement at the flash of cash waved in front of their smudged and filthy faces.

'Where'd you get that sort of dosh?' Ritzy asked, as she grabbed at the filthy lucre and began a tug of war with Chas.

'Never you mind,' and he released the pound, which Ritzy immediately stuffed into her hollowed out bra containing her emaciated sparrow tits and a wad of tissue padding. Chas continued, 'There is another one if you do what I want exactly right and, if you don't,' he patted the concealed handgun, and Ritzy, as well as the other observers, got the message, double impressed with this transformation in Chas Larkin. The boy not only looked like he had grown into a young man, but he had *chutzpah*, and they watched him bend down and pick up the small attaché case that Ritzy recognised as his mum's.

'You on yer toes then, Chas? Can't say as I blame yer,

especially if you've come into some sausage and mash, and I would get as far away as possible if I were you.'

'Ritzy.' Chas fixed the dockyard doxy with a frigid stare. She was again chilled. 'Just go and do as I ask. Get out sharpish and come back to the dock gates and I will meet you beside the phone box,' and he pointed to the red, glazed, telephone box. Message received, and he watched his mum's friend wobble off on her high heels in the direction of Dad's.

Chas followed at a discreet distance and disappeared into the back yard of the pub as Ritzy entered the public bar. Chas bided his time. Eventually he tried the back door. It was unlocked as it usually was, and when he heard the uproar from the bar, he stepped into the back store, placed the case beside the gas main and meter, all as instructed by Roisin. He departed, and if anyone cared to observe, Chas walked a lot easier. He did not drag his foot so much, in fact, he felt like he was walking on air. So, this is chutzpah? Roisin had explained it to him. He had gained in confidence, not quite untouchable, but he felt bold, able to take on whatever the world threw at him and, after today, it would likely be a lot more than he was accustomed to.

Casey knocked on the commander's door and walked in saying, "Come".

The commander flicked his eyes at Wade and then to the ceiling, as if to say *God save us from Irish wide boys.*

Casey walked to the commander's desk and made an expressive show of slapping down the crime scene photo. 'Anything grab your attention here?'

The commander looked at the photo as if it was radioactive. 'Is that Limp Eric? Or more to the point is that Limp Eric's brains on the wall, not that he had much of them.'

Wade cut in, 'Well, he has even less now, and they're not working very well.'

Casey and the commander chuckled.

'I suppose we're looking at the message on the wall?'

'Bingo, commander.'

'Wade, please, some respect for my rank please.'

'Sorry, sir.'

The commander smiled, 'You're okay, but in front of the troops, for my sake if not your own, please'

'We finished with the feckin' love-in have we, this ting...' and Casey pointed to the photo, '... with the O'Neills, is ramping up. So, what does it mean for us around here?'

Wade looked at Casey conspiratorially, *the O'Neills did not exist, right?* Paddy returned her look with a stony face, revealing nothing, except it did make Wade think she was a tad out of her depth, but she was determined to hang on. She continued to tread water.

The commander applied his serious face. 'Well, Paddy, what do you think is happening?'

'Haven't a fucking clue...' and the commander, Wade, and Casey looked at each other, it was inappropriate to laugh, but it was funny, and then Casey applied his serious face, *'The O'Neills say hi* sir, it's a coded message.'

'Oh, shut up,' the commander responded, flapping a hand at Casey.

The commander still had to learn about Casey's face changes, not just the wind changing, but time for everyone to change with him. So, Wade explained, 'This is serious sir. A special telephone line has been set up that must be manned at all times by only people we can trust. We will also need to keep an eye on Old George as the Nick telephone exchange is just behind his desk and that line is going straight into there as a direct extension from Scotland Yard,' she looked at Casey and he nodded. 'Actually, it is MI5, if you get my drift?' and she fluttered her hand.

The commander nodded he did, his face now suitably serious. Casey continued, 'Only the IRA know this telephone number and so any call on that line, and with the correct code, is direct from them. We will never get a chance to trace, because whatever message we receive will be short, sweet, and deadly. It will tell us where they are planning a bomb and how long we have to get the area cleared and, it will not be long, so we can't afford to feck about.'

'Jeez, Old George?'

Wade answered, 'Old George is a bit moody,' and she shuffled her shoulders and raised her eyebrows, to indicate he was not trustworthy.

'What Wade is saying, is, we cannot take any chances with leaks, but we also cannot just remove the desk sergeant without raising suspicion. So, we need to keep a close eye. The line is established in the switchboard room, separate from the other phones, and soon we will have a *special officer* manning the phone all the time, but they will actually be MI5,' and Casey waited for the penny to drop, that he had spies in his *nick*. It hadn't dropped, 'I need you to understand, we cannot tolerate any interference. So, watch Old George and anyone else carefully, understood?'

The commander nodded, 'Bleedin' 'ell,' the penny dropped, 'I need a cuppa Rosie,' and he looked to Casey and Wade who shook their heads. They did not need tea, maybe something stronger, and all of that was interrupted as the commander took a phone call and immediately passed the phone to Casey like a hot potato.

Casey listened, handed back the phone with instructions for the commander. 'Our first coded call. We have five minutes to clear Dad's pub, they're about to blow it up.'

'The commander leapt up and immediately ran around the room like a headless chicken and called out to his PA. Phyllis stepped in and she immediately told him to shut up, sit down, dispatch patrol cars and to get instructions out to evacuate the pub. 'The clock is ticking, ' she emphasised as she patted his bottom.

Wade looked at Casey, then to the sassy PA, back to Casey, her mouth wide open as another penny dropped into her slot. 'Yes, Phyllis is one of us?' Casey whispered, answering her inquiring look.

`One of us? I know I'm one of them, but am I now one of you?' Wade asked, butterflies unsettling her stomach, anxious, not knowing what reply she wanted to hear.

Casey smiled. 'Of course you're one of us.'

Wade grinned like a Cheshire cat, she had her answer, and was surprisingly relieved. 'Right, suppose we'd better get to Dad's then.'

22

THE PARTY WAS IN FULL SWING, THE PIANIST THUMPING OUT honky-tonk tuneless, but well-known songs, and the ribald, equally disharmonic singing rocked the rafters. The real crumpet had been returned and ceremonially placed in its rightful place, on the back bar, under the glass dome of the display case. The decibel levels of the partying increased proportionately as the beer flowed freely, and it was some time before anyone heard the phone ringing. Eventually young Bessie, irritated at the incessant ringing, answered. She listened, then rolled out a peeling laugh which was lost in the atmosphere of genuine rejoicing and those phony, fractured whoops, from people who knew they would rue this day, the day the real crumpet had been returned. Ritzy took the ten bob note from Madge, excused herself, but before she could dodge away, she was collared by three Saint

Boys. They had been instructed to escort her back to Chas Larkin and do him in, and that would round off a brilliant day for the Saints. They could then focus on the O'Neills.

'Fuck off you bleedin' loony, who is this anyway?' young Bessie shouted down the phone. The police repeated the message, which was again lost in the rowdiness. Bessie said to hang on, and she rang the last orders bell until she got silence. 'Shut the fuck up the lot of yer, I've got the Old bill on the dog,' and she waved the phone so everyone knew to shut up. She returned to the phone call and heard the message loud and clear, she looked to the melee of confused family and patronising patrons, presenting her own equally bemused look. She passed the phone to Madge.

'Allo, Madge Saint 'ere, who is this?' She listened and then questioned, 'you're 'aving a bleedin' larf ain't yer?' and listened some more as she heard the officer reiterate that this was not a hoax. Madge shouted out to the bar, 'Some jeffing woodentop is saying we got a bomb about to go off in 'ere and we should get out,' and she hung up just after telling the filf he could stuff his bomb where the sun don't shine, by which she meant it may have an efficacious benefit for his constipation, and that well received rejoinder fell on stony ground as the approaching police bells broke into the now deathly silence.

A customer and young Bessie stepped outside to take a look, confusion as the squad cars pulled up some distance from the pub. Young Bessie went to speak to them. The customer shouted back to the patrons in the bar, 'The filf are saying for us to get out, they're clearing the...' He never got the chance to finish, the bomb went off and he was blown clean across the street accompanied by shattered windows, the glass fragments spraying the walls of the houses opposite like they were being machine gunned. Dad's was on fire. It was a small bomb, designed to ignite the incoming gas main. The pub was now an inferno as those who could, made their way outside, but many more lay dead or unconscious as the Fire Brigade arrived, shut the gas off in the street and began dousing the flames. It wasn't so long ago this was being done on a regular basis in the blitz, and there were still some firemen who could recall the experience and knew exactly what to do.

Ritzy was being scurfed along, held by her collar, occasionally falling and scraping her knees. 'Oi, me bleedin' stockings,' but it had no effect on the thugs who continued tugging. Upon turning a corner, they saw the phone box where Chas Larkin was supposed to be waiting, but he wasn't. The thugs sought a reaction from Ritzy as they neared the box. 'Don't look at me, this is where he said he would be,' and one of the bruisers back handed the tart. She went flying and was left sprawled across the pavement, where, as the thugs began to lift her for another right hander, Ritzy could see a cool cucumber, red-headed girl, leaning against the phone box she had recently made a call from. She was expecting them. Chas had known Ritzy would not be able to resist questioning.

The goons dropped the tart to the ground and as Ritzy looked up, ready to make her getaway, there was an almighty explosion. It shocked everyone, except for Roisin, who walked casually to the stunned Saint boys and in a strong Irish accent, 'You heard of the O'Neills?' she asked.

They nodded they had, seemingly distracted by the pyre that was coming from around the Dad's pub area. 'Yeah, what of it?' repeated by one of them as the local tarts came running to the aid of a scrabbling Ritzy.

'Oh, just they said to say hi,' and Roisin revealed the gun she held in a handbag and expertly shot all three of them in the forehead and, as she toe poked the bodies to make sure they were dead, she pulled a pound note from the same bag and gave it to a nearby hysterical Ritzy. 'Now, Ritzy love, you are paid,' a strong Irish accent, 'and the O'Neills tank you, so.'

'What shall I tell the police?' Ritzy asked and she looked at the bodies of the men, pools of blood under their head, draining to the kerbside, forming a sluggish river to the road-side gulley.

'Say you saw a red-haired girl who said she was Roisin Dubh, got that? Pronounce it Rosheen Dove?'

Ritzy said okay to thin air. Roisin had disappeared.

'Jesus, why did they not get out?' Wade asked, as she, the commander, and Casey stood behind the police barriers, watching the firemen do their job.

'They thought it was someone 'aving a tin barf,' Young Bessie said from behind the police car.

The commander mumbled, 'They thought it was a joke?' mentioning, whilst in his state of incredulity, 'the Fire Brigade expect at least twenty bodies, more injured and burned, some managed to get out and have been ushered away to the end of the street.' They looked and there was a small gathering, not many had made it, but Wade recognised Young Bessie being held back by a constable. The commander shook his head in disbelief, 'Seems they were celebrating the return of the crumpet, which, I also presume is now burnt to a crisp and gone forever. Praise the Lord. As are a good many Saints, and that's another blessing.' He looked to Wade who was with Young Bessie, 'Someone said there were Larkins in there as well, so a bonus for us crime fighters,' and he grimaced when he wanted to laugh, but not in front of a powerful Saint lady.

'There's a St Crumpet?' Casey asked. 'I'm a Catholic and thought I knew all the Saints, but never heard of that one,' and the commander and Wade looked at the dipstick Irishman, the commander suggesting they return to Arbour Square.

Wade took a last look at the scene, the shell of Dad's still on fire but coming under control. Some of the Saints and Larkins were returning for a closer look, the semi-detached Arries, hardly touched. Curious, she thought.

Casey saw Wade ruminating, 'You thinking Arries is hardly damaged?'

'Bit of expert bomb planting that, and if I had to guess, I would say it was a small device beside the gas main, so a blast, but mainly a devastating and well positioned fire. If they had evacuated as they should have, we would not be looking at such a death toll.' She thought on, and then voiced her gestating thought process, 'Maybe the bomber knew it would be treated as a hoax and this was the result they sought?' She speculated some more, 'Cleared the gangster way, but for what?' Wade hemmed, Casey said she had the right of it, and she bowed to his *superior* knowledge. They had not had to experience such events in London, but in Ireland, in the north especially, it presumably was not so rare an event. 'The O'Neills?' she suggested, in jest rather than a serious proposition, but she noticed Casey took the hypothesis seriously. 'Blimey, what the bleedin' hell is 'appening? Still vacillating, and with Casey in tow, she trudged toward the waiting patrol car, halting as they were approached by a constable propping up and comforting a distraught woman, who, judging by her attire and smeared painted appearance, had to be a dockyard floozy. As they got closer, Wade recognised the woman from the Larkin funeral. The constable spoke to Wade and Casey, the commander had gone off to do some commanding, as Wade had recommended.

'This is Ritzy,' the constable said and, in a very nice way, explained she was a local woman, not mentioning her trade at all. He didn't need to, and Ritzy looked up, warmly appreciating the kindly gesture.

Wade shared the constable's respect. 'Hello Ritzy,' and Wade commented on the state of the woman, 'you look a right two and eight, were you in the pub?'

'No, but I need a bleedin' drink.'

Wade and Casey subliminally agreed, and Wade steered them away from the scene to another nearby pub, past Arries where some of the Larkin men were milling around. Odd, Casey whispered, but Ritzy answered the Irishman's perplexed look. 'The Larkins and Saints rub along. They went to school together and like each other, this is not so strange if you know the locals, and, some Larkins may have perished inside as well.'

They set off again, the constable with his arm still around the sobbing Ritzy, who continually remonstrated that he needed to do something about the three bodies at the dockyard gate. 'I know Ritzy sweet'art, we have some people there. You 'ave your drink and tell these officers all about it okay.' Ritzy settled as the constable made to leave, then he dragged the prostitute to the floor as a shot rang out over the din of the firefighters. A Larkin thug dropped, another shot, and another Larkin, another, and then it dawned on people to run for cover, but not before three more Larkin men had been gunned down by the sniper.

From behind a patrol car, where the constable had pulled Ritzy, Casey and Wade surveyed the area, now completely clear of spectators. The firemen had departed the scene, no longer able to rescue anyone still trapped in the inferno. Was this the intention? The cries from inside Dad's soon silenced as the fire returned to its original fervour, to go about its unholy business.

Wade grabbed a loud hailer from a nearby officer and called out for everyone to stay under cover, a rather unnecessary command she later thought, but it did get silence. There was just the sound of the ferocious fire, no longer being quenched, and then a shrill response from inside one of the nearby houses, "The O'Neills say hi", in a thick Irish accent.

After about five minutes of stagnation, no further shots, the fire brigade resumed their business, and a patrol of police officers ran at the house, broke down the door, and in a circumspect manner searched the premises. All they found were some discharged shell cases in an upstairs bedroom, and a petrified family locked in the coal cellar. They reported that a red-haired Irish girl had shut them in at gun point, she had a pistol and a rifle slung over her shoulder and the girl had said to tell the police, "The O'Neills say hi".

This intelligence was relayed back to Casey and Wade. 'The Black Rose?' Wade asked.

Casey nodded, gesturing with his head to Ritzy, and Wade steered the wobbling tart into the pub. 'You could probably do with a brandy, yeah?' Casey asked unnecessarily.

'Make that a bleedin' treble darlin' I've 'ad a right scare I can tell yer.'

Chas walked away with Roisin, both pleased with themselves. 'You're walking a lot better there, so you are, Chas,' Roisin observed, as she stuck out a hand and hailed a passing black cab. The cabbie was a little circumspect as he took in the look of raggedy Chas but responded positively to the proffered ten bob note and instruction to an address in the West End of London, Saville Row.

CHAS FINDS HIS CHUTZPAH

23

AFTER THE THIRD DRINK, CASEY PULLED THE BALLOON GLASS from Ritzy. It was time she told them everything, and she did, remarkably concisely considering how shaken up she was and the alcohol she had imbibed. Casey gave her a pound note and sent her on her way, her internal equilibrium returning, if she was not so steady on her feet.

Casey and Wade had refrained from drinking, steadfastly firing questions, and now, back at Arbour Square, they evaluated the responses they had received from the one person, other than Nadia, who had a close relationship with Chas Larkin and, one thing they agreed upon, they needed another trip under the Thames and a briefing with the major.

Young Bessie, Nan, and Maude Larkin, survived, but Madge and Mum Bessie had perished, along with the remaining brothers and many foot-soldiers. All that remained of the Saint inner circle, power base, was Young Bessie and Bernie, *I only asked*, and some minor players. The Saints had been all but annihilated. The Larkins had lost six key soldiers outside the pub, and inside, all the brothers. Nan Larkin counselled comfort to what remained of her own family, as well as condolences to Young Bessie and Bernie, as they all gathered in the snug bar of Arrie's. The scent of the charred remains of Dad's was all pervading, reminding them of the serious position they now found themselves in.

'Clearly we have underestimated the strength and abilities of these O'Neills,' Nan Larkin said, opening up this hastily arranged extraordinary meeting of the two clans. 'Bessie...' the young woman looked up, '... you will no doubt take charge of your family...' and she waved her hands to suggest, what is left of them, '... and to balance things I am going to handover the reigns to my granddaughter, Maude. I believe that you two will make a formidable team. I have always thought this, and now... well, it is time.'

Maude, presenting the image of a demure, butter wouldn't melt, gangster moll, looked up from her toying with a beer mat, seemingly not so shocked to hear her name put forward as head of the Larkin family. Her gaze remained fixed on Nan, who continued. 'Maude darlin', time to come out from under your rock. You are the brightest of our bunch and I want you to work with Young Bessie,' not everyone saw the wink from Nan to Maude. What was all that about? Nan continued, comfortable with the raised eyebrows, things were panning out very well. 'It is important we reinforce control of our networks and let that message be conveyed on the streets. It is time for me to step back and let you youngsters have your way, so Bessie, Maude, what do you want to do?'

Young Bessie leaned her elbows on the table, rested her chin into her hands and looked up through her eyebrows. She already knew she would be in charge of the Saints at some time and was prepared. She had however, not anticipated Maude being given control of the Larkin family but, they were old schoolmates. The two young ladies acknowledged each other, they had a bond, and Bessie felt butterflies in her stomach as she anticipated working closely with Maude; something she had always wanted but could never say.

Bessie went to speak but was beaten to it by Maude. 'We should put out a missive that we want to meet with the O'Neills and, this is to have the reassurance of a truce and safe passage.'

Bessie went to concur, but was again interrupted, this time by Bernie. 'Can I make a suggestion?' he was still mourning the loss of Limp Eric, not so much his decimated family, he loved the man, but was energised that he had a place at the table. He had always resented being considered a dimwit.

Bessie loved this sole remaining brother of hers, if you discounted *Mickey the Cabbage*, as young Mickey Saint was now being called. She was sensitive to his plight about his sexuality, 'Please Bernie, *I only asked,* but it was you who actually thought the O'Neills did not exist, is that right?'

Bernie nodded, 'I think they may exist, but not here, in this part of London, but maybe somewhere else and they are pulling strings on our manor. This Roisin, she's an O'Neill, or so we think. Anyway, I sent messages back via granddad's old contacts and you recall Ritzy said the message "the O'Neills say hi" was given by this Roisin as she shot Bobbie, Jack, and Ted, well, she is reported to have said clearly her name was Rosheen Dove.'

'And your point, Bernie?' Bessie asked, patiently.

Our people in Cork came back and said this was *the Black Rose* and should be treated with extreme caution. Well, I think we know that now.'

'What are you suggesting, Bernie?' It was Maude, intrigued and impressed by Bernie whom she had considered an idiot up until now.

'The message should be gotten to Chas Larkin.'

Bessie snuffled a laugh, 'But Larkin's barkin', everyone knows that.'

'Radio fuckin' rental and an A-one certified loony and he's me jeffing cousin,' Maude said, in all seriousness.

Bernie was not to be moved. 'I hear you both but, whatever he may be, I think he is not mad, other than he may be hell bent on revenge. However, he is the only one who can get to this *Black Rose,* and through Chas we might find out what she wants? And then, we might be able to sue for peace with the O'Neills... do you not think?'

There was silence in the small, comfortable bar, snug as its name suggested, as it was uncomfortably crowded with the new pretenders, the acrid smell of a still smouldering Dad's serving to agitate the emotions, but Maude and Bessie knew, as did Bernie, it was a level-headed approach needed now. To those who could see the bigger picture, this was the opportunity for a new beginning. The old days of *violence first, think later*, had not served them well in these latter days and Maude said as much, which received full backing from Bessie.

'How do we get a message to Chas then Bernie?'

'Do I still have to be called Bernie?'

'Shut it Bernie, *I only asked...* okay.'

'Okay Maude,' and the big man, not so much brawn as a sensitive tub of lard, responded, accepting his name, content with his new position in the family. I think a message via Ritzy will no longer work, she has served her purpose for Chas, as I am sure she was used by him as a distraction with the return of the crumpet. So, he could place the bomb.' There was an intake of breath, not because of the mention of the bomb, but at the acuity being displayed by a man who hitherto had been considered, first and foremost, a man, and thus low down on the hen-pecking order, and then a dozy bastard to boot. But Bernie, *I only asked*, was showing himself to be anything but.

Bernie waited for the realisation of the fact that he might just know what he is talking about, to settle in, before he dropped his bombshell. 'There's a new police Inspector at Arbour Square, a DI Casey, and Irish...' he paused, '... been here about two weeks...' he waited again; did he need to say more?

'Fucking Ada,' Maude ejaculated, as things began to dawn on her. 'About the time we started to 'ave trouble with these O'Neills, the Saint crumpet goes missing and, we start hearing about this Rosheen bleedin' Dove tart.'

Bessie leapt at the logic. 'And Chas's mum gets her brains bashed in.' She thought on, 'Fuck me sideways, could that have been Chas?' She thought some more. 'Not bleedin' likely, bet it was this Black Rose. Didn't Mickey the Cabbage's mates say this Rosheen girl rescued Chas at school and carted him off? Apparently gave the headmistress a good hiding as well, and Chas winds up in hospital, probably after the beating he took from his mum. She always was a violent mare, especially if she'd had a drink.'

'So, this Rosheen steps in and does the biz on Betsy Larkin?'

Bernie nodded, 'Looks that way. So, we send a message to this bog dweller cop.'

'No.' Maude stepped in, 'We need to get to Chas's doctor, the wog girl, you know, whatever her name is, the foreigner?'

'She's Palestinian, and I do not like the term *wog,*' Bernie interjected.

'Ooh err, get you.' Bessie said, her respect growing all the time for her up until now dozy sod of a brother, as she took in Bernie's serious frown. 'Okay, Maude, Bernie, we contact his doctor?'

'Send a strong-arm team, no violence, just the suggestion of it.' Bernie further counselled, and the order was dispatched.

'You do know this is kids' stuff don't yer,' Wade said to the back of Casey.

Casey and Wade had just gone through the rigmarole of the Caretakers' room, the tunnel under the Thames, and were now pacing down the second-floor corridor to be met by the prim and business-like PA, who, with a casual wink and a smile for Casey, expeditiously shuffled them into the corner office, where the booted and suited, shiny faced major waited for them.

The major gestured for them to sit at the conference table while he paced up and down, stopped, spun on his military toes, and looked out of the window, marching time, smoking an imaginary cigarette; Wade presumed he was trying to give up, but still clung to the rituals. She was, however, intrigued by the presence of a tiny, timid, mouse like man, his face twitching as if he had no control over its movement, or maybe he had the scent of some cheese. The nose held circular wire framed, National Health type glasses, and he had a shock of red hair that also appeared to have a mind of its own, much like the face that peered over the top of the table like a moon man.

Eventually the major turned to face them and, with a flourishing extended hand, uncharacteristically flamboyant, he said, 'Casey, you know Hemmings,' and Casey nodded to the moon mouse. 'Er, Wade, this is Simon Hemmings, Irish desk. I've invited him to brief on the latest intelligence, which may go a long way to explaining why we have such *Irish* activity in London and, why this may be a wing of the *IRA,* and more importantly, why we may have imported the *Black Rose.*'

Hemmings shrunk back in his chair, not happy being the centre of attention and, even more nervous, if Wade was any judge, of the galloping major who had taken off at a pace around the room after he had challenged the diminutive man to get on with it. Hemmings gave the appearance of needing the toilet as soon as may be. 'Well man?' the major asserted, halting his route march, to reinforce the reprimand, before continuing his pacing.

Hemmings straightened on his chair, there was hardly any height difference, but it did give the intelligence officer some semblance of confidence, until he spoke, his voice so soft it was an unintelligible whisper.

The major barked, 'Speak up man,' and Hemmings reacted like a startled rabbit.

'Well, er,' he gazed back at the major, who looked like he might barrack the poor man again but thought better of it and, with this degree of unreliable assurance, Hemmings continued, marginally louder. 'The intelligence we have, er, has confirmed your theory Paddy. Someone in the City of London is funding not only the IRA, but also the UDA,' then for the benefit of Wade, he explained, 'the Ulster Defence Association, they are an extreme group that we have always thought to be unusually well funded, set up to oppose the Catholics in the North of Ireland. '

Casey interrupted, and Hemmings looked relieved at an opportunity to gather himself. 'I take it you can confirm this and, has this anything to do with arms and munitions being shipped by the Saints out of the East India Docks?'

'It has been going on a long time,' Hemming confirmed, 'but for some reason we have never done anything to halt the trade? Import and export, but more importantly, in some instances, sourcing from our own arms manufacturers.' He left that to simmer in the stultified silence, before confirming what this should suggest to everyone at the meeting. 'This suggests, er, self-interested Governmental interference, maybe?' and he wobbled a nervy, twitching hand.

'And you think it is about money to our industry, regardless of the damage that may be done in Ireland... and, here in Blighty?' Wade asked, and Hemmings nodded. 'And you also think this has something to do with wheels within wheels in the City of London and, government ministers in the pockets of some unscrupulous Funder?' Hemmings nodded again. Casey made to intervene, but Wade was not finished. She was beginning to seriously impress him, Hemmings, and the major. 'And you think things are starting to be taken seriously in England because...' and she counted off her fingers, '... One, we are expecting a campaign here on the mainland and we will be blown up by our own bombs, funded by our own people? And two, we may have to send troops into Northern Ireland* where the same will apply, except our boys will be stuck in the middle being riddled by our own bullets?' Hemmings nodded again. Wade had the right of it.

** Troops were first sent into Northern Ireland in 1969*

'Well, I am impressed Wade,' Casey commented, 'you follow Irish politics?'

'Only recently, I looked it up. You, all of a sudden appearing on my doorstep and, it wasn't because of the Saints and Larkins, well, not directly, but I do not like that our government have been allowing this to happen. Happy, or so it seems, for the Irish to kill each other, take the money and run, but now, volte-face, it's about to blow up in our faces, literally.'

'Ahemm, Wade, steady on now, Queen and country and all that.' The major asserted, standing to attention as if on parade in front of the royal family, realising, too late, that it was also an incendiary remark to Casey.

'Not my feckin' Queen, or my country it's not and, I am just as resentful as the IRA at what the British feel they can do or not do, playing with the lives of my people.' He paused, and took stock, 'And while we are at it, messing with my country. I am, however, no supporter of violence. I am sick of it.'

Wade gave Casey an old-fashioned look, *he was sick of the violence?* Needs must she supposed and thought Billy Big Head likely deserved what he got. 'So, Mr Hemmings, I presume you have intelligence about who is funding this deadly debacle?'

'Yes,' Hemmings replied, seeking comfort back in the chair, looking as though he wanted to slide under the table, but only after he had launched his final bombshell, 'and our people have not been able to track *The Black Rose* in Ireland. We have no firm evidence she is here, in London, apart that is, local hearsay.'

Casey stood, a prelude to leaving. 'Oh, she's here alright...' and he turned and left, Wade having to make her farewell gestures to the Major and Hemmings on the hoof.

24

Wendy prepared a lovely dinner, set the table with a candle. It was going to be a pleasant sojourn, two lovers, at least until she pressed Flora for some salient facts about her life and how this would affect her own. She was determined, and she lounged at the end of the table as she heard Wade turn the key and call out, she was home, 'Mmmm that smells divine darling,' said as she entered the living room and looked across to the stage set dinner table. 'Oh, I say, what's the occasion?' and Wade racked her brains to make sure it wasn't one of these anniversary dates of events that were so important to Wendy; she couldn't think of anything.

'Relax darling, it is no special occasion,' Wendy said, as she lifted herself from the chair and slinked across to greet her inamorata, her lady love, with a passionate kiss. 'There, I just want a special evening with you.'

Wade felt warmed and sensually aroused as she slid, slowly, inexorably, into the Venus fly trap.

Casey returned to the Section House, poured himself a tumbler of Jameson's, stared at himself in the long mirror on the back of the door and raised his glass in salute, ' *Tá rudaí ag dul go maith Paddy*' he said to himself in the Irish, swallowed the whisky and relished the burn. 'Things are going well for Paddy,' he repeated to himself in the looking glass.

Nadia was on duty so would not see Casey, and she was okay with that. She needed a bit of time to consider their relationship. Did they have a relationship? The more she thought about it the more she thought he was a lovely slippery eel and could not be sure that all he said was the truth, or the whole truth at least. Although he appeared to speak with absolute sincerity, she had no way of knowing if this was the famed blarney? All this she muttered to herself as she left casualty and wandered down the corridor. She noticed three men hanging around outside her office and thought nothing of it. 'Can I help you gentlemen?' she asked, as she unlocked the door, to be immediately bundled in and as she fell to the floor, she heard the door slam. Now she panicked. Now she wanted Padraig to walk in.

Chas checked into his room at the Ritz on Piccadilly, it had been reserved for him and, although he was way out of his comfort zone, you would never have known, as he allowed the Bell Boy to take his new case, containing his newly acquired clothes, and accoutred in a dapper way, he looked the part and, he was ready to play that part.

Young Bessie sat with Maude in the lounge of Maude's house and they made plans, a shared growth of the Saints and Larkins, teamed up. They had dismissed the heavies who had reported, following the intimidation of Chas Larkin's doctor and enjoyed a tipple of gin to toast a job well done. They were confident the message will get to Chas Larkin and onto the O'Neills. Yes, this was going well, Maude thought and now for the cementing of a future, to enact the plan her Nan and she had concocted and, core to that, if the Larkin family were to effectively accede to the East End throne, was the willing subservience of Bessie Saint.

Scotch 'Arry called at the Section House reception, wrote Casey's name on a piece of paper and the Desk Sergeant telephoned Casey's room. Ordinarily there were no phones in the rooms, but Casey had insisted, and he got one.

After a few rings Casey picked up, croaked a response to the annoyed sergeant and said he would be down to meet the incomprehensible drainpipe snitch. Following a brief stroll around Arbour Square, Casey learned that Chas was on the missing list, which Casey expected, but more worryingly, Nadia had had a visit by some goons. Scotch 'Arry had seen them, seen that Nadia was not hurt, but more worrying for Casey, she had not been in contact to tell him; she didn't trust him. Scotch 'Arry confirmed he had followed Nadia to see her safely ensconced into the home of Wade and Wendy Richards.

25

WENDY HAD HER FLORA IN A LOVELY PLACE, FED AND WELL-watered, the mood sublime, lights dimmed, candlelight, soft music and their chairs close together, holding hands. Looking into Wade's eyes, Wendy commenced her questioning, 'Darling?'

'Mmmm?'

'What you are doing at work, can you talk about it?'

Flora was stirred, but only a little, 'Normal stuff, you know?'

'What's normal about bombs, people being gunned down?'

Flora, now more alert, 'Nothing that should bother us.'

'No?'

'Not really...' Flora dragged this out, she never could lie to Wendy.

'So, maybe just a little?

'Maybe...' wide awake now.

'You know I love you, don't you?'

Shit, here it comes Wade thought, her nerves jangling. 'And I love you too, sweet'art.'

Wendy smiled, she loved it when Flora said she loved her and felt bad, but she needed peace of mind. 'Can you tell me...'

The doorbell rang.

Saved by the bell, Wade thought, standing, dragging a caress across Wendy's shoulders. 'I'll see who that is?' Looking at her watch, 'It's after eleven, this is not right.'

'Don't go darling, please, leave it, whoever it is will go away, come back.'

The bell rang again, and Wade stepped to the hall door, looked back, gave Wendy a *don't worry* look, disappeared and Wendy could hear the not so delicate clop of her sweetheart's feet on the stairs; no ballet dancer her Flora but, she did love her.

There was silence, Wendy straining her ears, and after a while she walked nervously to the stair landing. She could just hear muffled sounds, crying she thought, but could not see. She crept down to the half landing and, cranking her head around the dog leg flight, she saw Flora cuddling another woman but could not see who. Her hackles rose, 'Flora?'

Both hugging women looked up, Wade erect and alert

and Wendy could see a slumped Nadia, clinging to her Flora. Nadia released that grip as she saw Wendy descending the stairs to the compact hallway, her arms open to receive the weeping psychiatrist. Thank fuck for that, Wade thought, not sure she would have been able to comfort the distraught doctor. Wendy had a way for these situations, and she should know, it was how they had met. She, distressed and needing comfort and that consoling physicality blossomed into love. Wade remembered all of this, the feelings she felt when Wendy first put her empathetic arms around her, as she watched from the entrance lobby, Wendy holding Nadia, whispering words of reassurance, and gently steering the woman, the floodgates of tears well and truly opened, ascending the stairs, around the landing and out of sight, still audible as they disappeared up the return flight, the landing and into the flat.

Wade kicked the door shut, probably a bit harder than was necessary, had a flutter of guilt about disturbing the neighbours. Then said out loud, 'Ah fuck it,' and trudged the stairs, a sense of trepidation. This did not bode well for her anticipated night of intense lovemaking, after she had assuaged whatever was bothering Wendy. What was she going to ask anyway, Wade thought, with a flush of relief? Maybe this had been a close shave?

Young Bessie Saint and Maude Larkin were still squirreled in the lounge of Maude's house. They had plans to make and didn't need the tosspot family interfering. Those not dead or injured, were left to get sozzled in the bar of Arries, dealing with all that had happened in the past few weeks by seeking temporary oblivion. Bessie and Maude however, had no time for lassitude, they had two families to save and a reputation to re-establish, and Maude, with her Nan behind her, knew exactly how to do it. She just needed to get Bessie on board. Bessie was the brains, though Maude and Nan considered she lacked the aggression, but Maude had plenty enough for both of them.

'That was a lovely dinner, Maude, and you have a beautiful home,' Bessie said, rising from the armchair and heading to collect her raincoat for the short step back to her own house. It had been a fine misty drizzle all evening which beneficially dampened the smouldering Dad's shell of a pub, now a physical manifestation of the smouldering mood of the families. Maude had a sizable end of terrace house that had dodged the bombs and been fixed up by the family, Nan Larkin mysteriously insisting Maude be well accommodated, and the family now knew why. She was to lead the Larkins, nobody aware this was also to include the Saints.

'Bit big for me on my own,' Maude replied, luxuriating in helping Bessie into her coat. 'I need someone to help me wiv it, to do the looking after... you know?' And she paused as Bessie turned an enquiring look upon her old school friend.

'To look after me... proper like, steer me as well, you know? I can be a bit of an 'andful, but you know that, eh?'

Bessie was perplexed at Maude's expressed domestic desires, but it felt nice as she stretched out her arms to have her coat helped on for her. 'Thanks luv,' and Bessie turned and leaned into Maude and pecked her on the cheek; she lingered. 'We make a good team you and me.'

'We do that Bess, we've always got on, since school,' and she leaned back into a laugh, 'what a laugh we had there, eh?'

Bessie joined in the comfortable banter as she reached for the door latch, 'We did...' opened the door a little, stopped, and turned back, '... Maude?' She had a serious frown.

Maude stepped closer, 'What?

Rather breathily Bessie responded, stepping closer into Maude's personal space, as if to impart a secret. 'We have to join the families,' and she left that statement to hang in the electrifying atmosphere. Maude kicked the door shut, it made Bessie jump, the noise, and the aggression from Maude. 'Shit, that made me jump.'

Maude laughed, and hugged Bessie. 'Sorry sweet'art,' and she placed her hands on both of Bessie's shoulders, tilted her back and faced her guest, 'We need to join the families, eh? And how do you suppose we should do that?'

'A marriage?'

'A marriage, who?' Maude offered a face that she hoped

showed she was puzzled, even though the thought had crossed her mind also.

'We need to grow the families, also, together.'

Maude was getting frustrated. 'Bess sweet'art, spit it out. You've obviously fort about it.'

'Haven't you?' Bessie looked intently at Maude.

Maude offered a pretence of stirring her memory banks, a frown that morphed into a warm smile, of course she had thought about it, and so had Nan. 'School?' She offered a tentative answer.

Bess nodded, 'You remember?'

'I remember. We ran the school together, best time I've ever 'ad,' and she stepped back and sat on the stairs.

Bessie joined her, close to Maude like they used to do on the school steps. 'Remember when we duffed up that teacher? What was her name, a student on work experience?'

'Miss Chalmers,' Maude replied, instantly recalling the young lady they had tormented. 'You thinking of the stock cupboard?'

Bess nodded, and the demonic grin on the two gangster ladies broadened. 'Fuck me gently, I still get off on that.'

'You do?'

'Yeah, well you, 'ave to fink of sumfink while yer 'aving a, you know what, don't yer?' 'A, J Arfer Rank.'

Both young ladies shared thoughts of the time they had beaten up this nervy student teacher, thrown into the lion's den, for work experience. They had dragged her to the stock room, stripped her naked and made her perform on them, one at a time, while the other abused the poor young woman intimately.

'Blimey, I didn't 'arf fancy Chalmers. Whatever happened to 'er?' Maude enquired.

'She had to disappear didn't she. I told Madge and she had a couple of the boys do it.'

'Shame.'

'Yeah, but to be 'onest, what we did was not 'er cuppa tea, know what I mean,' Bess asserted, reasonably vindicating their actions.

'Yeah, shame, would have liked to have kept 'er,' Maude said, into the ether, as if this was a new casual thought. 'So, Madge helped?'

'Yeah,' Bessie replied, nonchalantly, still dreaming of the stock room.

'You told Madge about me?'

'Yeah, of course, why d'you fink you and I were chosen to run the families?'

'Jesus fucking wept.' Maude was carrying off the pretence magnificently, and she was sure Nan would be pleased with her consummate acting skills, though not everything was acted, she did truly relish the time in the stockroom.

'Did he, darlin', can't answer for Jesus, but I did enjoy a lovely butcher's hook up yer skirt when you were sitting opposite me tonight. It was all I could do to think about the families and those fucking O'Neills, you did that deliberately, didn't you?' Bessie enquired, already knowing the answer.

'What, open my legs, or wear stockings and little knickers for you?'

'Did you?'

'I did,' and Maude leaned into Young Bessie, the new Saint thug, lady leader, the brains, and with a whisper of hot breath on her neck, 'we should get married,' and she grabbed Bess's hair and roughly turned her head to face her. 'I want you, for my missus.'

Still with her head in a vice like grip, and strangely enjoying the dominance of her childhood friend, 'You love me?' Bessie panted.

'I do, always have, and you love me.' It was not a question. Maude squeezed and Bessie squealed, but did nothing to stop her friend who leaned in and planted a forceful burning kiss. 'You're mine... to all intents, my missus, and that is how you will behave.'

'I am? I will?'

'You are, and you'll do as you're told, right?' It was all as Nan Larkin had predicted. Maude would bring the families together and lead them, young Bessie her subservient Queen, offering wise counsel. A necessity as Nan knew Maude could be a bit headstrong and would need steadying. 'You agree, you are mine, Bess?'

'Yes.' Bess was not sure what had happened, but she was deliriously happy. She had always imagined herself in the stockroom with Maude doing to her what they had done to Miss Chalmers. 'I love you Maude.'

'I know.'

'You do?'

'Yes, and you will be an obedient wife?'

Bess thought for a bit, this was getting even better, 'And if I don't?'

'I have a cane upstairs, the one we used in the stockroom.'

Bess mewed, 'You took it, for me?' Her body language said she had already submitted, and she leaned into her lifelong love, encircled Maude's waist, and hugged her. 'I will be your obedient wife.'

Bessie did not see the malevolent grin on Maude's face, she was in heaven and responded when Maude suggested in a way that brooked no argument, she should go upstairs, and Bess obeyed. The families were now enjoined, but more significantly, the Larkins, always the poor cousins of the two gangs, were in the ascendancy, albeit the Saints brains would steer the new battleship.

26

THE O'RIERDONS WERE A STRONG IRISH FAMILY THAT SINCE leaving Cork, in Southernmost Ireland, many generations ago, had established themselves in Kilburn, north-west London. Exiles they may have been, but they maintained the family traditions along with their Cork ties, and their Irish star had risen since that auspicious day Dah O'Rierdon had brought home the cockney waif run away from the East End, Chas Larkin.

Aoife O'Rierdon, Ma, was as good as her Gaelic name translation, Eve, and she nurtured Chas for those few days, tolerating his guttural pronunciation of her name as Weef-fah, before tempting him to take a bite of the forbidden apple of revenge. She had shown him a better way of life. Better for them and their cause, though also, seen in a prudential light, and Chas did, not bad for him also. Chas saw a clear path to fulfilling his one dream, violent retribution, on the Saints, and even his own family.

At the lap of Aoife, he had listened intently to the stories from the auld land, the myths, the legends, and the pain of the people under the long and brutal rule of the British. But what attracted Chas, what Chas identified with most, was the Irish never gave up, and eventually they prevailed, albeit six northern counties were annexed, which he took to mean, had been kept by the British as part of the United Kingdom. He recalled Paddy telling him of this when he had visited him in the hospital, and he could understand why this would rankle with the Irish, not least, as he was told, the Catholic minority in the north were treated so poorly. And all in the name of religion. Well, religion and a desire for a united and free Ireland and that didn't sit well with the predominant Protestant, loyalist, people of the North.

Chas sat at the O'Rierdon dinner table like a normal family would, at least like he imagined a normal family would, and he had always dreamed of. It was during the O'Rierdon family mealtimes that he listened to more Tales of the Emerald Isle, and in particular he latched onto the story of *The Black Rose.* Aoife explained that Roisin Dubh, translated as Black Rose, and she was a mythical defender of the oppressed, an Irish Valkyrie, who walks among the people unobserved, seeking justice, and wreaking revenge. Fixated, Chas devoured all knowledge of the Black Rose and learned that always in every generation there is *A Black Rose*, and slowly, the myth was translated into the here and now. She was here, in London, to lift the darkness of Chas Larkin? He hoped this would be true, he had always wanted a defender, and he prayed *The Black Rose* would come for him. It was his fate.

Aoife did not disabuse Chas of his conviction, it gave the lad some comfort, she could see, and it also gave them an ally in the East End and one so knowledgeable in the ways of obscuration and, hallelujah, access to the Saint's munitions warehouse, and so the O'Rierdons told Chas Larkin they had summoned *The Black Rose,* and she would visit him.

And now, nurtured by the O'Rierdon family and Roisin, Chas had grown. Funds were sought and provided. The boy had done well. However, the campaign needed stepping up, and a born-again Chas was transformed; he was ready.

Wendy drifted into the lounge, sat Nadia down at the table, poured a glass of water and passed it to the distraught doctor. Wade watched all of this from the living room door, trying not to be irritated, which became more difficult after Wendy cast her a wizening look.

'What?' Wade responded, pushing out her neck in a provocative manner as she stepped into the room, and she herself became provoked. Nadia had taken her seat, the one squashed next to Wendy.

'Flora, be a dear and fetch us some coffee please,' and Wendy returned her focus to the sniffling Nadia. 'Coffee?' She repeated as Wade had not moved, and then to Nadia, 'coffee?'

'Yes, please,' Nadia's staccato reply as the woman dry sobbed, her breath catching.

'Now, while Flora gets the coffee, why don't you tell me what this is all about?'

Nadia looked up, could see how irritated Wade was, 'I'm sorry, Flora, but I think you should hear this... as... as a police officer.'

Wade required no second request, dragging a chair opposite Nadia, who was sat in *her seat*, next to *her Wendy*, and offered a glance to *her* beautiful lover that said *Ner,* which received a fleeting confused response from Wendy. Wade considered another *Ner* when Nadia focused on her and not the psychiatrist, and then she became lost in the story, no longer troubled with her ladylove, as Nadia gabbled it out, halting every now and then when she slipped into her own language as the emotion took hold. Wade was momentarily amused at Nadia's use of the occasional cockney phrase.

Nadia conveyed the essentials: she had been roughed up, by, she assumed, some Saint heavies, demanding she reveal the whereabouts of Chas Larkin. Wendy leaned into the slowly calming doctor, to put a settling arm across her shoulders. She went to offer some additional comforting words, but was interrupted by Detective Sergeant Wade, now bolt upright in her chair, a fully functioning law officer. 'And?' Wade asked, probably harsher than she should, but her experience told her that when a victim was in this state, often an officious approach yielded speedier results, much like a slap halted hysteria and, Nadia had not been far off being hysterical. This did work, Wendy looking on impressed, as Nadia responded to expert interrogation.

'And?' Nadia enquired, confused.

'Yes, what else?'

'Well, I tried to get Padraig, but he wasn't at the Station.'

'And?'

'And what?' This time Wendy stepped in, concerned about the emotional state of Nadia, and now demonstrably irritated at the strength of Flora's questioning.

'Wendy, please,' and Wade turned back to Nadia, 'and?'

'I don't understand?' Nadia looking like a lost soul.

'Yes, you do. You have an opinion on what happened, what is it?' Wade probed.

'Oh... well, I er... I think they went easy on me.' Nadia's wide brown eyes began to brim once again, and Wade knew she was about to get some more informative detail, but the doorbell sounded, again.

'Oh, fuck it, it's like bleedin Piccadilly Circus in 'ere tonight and Wade stood, knowing it would be her role to answer the door, just this once resenting it.

'Flora, please, just answer the door.' Wendy said forcefully to her fulminating partner.

'See?' Wade murmured to herself, 'It's me, I have to answer the bleedin' door,' as she strode across the room, halted to converse with herself, and the doorbell rang again, conveying the message that whomever this was at the door at this ungodly hour, had little patience.

'Stop muttering and answer the door, please... darling,' and Wendy gave Flora a Brahma of a smile, and all of the vehemence Flora felt, melted away, and only returned halfway down the stairs when she realised how this woman she loved could play her, and by the time she wrenched open the door, she was, once again, in a fully-fledged foul mood. 'Yes?' she almost shouted at Casey, as he stood on the front step, leaning into her face. She was about to give him both barrels, but it is rare she ever saw a man crying.

'Nadia?' was all he managed to say.

Wade stepped aside and with a flourishing butlery bow, she waved him in, and as her arm swept up from the floor, she gestured upstairs with her head. Casey stepped over the threshold, thanked her kindly, and tore up the stairs, two at a time, leaving Wade, once again that evening, to close the door, and join the *party* after it had already started.

Young Bessie and Maude had consummated their new relationship, the ground rules having been established by Maude, and enthusiastically accepted by Bess; Maude had decided she would call her Bess, and Bess liked it, loved it, she had always loved Maude, had fantasised about her since their shared school days, in particular the stock room. However, the adversarial stances of their respective families had prevented any positive moves, but it seemed that the Saint and Larkin grandmothers had seen something that would save both families in their hour of great need. They had lost a lot of personnel, the *Inner Circle*, and serious ground to the O'Neills over the past weeks, so a new start was needed, otherwise they would lose the hearts and minds, but more importantly, the fear, of their followers. The Saints had lost their crumpet in the Dad's inferno, giving the Larkins an opportunity that made grand-maternal sense.

'We will run the families now, you and me, Bess, my love,' Maude said as the two women lay together in their *marital* bed, Bess enjoying the sensation of Maude smoothing her bottom, tantalisingly sore.

'We will?'

'We will. You as my wife in name, beside me, we will enjoin the families and take back our conjoined manor from the O'Neills, and we will start tomorrow with a family meeting at Arries. We will rebuild Dad's but as an extension to Arries, as a further sign of unity brought together by our union. We will call the new pub Dad's Arris,' and she laughed, 'the Dog and Duck bum,' and they shared the laugh.

'You've thought about this?'

'I have Bess, and we will make it work, grow the family

again, you will have our babies.'

'I will?'

'Yes, you will,' Maude asserted, smoothing Bess's bottom some more and allowing Bess to respond to her more intimate fondling.

'Yes, I will my love, I will do anything for you.' This was all Bess had ever craved, to share her life with Maude.

'No, I'm not getting any fucking coffee, you get it.' Wade stood firm, asserting her reluctance at being side-lined.

Nadia parted from Casey's embrace that she had run into as he entered the room. 'Please!' she asserted, 'I don't want coffee, and Padraig can do without for the time being. Let us sit down, we have a lot to talk about.'

Casey mumbled he would have liked a coffee, and Nadia told him to sit down and shut up, she would get one for him later. Wendy and Flora stopped their squabbling to look at a restored Nadia, directing Casey, Wade amused as her guvnor demurred, and she couldn't disguise her look. Wendy told her to take the smirk of her face and also sit down, which she did, and this elicited a reciprocal smirk from the lovelorn Danny Boy eejit.

All seated, Nadia opened up the conversation, meaning to discuss the visit of the Saint heavies and all that this meant, but she became side-tracked. 'Padraig, how did you know I was here?' And she thought on, while Casey tried to sidestep her headlights, as would any self-respecting startled rabbit, if it had not been so besotted and addled. 'Are you having me followed?'

'That's you done up like a kipper, Paddy,' Wade joked, only to be told to shut up by Wendy, 'but?'

Wendy leaned to her lover and pressed an index finger to Wade's lips, 'Shut it, sweetheart, please.'

'Kipper, kipper,' Casey mumbled, and Nadia expertly brought him under control.

'Padraig?' Nadia pressed her interrogation. Casey tried to answer, but was interrupted as Nadia came to her own conclusions, and questioned him further on those; was he needed he thought? 'If you had me followed, why did whomever was doing the following, not intervene when I was set upon?'

Here Casey did feel guilty, and in that moment, he knew he should have put someone on the tail of his lovely doctor who was not such a coward.

Wade sloped her head knowingly. 'You didn't use that Frankie Howard, Scotch 'Arry did you?'

Wendy enquired, nicely, before she really lost her temper, 'Frankie Howard? Scotch 'Arry?'

'Coward sweetie, Frankie Howard,' Wade replied, leaning in to kiss Wendy only to have her attempt expertly dodged, as Wendy made for the follow up.

'You knew? And you didn't tell me?' And she thought on,

'You're not having me followed, are you? Am I in danger?' Wendy kippering her lover, and Wade looked well and truly smoked.

'Well...' she said nothing else, knowing fatalistically, that this will be a matter of discussion before bedtime and Wade, as usual, would have no strength or indeed linguistic skill, to combat Wendy's comprehensive arguing ability. Her brain always became vacant in their before bed *talks*.

'We can talk about this later,' Wendy asserted, reinforcing this with a dangerous smile that Wade recognised, confirming her theory, and so she commenced trying to think of answers to the notional questions, forgot it all, and settled, looking forward to the makeup sex. Wendy of course knew Wade well. 'And don't think there will be any makeup sex, not until I have had the truth out of you.'

'Kipper, kipper,' Casey mumbled again, until Nadia knocked the salacious grin from his charming face, with a look that said she will tear the skin off him.

'And none for you either, until I have the full truth,' Nadia said, stunning Casey who could not answer, aware of a whispered, "Kipper, kipper" from Wade, and he didn't mind in the least. Was Nadia suggesting tonight, was the night?

Wendy returned the focus of conversation back to the evening's events, aware Nadia and she had both Wade and Casey in a vulnerable position where they were most likely to get to the truth, and after a while of drooling gibberish from Casey, he spilled at least some of the beans.

27

Even the weather was benign this Friday morning, no more of the insidiously saturating summer drizzle. The morning brighter, promising sunshine, a propitious summer solstice weekend ahead, the augurs looking well, but for whom?

Chas, he was tucked away in a luxurious room in the Ritz, his mission charged, as was his passion?

Maude and Bess, a new and prosperous looking relationship, the families enjoined in a most extraordinary way?

Wade and Wendy, a shaky chat before bedtime, but the makeup sex made up for everything, least Wade thought so?

And what of Casey and Nadia? Although Nadia had reservations, her heart led, and she took Casey, her gibbering nervous wreck of a prospective lover, home, where she reasserted her new ground rules, primarily about him no longer being shifty about what was going on, especially where it will affect her, before they effectuated their seedling bond. Not brilliant Nadia thought, but good prospects... she hoped.

Nadia was into the hospital early Friday morning, leaving Casey in bed, bemoaning the fact she would not take the day off. She'd kissed him goodbye, chuckled at his attempt to cover up the disappointing night before, suggesting he had his sea legs now. She told him to get his life sorted, and that left the Irish copper befuddled, which amused Nadia all the way into work, enjoying the walk and the improvement in the weather, her spirits deflating only when she saw a man waiting outside her office, pacing. She slowed her step, wary after the previous evening's encounter, but even from a way down the corridor she could recognise a well-tailored suit. This was a fine-looking young man, and as she approached so the gentleman turned to face her, he smiled, it was a beatific smile, no malice, and genuine pleasure in seeing her.

Nadia's trepidation did not desert her, but still she walked to her office with hardly a falter in her gait and, still some distance away, she exhaled a perplexed sigh of relief in recognition. 'Chas? Is that you?'

Chas stepped to meet Nadia who had halted some ten feet from her office, shocked at the transformation in her patient, still with the hint of yellowy staining around his eyes, and as he approached, she became aware that he walked with only the hint of a limp.

Chas followed Nadia's gaze, 'Handmade shoes,' he explained, 'remarkable what a difference it makes, but still, sometime, I would like that operation you mentioned.'

'Of course,' she answered, but really, she wanted to ask, how can you afford them, the suit... and the rest? This was some wash and brush up. In short, a total transformation?

'Saville Row,' he explained, as Nadia took in the look of her patient who lofted a foot, *'John Lobb,'* and from behind his back he produced a hat, 'and next door in St James', *Lock and Co*, hatters.'

'Well, Chas, you took my breath away. Truly dapper, nobody would recognise you, but...?' She was lost for words.

Chas beamed, and again Nadia was taken aback, here was a handsome young man and she had never seen him smile before, apart from the devilish grin he had when his mother's body had been blown to smithereens. He ran a flowery hand down his svelte image, 'How can I afford this?' Chas had thought of an answer, knowing the question would be asked and he couldn't say the IRA. 'The family stash. I've always known where the various caches of loot have been hidden, and now, they have all been removed and relocated. So, you could say, I am a self-made man.'

'Isn't that a bit dangerous?'

Chas batted away her concern as lightly as flicking a fly

that had had the temerity to land on his new togs. 'You wanted to see me?'

Chas's beaming expression was infectious, and it buoyed her already elevated mood and, bending to unlock her office door, she replied, 'A once over, make sure you're okay.'

Chas insisted that Nadia enter first. A gentleman as well, she thought, as she took up her seat behind her desk, gesturing for Chas to collect the seat by the wall and bring it to sit beside her. She took out a medical torch and gently holding his face, she tilted it so she could look at his eyes and felt the rough sensation of a beard finally growing, making up for lost and stunted time. She examined him and was satisfied the operation had been a complete success, both eyes. 'Well Chas, perfect, even if I say so myself.'

Chas had not lost his youthful gleam and thanked her for all she had done for him. 'Is that it?'

'Yes, I will send a report to your family doctor, but I would like you to do one more thing for me please.'

'Anything?'

'You recall Wendy Richards; she came to see you when you were in the side ward?'

'The trick cyclist?'

'The psychiatrist, yes,' Nadia replied, struggling not to laugh.

'I would like you to see her.'

'You would?'

'Yes, please, you have suffered a lot and this sort of thing can affect you badly.' Nadia thought for a bit, recalling a picture of Chas as he had waited outside her office, 'I noticed you didn't mind stepping on the cracked floor tiles just now, are you no longer superstitious?'

'The thoughts are still there, a bit like an electric current, but Roisin has shown me how silly it was and I'm gradually kicking all my superstitious habits,' he shrugged, *how stupid he had been*, and for Nadia, another devastating smile that smacked her right in her solar plexus.

Steadying her breathing, she responded to this remarkable vision of transformation, the like of which she had never seen before, and wondered what Wendy would make of it, recalling her last comment, Chas was "a fruit cake", and picking up the phone, she dialled the number for Wendy Richards' office. While the call rang out, she turned back to Chas, 'Well, I am pleased about that, mention all this to Wendy as well will you,' and she returned to the phone as Wendy answered, still not able to take her eyes off Chas. 'Hello, Wendy, yes, I am a lot better, thank you. I have Chas Larkin with me.' Nadia listened to some exchange from Wendy but decided to interrupt her. 'Wendy, I want to send him to you and let you give him the once over, though he seems remarkably well to me.' She listened some more, 'Look, see him now and you will be amazed at the transformation, trust me, okay,' she hung up.

'She'll see me now?'

'She will,' and Nadia drew a little diagram of corridors, Chas stood, took the proffered note, 'and Chas...'

'Yes?'

'Be honest. Tell her everything you feel, it will help you. Wendy is very good.'

'I will and thank you for all you have done for me, I will never forget,' and Chas turned on the ball of his good foot and disappeared out of the office.

Nadia drilled her fingers on her desk, something was not right? She picked up the phone and called Arbour Square police station. Neither Casey nor Wade were there.

Casey and Wade were in the Major's office. Wade, taking in the view across the Thames to Parliament, swung her gaze to the Scotland Yard building, from whence they had set out to this building, instead of going through the front door like a normal person. She pictured the Thames and imagined the tunnel beneath, a shiver of apprehension, before she turned to give a bit of her mind to Casey, who seemed too thoughtful this morning for her comfort. He was sat at the table, fingers steepled, preoccupied, and if she was any guesser, and she was, he was thinking about last night with Nadia and, judging by his look, she suspected he had been shite in the bed department. She pressed home her hypothesis, 'Don't worry Paddy, you and Nadia will get better over time.'

Casey, still in his dream, answered without any male doughtiness, or bravura. 'It took me by surprise. I was nervous.'

Wade felt unusual compassion for the vulnerable man, 'It's because she is important to you. It mattered.'

'But...'

'Oh, shut up for fuck's sake,' empathy exhausted, 'Nadia will understand, women have to, it is our lot, well those that prefer men that is,' and she fluttered her eyes. 'All she wanted last night was some physical comfort, not a mind blowing, jeffing orgasm...' and she looked at Casey's face, she may have overstepped the mark, thought, in for a pound, '... not that a mind-blowing orgasm would not have done the trick, but I'm sure you'll get there.'

'Wade!' He was stunned and she chuckled at his discomfort, thought of some more home truths to chuck in to dampen the male ego, confident Nadia could restore this with a flick of an eye, or a little white lie, like, "It was lovely in bed with you last night" and, eh voila, job done, as Wendy would say. And then Wade had a discomforting thought but dismissed it; she knew she was good in bed.

Fortunately for both Wade and Casey, and the uncomfortable conversation, for Casey that is, the major entered with Hemmings trailing behind, like a faithful hound, low to the ground and Wade could not stop herself imagining a sausage dog. Hemmings had a hang-dog expression, not all was well in his world of espionage.

Aoife O'Rierdon walked confidently along Gracechurch Street in the City of London, she had a meeting with the young Vanessa Thyme, daughter of the current Managing Director of Brockeln Bellands*. This was an enigmatic City of London hybrid company, a mix of stockbroker, financier, and in some areas, banker to the shady side of the world, although you would be hard pressed to define the actual role of Bellands, or prove any misdoings, a company originally out of Frankfurt, Germany.

** See Dead No More - Rhubarb in the Mammon - Bellands in the twenty first century.*

Bellands was a seriously influential family firm, of what, nobody truly knew, except they wielded power, money, and if you were able to probe, malign influence. The firm was discreetly managed by the matriarchal line. Originally made up of two German families, Brockeln and Belland, until the Brockeln men had been conveniently dispatched in the First World War and the men of the Belland family, those that had survived, had been suitably manipulated to stand as figure-heads of the firm until their usefulness had expired, a new male heir in the wings, ready to take up the position on the company parapet. It would then be time to dispatch, by means of a sad accident or whatever amused at the time, the extant chief executive officer. It was a sad fact that the heads of Brockeln Belland, over the years, had never lasted much longer than the need to produce heirs, first and foremost a daughter, for this was a firm run insidiously by the female line; a sacrificial son would be useful, but not absolutely necessary as other *rams to the slaughter* could always be found amongst the mainly dim, but enthusiastically ambitious, masculine cognoscenti of filthy lucre in the City, even if there was only a tacit familial link.

Vanessa Thyme had produced a daughter and was working on a son with her just tolerable husband, out of the Thiemann Teutonic stock. The marital name had been anglicised to Thyme, for convenience. Vanessa had discounted her husband as CEO, he was useless, and as soon as a son was provided, he would be disposed of in the time-honoured way. Vanessa's mother had installed a cousin, Mark Sohre, in the puppet role that circumstances being as they were, may have run its course. So, Vanessa needed a cousin for the soon to be vacant managing director role. Not that the position was yet vacant, but it soon would be. The cousin had been educated and primed to take over the firm as a contingency, the previous Managing Director having sired a son as a backup, in case Vanessa's mother could not produce the expiatory boy. The current patsy managing director had outstayed his welcome, in so much as he had drawn unwanted attention from the British Intelligence services regarding their funding of, what is so amusingly described by the British as, the *Irish Troubles*. The funding of both sides in any conflict was not the issue here; Brockeln Belland had been doing this for over two hundred years. The serious *point of departure* was that the current incumbent had a loose mouth around the ladies and careless pillow talk costs money and, in the case of Mark Sohre, lives. Namely his own.

It was for this reason the Grand Dame of Bellands had handed a first serious task to her granddaughter, Vanessa Sohre, a task for which she was well prepared. Vanessa had informed MI5, via a circuitous and safe route that the MD of Bellands had been funding the Saint family, who in turn, had been supplying arms to both the IRA and the UDA, which in itself did not seem too bad, but the killer punch was that the *conflict* was to be brought to the British mainland. It was made clear that sole responsibility lay with Mark Sohre and that the firm of Bellands were highly embarrassed and, wished to distance themselves. So, with the Authorities covered off, Vanessa had arranged to meet Aoife O'Rierdon at the Bunch of Grapes pub off Lime Street passage, to cover off Bellands' future.

28

'WELL, THAT IS ONE HELL OF A TRANSFORMATION, I HAVE TO say, but the lad may still be a fruit and nut case.' Wendy had telephoned Nadia, following her interview with Chas Larkin, and arranged to meet up lunchtime for a sandwich and a cup of tea, in Nadia's office. 'I cannot work out if this was denial, the way Chas had gotten through his torturous childhood, well, that and his superstitious habits, which he does seem to be on the way to kicking now, but there is still something not quite right.'

'Not right, how?'

Wendy had to think for a while, still unable to put her finger on what it was that irritated her synapses. 'I look into his eyes and see nothing, but that would not be unusual with a person who has suffered so much trauma in their short life, but...'

'Yes?' Wendy thought for a bit longer, chewed her finger and looked to pick up a pencil from Nadia's desk. 'No,' Nadia said firmly, taking the pencil out of range. 'Come on, spit it out.'

'Well...'

'He has no soul behind his eyes, has no vulnerability?' Nadia said what she thought, frustrated waiting for Wendy.

Wendy appreciated Nadia's perceptiveness, not so much her impatience. 'Yes, that is it,' and she thought on, '... he's lost his look of helplessness, but... my problem is, I cannot work out if we are now seeing the real Chas and, his pathetic look previously, was...? No, it cannot be, it was all so real. But the lad now has...'

'What?'

'Chutzpah.'

'Chutzpah?'

'Yeah, brass neck we sometimes call it. The thing is, I can't work out if he has always had it, and maybe the strength being repressed, or he has miraculously acquired it?'

'You think he has put on a show in his childhood?'

'No, I cannot be that easily fooled. He clearly has had a traumatic childhood, what I am thinking is that he worked out a way to deal with this and, maintained the *put-upon facade* in the recent months and, if I had to guess...'

Nadia interrupted, 'Since this Roisin appeared?'

'Yes, and I would really like to talk to that girl, woman, who knows, I can't get a straight answer out of him...' and

Wendy paused, in thought, '... whatever, she has certainly performed a miracle on Chas Larkin, but one I think makes the lad unstable. You just do not recover from a life like that, that quickly, without there being a price.'

'What do you mean?' Nadia asked, intrigued, a plan forming in her head that she would be reluctant to pass onto Padraig.

'I mean, it should take years of therapy to get the young man back to any semblance of normality.' She pondered further, 'This is not right.'

'I was thinking of suggesting to Padraig that he look into Chas Larkin's recent life, since Roisin came on the scene, all these events that are covered up in a conspiracy of fear, retribution from the O'Neills, the school incidents for instance, the murder of his mum?'

'I have thought of asking Flora this as well.'

'You have?'

'Yes, but Flora says Casey knows Roisin Dubh does exist, and then she goes off in a dream.'

'Padraig has said this to me also, but he's not telling me all, I know, and, he was very preoccupied last night, as well as being shit scared about going to bed with me,' Nadia replied, enjoying the stunned look on Wendy's face.

'Nadia!'

'Don't look shocked, I am not as pure and innocent as my image or background may suggest and, I think I may have shocked Padraig last night, but that is his problem, he needs to grow a pair,' and the pair of ladies looked intently at each other, Wendy not able to prevent a spluttered exclamation that did not drift into extreme profanity. Nadia settled Wendy with a look, 'I will give him a bit of time though, as I said, I think he is preoccupied with this investigation and I did rather surprise him last night.'

'So, you think perhaps we should do a little background check on Chas Larkin ourselves?' Wendy asked, changing the subject.

'I do, and I think we should start at his school. What could be more normal than two doctors having the welfare of their patient at heart, visiting the school, and checking on the boy's behaviour when he was there?'

'Isn't it the school holidays?'

'Yes, but I expect some staff will be there and it will be better than having a load of screaming kids around our ankles while we probe.'

Wendy and Nadia agreed and felt there being no time like the present, polished off their lunch, and set off for Chas's school.

The word was out on the street, the Saints and Larkins were meeting, and if rumours were to be believed, they were forming an alliance; just what everyone needed, a stronger villainous family running the streets of their manor, just as people had gotten used to the idea that things might get better, after so many of each family had met their inglorious ends. So those patrons of Arries and the former pub, Dad's, had been summoned for an afternoon meet; no refusal would be accepted.

All her dealings with Brockeln Bellands had been with Mark Sohre. Aoife had never met Vanessa Thyme and was wary as she entered the *Grapes* pub. The City boy traders were hard at it, liquid lunches fuelling boasts and counter grandiloquence, money made, companies trashed or made, peoples' lives crushed and rarely made. It was so crowded Aoife could not see how she would find the lady she was due to meet and this made her nervous; a lot rested on this. She felt her elbow grabbed and involuntarily, she was steered to the back of the pub, and was behind the bar before she'd had time to look back at the stunning blonde, blue eyed, elegant woman, directing her. A woman a lot taller than herself, and Aoife was unusually tall.

Vanessa smiled and Aoife chilled, and did as she was told. She stepped through the door held open by the barman who saw nothing out of the ordinary, the traders oblivious, thoughts only for themselves. The door closed and Aoife faced a steep flight of narrow stairs, this was an old City building, and the back of house had the appearance of a

Dickensian hovel. Aoife, impelled by the presence of Vanessa, stepped and rose steeply up the stairs that creaked unnervingly. At the top was a small landing with two doors, she was steered to the right and for the first time the dominant lady behind her spoke. 'Open the door Aoife,' a surprisingly gentle voice.

The lady had pronounced her name correctly and Aoife felt flattered, but still cautious. The door opened into a bare room, distemper on plastered walls that looked as though it clung to the lathes by nothing short of a miracle. Bare, uneven floorboards that groaned more than the stairs. Vanessa still had hold of Aoife's elbow, a firm grip that would likely produce fingertip bruises, but this was not on the mind of Aoife, or Vanessa.

A few paces to the centre of the small room and Vanessa scraped back a utilitarian chair from the modest square wooden table. 'Sit,' she instructed, finally releasing here hold. Aoife sat; the chair wobbled. Vanessa did not immediately take up the vacant chair on the opposite side of the table but promenaded around the room like it was a stately hall. Aoife watched the statuesque woman, who walked so elegantly on impractical stiletto heels. Nothing was said, just an eerie silence, only the muffled voices of the ignoramus robbers in suits below. There was the hint of a breeze from a small sash window, offering precious little daylight as the walls of neighbouring buildings crammed into the valuable City space, and like everything in the room, the window was in need of more than a lick of paint. The breeze wafted, a bare light bulb that swayed on its platted flex, creating spooky shadows as Vanessa toured the room.

A knock, and the door opened. A lad with a gammy leg that he dragged behind him, entered with a tray of drinks; Aoife was put in mind of *Tiny Tim*. The boy put the tray on the table, laid out two starched linen napkins, stood back, and with a voice that suggested a cleft pallet, 'Will that be all, Madam?'

Vanessa turned and stepped to the chair and as she sat, she spoke, 'Thank you, Michael,' and the boy, his leg trailing, disappeared, the sound as he thumped down the stairs reverberated.

The two women sat at the square table. Vanessa served the drinks that Aoife had no idea of the identity. Noticing Aoife's questioning look, 'Champagne cocktails, what else?' Vanessa responded, and sipped, taking clear pleasure in the drink. Aoife copied the action of this sophisticated woman sat in front of her, including the facial expression of appreciation of the sparkling strong drink that tickled her nose and momentarily took her breath away. Vanessa smiled warmly. 'I have always admired you Aoife, the way you run your family.' Aoife said nothing, she was experienced in these matters and knew you spoke only when absolutely necessary. People like Vanessa could take offence at the smallest thing and have a manner that suggested she would enjoy tripping you up, either to embarrass, or for more malevolent or devious reasons and, the consequences could be dire and far reaching. 'You have always run your family in a way that I approve.' Vanessa pondered while she took out a small handkerchief, drenched in the most exquisite perfume, rubbed the table clean, before she returned the cloth to her handbag and rested her elbows, lowered her head through her shoulders and looked Aoife directly into her eyes.

Nothing was said for a few minutes. Vanessa challenging Aoife, very much as the Irish woman challenged the butterflies in her stomach, steadfastly still, waiting.

Eventually Vanessa nodded, as if approving of the steely nerved woman in front of her. 'So far so good, Aoife.' Aoife continued her silent response. She played the game. 'We need certain things to happen and I want you to arrange them for us. You may rest assured you will be more than adequately recompensed in return for this, small favour.' Still Aoife maintained her counsel. Vanessa admired this in the woman. 'Time for *the Black Rose* to up the ante. You can arrange this?'

Finally, and Aoife responded. 'It might depend on what you wanted done, but certainly I can get a message to Roisin Dubh.'

Vanessa liked the answer from this wily woman. So many times she had had people in front of her who readily agreed to do her bidding, regardless of risk, or even knowledge of the task. 'I have need to rid myself of Brockeln Bellands' Managing Director.'

'Mark Sohre?'

The dialogue was becoming freer. 'Yes dear, he has...' and she drifted as if in a dream, wobbled her head in a most considerate manner, '... shall we say, overstepped the mark?' And she allowed herself an evil titter at her joke.

'Not my business. What are you not telling me?'

Vanessa's cold grin returned, this was going to be dangerous Aoife thought, and then she was proved correct, but certain things had to be done if the *Cause* was to remain adequately funded. There was always a price, and then there was the family cut, naturally.

'Hemmings, cough.' The major said abruptly, just after they had all sat around the table. The small man offered up a pathetic clearing of his throat, looking like he wanted to step over to the leather chesterfield to steal one of the scatter cushions, not scattered, but perfectly aligned in regimented order, with a view to sit upon it to redress the height balance at the table. 'Not cough, spill the beans,' the major softened, 'please... my dear old thing.'

'Oh,' Hemmings said in a voice that you would only hear if you had super bat ears.

'Speak up, man.'

'Yes major,' they heard that, but only just, and before the major could frighten Hemmings more, Wade noisily scraped her chair as she stood, and moved to sit next to the intelligence officer, gesturing for Casey to do likewise with a chair the other side of Hemmings. Thus bracketed, the tiny man felt cushioned from the vocal bullying of the major and commenced his briefing.

'Er, er, Brocken Belland is a City of London company of, shall we say, dubious heritage.'

'Aren't they all,' Wade responded with a chuckle, and was suitably admonished by a cautionary glance from Casey, and a frigid military stare from the major. Wade harrumphed.

'I said last time we were aware that a City company was funding the Irish *troubles*...er, both factions, IRA and UDA.' Hemmings waited and Casey and Wade wondered what was happening, before realising they were required to nod acknowledgement of the retained previous briefing, so they nodded, and the major humphed. 'We now have solid evidence of this fact.'

'You do?' Casey reacted energetically, standing to demonstrate his dismay and almost scaring the Intelligence officer out of his skin, 'First I've heard of it.'

'Er, why would you necessarily hear of it before us, Mr Casey?' Hemmings seemed to grow in confidence, knocking Casey back for a moment.

Casey sat, tentatively, prepared to leap to his feet anytime his comprehension of the situation is questioned. 'Well, I keep my ear to the ground is all I meant,' and Wade raised her eyebrows. Hemmings may look like a Lemming about to throw himself off his chair onto a chesterfield, but she thought there was more to the diminutive man than was immediately obvious.

'Yes, well, information off the street is always valuable and perhaps you might feel able to share that with us next time, Mr Casey.' It was not a question, Hemmings was asserting himself, and Wade got a sense of just how such a man had risen in the ranks to be able to sit at this table.

'Maybe I will, but what are you telling us now?'

'We are sure that Mark Sohre, Managing Director of Brockeln Belland, has been supplying illicit funds for arms trading. We have our doubts about the whole company, and we are gradually infiltrating and hope to have some under-cover officers in positions of responsibility soon, able then to give us chapter and verse.'

'You want Mark Sohre taken in now?'

'Yes, Miss Wade, we do. We think we can get a lot of information out of him, he is...' and here Hemmings chuckled, and Wade thought he had a lovely warm face, '... he is not thought to have very much backbone, if you get my drift.'

'So, we can break him and give our undercover guys a bit of a lift up?'

'Indeed Mr Casey,' Hemmings agreed, 'this was exactly what we had in mind, but the question is, how do we bring him in without alerting the company, so they have time to cover their tracks?'

'And this is what you need us to do?'

'Yes, Miss Wade, thank you, exactly, er...' and Hemmings retreated into his shell, job done, and shortly after an interminable speech for the major, Casey and Wade excused themselves to return to Arbour Square to get their thinking heads on.

29

Nadia and Wendy stood outside the main entrance to the school gazing up at the stone dressed portal set into red brick, a flight of five poorly maintained stone steps rising to a pair of impressive, but intimidating, oversized timber doors. 'How could anyone think this was good design for children?' Wendy observed, her eyes fixated on the doorway while her nose scrunched at the smell of liberally applied, and largely ineffective, disinfectant.

'I imagine the patronising forefathers, those from the superior echelons of society, that is, built the school to reflect their own ego and to a scale that would deliberately intimidate children, so they learned first and foremost their place in society, rather than make them feel welcome to embrace a mind-expanding education.' Nadia further observed, mellowing slightly, 'Still, at least they built a school,' her fingers pinching her nose to dodge the aroma of dog shit barely disguised by bucket loads of whatever disinfectant was sloshed around that morning and, gesticulating with her other hand, she suggested they enter. 'The aroma may be more acceptable inside,' she said, 'shall we?'

'Yes, let's,' and the pair of doctors ascended the steps, pushed at an open door, relieved they didn't have to knock to summon entry and stand around waiting in the delusive antiseptic miasma. They passed immediately into a large vestibule to be greeted by the smell of institutional floor polish on lino tiles, only marginally surpassing the disinfectant aroma. The voluminous entrance hall, with its drab colour scheme and smell, screamed Institutional oppression.

After a brief moment of assimilation, that State oppression was given a voice, 'Yes? Who are you, and what do you want?'

Wendy and Nadia turned their awe-struck gaze from the interior design of ersatz grandeur, to a tiny hatchway that encapsulated a woman of patent impatience, the tableau akin to a painting of the Gorgon on the wall of this otherwise bare and echoing chamber. The doctors, as if turned to stone, were inanimate in shock, unable to move or respond. Eventually Wendy whispered to Nadia, 'God, how terrifying, can you imagine how the children must feel?'

The whisper echoed and was clearly audible to the termagant custodian of all that was sacred, Myth Medusa, and from her tiny window she issued forth, 'The children around here have precious little fear, and it falls to us to bat some respect into them, if they are to have any hope, going out into the world.'

The Gorgon had spoken, and it was as if the shockwave of vehemence and flagrant dislike of children hit the statues of Wendy and Nadia, the vehement remark like a lightning bolt fracturing their stone encasement. With barely contained bubbling anger, they approached the reception hatch, to explain their mission. Nadia, in a stunned silence, preferring to keep her counsel lest she lose her temper, for she had already seen the result of such attitudes on Chas Larkin, and wondered just how many more children had been emotionally and psychologically, as well as physically, damaged?

Wendy spoke, 'We are doctors from the hospital and have been treating a pupil from here, Chas Larkin.'

Before Wendy could get further, she was interrupted by a tirade of Medusian invective, 'That nasty piece of crippled shit, in the hospital, is he? Best place for him, lady, would be the loony bin after all the trouble he caused here.'

'Trouble?' Wendy pushed, worried that at any moment the snakes would appear in the harridan's hair and they would be done for.

The snakes remained tamed for the time being as the woman thought how to respond to two ladies who displayed little fear; not what she was used to. She sucked on the stub of a cigarette that had been stuck to her bottom lip wobbling in time to her speech and, Wendy and Nadia watched as the glow of the fag grew bright and intense, reducing in length so rapidly that they later swore they could smell the acrid aroma of singed lips. Expertly, and with finely pinched, nicotine-stained fingers, the receptionist detached the butt and flicked it at the lady doctors. Wendy dodged the incendiary missile, but it hit Nadia in the face. There was no hurt other than shock, but Nadia did react and the fiery woman that Wendy had sensed bubbled below the cool exterior, exploded as she dived for the hatch. The Gorgon was too slow to avoid her hair being grabbed and all in the same swinging movement, Nadia slammed the woman's head onto the countertop with a crunch that resounded around the echoing vestibule. Blood spurted from the nose of the receptionist, the first line of defence for this school, but Nadia offered no respite and pressing home her advantage physically, she squeezed the face firmly down and, lowering herself to the level of the counter, she spoke in a gentle manner that defied the recent display of aggression. 'Now, are we going to have a civilised chat about Chas Larkin, or do I have to come around there and put my boot up your arse?'

'Nadia, please,' Wendy counselled, secretly relishing the picture of the Palestinian action woman.

Nadia released the hair, subconsciously checked her hand for snakeskin and stood erect as the prone woman brought her hand to her nose, took it away to reveal it bloodied and, recovering some pride, 'Look what you've done. You're for it now, I'll tell the headmistress...' she thought a bit, '... I'll call the police,' she threatened.

Nadia was not going to be intimidated. 'Call the police, Arbour Square, and ask for DI Casey, he is the officer looking into the abuse at this school,' it was not exactly the truth, but Nadia noticed her verbal spar had hit the mark and, if she had her way, she would get Padraig to investigate what actually goes on at this school. She had seen and heard of too many incidents in the local schools where children were physically and emotionally abused, and it had to stop.

'I agree,' Wendy said.

'Did I just say that out loud?' Nadia asked, but did not need an answer as the receptionist displayed the fear of authority and consequent action that likely the children felt every day.

Dabbing her nose with a handkerchief, the receptionist was now suitably pacified in order to be interrogated and Nadia deferred the first questions to Wendy; sort of good Doc to Nadia's bad Doc.

Wendy, her face plastered with a reasonable visage, asked away in her soft, butter wouldn't melt voice, 'What is your name?'

'Maddy,' the lady answered, the irony lost on her, but not Nadia and Wendy, who smothered a chuckle.

'Well, Maddy, we want to find out what happened on the day Chas Larkin ran away from school, you remember?'

'Remember?' Maddy responded, 'Remember?' the lady of

indeterminate age, but had to be at least sixty and smoked a similar number of cigarettes a day, which in turn, had ravaged her skeletal face, responded. No longer dumb struck but reenergised, unable to disguise her surprise that the day in question had not gone down in local folklore and should be known by everyone.

'Yes, remember. Tell us what happened, please.'

'Remember?'

This was getting tedious, so Wendy prompted, 'Maddy, we know only that there was an incident in the boys' toilets, Mickey Saint *the cabbage* was assaulted, and afterwards in a classroom there was an altercation with the Headmistress, after which Chas Larkin ran away.'

'Altercation?'

Wendy felt the bile in her stomach begin to rise as the interrogation was interrupted by a shrill authoritative voice, a bit like Lady Bagnell referring to a handbag, 'Altercation!' the word was screeched across the expansive vestibule, it echoed, and brought the Gorgon to attention as if being addressed by her sergeant-major on the parade ground. 'I'll say it was an altercation and, if anyone was assaulted, it was me,' and the agitated authoritative woman, looking like a jolly hockey stick teacher, straight out of the *Kennel Club*, encased in tweeds, was angrily shuffling on the spot in her soft soled suede shoes. After the short and stubby woman had presumed she had asserted her authority, in this her domain, she strode determinedly across the polished hall floor to confront Wendy, but not taking her eyes off Nadia, as if she had never seen a middle eastern person before. 'Did you hear what happened to me?' she challenged as she approached, her crepe soles squeaking, diluting the intended strike of fear, so much so, Wendy and Nadia could not disguise their amusement.

Wendy, however, not in a mood to be intimidated, countered the woman, whom she gathered was the headmistress judging by the fawning going on by the bloodied sycophantic receptionist, who had left her office and joined the *altercation* in *her* vestibule. 'Stop!' Wendy shouted, putting her hand up like a policeman on point duty. The headmistress did stop, a look of shock on her face as if one of her pupils had hit the hockey ball into her face. 'We are here...' and she waved her hand to encompass Nadia into the conversation, '... as doctors who are treating Chas Larkin and you may assume we know little of what happened on that day.'

The headmistress looked like she was loading up her shotgun in order to discharge both barrels, when she was disarmed by a gentle but firm voice from an attractive and decorous young lady. 'Headmistress, please,' the command potent enough to stop the head of school in her squeaky tracks.

'Miss Doyle, I do not think you need be involved in this conversation. Do you not have work to do?'

'Miss Doyle, junior schoolteacher,' the young lady introduced herself as she noiselessly crossed the entrance hall to shake the hand of Nadia, and then holding onto Wendy's hand, she spoke whilst continuing addressing Nadia and Wendy. 'If you are investigating the abuse at this school, you may rely upon me to stand witness.' She dropped Wendy's hand, unaware the effect the physical contact had had on the psychiatrist; Nadia noticed.

'Wendy, focus please,' Nadia despatched her rebuke, of sufficient strength to shake Wendy back to reality, but it had also given time for the headmistress to regain her authoritative confidence.

'Miss Doyle, if you do not mind, I will handle this,' and returning to Wendy, 'I cannot imagine why Chas Larkin is not already locked up with the key being thrown away, that boy is seriously disturbed.'

Wendy reacted, right into the face of the stern Head. 'If he is disturbed, I could look no further than this school and the way the lad had been allowed to be bullied, not only by other pupils, but also the staff.'

'Absolutely,' Miss Doyle interjected. 'I will be able to give you chapter and verse and, if Chas Larkin reacted violently, my only surprise would be that it took him so long and, I refer not only to this school but the regular abuse he received on the street and in his family home.' She took a deep breath, clearly emotional, it was as if she was releasing feelings pent up for so long. 'I reported this to the police on many occasions and they did nothing.'

'You reported to the police?' The headmistress was

stunned at this clear show of disloyalty by a member of her staff.

'I did, and I am not sure I would ever trust the local police, they seem to have their fingers in so many pies, and it did not surprise me that they did nothing.'

Nadia stepped in, thinking Padraig had said much the same thing the other night when he was explaining how preoccupied he was. A poor excuse for his lack of performance that she found charming, if not a little frustrating. 'Can you tell me which officers you refer to, please?

Miss Doyle seemed more than willing to oblige Nadia. 'Yes, it was a desk sergeant, George something, people called him *Old George.*'

Nadia made a mental note to let Padraig know. 'Miss Doyle, can you tell us what happened the day Chas Larkin ran away please, and we are particularly interested in his relationship of dependence upon a girl, or maybe a young woman, called Roisin?'

'Roisin?' Miss Doyle replied, and this was echoed by the headmistress and the receptionist, "Roisin?"

'Yes, please.'

The receptionist now added her intelligence to the conversation, feeling that as a local woman and more in tune with the pervading feeling of the area, she ought to supply the confidential information. 'You do know we have been threatened with the wrath of the O'Neills if we tell,' and she stood back, folded her arms as if in a defiant challenge. The gauntlet had been thrown to the ground and whoever picked it up would likely incur the Irish family's ire and anticipated violent reaction.

Miss Doyle stepped in, wishing the O'Neills were there now, if only to knock the smirk off the receptionist and headmistress's face and, addressing both Wendy and Nadia, 'I am pretty much finished for the day, perhaps we could go somewhere less intimidating to talk?'

She received a satisfied agreement from the lady doctors and Miss Doyle said she would collect her things and join them outside, shrugging off the violent look of disapproval from the headmistress. A look noticed by Wendy and Nadia, and after Miss Doyle had disappeared, they considered it prudent they take their own leave and they did, offering no departing pleasantry to the two fulminating institutional women.

There was a telephone box opposite the school playground gates and Wendy chatted to Miss Doyle while Nadia made a call to Arbour Square, pleasantly surprised she was able to get hold of Padraig.

30

THE TIME WAS SET FOR LATE AFTERNOON, THE PEOPLE WHOSE attendance had been requested, aware this was not optional, were slowly arriving, the lure of free carousing too attractive to resist, before you considered the risk of lots of pain if you decided you had something better to do. The Saints, and many of the Larkins may have been seriously depleted in the last day or so, but the strength and fear of the resident tormentors was too ingrained into the psyche of the local people to ignore any threat, implied or explicit. The doors of Arries were locked after a time and liberal drinking commenced and continued, because it was free, or maybe most patrons required lashings of Dutch courage?

The wizened old grand dame, Nan Larkin, was shrunken into her matriarchal chair, brought out of the Snug for this special occasion. Reduced in physical stature she may be, as old age crept inexorably on, but Nan Larkin packed a mean verbal punch and had all of her Machiavellian wits about her, so much so, nobody would contest her authority. However, this was to be an afternoon where she would handover that power at a gathering of the two clans, those that had survived, along with the requisite hangers-on. With her scratchy voice, she called Young Bessie over to her. 'Pull up a chair Bessie.'

Bessie did, but didn't sit. 'Bess, call me Bess please, Nan. Maude prefers that.'

'Yes, she's right, it suits you. New start and all that,' and Nan Larkin offered a toothless grin, patted the seat of the adjacent straight-backed chair, 'sit with me, things won't start for a while. Maude's waiting on a phone call.'

Bess leaned down to Nan's ear and whispered, 'I can't sit Nan, it stings.'

Of course, Nan knew what Bess's problem was. She had talked all of this through with Maude some time ago, and this morning received Maude's report and took pleasure in seeing a well-conceived plan rolling out and, in a perverse way, delighted in the discomfort of the Saint girl. Nan crooked her arthritic finger and beckoned Bess back to her face and took the opportunity to pat her behind. Bess squealed, and that brought Maude over.

'Nan, don't tease Bess.'

'I just wanted her to sit next to me,' and a wicked smirk

passed across Nan Larkin's face, unnoticed by Bess who had eyes only for Maude.

Maude returned a stern look to her *wife*, 'You don't want to sit next to my Nan, darlin'?'

Bess leaned over to her lover, *wife* in all but law, and whispered, 'It hurts my love', you know,' and she made a gesture with her mouth to suggest a sucking in of breath.

So that her Nan could hear, Maude replied, 'Unless you want me to take you upstairs...' and she allowed the consequences to sink in, '... I suggest you sit down.' Bess was shocked, yet titillated, and gingerly she lowered herself onto the seat of the polished wooden chair.

Nan, in her dotage, kept her feelings close to her chest, but held her enmity firm, despite gestures of friendship with the Saint hierarchy as and when it was needed. She had a soft spot maybe for the late Madge, whom she had been at school with, however, she had taken significant comfort in the recent demise of so many Saints and even those within the Larkin clan who, in her mind, represented trouble and were best removed. The remainder of those she considered expendable could wait until a suitable opportunity arose. Nan had the Larkin family where she wanted it, and with the Saint heir subjugated, as much as she needed, sitting uncomfortably next to her. Nan, and by extension Maude, needed only the *wise counsel* of Bess Saint, the brains. The soon to be retired matriarch, relaxed back into her special chair, satisfied with a job well done and not an ounce of blame on them, thanks to these O'Neills.

Nan leaned across to Bess, 'Just do as you are told and life will be good for you, and Maude,' and she winked, rather unnerving Bess.

Maude grabbed for Bess's hand, a loving gesture, and Maude followed this up with a kiss full on the lips. 'I love you Bess, my wife.'

It was all Bess needed to hear as she gazed back into Maude's eyes, not seeing the furtive wink from Nan as Maude tugged Bess off her seat and towed her to the kitchen out of sight of everyone, though the behaviour of the two ranking family members was noticed. Despite a reputation of intolerance, relationships between same sex couples were accepted in the East End, it had to be as so many of the gangsters in the neighbourhood shared similar proclivities and, if these two ranking members of adversarial families preferred each other's company, who were they to say anything about it.

In the deserted kitchen, Maude lifted Bess's cotton dress and pushed her against the wall. Bess emitted a squeal of exquisite pleasure at the touch and coolness of the ceramic tiles, after which Maude elicited pain from the submissive woman as she cupped Bess's buttocks firmly, before she planted a powerful kiss. 'Do you love me?'

'Yes,' Bess replied. 'I've always loved you.'

Maude smiled, looked at the frown on Bess's face, 'What is it?'

'Your Nan knew, she even patted my bum.'

'Of course, she knew, she has known about the two of us for years.' Maude released Bess, her dress dropped, and standing back to take in the full picture of her obedient woman, 'All of this was Nan's idea.'

'All of what?'

'Me and you for starters. She has always admired your insightful intelligence, aware also how much you loved me and picked up on your submissive nature, as did I.'

'You did?'

Maude sighed, this was a pleasant interlude whilst she waited for the telephone call, she looked at her watch, which was late, but sometimes she thought, despite her general acuity in the family business, Bess was a bit dozy. 'I did,' and she beckoned Bess to her with a crooked finger, Bess came, 'remove yer knickers, now.' Bess didn't think twice, she did as she was told and handed her French drawers to her lover, 'Thank you - see?'

'See what?'

'See how you did as you were told by me. You have always been like that and now we have been blessed with the leadership of the enjoined families, see?' Maude wasn't sure if Bess did see, but she said yes anyway, another example.

'Why are we waiting in the kitchen?'

The phone on the wall beside Bess rang, making her

jump. 'For this,' Maude replied taking the receiver and putting it to her ear. She listened, looked at her watch again, and responded, 'Okay, two hours, bye,' and she hung up and spoke to Bess, 'we have an hour or two, I'm going to fuck your brains out,' and gesturing with her head to the rear staff stairs, 'get upstairs,' and Bess did as she was told.

Casey and Wade made it back to Arbour Square to be confronted by the desk sergeant who handed each a sheaf of scribbled notes, telephone messages. Wade shuffled her billet-doux, getting them into time order and started to look them through before Casey suggested they retire to their office. He had skimmed his notes and already had the gist.

They trod the stairs silently. Casey held the door of the CID room for Wade and she passed through, a nod of thanks, and the pair made their way across the expansive space to the Aunty Terrorist Room, their office. Silence in the room marked the respect the pair of detectives had acquired in just a short time, not least of which the fallout of violence since DI Casey had appeared in their nick. This did not go unnoticed and there were circumspect conversations.

Casey held the office door for Wade, this time she thanked him, offering up a perplexed look and, as he leaned back on the closed door and it snapped shut, she asked,

'Thanks for holding the door. Did you notice the quiet as we entered, odd?'

'I think the woodentops have finally made a connection between the recent violence and my appearance on their manor.'

'Well, a blind bat with cotton wool in its ears in a well-lit room could see that, but why now? Something has happened, and I need to go and ask what it is,' and she made for the door, but Casey remained leaning against it. 'You will need to shift yer arse for me to get out yer dozy sod.' Casey grinned. 'Okay, bog dweller, what is it, and take that cheesy grin off yer boatrace or I'll knock it off for yer.'

The phone rang and Casey left the door to answer, it was Nadia, he said. He listened as she passed on her message, he asked where she was, 'You're where? with who?' He listened some more, Wade hardly failing to catch the drift of the conversation and enjoying every moment of her Guvnor's discomfort. 'Yes dear,' he said, as he closed the call and replaced the receiver.

'Marching orders?' Wade asked, barely able to disguise her amusement.

With a confounded look on his face and a flourish of his arm, Casey gestured for Wade to sit down at her desk. He had pacing to do and there wasn't room if another person was standing.

Wade sat and Casey paced. 'Oh, brilliant I have to watch the Great Meringue Brains Trust walk up and down pontificating while I sit like a church mouse, is that it? Well, I reckon the dipstick filth out there,' and she waved her hand in a flowery gesture to the CID room, complimented with a limp wrist to indicate their detective comrades couldn't detect themselves out of a brown paper bag, 'have done a bit of detecting, at last, and are only now starting to see a link between Chas Larkin and this Black Rose tart.' She waited for him to respond, he didn't, he continued his pacing, and as he passed her for the umpteenth time, she tripped him. He toppled onto his desk, twisted, and fell into his chair, the momentum driving him back the short distance to the wall, where his halt in backward momentum translated into him twisting to and fro on the swivel chair. He steadied himself, approving Wade's masterstroke as she wiggled her fingers as if saying hello to a five-year-old. 'Hello, tosspot, what conclusions have you come to while you've worn out the soles of your daisy roots?'

'Daisy roots?' he asked.

'Boots bozo, so, anything, let me into your great master plan, please.' Casey looked stumped. 'Brilliant, not a bleedin' clue. D'you want to hear what I think we should do?'

Casey was looking down at his telephone messages, all of a jumble on his desk, whereas Wade had sorted her own while the Maestro Aunty terrorist had paced the floor like Sherlock Holmes. He looked up, 'Yes please *stor'*

'Stor, what the fuckin' 'ell is that?'

'Darling in the Irish, *Ghile gra amhain,* darling loved one.'

'I'm not yer bleedin' loved one, darlin',' she responded in a brazen cockney, cod Irish, accent that made Casey smile, 'and, if Wendy heard you say that she'd knock yer block off, as would Nadia I suspect. How did that really go by the way?' She felt like winding him up again, having already got the gist he had failed as an ardent lover.

'How did what go?'

'Your night of passion with the gorgeous Nadia?'

'She is gorgeous, isn't she?'

'Oh, you lovelorn tow rag. So, you were hopeless then?'

'How?' and Wade picked up a note and fluttered it in Casey's face, he looked done in, and made a grab for the note to see what it said, but Wade was too fast for him.

She momentarily felt sorry for the deflated ego sat in front of her, and so applying her male puncture repair outfit, she pumped some air back in. 'I think the Doc loves you, so don't worry, by the time you both draw your pensions I imagine you might get it right,' and she rolled back laughing and responded to a knock on the door, 'Yeah?'

The door opened and a pimply young detective constable, with greasy hair draped over his dozy forehead, poked his timid head around the door, 'Er...'

'Spit it out Jezzer,' Wade instructed. 'I presume they've sent you in here to ask where you can find Chas Larkin. That right?'

'Yes,' Jezzer replied.

Wade picked up a few of her notes, stood and walked to

DC Jezzer, shuffled the sheaves of paper, then read the notes one by one. 'Well, he had a check-up with the Doc this morning,' next note, 'went to see the trick cyclist as his bonce needed a bit of sorting,' another note, 'and left the 'ospital about an hour ago. Did your man not spot him?'

While Wade was preoccupied with the dozy Detective Constable, Casey leaned across the desks to filch the note with which Wade had taunted him. The message was from Wendy, telling her if she wasn't home for the postponed dinner by six, she would be on the naughty step.

The DC left, none the wiser about where to find Chas Larkin and Casey threw the note back onto Wade's desk.

'See what you wanted, me on the naughty step if I don't get home before six, because our lubbly jubbly romantic dinner was spoiled last night by itinerant visitors in various states of distress?'

Casey retaliated, 'It said nothing about Nadia and me last night.'

Wade beamed a victory smile. 'No, but I guessed right didn't I, you macho prairie 'at.'

'Prairie 'at?'

'Pratt, twat, dipstick, bleedin' bonzo brains, or in the Irish if you like, you feckin' eejit.'

Casey grinned. 'Well, last night, I was worried about what had happened to Nadia, and completely thrown out of kilter by the offer to sleep with her, so...' he thought on, '... and I worry about who to trust. Old George, for instance, who we have already considered a tad moody...' and he waggled his hand to show the bloke could not be trusted, '... and, by all accounts...' he pointed to the phone, '... Nadia informs me, the desk sergeant is right out of the window.' He went on to explain about the teacher, Miss Doyle, the scene in the school vestibule and after passing on the misgivings of Old George, she passed on the intelligence regarding the O'Neills.

Wade responded, feeling sorry for him, a strange emotion for her. 'Look Paddy, I know Old George is dodgy,' and she fluttered hand in mid-air to mimic his previous gesture, 'and I would never share any information with him unless I wanted it shared all around the manor, oh, and for the record, I could not give a toss about your inability to pleasure a woman.'

'Oi!'

'Shut it. You need to wise up man. Nadia was truly scared last night, and she clung to the man she loves, leapt on you as you came into the room, did you not notice, especially from a woman who up until that moment had shown only reserved affection?' Wade watched as the notion sank in, at last. 'Der, what is it about blokes eh? Thank fuck I prefer women, and...' Wade stood, a menacing look on her face as she leaned over him cowering in his swivelling chair, '... if you hurt her, when you disappear back into the mire of MI5, or back to Ireland having completed your murky mission here, that I now think I know about,' and she took pleasure in the mystified and then scared face on Casey, 'Paddy, so help me bleedin' Gawd, your Deity as I don't believe in all that mumbo jumbo, I will find you and cut off your largely ineffective willy, got that?' Casey nodded, 'Good, now, do you want to hear what I think we should do, since you 'ave not a bleedin' clue?' Casey nodded again, and Wade told him he should be thankful for the women in his life, because currently Nadia and Wendy were doing what, she had previously argued, they, should have done ages ago, and that was speak to the school and find out more about Roisin, the Black Rose, and then she had a light bulb moment. 'Oh, fuck me gently. You don't want us to find out about *The Black Rose* do you?' Casey did not speak, she recalled his reluctance to pursue the woman at the cemetery, and Wade had the answer she sought, written across her bog dwelling boss's face, but even so, before she is stuck on the naughty step tonight, she resolved to get Wendy's feel for this Roisin and her relationship with Chas Larkin.

31

Ironically, just as the great and definitely not good, were gathering in Arries for a gangland, extraordinary general meeting, Vanessa Thyme attended the regular fortnightly Board Meeting of Brockeln Belland. Though not a director, or having any title within the firm, everyone knew it was Vanessa, her mother, and grandmother before her, who ruled as an illusory complaisant dictatorship.

Mark Sohre took up his place at the head of the table, serious, head bowed deferentially. A period of thoughtful reflection before he looked down the lengthy expanse of polished mahogany, past the vacuous faces of toady directors, directors without Porte-folio, and non-executive directors, those there just to put in six hours a month and collect their pay-off, mostly politicians. Eventually his gaze reached the opposite end. The head? Who was to say, and sat in her mother's seat was his younger cousin. Where was her mother? Vanessa had been attending recent meetings but usually took up a seat alongside her mother, a foot or two behind; she was being coached. Vanessa's solo appearance this afternoon undoubtedly meant mother had considered her daughter suitably prepared.

Mark Sohre, the Managing Director, was about to find out just how prepared she was.

A tap on the door and a butler entered, a white starched cloth draped over the forearm of his tailed penguin suit. He walked to Vanessa and reverentially handed her a folded note that lay on a silver salver. She read, scribbled a response, which she placed back on the proffered tray and the butler, head bowed, backed away, turned at the door and left the room.

All eyes that had been on the butler and the exchange of notes, reverted to Vanessa as the servant departed. Silence reigned, and a frigid atmosphere pervaded the board room. A pronouncement was due from Vanessa. They were not to be disappointed, her pencil point, deep blue eyes, zeroed in on Mark Sohre, and the managing director felt the blood in his veins inexplicably freeze, and the familiar pulse in his eardrums struggling to maintain rhythm. Ordinarily he was a confident man, after all he was MD of this very successful, if secretive, firm and, in his way, he had made a lot of money for it and the family, albeit many of the suggestions had come from Vanessa's mother. He had though been the one to carry the policies out, so why was he nervous? He put it down to the fact Vanessa had taken her mother's place at the table without his prior knowledge.

He decided to take the initiative. 'Your mother not attending today, Vanessa?'

The chalk white, bedizened face, made no movement. The stare was maintained, no flickering of the eyes or hint of emotion from the crackerjack crimson red lips, it was as though any smile would fracture the decorated face and Vanessa's mask would crack. Mark had often wondered why this beautiful woman wore so much make up, she did not need it, not realising that all virago beldams had a face for public scrutiny and, if you were the focus of that face, you would already be in the viperous clutches, slowly dying an eventual painful death. Vanessa's face, though masked, had a look, and Mark had seen this look before, on her mother, his aunt.

'Vanessa?' he asked, and he saw the remaining director cannon fodder visibly shrink back into their seats, probably wondering why they were there, having to remind themselves they made a load of money for precious little effort, just the odd smoothing of the way in certain government circles, but with that came a price and, so long as they were not paying that price, they took the money and skipped away. Today, it looked like Mark Sohre was being asked to pay up.

Vanessa's chair scraped on the polished oak floor, the painful sound like the fingernails of a teacher grazing the blackboard, a harbinger of doom. Someone was not going to make it through the day and, as Vanessa stepped slowly past the serried ranks of sycophant directors, gliding slowly and effortlessly along the length of the table, each and every one of the attendees breathed a sigh of relief as the *Cruella DeVille* of the City of London passed them by, this time. Mark Sohre's face at first showed dread, then panic, as Vanessa pulled up beside him and tapped him on the shoulder. The *death tap*, is what the Traders called it, and they all lived in shudder-some fear if ever a member of the female line of Bellands passed them by; would they receive the tap? This time though, *Cruella* had settled beside the current Managing Director, and Mark Sohre knew he had just been fired.

He stood, thought about pleading his case, but knew it would be a waste of time. He looked around the table, no eye contact from any of those sat counting their money in corrupt minds, relieved not to get the *tap*. What a stupid expression Mark thought, thinking at the same time, he had enough money, he could retire and shake the worry of Bellands out of his life, and as he thought this he smiled. It was a relief and now he thought about it, he had never expected to get the job anyway, it was only the unfortunate accident of his cousin Roger Belland that enabled him to step into the *Dead Man's* shoes, never realising it was not a pair of shoes but a chalice he was being handed, and it contained an insidiously slow acting, but inevitably fatal, poison.

Vanessa remained unmoved, emotionally or physically, she had been trained well at a Swiss finishing school and she knew how to deal out a *tap* when it was needed. One of the first things she had learned as a young girl. She had seen her mother do it many times and loved the drama of the gesture, the fear in the faces of the men dealt the final salute.

Mark Sohre stepped around his ice maiden cousin and made his way out of the Board Room, barely able to contain his joy at a release from what had been a nervy tenure at the head of this company. Seven years, the same number of years as his predecessor, he thought, and as he headed for his car, parked in Gracechurch Street. He tried to think of the MD's before him, how many years was it for them?

Back in the Board room the butler returned with another message and this time he whispered it into Vanessa's ear. 'Speak up, Watkins.'

Watkins did speak up. 'We have had a message from the City of London police, Ma'am.'

'And?'

'They said we have been targeted by the IRA.'

'And?'

'Geoffrey Thyme, your brother, is outside. Shall I show him in?'

'Yes please, Watkins.'

And the police Ma'am?'

'Tell them to fuck off. We will never be held to ransom.'

'Very well, ma'am,' and the butler retreated and, holding the door he summoned entry to a smartly groomed and accoutred young man. The door closed and Geoffrey walked stiffly to Vanessa, air kissed her cheek; he knew better than to risk damaging his sister's mask. 'Hi Sis, what was all that about the police?'

Vanessa held her finger up for silence, she got it, and for nearly two minutes the attendees, including Geoffrey, hardly dared breathe, before there was a loud explosion from the street outside. The glass in the Board Room, even this high, twelve stories, rattled. 'That,' Vanessa said. 'Now, take your position, Geoffrey,' and she pointed to the recently vacated dead man's shoes, seat, 'we have a lot to get through this afternoon.'

Wade was about to give Casey the lowdown on her recommended next moves when they got the call, "The O'Neills say hi", a City of London target. They had five minutes and no time to get across to the City. The company, Brockeln Belland, had been informed but the telephone officer had to report they had been told to "Fuck off, nobody held them to ransom".

That was it and after taking a note of the address, they headed down to get a patrol car to give them a lift, Wade calling after Casey as they flew down the stairs, two at a time, 'Brockeln Belland, isn't that the firm Hemmings mentioned?'

'Yep,' Casey replied, 'interesting eh?'

By the time they reached the desk sergeant, been through the Jobsworth rigmarole that the City of London was not their turf and, ordered a patrol car to take them into the City and, finally got the message through that it was urgent, they got the car they wanted and then waited patiently beside the desk sergeant's counter. The telephone rang and Old George answered, 'What? What the fuck?' he looked up at Wade and Casey.

'What?' Wade asked, not looking at the sergeant but at Casey, he looked like he already knew or couldn't care, and then back to the desk sergeant, who was a fuming gibbering wreck. 'What?' Wade said to Old George.

Gently replacing the phone, the desk sergeant, with a look of shock on his face, explained, 'A car has exploded on Gracechurch Street in the City, killing the driver and injuring some passers-by. What the fuck is happening and, while I mention it...' his already sour face turned to one of implacable anger and he pointed an accusing finger at Casey, '... you wanted to go to Gracechurch Street...' He paused and summoned his resolve to rebuke a senior officer, something Old George considered his right as he had gained his stripes in this police station, and still with his outstretched accusatory arm and pointing index finger, 'This all started since you arrived.' The sergeant thought for a moment, a painful process Wade felt, examining the long service screwed up face of the *old school*, tell-tale, bobby. 'You,' still pointing to Casey, 'you,' and he looked like he could not believe what he was thinking and about to say, 'you're fucking IRA aren't you.' He went for the telephone on the desk, but hesitated, responding to a resounding metallic click, Casey had cocked his gun and had it straight arm pointed at Old George's forehead.

Wade saw in her mind's eye the brains of Billy Big Head splattered all over the Gallows pub and thought of Limp Eric's brains, and now it looked like it was all about to repeat itself, but with Old George's grey matter. 'Fucking Ada, Paddy. What's the matter wiv you?' Wade exclaimed, thinking she needed to calm this situation, at the same time beginning to wonder if perhaps the desk sergeant hadn't hit upon a home truth.

Casey ignored Wade and gesturing with his pistol, he hustled the desk sergeant into the telephone exchange room, where the two lady operators heckled the backing in sergeant before screaming upon seeing Casey's firearm, his face suggesting he was not frightened to use it, and then he did.

Casey shot out the control box, the noise of the gun a resonating explosion in the confined space. The two ladies, holding their ears, dived under the exchange desks, which Casey then shot out and as Old George tried to take Casey on, he sideswiped the sergeant across his head with the white-hot pistol, knocking him out. A deft flick of a back heel, Casey kicked the protruding legs of Old George back into the room, snapped the door shut, locked it, and slung the keys under the shelf of the front desk. 'Right then,' he said to Wade, 'shall we find that patrol car?' And he sauntered off, casually holstering his gun, as a number of officers came running out of the canteen in a blind panic, swearing they had heard shots, looking to Wade for an explanation.

Wade didn't know that she could offer any account that would make sense, as it didn't make sense to her either. She shrugged as she heard Casey call after her, 'Oi, bagbird, you coming or chewing a brick?' Casey had popped his head back through the double swing doors and in an authentic cockney accent, chivvied up his bag lady.

'Give us five minutes, then get the cavalry out,' Wade said to the plod, now looking at two mad women banging on the porthole glass of the telephone exchange door, their muffled screams an eerie intrusion into the stultified atmosphere of the police station vestibule. Wade spun on her heel and sped after Casey who was holding the rear door of the Jaguar police car, slamming it shut behind her as she dived lengthwise in, wondering why she was doing this? Righting herself in the seat, she looked out the car window, nobody was chasing her, and she watched Casey casually stroll around the bonnet of the patrol car, step into the front passenger seat and calmly tell the driver, 'Gracechurch Street please, as quick as you like.' He leaned to the dash and flicked the switch for the car's alarm bell. The driver sat there stunned, as the peeling bell rang out. This was not what Casey wanted. 'Oh, fuck it,' he said as he leaned across, opened the driver's door, and pushed the shocked constable out. He slid across the seat, whacked the gear lever and stuck his foot on the accelerator, to the floorboards, and as the car screeched off, the tyres calling for help, Casey shouted back to Wade, 'Where the bleedin' 'ell is Gracechurch Street?'

32

MAUDE STOOD BESIDE THE PIANO IN THE PUBLIC BAR, unnecessarily hushed the pianist who had already frozen midway through *Nellie Dean*, a favourite song of the Larkins, there once being a well-known Larkin, Nellie, who married a Jack Dean in the late nineteen hundreds and were reputed to have owned a mill by a stream. She called for order and announced there would be a delay to the proceedings, they were expecting someone who had to make a call into the City of London. She apologised and announced free drinks would continue, which received a less than anticipated enthusiastic response, people were naturally nervous, and then Maude kissed Bess, passionately, in front of them all.

Dead silence.

'Ooh err missus,' Bernie called out, breaking the ice and the patrons speedily returned to a boozy contrived jollity, wary of the *slow drinkers;* these were the soldiers, men and women, ready for action at any time, it was their job.

'Nice move Bernie,' Maude said, as she slipped through the crowd tugging an embarrassed Bess, accepting the plaudits from the crowd, punters only worried what this would mean for them? Business as usual, or new rules to learn?

'Who are we expecting my love?' Bess asked.

'You'll see.'

Nadia replaced the telephone receiver and walked the zigzag short distance of hospital corridors to Wendy's office, she had caught up on her messages, nothing urgent so felt she should sit with Wendy and chew over what they had learned at the school. As she walked the polished corridor floors, shoes squeaking, her thoughts were not on Chas Larkin, but on Padraig; who was he? What was he? She was pretty sure the man loved her, but was circumspect about her own feelings, beyond physical desire. He was an attractive man and that presented her with another dilemma, was she captivated by the aura of danger that emanated from every pore of the man? In the greasy spoon cafe, Wendy and she had a diabolical cup of tea, while they gathered a lot of information from Miss Doyle who seemed immune to the beverage and her stale Eccles cake and, following the discharging of her conscience, she said she was off into the broad horizon. The

East End of London had become a most dangerous place. She also presumed she would have become persona non grata, having grassed and told all and feared not only the wrath of the O'Neills, the Larkins and the Saints, there was also the School Board.

Nadia tapped the door and walked in. Wendy was standing beside the window, the late afternoon sunlight reflected bright on her face, illuminating a radiant smile as she welcomed her colleague and friend, a waved gesture to suggest Nadia take a seat and she dragged the visitor's chair that resided the opposite side of her desk, to be beside her own. 'Here,' she said, pointing. Nadia adjusted the chair's position to provide for her a comfortable distance, sat, and smoothed the skirt beneath her white coat, crossed her legs whilst following Wendy's eyes. She unfolded them and smoothed her skirt again.

'Oh well,' Wendy commented out of the side of her mouth, flapping her hands, engaging in a shared smile at the brief intimate knowledge.

'So,' Nadia opened up, to disguise her blushes with a business-like persona, 'what have you concluded about Chas?' She thought on and Wendy allowed her a passage of consideration, 'Apart from he's a fucking fruit cake,' she said, sloping her head and quoting Wendy's previous assessment of Chas Larkin's mental condition.

After a short period of silence, to emphasise the importance of her impending revelation, Wendy ventured forth with her diagnosis. 'Still early days. Chas Larkin is a complex character.'

'Yeah, well, that's obvious... ' Nadia interjected, and accepted the reactionary stare from the psychiatrist with some resolute fortitude, but wanted to cut to the chase, '... but, is he dangerous?' There, she had asked it and now she could relax and listen in on the more expert analysis.

Wendy leaned back in her comfy chair and it was Nadia's turn to look at her friend's legs, but immediately averted her gaze to Wendy's serious azure eyes, her face animated, her body tightly coiled, a spring ready to be released? 'Dangerous? Hmmm,' and she wobbled her head in more reflected thought, 'I suppose that might depend on where you stand in his long list of hurts that in his cold and calculating mind require addressing.'

'Revenge, you mean?'

'Yes.'

'And?'

Wendy sat upright and leaned into Nadia's personal space, her spring beginning to unwind. Nadia backed away, just a little. 'There is more, much more,' and resting her elbows on her knees, she steepled her fingers and brought them to her lips, thought on as her eyes swivelled to her desk for a pencil to chew. Nadia saw and frowned. Wendy sighed, but continued without her pacifier pencil or fingertips. 'Chas Larkin's burning desire for revenge, so coldly concealed, might be considered the least and perhaps the easiest condition to treat, or at least begin to treat. What worries me the most, however, is this growing ability he has acquired to bury his feelings and desires beneath an increasingly cold, apparently benign, face.' She paused and Nadia waited with bated breath. Here it comes she thought, and it did, 'Roisin, however?'

'And?'

'And...' Wendy leaned back and stretched, folded her arms behind her head and swung a little in her chair, impressed by Nadia's perceptive mind. 'I believe Chas Larkin has a delusional sense that he is *untouchable,* that he is protected in some mysteriously ethereal way. At least I say it is ethereal, but he says it is his newly acquired friend, Roisin, and the way he talks about her appearing when he needed her most, makes me think he has conjured this unworldly *guardian angel* out of thin air. In fact, even more so since we have the latest gen from Miss Doyle.' Leaning forward and bringing her arms out to rest on her knees again, Wendy peered deep into Nadia's deep brown, almost black eyes, because she wanted to observe her reaction and maybe get her to press for more information from Paddy, as she will from Flora later. 'I would be convinced of all of this, except, as you know, Paddy says *the Black Rose*, this Roisin Dubh, does exist. But then again, I am also not totally convinced by his mythological inspired blarney and, he may just be away with the Irish Faeries himself. So, there you have it. In summary, I do not have a clue, except Chas Larkin is most certainly barkin' mad.'

'Where is he now?'

'Haven't a clue. He left my office this morning buoyed in spirit, in his best bib and tucker and, God only knows where that lot came from and, who paid for it? He said he'd spent the night at the Ritz. Can you believe that?' Both ladies shared a circumspect look, not sure whether to laugh at the funny side of all this, half wondering if Chas Larkin had actually stayed in the Ritz Hotel, or with Ritzy the dockyard floozy. Wendy continued, 'I do not believe he had knowledge of a Larkin stash of loot, which was his explanation when I asked.'

Of course she asked, Nadia thought, aware she was too nervous to throw the obvious question at Chas when she had examined him this morning, but Chas had offered the information in response to her enquiring look.

Wendy continued following the money, 'He would have been too far down the pecking order of that family to be privy to the sort of intelligence that would enable him to know where ill-gotten gains might be stashed. Wendy pondered and Nadia realised the psychiatrist was about to float a hypothesis that still had no substantial thought behind it. 'This guardian angel,' and she allowed herself a tight grin, 'no doubt flush with money, who knows, must at the very least have given Chas his newfound chutzpah, unless...?'

'What?'

Wendy ignored the question, she wasn't ready to float her real thoughts just yet, and Nadia, in her view, wasn't ready to receive this bit of perceived wisdom, so Wendy skirted around it. 'Chas did seem to know exactly what he was going to do and, to be honest, I am not worried about the money so much as the rapid change in his persona and behaviour. This sort of thing just does not happen. In short, I believe he is a ticking time bomb, but I would not be able to justify him being taken in, under arrest, or even protective custody.' She thought, confusion written across her face, 'Though who is in need of protection, Chas, or the public, I am unsure.'

'What were you nervous of telling me?'

'Nothing...' But Wendy delayed too long, her answer drawn out, forgetting she had an astute woman in front of her.

'Should I tell Padraig?' Nadia prompted, already thinking she knew where this was leading. 'He has already said he thinks Chas may have done for his mum, before he likely arranged for the blowing up of the woman's remains.'

'I asked him about his mum and after we got past the vile and insidious remarks, he suggested it was Roisin who had come to his rescue, and when you think about his injuries, how could he have done that to his mum, bearing in mind also, he was as blind as a bat?'

'People can do some mighty impressive things when their adrenaline is flowing, however badly injured,' Nadia observed, 'and there is still something you are not telling me?'

'Should I tell Flora?' Wendy responded, deflecting the one question she did not want to answer. 'But, all of this is in the realm of patient confidentiality, unless I considered he was a danger and although I am convinced he is, I cannot prove it beyond my professional instinct and, do we tell Flora and Paddy what we have learned from Miss Doyle?'

'Wendy.'

'Yes?'

'I think Padraig knows.'

Well, here was her opening, Wendy thought, but should she take it? In her way she could see that Nadia was herself quite vulnerable. She had allowed her straight jacket of professional restraint to drop and fallen for a man who very likely could be dangerously unstable, but whether they would concur on their conclusions, that would be the question? She forestalled her thoughts for the time being, 'As does Flora, she knows something, but how much I am not sure?'

'What do you mean?' and Nadia shuffled forward in her chair to meet the already crouching psychiatrist, as if to share a confidence, not to be listened into by any bystander. Wendy had an instinct that Nadia respected and wanted to hear what she had to say about Flora Wade and, was it similar to how she felt about Padraig Casey?

'Well, Flora thinks Chas Larkin is dangerous, but also

sees that leaving him out there,' and she waved her hands as if to encompass the wide world, at least the East End, Chas's world, 'might produce some enlightening results. But, in what direction I don't know and, I also think it is different to what Paddy thinks or wants.'

Nadia Sighed, 'I agree, but what?'

This was it, she owed it to Nadia didn't she, to tell her friend just who she was getting into bed with, literally, and she chuckled just a bit. It was picked up by Nadia.

'What? You laughed to yourself there, what were you thinking?'

'I was thinking what or how much I can tell you, not about Chas, but the man you are getting into bed with.' She paused while Nadia blushed. 'See what I mean? That was the little laugh I had to myself. How was it by the way?' Now Nadia's face burned, she sighed, a powerfully exhaled breath that cooled Wendy's own face. She was not sure she should have asked that, but Nadia seemed willing to talk, so she pushed. 'Good, bad, indifferent,' and she looked deep into Nadia, 'Aaaah...'

'What?'

'So, it was worrying? Not affirming of the relationship, but presenting you with more questions?'

'Yes,' Nadia realised the barriers between Wendy and herself had been taken down, there was no defence. She realised also this was a clever technique the psychiatrist had used, but what was truly worrying, she did not mind and, more surprising, she welcomed the intrusion into her innermost thoughts that ordinarily she would guard from absolutely anyone. Nadia felt she needed to back pedal, 'What is it you are sensing about Padraig? What is it that you are nervous of telling me, and how does this relate to Chas Larkin?'

'I don't know for sure, but Chas did mention a family in Kilburn,' she flipped open a notepad on her desk, found the page she wanted, read, and closed the book. 'The O'Rierdons, and this family, he tells me, had taken him in and looked after him when he had run away one time. Seems this became a regular occurrence he said, also mentioning that he could be away for days and nobody would notice he was missing, and that has its own psychological ramifications. However, if he was vulnerable, as I have no doubt he was,' she thought, 'and likely still is, he would have been highly suggestible,' and she sighed again, but with a grimace of resolve. 'The thing is, if these O'Rierdons were an unscrupulous bunch with a motivation other than the milk of human kindness, well, Larkin would be a lamb to the slaughter, a ballistic missile ready to launch after subtle priming and considered aiming.' Both women locked heads. Wendy continued her pontificating, 'Now, what if Paddy is investigating the O'Rierdons and nothing else? Not the Saints or the Larkins, not even these illusive O'Neills; what if...?'

'Yes, what if?' Nadia responded, her own thoughts beginning to find some fertile ground. 'Oh Padraig,' she said to herself, as Wendy thought, Oh Flora, what are you up to?

'Get yer arse to the front and onto the dog and bone and call the nick.' Casey ordered Wade, as the Jaguar slewed out of Arbour Square, across Commercial Road, careless of any thought for traffic, causing oncoming vehicles to swerve, her repost drowned in the ensuing cacophony of horns and hurled abuse; drivers and pedestrians, always pleased to have an excuse to launch insults at the police.

Back on the straight and not so narrow road and gathering her senses, 'No chance of you stopping then so I can get out, walk around, and then get in the front and then use the phone?' Wade replied, angry, and not a little concerned that her guvnor had totally gone off the reservation.

'Just do it. I have to stop the cavalry gunning for us.'

'Us? You mean, you, surely?'

'Wade, stop yer bleedin' moanin' and get on the blower.'

Wade began her indecorous clamber from the back to the front seat, contemplating clumping her guvnor as he commented on espying her knickers. 'Keep yer mince pies off me Alan Wickers and on the road, you pervert,' and she kneed him in the side of his head, which all things considered may have been a mistake, as he swerved and scraped the side of a parked car. Not that any of this seemed to bother him. To Wade, Casey seemed more preoccupied thinking of a *smart Alec* response to her barbed comments and continuing to drive like a cowboy on a runaway horse.

'Nothing perverted about what I was looking at sweet'art,' and Casey for the first time in a while snorted a laugh.

Wade groaned. He was enjoying this she thought, and reflecting, as she was settling on the passenger seat, adjusting her skirt, so was she. Explain that, she thought? She took the telephone radio receiver out of its bracket and aggressively twiddled some knobs and soon got the control room. 'Control?' she called, and the box on the dashboard squawked back, "Well who else would it be, dear?" God help us from the dreaded wit of the control room she thought, thinking maybe Casey should have shot that lot out as well. 'This is DS Wade, with DI Casey, get a message through to Arbour Square, please,' and she looked at Casey, 'well, what's the fucking message?'

"Yeah, tosspot, what's the fucking message?" the squawked response.

Wade had to laugh, even though she feared for her life, certain Casey would crash anytime and, if he didn't, they would be gunned down by an armed unit that had to be already on its way.

Casey grabbed the telephone and dismissed Wade's almost violent objection, 'Hallo, DI Casey here.'

"Oh, watcha darlin', you the bog dweller with the gorgeous arse?"

Wade snatched the phone back, causing the patrol car to sideswipe some more parked cars. Casey unconcerned about the trail of damage, ploughed on, reliant upon the warning bell being sufficient to make people get out of his way, and if they didn't, well, it wasn't his fault. Wade spoke into the telephone, 'Listen there is nothing gorgeous about his backside unless you refer to his face that looks like a fat bum with verbal diarrhoea.' The control operator thoroughly enjoyed Wade's jest, jettisoning raucous laughter.

Casey snatched the phone back and after a brief tussle that involved the paintwork of several oncoming cars, he finally conveyed his message. 'Oi, sweet'art, Arbour Square, okay. Tell 'em the desk sergeant's a squealer and he's to be locked up. I'll sort him later.'

"What, Old George, a duck's arse?"

Replying to the operator who seemed reluctant to pass on any message that would get "Old George" into trouble, 'Oi babes, just do as I say, okay?

"Alright, alright, keep yer girdle on honey. Is that it?"

Casey moaned, while he contemplated running over the police constable stood in the middle of the road with his hand out, suggesting he should stop the car, but decided in the end to hand the phone back to Wade in order to best be able to veer around the bobby who looked like he had done himself a mischief in his underpants department.

'Jesus, Paddy, steady on... less haste and all that.'

'What else do you want me to pass on,' Lady Squawk

demanded, patience clearly not one of her virtues and Casey pictured a harridan parrot chained to a perch in the control room.

'Paddy, what else?' Wade asked, rather more serenely than she felt, aggravated by the Danny Boy grin that suggested her Guvnor was more than a bit mental.

'Tell them to get the Sweeney to meet us at Gracechurch Street,' he ordered and then explained, 'we may need a bit of back up and, tell them also we will be going into Kilburn and, most important of all, call off any tooled-up cavalry that may have been organised to intercept us. Alright sweet'art, can you 'andle that?'

Wade restrained her ire at being patronised by a moron crap driver and passed on the message and, after she had replaced the radio phone, she swivelled in her seat. 'Oi, Dorothy, you irritating ponce, yer bleedin' accent is slipping.'

33

MAUDE STOOD BESIDE THE BACK BAR TELEPHONE, DRUMMING her impatient fingers and almost jumped out of her skin when the piercing bell broke into her reverie. She snatched the phone out of its rest, 'Yes?' She listened, 'Kilburn? Why there? Well, when the bleedin' 'ell will you be here, this lot will be as drunk as skunks by the time you get 'ere...' and she turned the phone to face the bar so the caller could hear the party in full swing, the piano banging out the old songs, the crowd singing along, '... hear that? Well guess who's paying for all this as they drink me out of booze, house and home? Me, that's who.' She listened some more and then banged the phone down.

'Who was that?' Bess asked.

With her hand firmly on Bess's bottom, 'I will tell yer, but it's a secret for now, okay?

'Yes, my love.'

The Flying Squad were already at Gracechurch Street. They had been called out as soon as there was an explosion, their trigger fingers twitching but not sure who to zero in on and now told to expect police detectives Casey and Wade and, they would be off to Kilburn, West London. They were doubly excited, it could only be the O'Rierdons, a family always on their radar and their adrenalin levels rose, their training kicked in; the O'Rierdons had a rep and they would need their cool thinking heads. Like clones of each other, the six flying squad officers tapped their concealed shoulder holsters, leaning back in an insincere display of casual indifference, onto their two cars. The Flying Squad were maverick officers, all of whom considered themselves the elite and arrogantly carried out their duties in whatever manner they felt appropriate, the end justifying the means in their view, a cut above the rest. They watched on as the fire brigade organised themselves, some leaving the scene having dowsed the flaming car, the remaining crew left to deal with the charred body of Mark Sohre; the driver had been identified by the still trembling office Commissionaire who had witnessed the whole thing.

The scene was one of shocked silence, just the thrum of

the fire appliances and the excruciating grating of metal being clawed back to free the remains, which was soon interrupted by the approaching sound of a police patrol car bell and the eventual screech of tyres as the Jaguar slewed to a halt, just before the police cordon. A man exited the driver's side, as if jettisoned by the force of a woman who continued her haranguing as she stepped out. Casey and Wade brushed aside a police constable's objection to them crossing the invisible line, without interrupting their continual exchanges of invective, which Jordan of the Flying Squad thought was mainly about the nationality of the man, Irish or a "fucking cockney"? The battling detectives made their way to the smouldering car, looked in, pinched their noses, momentarily elevating the intonation of their fiery verbal discourse, and shared agreement expressing distaste at the smell, before they headed to the Flying Squad officers, now upright and ready to roll.

An officer stepped up to greet them. 'DI Jordan,' a tall lean man whose purple veined face suggested an experienced drinker, not long for this world and already looking several sheets to the wind; the Flying Squad noted for their ability to imbibe whilst on duty, well, anytime really. Jordan addressed Casey, which involved stepping between the warring pair, arms stretched pushing them apart, ignoring Wade, not realising this left him vulnerable. 'Sweeney,' he announced unnecessarily, 'told you need us?' And the man beamed at the importance of his crew, whilst Wade stepped back from the alcohol fuelled breath, feeling she might need to interpret the slurred speech for her Guvnor of unknown origin.

Casey looked at Wade. Wade looked back, challenging and pushing Jordan to one side, thrusting her nose in his face and then into Casey's. "What?" both Jordan and Casey replied.

'Sweeney fucking Todd?' Jordan said with vehemence as his squad laughed at Casey being pushed around by a girl and not afraid to mention it in amongst the cat calls, and now right into Wade's screwed up face, enjoying her revulsion at his breath. 'You asked for the flying squad you bleedin' dipstick.' Wade moved her chin away to allow Casey to step in and brief the Flying Squad officers who circled like kids in a playground, witnessing and enjoying a fight, hyperactively energised, Jordan stepping from one foot to the other as if he needed the toilet.

Jordan defused the unseemly battle of turf and rights of leadership from one playground gang to another. 'The O'Rierdons, in Kilburn?'

Wade quietened, this was all news to her, and so she listened intently. She could always bash Casey later.

Casey flicked his head and strode to the vestibule of the office building, the Sweeney officers following, Wade playing catch-up, which did her humour no good at all. Casey was oblivious.

They found a quiet part of the spacious and voluminous vestibule and gathered, heads down conspiratorially, Wade, a newcomer, muscling in and bristling, her ire temporarily defused by a nervy Sweeny officer, stepping into the noisy, hush-hush ring, and once he had inveigled himself, he directed his attention to DI Jordan. 'Guv, message from Arbour Square, the cavalry's been called off.'

'Fank fuck for that,' Casey replied.

Wade grabbed Casey by the lapels of his jacket, looked to Jordan. 'Excuse me boys. I need a brief word with my tow rag of a guvnor. Won't be a minute.' And she fumed as she tugged Casey away from the gathering storm of testosterone laden police officers, just one step away from being gangsters themselves, and all to a man looking like they didn't fancy their chances with Wade.

She steered Casey to a small alcove. 'Right, you,' she said, as she slammed him against the marble lined walls of this Financial Institution, a building full of slippery bandits, trying very hard to give an aura of respectability. 'Spill the bleedin' beans mate and start by telling me just who you are, and then, let me in on these O'Rierdons... comprendeh?'

Despite the locking up of Old George, the O'Rierdons had been tipped off and were gathering their own resources. Not a greeting party, although in the opinion of Aoife O'Rierdon this was long overdue, Casey having been a thorn in their side for many years. "Feckin' MI5", she said, but the confrontation would have to be delayed as they had pressing business in the East End. She fumed to herself as she ordered her troops over the phone. They were to meet at the Saints warehouse in the East India Docks. Her consoling thought was that while they were in the East End, Casey and his moll, Wade, and whomever he dragged along with him, would be heading West, where Kilburn would be empty of O'Rierdons.

DI Jordan cautiously approached Wade and Casey. 'Sorry to disturb your little tete-a-tete, only we've just had a dickey bird from one of our snouts that the O'Rierdons are on the move and, if our informant is correct, they're gathering at the East India Docks. I can only imagine it is to pay a visit to the Saint warehouse to 'elp themselves to all their goodies, know what I mean? What d'you think? Shall we buzz over there and maybe gather a few reinforcements along the way while we're at it?'

'No!' Casey shouted, energised.

Wade stood back and had to rely on her cockney bog dwelling guvnor knowing what was happening as it looked like none of this was coming as a surprise, except perhaps, things were moving faster than anticipated. 'Well?' Wade asked, trying to knock Casey back into the here and now.

'This is all a bit faster than I expected.'

'No kidding Brains.' Wade interrupted, having just had her own assessment confirmed, noticing Jordan leaning in to learn as much as he could, or he may just be inebriated. Yeah, that would be it Wade thought as she declined the offer of a nip from the proffered hip flask.

'So, get over to the East India Dock?' Jordan asked, wiping his lips with the back of his hand, stoppering the flask, and returning it to his jacket inside pocket.

Wade caught a glimpse of an enormous handgun residing in a brown leather shoulder holster. 'Fucking Ada, Jordan, you bringing the artillery?'

Before Wade could offer any suggestions of her own, like perhaps her Guvnor could be dropped off at the loony bin on the way to the docks, Casey calmly repeated his decision. 'No. I need to make a call.'

Wade interrupted again, 'What, no? No, we shouldn't go to intercept these O'Rierdons, who I am gathering are a nasty piece of work, gang?'

'No, we hold off from the docks for a minute. I want the O'Rierdons' thinking they have the manor to themselves.

Jordan nodded, he understood both points of view and he explained for Wade's benefit all about the Irish family while Casey crossed to the reception desk, asked for the telephone, and made a call. Wade resented that Jordan demanded her attention. She wanted to eavesdrop on that call but was committed to listening to the slurred report on the O'Rierdons. Oh well, she could always pump Casey later, she thought, as she asked Jordan to repeat what he was slurring.

The half pissed elite officer started again, seemingly pleased to be the font of knowledge. 'Into everything, thieving, drugs, violence and, we suspect, may have links to the IRA? The new boys on the block so to speak, but whether they are true nationalists or milking the money from them, as were the Saints of course, we still have to gather. My money's on them just being downright scoundrels and sooner or later, they will get their comeuppance. If not from us, maybe from the Irish? What say you, Casey?'

Casey was back from his call and Jordan was already beginning to suspect this Arbour Square DI knew the O'Rierdons better than any of them and, his suspicions that not all was kosher might be correct and, if so, he and his lads would need to be on their metal today if they were to survive. They could be walking into a hornet's nest, so he broadcast to his team, 'No more drinking lads until we put the O'Rierdons to bed, okay,' and he received a nod of assent from his men with the sound of their flasks being stoppered. Now with his business head on, Jordan pressed Casey further and Wade marvelled at the transformation. The Sweeny DI was alert, no longer intoxicated. How could he do that she thought?

'So, DI Casey if that is who you are, what are we walking into?'

Wade thought she would like to ask the same question and watched on as Casey grinned, flicked his head to a nearby glass and stainless steel low table surrounded with leather chairs, looking most attractive but excessively uncomfortable. 'Let's sit and I will brief you.'

34

WENDY AND NADIA FELT DESOLATE. WELL INTO THE WEE hours they had sat and talked the whole thing through yet felt no further forward. What could they do, except interrogate their partners when they got home from whatever operation they were on?

'We need to do something,' Nadia commented.

'Yeah, but what?'

'Is Scotch 'Arry still following us?'

Wendy walked across her office, opened the door a crack and saw the maundering stick thin shadow lurking in the corridor. She looked back to Nadia, 'Shall I call him in?'

'Yeah, let's see what he can tell us?' and she slapped her forehead, 'if we can understand him?

Wendy got Scotch 'Arry's attention and summoned him

into the lair of two very clever women, but how good were they at interpreting Glaswegian?

Chas made the call from the same telephone box where previously he had met Ritzy, she was there now, as were the other working girls, pressing their backs to the dockyard perimeter wall and pressing Chas for a little money. Chas had come into some wealth and they wanted a share in it. Chas called Ritzy over. She almost fell into him as he rummaged around in his trouser pocket, an action Ritzy was trained to observe.

'Ritzy,' Chas said, waving a fiver that had the tart with the heart's attention. This was an enormous sum.

'Yeah, Chas?' Her eyes fixated on the money and trying to work out how she could get out of sharing this with her fellow dockyard floozies.

'I need you and your girlfriends,' and he looked up to the line of girls all easing their seedy way towards Ritzy and Chas whilst attempting to give the appearance of not moving, but they just kept getting closer. Chas enjoyed the subterfuge, 'I need some help,' and he beckoned the girls to him.

'What d'you want wiv this lot?' Ritzy asked, affronted.

Chas explained, he owed it to the girls to keep them safe, but unfortunately needed their cooperation and, most importantly, their presence at the gates this evening. Everything had to appear normal. 'Ritzy, there is something I need doing and it will earn you each a fiver, okay?' The working girls looked stunned, and all readily agreed, though should have realised that nothing is ever free, but the lure of the money was too much and so they gathered around while Chas Larkin, the new man, briefed them.

'Shit a brick, Chas.' Ritzy observed, and this sentiment was shared by her contemporaries, 'd'you fink we can do that?'

'Yes,' Chas replied, 'it'll be iffy, but I'm sure you girls can look after yourselves and at the end, there's a fiver for each of you.' He tapped his shoulder holster, 'However, if any of you split on me, well...' he did not need to say more. It was a done deal; they each could have a fortnight off from lying on their backs with that sort of money.

Chas stepped back into the phone box and made another call, a terse message, and he hung up and, as he exited the red box, he called to the working girls, 'Okay, get yourselves sorted. Ritzy, side gate, the main gate will be closed. I've a bit of biz at Arries,' and Chas disappeared down the street.

The girls looked on admiring the transformation, a young man changed from a limping gimp into handsome young man with only the hint of lameness. What had happened? They were about to earn a fiver for just leaning around and looking normal and then scarper when the balloon goes up, or at least a flare, is what Chas said.

After Casey had explained his rapidly arranged plan, he suggested they make their way to the East India Dock where they would secrete themselves in some of the derelict houses that bordered the dock wall, opposite the Saint warehouse, which was adjacent to the side gate, and here they would await the fallout. He informed them that some of the Dock Police, a separate force, and those Casey said he could trust, will be briefed by him, and he returned to the reception desk and made a call. This time Wade accompanied him and heard him instruct, presumably, the trustworthy Port of London Authority police.

Maude took a call and, with Bess she returned to the large public bar and, stepping onto the small stage the last order bell was rung, which got her the silence and attention she sought. Then she waited. It was an eerie silence, one that presaged menace. Just the look on Maude's face said that, and even the benign loving smile from Bess did little to disarm the atmosphere of dread of the rapidly sobering pub patrons.

A resounding thump at the locked doors. Thump, thump, equally as menacing as the silence it intruded upon, made everyone jump, except Maude and Nan.

Maude issued instructions from the stage, 'Open the door, please.'

Arbour Square police station was on red alert. Ordinarily anything happening in the nearby City of London, the business sector of the Capital City, never bothered them; the City had its own police force. However, the blowing up of a serious banking chief was nothing ordinary. Add to this the events of the morning, namely this maverick Irishman, thrust upon them only a few weeks ago, insisting Old George be locked up, and then shooting out the Police Station's telephone exchange, which shut down all communications, was something not to be taken lightly.

All officers had been called in. Overtime would be paid and steadily the numbers swelled through to late evening as the force gathered to be addressed by the station commander, who having been told they had a full complement, entered the room; the babble immediately ceased. The commander stood on a chair, he appeared to everyone in his number ones, his dress uniform, he needed to impress on his officers the seriousness of his intent. Most of all, he needed to stop those who would almost certainly leak information, from doing so, which was why Casey had shot out the telephone exchange and, why a separate, secure phone line, had been run into the commander's office before Casey appeared on the scene. The police station was locked down and isolated. There was concern and curiosity on the faces of the substantial police force assembled, all unaware of what was happening and distinctly unsettled.

This would become even more of a conundrum as the commander briefed them as to what they were expected to do. He opened up, 'You will be aware of what has happened this afternoon in the City, but not what is happening now. I can tell you only this, we will remain in this room until I receive a message that an operation being carried out on our manor is completed.' There was mumbling of confusion, one or two shouts for more information, and why they were to be shut up in their own police station? The commander hushed everyone, 'I am not at liberty to tell you yet what is happening, but yes, we are shut in, incommunicado, for several reasons.' And he counted his fat fingers, 'One, we have leaks, and it is important that you treacherous bastards in the pay of people we should be locking up...' it was clear how the station commander felt about this, '... do not allow information to filter out that may harm this operation. Other officers' lives will be at risk.'

There were shouts of anger at the revelation that another force would be trampling over their territory, all of which the commander silenced with a flamboyant wave of his hand. 'Secondly, and perhaps most importantly, we are secure here, not out and about, so we cannot be blamed for anything that happens, or indeed the fallout and consequences of what is likely to occur and, trust me, we are better off in here. So now, I need you all to settle down for the duration as best you can and I hope all will be clear by the end of the night,' and he waved both hands with crossed fingers above his head. It did little to calm people. However, they did as they were told and began murmuring to one another, speculating as to what was happening, Casey and Wade, headlining and, obviously on the missing list, then the O'Neills and, finally what was left of the Saints and the depleted Larkins.

The commander stepped down and, with Phyllis and a trusted second in command, they retired to the top floor office, to stand by the only remaining operative telephone and await news.

35

THE BANGING ON THE DOOR ALERTED THE PEOPLE IN THE Public bar of Arries, not knowing who or what to expect, other than it sounded like the police, which was not an unusual occurrence, or indeed unexpected, especially as they were locked in and drinking outside licensing hours. However, they were not expecting a smartly dressed and confident looking young man who bore a striking resemblance to the Larkin runt, Chas.

Chas stood in the frame of the door for a short while, basking in the impact his presence was having on this motley crew of hangers on, the vast majority already drunk, but not the wallflower soldiers, all of whom recovered some sentry poise after the shock of what they were seeing. Their eyes intently followed Chas as he stepped into the bar and strode confidently to meet Maude and Bess on the stage.

'Close and lock the door,' Maude instructed as Chas approached and, with only a hint of his former crippled gait, he stepped onto the stage to embrace his cousin.

'Maude,' he said as he leaned back from the embrace, his hands still on Maude's shoulders but looking at Bess.

Maude spoke deferentially to Chas and this did surprise those closest to the stage, who had all surmised Maude now ruled not only Bessie Saint and the Saint family, those that remained, but both families. However, it seemed obvious that Chas Larkin had something to say about that. 'Chas, you know Bess? She is to all intents, my wife, if you get my drift?'

'I do, Maude, congratulations,' and with a benign smile he stepped over to Bess, grasped her shoulders roughly and Bess squealed, he kissed her cheek, looked to Maude for a response. None came. Still with a firm grip, Bess was barely more than five foot to Chas's now straightened back, six foot and more, he bent down to Bess's ear. 'Welcome to the family. You will you do as you are told? You understand that?' the final sentence said so Maude could hear.

This time Maude responded, 'She knows the score, Chas. I love her and want her protected, you know what I mean?'

'I do cousin, ' and he turned to the stunned audience, crowding around the stage, jostling to be as near as possible to Maude, Bess, and incredibly, Chas Larkin, and all gave the required impression they were deliriously impressed with this transformation, but latent in their minds, was he still mad? Was he on their side and what side was that, Larkin, Saint, or this new combined family they had been hearing about and were still untrusting of? The mutterings were not lost on the acute hearing of Chas. In his days of defective sight, he had developed a strong reliance on his hearing, it sometimes being all he had to warn him of impending danger.

Chas addressed the crowded bar, and, despite the natural reticence of his audience, he sensed he had them in the palm of his hand. 'We are here this afternoon to mark the joining of the Larkin and Saint clans.' Well, there it was, confirmed. Was it a relief? Most did not know, but their opinions never mattered, ever. 'I wish for Bess to be recognised as the wife of Maude,' he let that news settle in, because it was significant. 'I will expect the respect and protection we would afford any other wife on this manor, to be now be afforded Bess. I hope this is understood?' There was a murmur of assent and Chas smiled as he turned from the crowd. 'Maude, the honours please,' Chas said to his cousin in a firm, self-assured, and clear voice so all could hear. He had a deep voice, whereas most people always imagined the hunchback cripple to have a squeal, but then again, he was so often being beaten up by Mickey *the cabbage* or his Mum, his voice had a natural default of high-pitched pain. The local people knew they had a lot to get used to and it would fall on their shoulders to spread the word, which they would do with relish, there being a certain cache to be had, counted in the few who had been invited to Arries this foreboding mid-summer's evening.

Maude stepped forward to stand beside Chas. 'Listen up and understand, day to day, me, with my wife,' and she turned to Bess, pulled her closer so she could put an arm across Bess's shoulder, 'we will run the family business, now conjoined, but with certain changes that you will learn about over the next few weeks.' She pointed to Chas, whose restored wide and brilliant eyes scanned the audience for doubters. Some he already knew and would deal with over time; others could not wait and would meet their fate that night. 'Chas Larkin will, however, be the de-facto head of the Houses,' and she left it there, the crowd further stunned by these new revelations, as Maude and Bess shuffled to the back of the stage leaving Chas out front.

Chas looked around, saw who he wanted to see, not difficult as Bernie stood head and shoulders above everyone else. 'Bernie, *I only asked,*' he called to the giant of a man, no longer considered a dimwit, 'can you come here...' and Bernie approached the stage, stopped briefly to listen to additional instructions from Chas, '... and bring Wally *the Weasel* please.' Chas's manner was restrained, the audience curiosity piqued, except for Wally, who looked to turn and run only to feel his shoulder in a vice like grip; Bernie had his man. Wally had no choice but to go with Bernie to the stage, dragged up and spun around so all could see. A gesture from Chas and he was forced into a kneeling position, his head jerked to look up. Chas ignored the pleading stare from the prone known grass, in order to continue to address the crowd. 'Wally has transgressed the unwritten law and if you lot don't know what that is, I will tell you and even write it down for you, so listen up.' He turned to a now petrified Weasel, 'Wally... Wally...' he began in a benign voice that had the audience on red alert. Wally relaxed a little, but he had misinterpreted the affectionate tone, until he saw Chas take a gun from inside his jacket. 'Wally, you done upset me and upset my very good friend Bernie when you fingered Limp Eric to the O'Neills.'

Wally saw the writing on the wall and began to energetically plead his case, 'I didn't 'onest Chas.'

'Mr Larkin to you,' and Chas looked around. Everyone now knew Chas was to be henceforth called, Mr Larkin.

'Sorry, Mr Larkin, but...'

'No buts, did you, or did you not squeal on Limp Eric?'

'But...' Wally squirmed, looking for a way out. Chas seemed to be reasonable, maybe if he was honest, he would get a reprieve, just a beating up? 'I only told Scotch 'Arry...'

'So, you ratted Limp Eric out?'

'Yes, Mr Larkin. I'm sorry, but everyone knows nobody can't not understand Scotch 'Arry.'

'Don't apologise to me. Apologise to Bernie.'

Alfie swung his desperate gaze to Bernie, 'I'm sorry Bernie. I truly am. I didn't know they would do for 'im, honest, you 'ave to believe me,' and he looked around to see if he had been believed, his look beseeching Bernie to forgive him. Bernie said he would, just before Chas blew Alfie's brains out. Blood and grey matter splattered those patrons who had crowded close to the stage for a better view. Well, they had a clear picture now. Who was in charge and what would happen if they transgressed the unwritten law which everyone agreed need not be written down.

Maude stepped forward and with her foot, pushed Wally's ironically limp body, missing half a head, off the stage. She swung her gaze to the crowded pub, but spoke to the wallflowers, 'Soldiers, we will need you this evening.' The bouncers stood to attention, while Maude rattled off a list of other names all of whom she asked to stay behind. The list was of people who had previously been co-opted into various nefarious jobs for either the Saints or Larkins, for the majority of these selected few had a penchant for violence, and other matters, which caused them to be marked out by Chas. The rest were dismissed, and a more grateful bunch of people pleased to be sent away from free drink you had never seen before, piled through the now open exit doors. Home to safety and to spread the unwritten word. Relief to be let off patent heavy duties, one such duty likely being to drop Wally the Weasel into the Thames.

Following the stampede of those relieved of God knows

what, there was silence in the bar. Chas spoke and broke the tension, 'Though this house give glimm'ring light, we will not tolerate dancing clowns,' and he stepped off the stage and strode to the rear exit door that was opened for him as he approached, and he passed through without breaking stride. The doors locked behind him and Maude began briefing the confused gathered gang, wondering if they were the dancing clowns, and what house glimmers? Saint or Larkin?

However, it was time to take on the O'Neills, at least this is what Chas had told Maude to say. It was to be a reckoning and this they understood, and even relished the prospect of what Chas had referred to as *A Midsummer Night's Dream*; the two last Saint and Larkin movements.

Wendy collected a lined writing pad from her stationery cupboard, and Scotch 'Arry responded to the questioning of Nadia and Wendy with written answers and, after a frustrating half hour, they were able to tell 'Arry they no longer needed him and he need not follow them all the time. His answer, roughly translated, was, "Fuck that, it's Casey what I'm frightened of". They did understand this, Nadia circumspect that her lover man might be even more dangerous than she first thought and both ladies resolved to accept that they would continue to be tailed by an incoherent Glaswegian, for the time being, although they struggled to see how he would be admitted to the Ritz Hotel in Piccadilly.

The extended mid-summer's evening twilight had faded to dark and a three-quarter moon in a cloudless sky, greeted them as they left the hospital. It was a warm and balmy night and they scooted off to catch a bus about to leave the hospital on its journey into the West End. Leaping onto the rear platform as it began to leave and, swinging on the pole, Nadia called back to the stranded tail that they would see him at the Ritz. Scotch 'Arry's response was unintelligible, but they got the drift as the Scot duck's arse bent over trying to catch his breath. There would be another bus along soon, he had time to make a telephone call to someone who would understand him, but most importantly, someone he could trust to get a message to Casey and Wade. He had to let them know that their other halves were on the loose, fancy free, in the West End of London. This news he knew would rattle their cages but could see no harm. After all, what could possibly happen?

The summer equinox evening had drawn into night, the moon bright in a clear sky, good surveillance conditions. No more the persistent fine rain. Wade and Casey set themselves up in a house opposite the Saint Warehouse in the East India Dock, not realising it was Chas's former hideaway. The

Flying Squad officers, along with a contingent of armed MI5 men, spread themselves in neighbouring houses in the bomb-damaged terrace, some with a full view of the warehouse and across the floodlit marshalling areas, others with a clear view of the side dock gate and the casual milling of the floozies. The appearance of normality was established.

By the time they had set up their positions, the O'Rierdons had arrived and a radio message from the Port authority police reported the small army of gangsters were gathered at the Saint warehouse. They were loading arms and materiel into several black vans. Casey asked them to hold their positions, 'We are here to observe,' and he added, 'to pick up the pieces.'

Casey was relieved Chas had managed to get a warning to the prostitutes to stay around so the O'Rierdons would not be alerted by their lack of presence. Chas had paid the tarts to drift to the side gate as the gangsters arrived and the Port Police steered the newly arrived Polish sailors to that dock exit. The danger would come for the prostitutes if it was learned they did not inform the families, but Chas wanted them warned so all appeared normal and they could clear the area when the action commenced.

Casey and Wade continued to look out of their fractured window, both had binoculars. Casey almost gave the game away as he jumped, being tapped on his shoulder.

'Shush Paddy, what the fuck?'

'What the fuck indeed,' Casey whispered in reply, to save

face more, as he looked down into the eyes of a short man. 'Hemmings what are you doing here?' The diminutive MI5 man was visibly uncomfortable, he was a brains trust, not a field operative, in short, which he was, he was scared and looking to get out as soon as possible. 'Well, what is it?'

Hemmings plucked up the courage to speak without stammering, 'I've had a message from Scotch 'Arry.'

'You have?' Wade asked, curious how he could understand if he had telephoned in, still he could have sent a written message she assumed. She looked and Casey and Hemmings were watching her, 'Oops, out loud?'

Hemmings answered. 'He telephoned, and I can understand him.'

'You can?' both Wade and Casey said at the same time.

'Yes, not difficult if you slow him down.'

'Well, what did he say?' Wade asked, frustrated.

Hemmings, anxious to get out, rushed his response. 'Nadia and Wendy are going to the Ritz.'

'The Ritz?' Wade interrupted.

Now Hemmings stammered, he did not like to be interrupted, 'Ye, ye yea, yes, w, w,' he rethought his words and found some fluency, 'they learned that Ch, Ch...'

'Chas Larkin?' Wade was losing patience.

'Ye, ye, ye...'

Casey sighed, and decided to interrupt. He already knew, and this truly got on Wade's nerves, 'You know, don't you?'

Casey nodded and Hemmings looked relieved he didn't

need to speak anymore. 'I knew Chas stayed at the Ritz last night, but I didn't know Nadia and Wendy would find out, and definitely never expected they would go calling.'

Wade looked at Casey's face, 'They're in danger...?'

Paddy nodded, as did Hemmings, who tried to speak, but gave up and left it to Casey. 'The room had been reserved by the O'Rierdons. They have funded Chas into his new status, and they will have likely left someone...' and he pondered, '... or something, at the room to make sure Chas did as they expected, and then...' he didn't need to finish, but Hemmings said it for them with a gesture, two fingers to his skull and a boom sound, rocking his head backwards.

Wade jumped up, 'Something?' she asked, already knowing he meant an explosive device. 'They don't want Chas to survive?' Casey nodded again and this final nod galvanised Wade. 'I have to go to them,' and she stood to leave but was dragged back by Casey, 'Stop.'

'Fuck off, Paddy, I'm going. If Wendy is in trouble I need to be there,' she thought on, 'Nadia as well.'

'Of course you do and I'm not going to stop you, but you need to know what you are dealing with.'

Wade looked from Paddy to Hemmings, 'Very dangerous, Miss,' he said with clarity, and a look of empathy.

Casey spoke again, this time calmly, 'Hemmings, take Wade please and get some back-up?'

Hemmings' nerves rose to the surface again and, looking

to Wade, 'I... I... c... can take you, and I... I... will try for h... he... help.'

'Good enough for me,' Wade replied, already halfway across the derelict floor to the rickety staircase, before Hemmings could get his tiny frame and little feet moving. All Casey could do was watch on and hope. This would be a considerable test for Wade and, he tried to calm his nerves for Nadia and Wendy both, for he could not leave his post.

36

Maude put Bent Ben in charge. She refused to allow Bernie, *I only asked*, to go along; he looked perplexed. 'Bess and I need you, Bernie. I never want you out on the job, if you pardon the expression,' and this elicited a chuckle from Bess and an appreciative grin from Bernie; he never liked the street battles. 'I have something else for you to organise and when that is done you will run the firm with Bess and me, okay?'

Even better he thought. 'What is it you need doing?'

'Not me so much as Chas and, the sooner the better in my view for all of our sakes. So, if you wouldn't mind organising the demise of Mickey *the Cabbage* please.' Maude said this in a manner expressing regret at what needed doing, and with a consummate compassionate voice that would fool most people, but not Bernie, or even Bess, and Mickey was her nephew and, shaking her head in feigned remorse, she added, 'It's no life for him like that, a bleedin' cabbage.'

Maude's motives were not compassion, she was simply translating the desire of Chas Larkin, whom she knew would not rest until they were rid of *The Cabbage*. It was psychological with Chas, and Maude understood. She understood also that before this Midsummer Night was out, she too would have rid herself of many demons. What a plan, Chas Larkin was a genius, she thought to herself and he had been in front of them all this time, used and abused. Well, no longer, although she did have reservations because it was clear to her and she saw it also in Bess's eyes, Chas Larkin was barkin' mad. But that was okay, he was on their side.

Bernie set off for the hospital with strict orders he was to allow the *staff* to do the business, that he should be elsewhere, where he can be seen, in the event someone tried to finger him for murder. Jack *the Dip* was going to do the business, with his delicate pick pocketing gift, he was to cut off the life support until there was no life to support, and then, restore things so natural causes would be suspected.

The Port police, from their positions inside the docks, reported movement approaching from both sides of the warehouse. They had been briefed by Casey that the two families, Saints and Larkins, were now enjoined, and would be out that evening to protect their stash of weaponry.

'Let it go off as it should, over,' Casey whispered into the radio as he watched Chas Larkin cross the road, bold as brass and dressed like he was off to a wedding, the hint of a hobble. The team watched him remove an old, boarded window panel. It moved with ease like it had been oiled and, with a slight heft, Chas was in and the window board closed behind him.

'That bloke has to be fucking mad,' Casey heard Jordan crackle over the walkie talkie to anyone who was listening in.

'The lad is motivated, nuff said,' Casey crackled back. When he had confirmation the Saints and Larkins were set up outside the warehouse, he gave the command for the Port Police to open up with a few rounds to distract, while Chas did his job.

The Flying Squad and Casey looked on as two short bursts of tracer bullets crossed the apron in front of the warehouse and as anticipated, all hell broke loose. The Larkin Saints fired on the warehouse and the exposed working O'Rierdons, most of whom dropped like stones, they did not stand a chance in the crossfire. Just one or two wounded were able to drag themselves back into the warehouse from where their companions returned fire.

37

HEMMINGS HAD A CAR WAITING A COUPLE OF BLOCKS AWAY. HE steered Wade into the back seat as the rattle of gunfire echoed in the compact streets. He instructed the driver to get to the Ritz and not to spare the horses. He explained to Wade that he didn't drive. He struggled to reach the pedals, 'Trouble with being a short arse,' he said, to the amusement of Wade. He had expertly defused her tension.

That time of night, close to midnight, traffic was light, and it didn't take long for the driver to reach the West End and he pulled up at the side entrance to the Ritz, on Arlington Street. Wade knew it, had often walked past this hotel in forays from her humble East End, into posh knob territory. She also knew a few of the staff, porters, and some of the bell boys, one of whom was taking a break, pacing, taking in the refreshing cool night air. It had been a hot day and it was likely still sweltering in the hotel. Wade let herself out of the car, not waiting for Hemmings who had to sidle himself across the seat to get to his door and she approached *Ding-a-ling* Jeff, a casual thought that things were likely to get hotter.

'Ding-a-ling,' Wade called out, shaking the bell boy out of his Midsummer night's reverie. He turned and saw a friend from his old street pacing toward him. His nerves jangled. He knew Flora Wade was police. What could she want, hoping she had not rumbled the little scam the boys had going in the hotel. Wade saw the look, 'Relax, Jeff. I'm not here to nail you for your shenanigans in the hotel. Good luck to you I say, fleecing these rich bastards. They can afford it anyway,' and Jeff relaxed. He had always like Flora and she had made him feel justified robbing from the rich to give, to... well, himself mainly.

'Flora, what the 'ell you doing 'ere?' Hemmings reached them. Jeff looked at the short man, 'Hi bleedin' ho, off to work we go?' It was all Wade could do to contain a serious outburst of laughter, reminding herself she had to save Wendy and Nadia and with that thought, her tummy butterflies recommenced their business of making her feel sick.

Jeff was a sensitive Bellboy, 'What's up Flora?'

Hemmings answered, unmoved by the *Snow White and the Seven Dwarves* reference he got all the time, a passing thought it was a stroke of good luck Wade knowing someone on the inside who could get them in without having to negotiate the reception desk and some frosty officialdom.

Jeff said he would help his old friend and neighbour, though he was not sure about her short mate though, who he gave a wide berth, whispering to Wade that he didn't want to tread on the little fella. 'What would Snow White say?' And chuckling, Jeff went off to see if he could find out what room a Chas Larkin was in.

Wade and Hemmings kicked their heels, waiting on Jeff's return, while limousines of the well-heeled drove up and discharged the knobs returning from the theatres and restaurants. As midnight neared, she hoped the hotel would quieten down so they could do their job without disturbing anyone.

Jeff returned; he had the information they sought. Chas was in a fourth-floor room on the west side, facing Green Park. Wade thought this would be helpful if the room did blow out. At this time of night there would be nobody in the park, relieved Chas did not have a room facing Piccadilly. 'Jeff, will you take Hemmings to see the Duty manager please, we will need to evacuate a part of the hotel near the room. Certainly, the fourth floor, Green Park wing.'

Jeff looked buzzed; this was the most excitement he'd had in a very long time. 'I will, Flora, what do you reckon then?'

'We do not know for sure, but the room may be wired with an explosive device.'

'Fuckin' Ada, a bomb, really?' And Jeff thought on, 'Shit on it.'

'What?' it was Hemmings getting in before Wade.

'The receptionist, bit of a looker, I quite fancy her.'

'Get on with it ding-a-ling,' Wade was in Jeff's face now.

'Sorry, well, she said she had just given the room number to a couple of lady doctors who said they were treating Chas Larkin. Ain't he the poor cripple sod from round our way?'

'Jeff, we haven't got time for this now, show me the back stairs up to the fourth floor and take Hemmings here,' and she pointed unnecessarily to the short spy, 'he's MI5. Get him to the Duty Manager and start getting people out.'

'Jesus, you, a spook?' Jeff asked, leaning over Hemmings.

Wade had no time. 'Jeff, move yer arse, please,' and Jeff did, tugging Wade up the short flight of red carpeted entrance steps, directing her to the side staircase and telling her the quick route along the Piccadilly corridor to the Green Park wing and, she dashed up the stairs while he took Hemmings into the main body of the famous hotel, like he was taking a schoolboy on a night out treat.

The Port police reported a severely depleted Saint and Larkin team were slowly easing their way to the warehouse, under cover of nearby buildings. The return fire was still consistent but reduced in strength; the O'Rierdons must have suffered many losses.

Casey responded to the call from the dockside commander on an open channel, 'When they are all in range, pull your men back and send up the flare.'

The order was acknowledged, and Casey responded with a message to the flying squad and MI5 officers. 'Okay lads, looks like we will not be needed. What say you we feck off to a safe distance and watch the fireworks, over,' and he lifted himself up as he saw the window board open up and watched on as Chas climbed out of the warehouse, but something was wrong, he had either been snagged or was being held by someone inside, either way, Casey knew he had to get down there to help. He radioed to the rest of his team, all of whom saw what was happening. 'Get yourselves out. I'm going to save the lad,' and he closed the call and made a dash for the street, negotiating the shaky stairs as fast as he could safely manage, flew through the non-existent front door and sped across the street.

Chas saw his rescuer coming. 'Get back, Paddy,' he called, 'it's gonna blow.'

Casey did not stop and drawing his pistol from his shoulder holster, he ripped the window board away from its tenuous attachment to the warehouse and, spinning across the window opening to avoid the hail of bullets that followed him, he took aim and fired, three times and the firing from inside the warehouse stopped. Chas was released and Casey tugged at the lad and together they made a mad dash down the street as a flare lit up the sky.

'Fuck,' Chas said, and there was an almighty explosion. Chas and Casey were lifted way into the air and blown along the street and, as they hit the cobbled road, so they rolled until eventually came to a painful halt. Casey was aware only of the searing heat from the fireball that was formerly the Saint repository of munitions for the IRA and anyone else who paid enough money and, he had to have broken some limbs. He dragged himself along the road to where he could see the inert body of Chas Larkin, thrown further away. He had to get to Chas and as he crawled nearer, he thought he heard laughing. He closed the distance and saw also some of his team running to their aid. Still the laughing continued, increasing in volume. A manic cadence.

'Take it easy, Paddy old son, ambulances are on the way,' DI Jordan said, and they could hear the bells in the distance, getting louder as the emergency services neared the site of this pitch battle, the incessant bells finally drowning out the crazed laughter from Chas Larkin as he raised himself up, rubbed the sides of his head as if the ambulance and fire engine bells were ringing in his ears.

'Jordan, do me a favour?'

'Sure Paddy, whatever you want. My boys and I have not had such fun in bloody ages, did you see that fucking warehouse go up, boom!' He looked back at a face made by Casey.

Casey was not impressed. 'Of course I saw it, you fucking turnip. I was in it.'

'Yeah, sorry, Paddy. You okay?' which was all he could manage on the empathy stakes as he retold how brilliant it was watching him and Larkin flying through the air, both like *Superman*.

If Casey needed any more proof the Flying Squad were nutters, he had it right in front of him and then, there was Chas, laughing like a Loony Bin drain, and he thought back to the day he was commissioned for this job, the Major saying to him that Chas Larkin was reported to be barkin' mad. Well, he had to agree. So, what happens now he thought through a miasma of pain that was starting to kick in as his adrenaline levels ebbed. Then he panicked. 'Nadia, Wendy,' he said to DI Jordan.

'Shit a brick, I'd forgotten about them,' he replied filling Casey with no confidence whatsoever. 'What about Arbour Square nick, shall we let them out now?'

'Blimey, I forgot about them,' Casey replied, and then both officers, one Sweeny, the other MI5, looked at each other, swung their gaze and saw Chas, limping towards them and, as Jordan lifted Casey upright, Chas put his arm around Casey and all three men hugged. 'Did you see that? BOOM!' Chas said.

Casey screamed, they were squeezing his broken limbs, thinking, yep, Larkin's barkin' alright, just before the whole terrace of houses collapsed.

38

WADE WAS UP THE STAIRS TWO AT A TIME, ZIGZAGGING, RIGHT then left as she flew down the Piccadilly corridor and, turning left into the Green Park wing, she saw Nadia. Wendy was a little way in front and about to turn the door handle to Chas Larkin's room.

'Nooo...! She shouted and launched herself down the corridor, pushing Nadia away as she reached a startled Wendy, who pulled the door lever. Wade heard the click, momentarily relieved at the pause. Likely a grenade, and she dived at Wendy smothering her just as the door blew. Wade could feel the blast on the backs of her legs, but sensed she was okay, apart from Wendy shouting at her. 'What the fuck? Get off me.' Wade was relieved, everything was okay. Wendy was back to telling her what to do and Wade thanked her lucky stars that swam in front of her eyes that she had been deafened by the blast.

Wade rolled off her lover and ran her hands all over her body to check Wendy for injuries. 'Good, you're okay, what the fucking 'ell were you thinking of?'

Wendy, oblivious of the alarms and the soaking she was getting from the sprinklers and, similarly deafened by the blast, could not hear Wade, or the shouts as people ran down the corridor from their rooms to get out. She felt unusually offended Flora was taking advantage of her state of shock to feel her up. 'Oi, get your hands off me.'

Wade, kneeling, leaned back onto her heels and looked at the face of the woman she loved, expressing disgust. So, she went back in and kissed her, gently at first and, as she sensed Wendy respond, so she pressed home and was warmed to feel Wendy's arms go around her waist, up to her shoulders and grip them, vice like. She was not letting her saviour and lover go, and she returned the passionate kiss, only to be interrupted by an embarrassed Bellboy. 'Flora, sweet'art, the police and fire brigade are on the way and they've suggested we leave the building.'

The spellbinding moment was over. 'Fuck me, Ding-a-ling. I was getting on brilliantly there, what's your game.'

Ding-a-ling turned a deep crimson. 'Sorry, Flora, just I thought we had better get out, although there's not a big fire, amazin' eh?'

'Yeah, bleedin' amazin', now, toodle-ooh,' and she wiggled her fingers goodbye, as she stood, offering a helping hand to Wendy, 'and pass me that fire extinguisher, there's a luv.'

Jeff passed the extinguisher and watched Wade walk through belching smoke and disappear into Chas's room. Nadia hugged Wendy while the psychiatrist looked over her shoulder to make sure Flora didn't see.

Jeff could hear the hissing of sprayed water and, after a short while, Wade called out. 'Okay, safe to come in,' just as the fire brigade trundled into the corridor, barging Jeff out of the way, and halted at Wade, who stood four-square, holding out her warrant card. 'Stop there me boyos, this is a crime scene. I've put the blaze out for yer, so you can go back to your little fire station and get some beddy-byes.'

The brigade watch commander pushed to the front. 'What's going on, Sam?' he asked the fireman.

'This bird's a copper and won't let me in sir.'

'I'm not a bird, I'm a woman, though he is right, I am a copper and I'm protecting a crime scene.'

The watch commander looked seriously put out, and tapping the badge on his white helmet, he said, 'I'm in charge here, sweetie,' and immediately regretted it as Wade gave him a right hander that knocked him back into Jeff, and then into Nadia, all three falling to the floor.

'Sorry,' Wade said, but you were getting on me tits.'

'Yeah, and that's my job,' Wendy said, and after helping

Nadia back up, she kissed Wade, whispered into her ear. 'Just let the little man in for a poke around darling, he will need to make sure the fire is actually out and then, we, can go back home to beddy-byes. How does that sound?'

Wade was completely suckered in by the wiles of her clever bonce lover, and her killer blow, being tempted into bed and flicking her head, she allowed the fire commander into Chas's room for a rummage and maybe put the odd fire out she might have missed. She wanted to go home with Wendy.

'Ah that's nice dear, but I think you should have put the fires out first. Then you can put mine out and, yes you did speak your thoughts,' Wendy said, enjoying the chuckling response from Jeff the bellboy.

'Is everyone accounted for?' the commander called out.

'Yeah. The occupant, Chas Larkin, we know where he is,' Wade replied.

'And the woman?'

'What woman?' Wade questioned.

Jeff answered, 'There was a young woman there as well, bit of a cracker an all, glorious red hair. Irish I think.'

Wendy looked to Wade, then Nadia, 'Roisin?'

'Has to be,' Wade responded, and all eyes turned to the commander as he stood there chuckling to his testosterone laden squad as he walked out of the room, helmet under his arm, and wearing a gloriously lengthy red wig, wiggling his bottom, and waving an airy-fairy hand as he walked like a model down the catwalk. 'What d'you think,' he asked anyone.

'Well, I think that answers one of our questions,' Wendy said to Nadia.

Wade was inexplicably offended. 'What bloody question?'

Wendy looked to her Flora like she was a dozy cow that needed milking. 'Oh, sweetheart, Chas Larkin was Roisin. He was the Black Rose,' and she looked at the dawning on her lover's face. 'You said you thought Paddy was not interested in tracking down Roisin, making it also very clear the Black Rose existed.'

Wade shook her head, pieces falling into place. 'That fucking Irish tow rag...' she stopped and looked at Nadia, then Wendy, '... if he is indeed Irish. He's been in league with Chas Larkin all along? Jesus, Mary and bleedin' Joseph, I'll ring his fucking neck.'

'Come on darling, let's get you home,' and Wendy whispered into Wade's ear, 'you saved my life just then. I think that deserves a good fuck, don't you?'

'Several actually,' Wade replied, wrapped up in Wendy's arms, neglectful of Nadia who now had a huge conundrum, like, what on earth was happening and, just who was Padraig, the man she was convinced she loved, despite everything.

As they reached the hotel lobby, order was being restored to the panicky rich people. Hemmings was there and ushering Wendy, Nadia, and Wade into a relatively quiet corner, he told them Casey, DI Jordan and Chas Larkin, had been caught up in an explosion and a collapsing terrace of houses opposite the Saint warehouse.

Nadia seemed remarkably calm, thinking to herself that if Padraig was dead, it would solve that little problem, though she would be sad of course, but frankly he was shit in the bedroom department. So, no great loss?

'Nadia!' Wendy said, a shocked look on her face. Wade looked upon the Palestinian doctor and wanted to say she knew what this was like, she often got caught talking to herself by Wendy. Still the makeup sex was good, but that might not help Nadia and Paddy, 'Flora!'

'Oh, fuck it,' Wade said, 'caught again.'

'Yes, but we can skip the row,' Wendy said raising her furtive eyebrows, 'and get straight to the makeup stuff, eh?'

Finally, they realised they had asked nothing of how Casey or even Chas Larkin were. 'Jesus, sorry Nadia.' Wade turned to Hemmings, 'Oi you, short arse, how's Casey and the others?'

Hemmings decided not to be affronted. 'They are in hospital, none too worse the wear considering they have been blown up and had a ton of bricks on their heads.'

'Thank God it was his head,' Nadia said, as Hemmings steered them to the waiting car on Piccadilly.

Hemmings said he would drop Wendy and Flora home and take Nadia to the hospital. 'Not on your Nellie, mate,'

Wendy responded, 'I want to see Chas. I need to make sure his synapses are firing, albeit likely in weird directions, and Wade here will want to make sure Casey is okay, won't you?'

'Not really,' Wade replied, watching the makeup sex disappear into the distance; luck of the Irish she presumed.

39

Nadia's ire with Casey thawed when she saw him lying in the hospital bed, bandaged, taped, and a plaster of Paris foot and arm. A look that comforted Casey, but for everyone else, it was a rare and too good to miss opportunity to enjoin in a good laugh at his expense. And, the Master of Ceremonies of this frivolity was Chas Larkin, who had his audience in raptures as he told the story like a practiced raconteur, the effect being to pour petrol on Wade's raging fires as she took in revelation after revelation, only a half of which she had already guessed. Of course, she now knew Chas was Roisin. It seemed that Wendy and Nadia had worked that out following their meeting with Miss Doyle at the school and, it had truly been Chas who lumped Mickey Saint and his mates with the length of four by two and, take the cane to the headmistress, after which all witnesses were sworn to secrecy lest they incur the wrath of the O'Neills. Chas Larkin had demonstrated his own abilities in retribution, if they had any doubts about his back up from the O'Neills.

Chas said he could not recall who had murdered his mum. He suspected Casey, as had Wade, but Paddy denied all and was quite convincing and, who could take issue with the man dressed to the nines in bandages. Nadia kissed him. 'Ahhh,' she said, 'my crap lover. I believe you, liddle diddums.'

'I told you, I was preoccupied,' his defiant response causing even greater mirth around his bed. The patient was done up like a kipper, fully smoked, the game up for him, so he confessed all, confident he had immunity from the law, though he was not so sure about the woman he loved.

He looked at Chas. 'I do not know who murdered Betsy Larkin...' and people noticed an ice-cold stare at Chas, who responded again with a manic laugh, '... not sure it matters though,' and he grinned. Letting Chas off the hook? 'I visited Chas in the hospital and sat beside his bed, you recall Nadia?' she said she did. 'I got close to him,' and he looked up and this time Chas nodded, the manic grin gone, replaced by a tear forming as he shuffled closer to the bed and took Casey's hand; roles reversed, Chas the comforter.

Chas took up the story. 'I told Paddy about the O'Rierdons, how they had taken me in. He already knew and this was why he was in the East End. He told me about the troubles in Ireland and how the O'Rierdons would likely be central to a campaign of violence in London and, eventually across the country. How he supported the cause but not the hurt to innocent people.' Chas halted, Casey was crying, and Chas gripped the man's hand tighter, and leaned in. 'He told me how his sister had been killed in an IRA bomb and his uncle murdered by the UDA.'

Casey was sobbing, old hurts surfacing, and Nadia took his other hand and squeezed, which caused him to screech in pain. 'Oh, be quiet Padraig, you baby,' and she leaned across and kissed him on the lips.

Chas continued while Nadia dabbed Paddy's eyes a little too hard, but as a doctor she had that sorted with just an admonishing look. Better than any anaesthesia.

Chas continued, talking about his hospital chat with Casey, 'I could relate to what Paddy was telling me, though I had already been indoctrinated by the O'Rierdons. Willingly by me, I should add, even though I knew they were taking advantage and, it was only later I suspected that after I had got them into the Saint warehouse, I would be killed, which you have confirmed was to be the case.'

Casey interrupted, 'Hemmings reported that MI5 also had Intelligence that the O'Rierdons were milking the IRA for their own wealth, something we had long suspected, and so it seemed to me like a good idea to tidy up the mess in one foul swoop, so to speak. Destroy the Saint warehouse of arms, with the O'Rierdons inside, at the same time, tidy away the unwanted, also so to speak, Saints and Larkins; job done,' and Casey allowed his cat who got the Irish double cream, smile, to infect his audience, surprised to get a sally of abuse back, mainly from Wade.

'Paddy!' Wade exclaimed. 'You can't go taking the law into your own hands like that.' She looked amazed and then thought on, 'Though, having said that...' and then another light bulb moment. 'Jeez...' looked to Chas, '... are you saying the Larkins now run the two families, and...' she looked to Paddy then Chas. 'Chas, are you running it? Fucking amazing,' Wade said shaking her head and chuckling. Wade saw Wendy looking on, confused, so she explained. 'Darlin' what these two saps have arranged is for the serious depletion of two nasty East End gangs, blown up and destroyed the IRA threat and, at the same time replaced it,' and she looked to Casey and again Chas, who nodded, 'with a *benign* gang who, whilst giving the front of dastardly deeds, would be working for us,' looked to Casey, 'MI5, am I right?' Casey confirmed she was right, and Wade continued with her conclusion, thoroughly enjoying them. 'And no obvious void to be filled by any other family considering staging a turf war. The only other threat was the O'Rierdons, who no longer exist. Stone me, bloody brilliant.'

Chas added a little rider to quench a little of Wade's thirst for knowledge, 'This was the gangs in West London dealt with, and we know we have none of sufficient strength to threaten what we have in the East End, but we will have to monitor south and north of the river, but we have help in that area, eh, Paddy?'

Paddy answered, 'We do Chas, a combination of Special Branch and MI5 are keeping an eye on a particular bunch in south London. So, we can be ready to step in if we have to.'

Wendy tugged Wade out of her reverie of discovery, 'You're a spy?'

'Oh fuck,' Wade sighed, sensing sex disappearing over the horizon as she looked to Casey, 'am I?'

Casey raised his bruised eyebrows. 'If you want to be. We could certainly use you, but maybe talk it over with Wendy?' He grinned, 'And then have the makeup sex?'

The aura of confession was interrupted. Maude, Bess, and Bernie *I only asked*, entered the room, brushing off the complaint of the ward sister that there were too many people around the bed. The sister's ire, however, was smoothed over by Doctor Nadia, the sister still fuming, but powerless to prevent the hospital rules being broken.

Here was this grand reunion that surprised Wade, Nadia, and Wendy, but not Casey as Bernie first of all kissed him, Casey spitting imaginary feathers, saying he didn't want to kiss no bloke, followed up by Maude and Bess, Maude imparting the good news that Bess was to be seen as her wife. This news set Wendy off. She wanted to be wife to Flora and Wade had no resolve to contest, indeed found she was excited by the idea and, wondering if tonight, when they eventually got home that is and, following the MI5 conversation, would it be makeup or honeymoon sex?

Maude told all from her and Bess's side, that the bad apples of the Saint and Larkin family had now been disposed of and the threat of the O'Rierdons taking over the East End, extinguished, and so, the manor could be managed without too much disruption, things would sort themselves out, without any threat of another gang muscling in, at least for the time being.

Wade tore herself away from Wendy to ask what she considered a pertinent question for a copper and thought maybe Casey should have been asking this. 'Hang on,' and she gave the evil eye to Casey. 'What you are saying is that this Irish...' and she stopped, '... or is he a cockney bozo...' she paused, '... anyway, this tart here,' and she waved in the direction of the injured Paddy, as all of her last ducks joined in a neat and orderly row. 'Are you saying Paddy engineered this war between the Saints and Larkins...' again she paused as more and more light bulbs lit up, dazzling her brain and looked to Casey in total illumination, 'you nicked the crumpet, helped Chas blow up his mum and showed him how to make the bombs?' She saw both Chas and Paddy titter, it annoyed her, 'And, with the collusion of Chas, Maude and Bess, you blew up *Dad's*?'

Bess interrupted, 'It got rid of some of the untrustworthy Saints and Larkins and enabled Maude and me to take over.' She smiled at Maude, pleased to be recognised as the brains of the outfit, whatever her personal relationship as Maude's wife, 'which will be run also with Bernie,' and she looked at Chas, 'and you, Chas - you still want to be involved?'

Chas gestured to Casey. 'I will be there, or thereabouts, but I think my place may be in MI5.'

'MI fucking five?' Wendy stepped in, worried for the vulnerability of Chas Larkin, 'Are you off your rocker?'

Chas replied, 'Yes, and who better to know that than you Wendy, but I would still like to visit you for counselling, would that be okay, would I make a good case study?' Chas grinned; he had his psychiatrist where he wanted her.

'How did you know I was doing a case study on you?'

'I guessed. I was right, yes?'

Wendy conceded with a sigh, 'Yes...'

'Good, so what do we do now, Paddy?'

'Hang on, I still have a few more questions before we talk about how many of us will become MI bleedin' five,' and Wade looked at Wendy, knowing that her lover could hardly criticise her after what she had just confessed and maybe they will not need that talk before bedtime.

'Okay, fire away Wade, and then I want you all to feck off, except for my lovely Nadia,' Casey replied.

Wade felt the wind had been taken out of her sails, but had to press home, realising this may be her only chance to get all of her questions answered. 'Okay,' and she began to pace, the crowd around the bed stepping back to give her room, as interested in the questions and the answers as much as Wade. She shook her head, where would she start? 'Were the O'Rierdons your sole target?'

'Yes.'

'Don't suppose you thought about telling me, you fucking arsehole.'

'Now, Flora, enough of that, just ask your questions politely, take the answers offered and you can talk about it later with Paddy, okay?' There was a threat of no sex behind the reasonable smile Wendy proffered. Wade knew all of her looks.

'Sorry,' she responded, anxious to ask her questions and get home before the wind changed. 'Are you really Irish?

'Yes, from Kerry, but I have lived in London on and off all of my life as my family responded to the various threats. So, you see, I can do a genuine cockney accent,' he replied in an authentic cockney accent. 'Next?'

'One last one,' and she dragged this out, because she was not sure she truly wanted to know the answer.

'Spit it out. You want to know if my name is Casey?'

'Yes, is it?'

'No, it is as you have wondered for some time, and Chas has known since we talked in the hospital. My family name is O'Neill.'

'And?'

'What?'

Wade had to ask even if it sounded truly silly. 'Are you the Black Rose? Not a bleedin' girl, but an Irish tart?'

He applied a wry smile; Wade was good, and they will work well together. 'Yes.'

'Black fucking Rose, more like a girl's bleedin' blouse,' she was angry with him, and looked to Nadia for her response. No sign of shock, 'You knew?'

'Not about the Black Rose,' Nadia replied, with not so much shock as Wade thought she should show. 'I eavesdropped on the conversation Padraig had with Chas when he was in his hospital room. I learned about his family, how they had suffered and how he had determined to resolve the issues, without violence,' and she put crossed fingers in the air, and everyone knew what she meant. 'I shared his feelings. My own people are oppressed by the Israelis and it will only get worse. I empathised, and from that time, I knew I loved him,' and she walked across to Casey and kissed him. 'Padraig, it is time you asked me to marry you.'

Just then a nurse poked her nose into the room. 'Is there a Bessie Saint here?' A timorous voice, aware of the Saint reputation.

'Yes,' Bess replied.

The nurse looked sympathetic, 'I am sorry to say your brother, Mickey, passed a short while ago. I'm very sorry.'

Bess looked at Maude; job done.

'Yes.' Casey said.

'What?' Nadia challenged him, 'you're pleased to hear of someone's death?'

'No,' and he smiled, 'yes, will you marry me?' he replied.

'I'll think about it,' Nadia answered, before she crushed him with a hug and a kiss that smothered his screams, 'oh, be quiet Padraig O'Neill.'

NOT THE END

The IRA campaign in London had been delayed...

...what next for Larkin, the Black Rose and Wade?

The next book in the Larkin series, it is 1969 and the ersatz peace in the

East End of London is threatened, as is the whole of Britain.

In

A DEADLY QUEEN

4 WARS

Dear reader,

We hope you enjoyed reading *Black Rose*. Please take a moment to leave a review, even if it's a short one. Your opinion is important to us.

Discover more books by Pete Adams at https://www.nextchapter.pub/authors/pete-adams

Want to know when one of our books is free or discounted? Join the newsletter at http://eepurl.com/bqqB3H

Best regards,

Pete Adams and the Next Chapter Team

You might also like:
Dead No More by Pete Adams

To read the first chapter for free, please head to:
https://www.nextchapter.pub/books/dead-no-more

ABOUT THE AUTHOR

Pete Adams is an architect with a practice in Portsmouth, UK, and from there he has, over forty years, designed and built buildings across England and Wales. Pete took up writing after listening to a radio interview of the writer Michael Connolly whilst driving home from Leeds. A passionate reader, the notion of writing his own novel was compelling, but he had always been told you must have a *mind map* for the book; Jeez, he could never get that.

Et Voila, Connolly responding to a question, said he never can plan a book, and starts with an idea for chapter one and looks forward to seeing where it would lead. Job done, and that evening Pete started writing and the series, Kind Hearts and Martinets, was on the starting blocks. That was some eight years ago, and hardly a day has passed where Pete has not worked on his writing, and currently, is halfway through his tenth book, has a growing number of short stories, one, critically acclaimed and published by Bloodhound, and has written and illustrated a series of historical nonsense stories called, Whopping Tales.

Pete describes himself as an inveterate daydreamer, and escapes into those dreams by writing crime thrillers with a thoughtful dash of social commentary. He has a writing style shaped by his formative years on an estate that re-housed London families after WWII, and his books have been likened to the writing of Tom Sharpe; his most cherished review, "made me laugh, made me cry, and made me think".

Pete lives in Southsea with his partner, and Charlie the star-struck Border terrier, the children having flown the coop, and has three beautiful granddaughters who will play with him so long as he promises not to be silly.

CPSIA information can be obtained
at www.ICGtesting.com
Printed in the USA
BVHW031429120421
604734BV00002B/226

9 781034 735762